BROWN GIRL
IN THE ROOM

BROWN GIRL
IN THE ROOM

Priya Ramsingh

TIGHTROPE BOOKS

Tightrope Books
#207-2 College Street,
Toronto Ontario, Canada M5G 1K3
tightropebooks.com
bookinfo@tightropebooks.com

EDITOR: Deanna Janovski
COVER ILLUSTRATION: Kavita Maharaj
COVER DESIGN: Kavita Maharaj
LAYOUT DESIGN: David Jang

Produced with the assistance of the Canada Council for the Arts and the Ontario Arts Council.

Library and Archives Canada Cataloguing in Publication

Ramsingh, Priya, 1968-, author
        Brown girl in the room / Priya Ramsingh.

ISBN 978-1-988040-33-2 (softcover)

        I. Title.

PS8635.A469B76 2017   C813'.6   C2017-904310-2

This book is dedicated to all of the lives that have touched mine.
All experiences—whether they felt positive or negative—have shaped
my perception, provided me with growth, and helped guide me
in the direction to create this story.

The meeting was already in session, and as she heard the hollow voice emanating from the core of the room, knots tightened in her stomach. She wondered if she should wait for a break in the meeting before walking in and slipping into a seat unnoticed. But standing in the familiar foyer brought back painful memories, fuelling her anger and pushing her on. Like the breath of air filling her lungs and inflating her purpose, she moved forward, and suddenly she was standing in the room, looking directly at the people sitting smugly in their seats of authority—the board of directors.

All eyes were at the front while the chair spoke. Sara hesitated, waiting for a moment. She took in a deep breath, closed her eyes for a second, and let the keys slip from her hand onto the hard floor. The clank was a switch, turning all heads around simultaneously. Instinctively, Sara froze. Fear filled her again, and she had to resist the urge to turn and walk out. Then she remembered Richard's advice: "You have to go. Face them in person. It would be good to see how they react when they see you walk in."

Face them in person. Face her fears and let them see her. He didn't offer to accompany her, which was out of character. He knew that she needed to do this alone, so he'd kissed her softly on the mouth and walked away, but not before she saw the admiration in his blue eyes. She couldn't let him down.

One more deep breath and her eyes focussed directly on the board chair. Despite the distance, Sara was certain she could see her cognac marbles narrow in recognition and her lips frown ever so slightly.

The other members of the board looked up, heads in unison, to see the tiny woman in the bright red coat who had disturbed the meeting. The chair paused slightly, but quick on her feet, she composed herself and resumed her speech. But Sara saw it. She'd been ruffled, even if it was just for a few seconds.

One quick look around the room, and Sara caught the wide eyes of her former colleagues. Weasels in the hen house, and Phillip was redder than usual. He looked at her, and then averted his eyes, looking down. Shame. It fed Sara's confidence.

She scanned the room and saw Mayree's smiling face beckoning her to the empty seat on her right.

Only when she sat down did Sara let out her breath. She waited a minute before taking off the scarlet coat, conscious of the stream of sweat that was tickling her sides. As she settled comfortably in the seat, she realized that it had been a good idea to walk in late.

Two years earlier

It was lunchtime, and Sara chewed her sandwich slowly, savouring every bite of the sharp swiss cheese and crunchy arugula. She ate in her cubicle so she could surf the internet, laughing at tweets and perusing job boards. When she saw the posting and looked closer to see the name of the hiring organization, Sara's stomach did a little flip, and she quickly closed the website window. Albatross Community Services was looking for a senior public relations officer. She was only three years into her current role, and had planned to stay for five before she moved on. But there it was—an opportunity to move into a senior position at a highly recognized organization.

She immediately called Catherine and spilled the news.

"So what are you waiting for? Apply!" It was the response that Sara expected. She often wished she could be a risk-taker like Catherine. Energetic to the point of irritating at times, and yet always the go-to person when Sara needed a positive push. She'd met Catherine in journalism school, and they'd immediately veered towards one another—a yin-yang friendship between a somewhat shy, brown-skinned Canadian woman looking for a stable career and a perky, Korean-born activist hoping to change the world. They were meant for one another.

"I know. I will. But I didn't want to leave this place so soon. I mean, I've only been here for three years! My plan was to stay here for five and then start looking."

"Three years is enough. Besides, you hate it."

"I don't hate it. I like my job."

"Yeah, you never like to talk about it, but I can tell that you're bored. Working with old people every day."

"Everyone gets bored in their jobs from time to time. We can't just jump from job to job every time there's a lull. And I don't work with old people, I just promote services for them. The office is filled with younger staff."

"Yeah, well they're all small-towners, and it's just not you! You want to turn into a bumpkin?"

Sara laughed. Once in a while, after a few drinks, she allowed Catherine to lead her into a joke-fest about small-town life.

"Besides, you can't plan these things. Who has a five-year plan these days?"

Catherine had a point. Sara loved her friend's free-spirited nature. It helped draw her out of her staunch, Capricorn box, a point that amateur astrologist Catherine often pulled out when necessary. "Yeah, that's true."

The small non-profit was located a fair distance outside Toronto, in a town that was still holding onto its Caucasian roots, having not yet been invaded by the influx of newcomers settling in Toronto and slowing creeping into the suburbs.

Sara spent her days as a publicist for the agency, which provided community services to seniors. The clientele were cookies from the same cutter—born and raised on the same street where they currently lived, with sons and daughters who married high school sweethearts, and grandchildren who attended the same primary schools that they had attended half a century earlier. It was a tightly knit community of people who attended homemade pie contests at Canada Day picnics in the town park.

Sara did not fit in. She knew it and the community knew it. But because of her job, her attendance at events was mandatory, even though she secretly felt that her presence just created discomfort. The slight widening of eyes when she approached was subtle, but the surprise couldn't be hidden under lowered lashes, despite the overly cheerful greetings. Kids however, were curious—drawn to her. Once, a tiny blond boy had reached out and held her hand, staring at the milk chocolate skin as if curious to see if the colour would rub off.

"Miss," he looked up, and she saw innocence in the bright blue, "are you from here?"

"Am I from here? You mean this town?"

"Yeah, I mean this place. Are you from another country, like Africa?"

She smiled at the comment because it wasn't unusual. How could she have such dark skin and yet not be African?

"No, I was born in Toronto. But my parents are from the Caribbean. Have you heard of the Caribbean?"

"Um, I think so. They are lots of islands where people go on vacation?"

"Yes, that's it."

"Okay. But did you ever visit Africa?"

"No, I haven't visited Africa yet. But I hope to visit someday. How about you?"

"No, I haven't gone there. My dad says it's not safe."

"Not safe?" The question blurted out with no permission.

"Yeah, lions and elephants running around. He says I have to wait until I grow up. But I want to see the lions."

A little sigh of relief escaped Sara. "Yes, he could be right. Maybe wait until you are older, but for now, you can see lions at the zoo."

"Yeah, we're going again soon. I want to see the pandas too! Have you seen them?"

"Not yet, but I hope to go soon."

His tiny head turned suddenly as a voice called his name. Sara looked in the same direction and saw a woman beckoning him, forehead wrinkled.

"That's my mom. I gotta go. Bye!"

After a few events, Sara decided that perhaps it made sense to stay in the background. After all, that's what a publicist did. They were supposed to be content overseeing the various details that would make the event successful and the participants happy. There was a lot of satisfaction in standing on the sidelines, watching her work unfold. It wasn't in her nature to pose in the spotlight anyway. The executive director was more than happy to work the rooms, shaking hands, rubbing shoulders, and performing her well-rehearsed smile, which to the elderly eye, appeared warm and authentic.

Luckily for Sara, her name sounded Anglo. It was a shorter version of her real name, Saraswati, given to her by immigrant parents, who were told by a pundit that according to "the book," this name was her destiny.

She was named after the goddess of knowledge and wisdom. And that was all the information her parents relayed. A Google search provided more insight: Sara learned that this particular Hindu goddess was the wife of Bramha, the Supreme Being, otherwise known as God or Allah.

She was forever thankful that her parents had the common sense to provide her with a traditional Hindu name that could be shortened to suit the unforgiving Western world. And so she was called Sara from birth. It was the first name that helped her get interviews because it was easy to pronounce. It was her last name that identified her as a visible minority, appealing to many employers who needed someone that could reach out to the changing population. It was the reason she got the job at Albatross.

Sara followed the receptionist's finger and walked down the hall in search of the kitchen. Concentrating on the unfamiliar path, she turned the corner to enter the doorway and suddenly pulled back to stop herself from running right into Mara, the executive director, whom Sara recognized from her job interview.

"Good morning." Sara managed to catch herself and spill out an eager greeting to the startled woman in the dark suit.

"Good morning, Sara." She stepped back slightly, realizing the closeness between them. Her tone was cool, but Sara felt relief at the familiar sight of the woman who had smiled at her comments about the reputation of Albatross.

"So, I found the kitchen on my first morning. That's a good start, right?" Sara watched Mara's mouth curve slightly upwards, but when she moved to the grey eyes, their stone stare triggered a stomach flip and had her pining for the exit.

"Yes, well that is a good first start for sure." Mara answered.

"Um, it's okay to put my lunch in the fridge?" Sara managed to say. There was no way out. It was her first day, and this was the boss.

"I'm not sure. You'll have to ask Margaret, the receptionist. She looks after the kitchen."

"Okay, sure. She's the one who sent me here actually."

Mara didn't respond, so Sara tried again.

"So, I want to thank you for this opportunity. I'm really happy to be here…" Her voice trailed off as she heard Mara's sharp voice interrupt.

"Good. Well, we are happy to have you here."

The words were curt, full stop, as the bony hands gripped the cup of coffee and Sara saw her back.

Mara Novak set the coffee cup on her desk and huffed out of her office into the ladies' room. She was alone and stopped in front of the mirror. A tired face stared back at her. At fifty-two, what did she expect?

Passing her hand over her hair, she tried to smooth the kinky curls that were a trademark in her family. There was no grey because of all the money and time she spent at a North York salon. But despite the deep-conditioning treatments, the coarse, disobedient nest refused to succumb and transform into the smooth, shiny mane she'd always coveted.

She turned slightly to see if her breasts looked perky today. Perhaps a little. But barely visible under the steel-coloured suit jacket. Somehow, the jacket had looked better in the mirror at Holts than it did under the dim lights in this community organization's modest staff washroom.

Or perhaps she was simply in the wrong washroom, inside the wrong building, in a mistake of a career choice. Most of her friends were private-sector professionals who prospered in posh leather and mahogany offices in the midst of the Toronto skyline. They left behind partially finished plates of duck confit after rushed lunch hours with clients at Canoe and Auberge du Pommier and competed in the race to slam down a platinum card before heading back to their offices, each of them stopping first in the kitchen to grab a leftover cookie or sandwich triangle that would plug the unsatisfied hole in his or her stomach.

How Mara wished for the privilege of those lunches. Often, she would sit silently at dinner parties when the conversation shifted to work. How could she say that she enjoyed her work in the community sector? She didn't dare admit that another company wouldn't offer her a top position, or any other role that was even vaguely comparable to where she was now.

She'd had high hopes after getting her MBA and landing her first administrative job at a hospital. She'd thought graduating at the top of her class would push her up the ladder quickly. So she worked tirelessly and managed to move to a mid-management position within five years. But there were always issues. Staff complaints about her lack of compassion, her "dogmatic style and condescending tone" were her downfall. She needed to work on her people skills said her superiors, but Mara didn't understand why. If she was too easy on her staff, they would not respect her.

Early in life, she'd learned that she didn't possess the looks that would help with popularity, so she knew she'd have to work hard. Being attracted to women didn't help. To this day, she kept her personal life hidden, even from her own parents.

Bullies tormented her as a teen. Her flat chest, Coke-bottle glasses, and hair cut short to manage the kinky curls made her a target. "Minus A" they would chant, referring to what they imagined was the negative cup size of her bra.

Everything changed the day the boys cornered her at the back of the school grounds and pulled down her pants to find proof of her gender. Humiliation spun through her like a whirling tornado and turned into a rage that pushed her to fight. She grabbed a boy by the throat with pinched fingers until he choked and fell gasping to the ground. He lay red faced, begging for air, as she lunged at another boy's throat, managing to grab skin before he quickly pulled away.

It was her eyes that made them back away. Suddenly, this quiet, nerdy girl had turned into a monster. Unrecognizable, with a rage and a determination that put fear into their hearts. And this fear manifested in their eyes—a look that changed Mara's life forever. It was the first time she realized the power that came with fear. And it was a confirmation that boys were not allies.

But the pretty girls weren't all that friendly either. The cheerleaders with slick ponytails were part of an unreachable social circle. So she admired them from afar. She often wondered what it would be like to be a link in that circle—sitting together at lunch, thighs touching, or walking home together after school and perhaps getting invited by one of the girls to come over and study in her bedroom. She imagined the smell of their hair, loosened from silky ponytails, and how soft their skin would feel under her fingertips. But they rarely looked her way, only to smirk sideways at her baggy clothes from time to time.

Mara suddenly realized she was staring at herself in the mirror, and her mind shifted to the woman she just left in the kitchen.

Young, milk chocolate skin, smooth, shiny black hair, and big doe eyes. And the breasts—so full and alert. Mara had imagined the way they would feel in her hand. Firm, soft, and even while the woman was addressing her, Mara was imagining hard nipples.

She shook the thoughts from her mind and realized working with her would be difficult at first, though she could manage. After all, the board of directors was adamant that she take some action to reach out to the growing South Asian community, who had recently started complaining about a lack of cultural sensitivity from Albatross.

That was the reason this person was hired—to do just that. And she was attractive, but that was incidental. The tinge Mara felt despite the dark skin was puzzling to her—she wasn't one of the blond cheerleaders from Mara's past. But this could be controlled. As long as the community was happy, the board would stay off her case.

She turned from the mirror and marched back to her office.

3

"How was your first day?" Catherine's question was genuine as she peered at her friend over a half-empty glass of draft.

"It was a bit strange." Sara was happy to talk about it with her friend. Giselle wasn't present, so it was easier to be honest, just one-on-one. "I have a small office with a window, and it's just across from Anna, the program coordinator—the one in the interview who asked me the diversity question."

"Oh yeah, the question you screwed up on?" Catherine teased, lifting her eyebrows accusingly.

Sara had been asked to explain what "diversity meant to her." Although it was a question she'd prepared for, having conducted various Google searches on the different ways "diversity" was implemented in organizations, she was still fuzzy on the term. Her rehearsed answer sounded contrived and vague, like a group of words thrown together for a bureaucratic key message that meant nothing. But apparently, it worked.

"I didn't screw up, or I wouldn't have the job, would I?" Sara retorted with a chuckle. "I just don't understand all of this diversity spin."

"You know what it means. It means they want to hire visible minorities."

"I know, but I don't get it. I mean, it sounds like they are coming out and saying, 'Hey, we're not racist. We hire everyone.'"

Catherine laughed. "Yeah, that's pretty much what it means. But it takes time ... multiculturalism is new."

"Actually, it isn't really, but I suppose more professional jobs are available to ethnic people now. It seems like a trend."

"Ah, Sara, get over it. You got the job, right?"

"Yes, true. I don't know. My coworkers weren't all that friendly. Anna said hello when she walked in but never made eye contact and avoided me the whole day. I just thought that if she asked that question, then she must be open to 'diversity.' I mean, that's why they hired me, right?"

"I dunno. It's hard to say, but it's early. She will come around. Some people just need to warm up to you." Catherine's comment was an indication that she didn't want to talk about work anymore, so Sara took the cue. She didn't want to waste the evening trying to figure out why Anna had been cold.

"Yeah, perhaps that's all it is."

"So what's going on in the dating scene? Meet any new guys?" Catherine's eyes were big and anticipating. She'd been dating the same guy for a few years and the excitement of the relationship had plateaued. So she was always looking for tidbits of Sara's online dating stories. But although Sara allowed herself to dovetail into a new conversation, her mind was still half on her first day in the new job.

During the morning, she'd tried to meet Anna's eyes a few times, but the plump woman just stared at her computer with a hard line on her lips. Sara worried that Anna was purposely avoiding her, but tried to dismiss the thought. It was too soon to start judging people. Maybe she was just being paranoid.

Sara heated up her lunch in the kitchen and ate in her office while reading through catalogues of the various programs that Albatross offered. Sara focussed on the programs that Phillip had highlighted, the ones that had the highest newcomer enrollment.

Despite her background, Sara really wasn't all that familiar with newcomers. She had been born in Toronto, and her parents had both left the Caribbean in their teens. Back in the sixties, Toronto was very Caucasian, and when you found someone from the same country as you, you immediately bonded. So her parents' marriage was inevitable. But despite the comfort of their shared culture, they made the decision to raise her as a Canadian, knowing that it would benefit her in the long run. And yet, here she was, saviour for Albatross Community Services, whose main clientele didn't speak English.

Sara wondered when Phillip would ask her what languages she spoke. It hadn't come up in the interview, but she wondered if there was an expectation that she spoke a South Asian language. Her last name, Ramnarine, was South Asian in origin, which could have been a source of confusion for Phillip and his staff. How could she possibly look South Asian and not speak Hindi, or Hindu as many insisted. How could she be from the Caribbean and not be black? It didn't fit.

Sara often bit her tongue when faced with such questions. She was patient and diplomatic, knowing that she wanted to educate, not discourage, and so she answered with facts. Sometimes, she really wanted to give an obvious answer, such as "Do you speak German? Because I thought all Caucasian people with blond hair came from Germany…"

But she didn't. It would be snarky, and it wasn't necessary. She could be patient and understanding, and now she was hired in a role where she was needed, and maybe not necessarily for her work skills.

As Sara was leafing through case profiles and eating one of her many sandwich variations, a movement caught the corner of her eye, and she looked up to see a woman walking into Anna's office. She stopped reading, swallowed the mouthful of sandwich, and watched.

The woman looked South Asian. Her black hair was pulled back from her face, revealing fair skin and a nose that stood prominently. She sat down in front of Anna's desk, and they started to talk. The woman carried a briefcase and a notebook, so she was obviously there for a meeting.

She waited for Anna to bring her over for introductions, but it didn't happen. Instead, the two talked for a few minutes, and the woman left, glancing at Sara as she walked away, with a hint of a smile.

The day passed slowly with much of the same. No contact with the staff until later in the afternoon, just before the day ended, when Phillip Williams came by and sat down in her office, on the edge of the guest chair across from her desk.

"So, Sara. Made it through your first day?" he asked. She was still getting used to the real Phillip, as opposed to the man she'd envisioned from his reputation. He was shorter than she had imagined, and there was something seemingly unnatural about his hair, a characteristic she never really noticed those times she'd seen him interviewed on television. She remembered the dampness of his hand when he welcomed her in the interview, and how she resisted the urge to wipe her palm on her pant leg.

"Yes. So far, so good!" she replied, turning to smile at him. "I've been doing some reading today, trying to get my email set up, you know, the usual first day stuff."

She was pleased to see his smile. "Great! Have you had a chance to look around the building? Check out the recreation centre that's attached to the office?"

"Well, I made it to the kitchen, but that's as far as I got. Maybe I'll wander around tomorrow."

"Yeah, it's a big building. Maybe you can ask Anna to show you around tomorrow. I'm sure she won't mind. She's been here a long time and knows a lot of the rec staff."

"Okay, I'll connect with Anna." She tried to sound cheerful when she said her colleague's name.

"So today was a busy day for me." His face started to flush as he spoke. "I had meetings offsite and wasn't here much, but tomorrow we will have a staff meeting so you can meet the other members of the team and the organization. Everyone is happy that you are on board! I know you're going to do some great work here."

"Thanks! I'm really looking forward to it." Warmth flooded through her insides, and Sara couldn't stop a smile from dominating her face.

He was already getting out of the chair as she spoke. Sara had hoped to talk a bit more about the clients and their expectations and issues, but Phillip was rushing out of the door.

"Have a good night," he said as he left.

At four thirty, Anna picked up her purse and walked out of the office without a word. Maybe that was just her way.

Anna walked into her kitchen and dumped her bag on the table. She walked into the washroom and flicked on the lights. Some wisps had escaped from the clip she'd used to pull back her limp hair, an unfortunate trait that she'd inherited from her father's side of the family. In the mirror, her eyes stared back through the glasses she wore every day. She had contacts but couldn't be bothered to put them in every day and clean them at night. Besides, her husband didn't really care what she looked like. They'd been together since high school, and the excitement had melted long ago.

She still had a pretty face. Prettier than the women at work, so there was never any reason to change her look. Anna forced the escaped strands back into the ponytail and re-clipped it. Sighing, she walked back into the kitchen to prepare dinner.

"Hi." Rob came in the side door from the backyard. "I'll need to cut the grass this week," he said.

"Maybe you should do it now." Anna turned and looked at him. Rob shrugged and opened the fridge.

"I'm making dinner soon, don't eat anything," Anna continued her orders.

"I'm just getting some juice."

"Well fine, but help me chop some vegetables."

Rob took a knife out of the drawer, and as he was walking to the sink, he heard Anna's voice, "Wash your hands!"

Without skipping a beat, he turned on the water and soaped his hands.

Anna didn't talk much while they were preparing dinner. Rob didn't ask if anything was wrong because he knew she would tell him when she was ready. Sure enough, during dinner she talked.

"New girl started today. They hired an Indian girl because they think she's

17

going to help with communications with the Indian seniors."

"Oh yeah? She started today?"

"Yeah. They put her in the office opposite to mine. I'm not sure she's going to bring anything new to the role, but they had to do it. The board is getting demanding and insisting we have to hire more people from the community. Makes no sense to me. Shouldn't people get hired based on qualifications?"

"Good point," Rob said through mouthfuls of salmon and rice. His mind shifted to the baseball game, and he wondered if he could finish his dinner in time to see the beginning. The clock said 6:45 p.m. and the game started at 7:00 p.m. But there would be the singing of the national anthem, and the commercials, so he could still be okay for time.

Anna continued to talk, and he made a point to look up every now and again and nod. But he didn't contribute. He knew that she had applied for the job, but that Phillip had told her she wasn't ready to move into a senior role yet.

The whole situation was unfortunate. Rob had known Anna since high school. She always had to have the top grades in class. He knew of her desire to win and make her competitors regret winning. So even though he loved his wife and wanted her to succeed, he suddenly felt for this new woman who had the audacity to accept a role that Anna felt should have been hers.

He'd been in the same homeroom class as Anna, who'd sat behind him. He liked the way she laughed at his jokes, and he was impressed by her sarcastic sense of humour. He'd never had a girlfriend before, and although he was excited by girls, he was very intimidated. Rob was close to his mother, who was a strong, sometimes overbearing woman. So he learned at an early age that it was easier for him to stand back and let the woman have the spotlight. When he met Anna, he realized right away that this was a girl who appreciated that gesture.

He started looking forward to mornings, just before the bell rang, when the two of them would watch the other students strolling into the classroom and make fun of their clothes and the way they acted.

"Wonder what she charges per hour." Anna remarked at one of the cheerleaders who wore short skirts. And then she watched his expression to see if he liked the skirts that showed off their athletic and shapely legs and flowed gracefully over their round butts. He'd learned how to scowl or wrinkle up his nose in distaste. It pleased Anna, who was bordering on the plump side with short, meaty legs.

"Gross," he replied. "Girls like that just want attention."

Rob found himself laughing at Anna's critiques and began to realize that he was developing a crush on her. He was very comfortable around her. He wasn't a tall, athletic guy like the preppies who played football. And he wasn't cool like the lean, wiry basketball stars who strolled confidently through the halls. Rob couldn't dance, and he couldn't play sports. He was smart and liked *Star Trek* and playing video games and watching baseball on TV. He also loved his mom's cooking, and he found it reassuring that Anna seemed to like her meals too. The full roundness of their midsections was a comforting commonality.

Although he loved to look at them, he knew that the blond cheerleaders with the bum-skimming skirts were out of his league. Even worse were the fashionable black girls who would surely laugh if he dared attempt to approach them.

Anna was his type. After all, she made him laugh and her eyes lit up every morning when he walked into homeroom. He noticed that she was always in her seat when he got to class, so that they always had enough time for a quick chat before the day started. By summer, they started dating and never looked back.

Now as she talked, he recognized a familiar pang of envy in her voice. But it was not his issue. Shoving another bite of the now cold salmon into his mouth, he looked over at his wife and smiled. "This is a great dinner, babe."

A wide grin brought her dimples out of hiding. "Yeah, I like it too. You're doing the dishes, though."

Mara watched the woman walk by her office. It was her second day, and something about her confident gait irritated Mara. Her simple outfit fit her body well—perhaps a little too snugly for work because she could tell that her stomach was flat underneath her tailored jacket.

She saw the woman glance into her office and heard a cheery hello as she passed. Mara took a sip of coffee without answering and turned back to her computer.

Sara hung her purse on the back of her office door. The executive director, Mara, seemed colder than she had during the interview. What had changed? Had she been trying to woo Sara so she'd take the job? Or maybe it was just the fact that now she was the boss, and being at the top meant having to be stern and commanding respect.

But it wasn't anything to be worried about, Sara thought. She just needed to do a good job, and then she could build a relationship with Mara.

Phillip came into her office as she was starting up her computer. He sat down, on the edge of his seat, his large belly protruding above his belt. Sara wondered if he didn't lean back simply because he couldn't.

"I have some projects that I would like you to start off with." He smiled and handed her a folder. "The program manager for the Passing the Torch program wants the brochure updated. We did the first one a few months ago, but it needs a change."

Sara opened the folder and saw the brochure sitting on top of a pile of documents. The smiling face of a young blond man chatting in the park with an older, silver-haired woman graced the cover.

"The program has been gaining momentum. It pairs youths with retired professionals, who act as mentors. You can see that the picture needs to be updated."

Phillip smiled at her knowingly, with a twinkle in his eye, and then leaned in a little. "The program manager is new. Maxine. She doesn't know much about publicity, so you'll have to work with her." He chuckled. "She will need some managing."

Sara made a mental note to tread with caution when dealing with Maxine.

"The Passing the Torch program is also celebrating its first anniversary. So we'll need an event. The details of this year's launch are in the folder." Then his face turned from amused to serious. "Maxine may want to pick the guest speaker, but you'll have to take control of that. Who knows who she will want to bring in? Besides, it's not her decision."

The tone of his voice made Sara wonder what she was in for.

When Phillip finished his talk, he walked out of her office and straight into Anna's. As he sat down and leaned back into the chair, Sara heard his voice, and she saw Anna's eyes flick in her direction. Anna hadn't spoken to her much since she started, except for a morning greeting and the odd answer to a question. But as Sara watched her interaction with Phillip, she saw their comfortable dynamic and the broad smile across Anna's face as she chatted casually with her boss.

Phillip didn't spend too much time in Anna's office, and as he walked out, he glanced at Sara with an upturned mouth in the shape of a smile, but she noticed his eyes were wide and almost fearful, in opposition to what his mouth was trying to do. Sara was pretty sure that Anna was not pleased with her presence. Was Anna just one of those people who didn't like change and was skeptical of new people? Perhaps Sara needed to win her over and build a rapport. Perhaps it was just a case of Anna mistaking her quiet manner for snobbishness, and making an extra effort to get to know her colleague was the key to overcoming her hesitation.

The year she turned twenty-five, she had been at her previous job for less than a year. Violet was the office manager who planned birthday celebrations for staff. She was the keeper of the employee events calendar and the purchaser of cakes for staff birthdays, new babies, engagements etc. The staff would assemble in the boardroom after lunch to wish the honouree well and enjoy a piece of cake and watch as they opened gifts.

Sara had attended many of these events at the agency and was secretly anticipating a birthday celebration. Two weeks before her birthday, she started hearing rumours about a change in the tradition. One day, she heard Violet talking to a few colleagues, clearly in earshot of Sara, who was refilling her coffee cup in the lunchroom.

"It's time for the cake tradition to end," Violet was saying. "I'm on a diet and can't handle any more calories. Plus we have been doing this for a really long time. I'm going to send an email this week to let everyone know that the tradition will end."

At first, Sara felt the twinge of disappointment, thinking it was a shame that her birthday was the next one in line, just as the tradition was ending. Perhaps Violet didn't know her birthday was so soon.

But when the email came, Sara felt tears welling up in her eyes as she read the words. No more cake, no more birthday celebrations. Why was she so upset about it? She usually went out for drinks with Catherine and Giselle. There was no lack of love, for sure. Still, she had been looking forward to a small celebration and some well wishes for her twenty-fifth birthday.

It took a walk around the building, letting the crisp, winter air clean out the toxicity, before Sara could put on a strong face and smile at the staff, whose eyes appeared sympathetic. Finally, Jasmine, an older lady who was the assistant to the executive director, said something to her.

"You know she only did it to spite you." Jasmine was known for her candour. "She thinks you are stuck up, so why should you have a cake? I heard her say it … Sorry to tell you, but that is how she is, and people should know it. She's also racist." The last words were given in a low whisper, with Jasmine leaning in closely.

So there it was again. Racism. The word dangled in Sara's mind. It seemed so cliché. Was it really that simple? Sure, she was working in a small town, and she was the only visible minority besides Jasmine who worked at the agency, but the premise seemed so backward, so shallow. She shook the word from her mind and picked up the second label: "stuck up." It startled her because she'd never heard herself described this way and wondered why anyone would see her as privileged.

Sara opened her mouth to allow the words to spew forward, and she watched as Jasmine's eyes widened in anticipation. But suddenly, she stopped. It wasn't professional. So she forced her lips to form a smile and said casually to Jasmine, "Maybe she doesn't know that my birthday is coming up."

"Are you kidding me? She knows." Jasmine was firm. "She is just like that. I bet she will continue the tradition when it's Suzanne's birthday."

She was the community liaison who was always out meeting with various agencies and local governments about partnerships. Sara often admired her streaked blond hair and sense of style as she energetically schmoosed at events. It didn't hurt that her family was quite prominent in the small town the agency called home either.

Suzanne's father was the former mayor and, along with her mother, ran a real-estate business in the area. Sara envied the way she walked in and out of the office according to her own hours and schedule, while Violet monitored Sara's lunch hour to make sure she didn't take longer than sixty minutes. A-listers would take extra time for personal errands or appointments, and Violet did her best to cover for them.

Suzanne's job entailed being out at meetings quite frequently, but everyone knew that she took full advantage of this schedule. Meeting venues were always close to the office since the agency was in the middle of a very small town. It would have been easy to go to a ten o'clock meeting and be back in the office for the afternoon.

But Suzanne never came back to the office. One time, on her way home one summer, Sara spied the blond waves blowing on a patio in the afternoon, a glass of draft on the table and tinkly laughter in the air.

She was never reprimanded and perhaps, Sara concluded, never even questioned. To complain would be futile, and it would only put her own job in jeopardy. Sara did not want to be the complainer. So she played by Violet's rules and reassured herself that this type of behaviour was the exception and not the rule. It had to be.

But now she was getting similar prickly vibes from Anna. Her colleague had spent the last few days avoiding eye contact and keeping her nose in the air as if she were trying to avoid a distasteful smell.

Perhaps the "stuck-up" label was indeed the reason. The clock said five minutes after noon. Sara got up and walked across the tiny hallway to knock on the open door. Anna looked up without a smile, eyes staring at Sara through her glasses.

"Hi, Anna. How are you doing?"

"Good, how about you?" Anna's answer was matter-of-fact, and she turned back to her computer as if engrossed in an important task.

"I'm good. Getting to know about the great work you guys do around here. I'd always heard about Albatross."

"Oh yeah?" There was a hint of a smile.

"Yes, for sure. When I was a journalist, we ran stories about your programs all the time."

"Where did you work as a journalist?"

Strange. Anna had been in her interview, so she should have seen the resume.

"In southwest Toronto. With a local paper. The *Community Reporter*."

"Oh yeah, right. I have heard of them. They cover our events sometimes."

"Yeah, but I think it's a different reporter now. So do you live close by?"

"Mississauga."

"So the drive isn't too bad?"

"Not really. It's about twenty minutes."

The small talk was painful, and Anna shifted nervously in her seat. As Sara thought of another comment, Anna got up from her chair and walked around her desk. "It's lunchtime already."

"Oh, yes, so it is. Are you going to the lunchroom? I'll walk with you. My lunch is in the fridge."

"Okay." Although the voice indicated dread, Sara persisted. There must be a common ground somewhere.

"Do you usually bring your lunch?"

"Sometimes. I usually go out on Fridays with some of the girls from the accounting department."

"Oh, that sounds nice. I haven't met them yet."

Anna opened the fridge and grabbed a black-and-white lunch bag. She politely held the door open so Sara could grab hers. Sara realized that she had a sandwich and there was nothing to heat up, but she stalled and opened the cupboard to get a mug for coffee, which she rarely drank at lunch. Anna lifted the lid off a container, and Sara spied potatoes and sausages covered in a dark gravy with curly pieces of mushrooms.

"That looks really good. Did you make it?"

Anna smiled at the compliment, and Sara felt a pang of hope. "No, my mom made it last night. These are leftovers."

"Looks like mushrooms. Oyster?"

"No, these are from the woods. My dad picks them once a year."

"Really? Wow, that's interesting. I heard that you can pick mushrooms, but I think you need to know which ones are poisonous and which ones aren't. I have no clue myself."

"Yeah, you really need to know. My dad's been picking them for years, since he was in Poland. Of course, the types you get here are a bit different."

The conversation was flowing.

"I guess a lot of people pick them over here? I wouldn't know where to go."

"In the forest. And lots of people pick them. My dad sees a lot of Orientals when he goes out."

"Orientals?" Sara resisted the urge to say "Asians."

"Yeah, they like to stir-fry."

"Oh yes, right."

The smell of her lunch wafted through the kitchen; Sara held her coffee cup in one hand, lunch bag in the other.

"Well yours smells really good. I just have a sandwich, which is what I bring every day, unless of course my mom has leftovers."

"Yeah, moms are good that way."

"Well, enjoy your lunch. Do you eat here in the lunchroom or at your desk?"

"I'm going back to my desk."

"Oh, by the way, I thought I could book some time with you to get some background information about your role. What do you think?"

"I'm free tomorrow afternoon." The answer was blunt.

"Okay, so about one o'clock? Does that work?"

"Sure. I'll put it in my calendar."

"Great, thanks."

Sara made her way back to her desk and wished she had bought some juice instead of the coffee. But it was a small price to pay for a chat with Anna.

As she bit into the tuna salad, she checked her email and saw that Maxine had responded to her request for a meeting. She'd sent a short email introducing herself and proposing a meeting to discuss the Passing the Torch event, and as she read that tomorrow morning would work, she felt a sensation in her stomach. Phillip's warning rang in her mind. She chewed slowly, making up her mind to read all the details about the program, so she would be ready to face Maxine the next day.

The smell of warm gravy hit her nose, and she turned to see Anna back in her office. Sara opened the binder and started studying.

Phillip popped his head in the doorway a little later and asked how she was doing.

"So far, so good." Sara turned away from her computer, grateful for the company. "I made an appointment with Maxine for tomorrow to discuss the event and brochure."

Phillip's eyes took on a tone of amusement. "Great! I'm interested to hear how it goes."

"Oh and I will be meeting with Anna tomorrow just so I can get an idea of her role and how we can work together."

The smile faded and the fearful eyes were back. "Great." The word came out flat.

Maxine's office was at the other end of the building. The meeting was set for nine o'clock, and Sara made sure she was early. As she approached the door, a tall, elegant woman with a neat afro smiled at her from behind the desk. Maxine stood up and extended her hand.

"Hello Sara, it is really good to meet you!"

Sitting down, Sara couldn't help but smile. "Very nice to meet you as well."

Maxine's grin was bordered by dimples, and she wore a silky, cream blouse that contrasted her dark brown skin. Flawless. That's how she looked, and while

Sara had her guard up as per Phillip's guidance, there was something very warm and comfortable about Maxine as she welcomed her into the cozy office.

"So Sara, when I saw your name, I guessed that you must be from the Caribbean."

"Well sort of. My parents are from the Caribbean, but I was actually born here." Sara felt a little twinge of relief.

"Me too." The dimply smile again.

"A coincidence." Sara didn't know what else to say.

"Well, usually it wouldn't be, if you think about how many people from the Caribbean live in Toronto. But it isn't really reflected here at Albatross just yet."

"Okay, I didn't realize."

"Well, many people don't realize, I suppose. But thankfully the board members realize that this needs to change."

"Yeah, that's what I was told in my interview. Albatross is trying to hire more staff that reflect the community." It was a factual, bureaucratic statement because Sara was being careful.

"Yes, that's the plan. However, the population has been changing for years, so we're a little behind in my opinion."

Sara was a little taken aback by Maxine's candour, but she was curious to know more. "Sometimes people don't realize, I suppose."

"Maybe. Or maybe they realize all too well. But that's a story for lunch. One day, we'll go out and we can talk. Today, I'm happy that you will be working with me on the Passing the Torch anniversary. I've been wanting to update this brochure for a long time, and I have some ideas about the event."

Sara waited.

"Do you know much about the program?" Maxine looked directly at her.

"I read a bit about the program and from what I understand it's a mentoring program where seniors speak with students about their work, so the students can learn?"

"Yes, that's exactly what we do. We have many seniors in the community who've had wonderful careers and some who've had just really interesting life experiences that they can pass along to students." Maxine's eyes were bright as she talked.

"The idea came up about three years ago when we had a seniors group and a youth group program scheduled at the same time in the community centre adjacent to this building. There was a break in the events, and the two groups went outside to the courtyard. One of the seniors started talking to a group of youths, telling a story about his career. He had worked as a chef in a downtown hotel back in the sixties. The story was so engaging, and the students were engrossed. As the break ended and the facilitators started ushering the groups back to their rooms, the senior passed along his number to one of the students, offering to talk with them further if they had questions..

"The facilitator of the youth group witnessed the entire scene and brought the idea forward. So we did a few surveys with the youths, their parents, and the seniors. The results showed that there was a need for mentors and an interest in the program among both youths and seniors. So we developed a plan and presented it to the board, who loved the idea. It took a bit of time to secure funding and get all of the details together, but within about a year and a half, the program was launched, and it is now going into its first anniversary."

"Wow. What a clever idea."

"Yeah, sometimes it's right in front of your nose, you know what I mean?" Sara nodded.

"So we need to do some more promotion. The brochure that we used last time was somewhat effective, but it's fairly outdated. The pictures don't really reflect the current audiences much anymore. What do you think?"

Sara squinted at the images. "Yes, you're right. From what I understand, the community is mostly South Asian, Caribbean, and African. So we should get pictures that represent that audience. I can help with that."

"Good," Maxine sat back in her chair, seeming satisfied.

Sara waited for a hurdle to present itself as Phillip had warned.

"So, you said you had some ideas about the event?" Sara asked.

"Oh yes, right. Well, we always have the same kind of event with the executive director saying a few words along with myself, as the program manager. But I thought we could get a few seniors and, of course, some of the youths to talk about their experiences with the program. We really need some first-hand stories. The only issue is that the program is very new, so we don't have any youths who have found successful careers yet."

"Sure, sounds great to me. Are there any youths who have found summer jobs or changed their career paths as a result of the mentoring program?"

Maxine smiled. "I'm sure we can find some."

"Okay. The personal stories will entice the media."

"Maybe we can talk to some of the ethnic media? There are a few Caribbean papers, lots of South Asian papers, and a couple of Somali papers." Maxine leaned forward with hopeful eyes.

"Of course. Don't the ethnic media come out for events now?"

"Nope. I've never seen them at our events, nor have I read a story about Albatross in the Caribbean paper. That's why you're here!"

Sara felt stupid. Of course, this was why she was hired.

"Okay. I've worked with some of them in the past, so let me do some research."
Maxine seemed pleased. "It's funny, isn't it?"

"I'm not sure what you mean." Maxine looked as if she held a secret that needed to be shared.

"Since I've been working with Albatross, the community has been relatively the same. Maybe there are a few more newcomer families, and maybe the demographics have shifted a bit to include more Somalian residents. But they've been here for nearly a decade."

It was clear what she was getting at. But Sara was hesitant to engage in the conversation. She was new, and it was her first meeting with Maxine.

"Well, it's only your first week here, and I don't mean to overwhelm you." Maxine seemed to have read her thoughts as she sat back in her chair and looked away. "Let me know your progress, and we can schedule another meeting to discuss the details."

"Okay, that sounds good. Looking forward to working with you."

As Sara walked back to her office, she realized that Maxine was indeed a strong woman, and although this meeting went well, it was still a good idea to keep her guard up. There was no reason why Phillip would warn her otherwise.

6

Maxine watched the young woman walk out of her office and felt uneasy. It was about time Phillip finally hired someone who reflected the community, but having worked with him for several years, Maxine wasn't sure his decision came from the right place.

She thought back to the day she was hired seven years ago. She had been given the job of program coordinator under Sharon, the program manager who had been with Albatross since it opened over thirty years ago. Sharon had built the seniors program from the ground up with the founders, Ronald and Mitzi Alderwood.

Sharon was a kind woman who was passionate about her work. When immigration started changing the face of the community, Sharon wasn't bothered like the other staff members. Instead, she kept focussing on the fact that residents needed the support. So Mrs. Singh was a vegetarian. Okay, well then that was a note on her file. And the concept of halal foods was simply similar to kosher foods. That wasn't so difficult. Some women wore hijabs and could not have male personal support workers or custodians enter their rooms. There were lots of female staff members who could step in. The adjustments took time, and were mostly about changing mindsets, but Sharon was a great leader.

Her approach was seamless. She treated each family, each senior as an individual regardless of their cultural background and made notes in their files according to their specific needs. She was steadfast in meetings, direct and calm when proposing accommodations, and she always handled challenges diplomatically.

But sometimes, Maxine wondered if Sharon had the right idea. The influx of immigrants prompted new marketing tactics to outline how taxpayers' dollars were being spent to make sure that ethnic needs were considered. The intention was to prove that the government was reaching out to all of its citizens, but it also put immigrants into separate piles, and, secretly, Maxine wondered if it encouraged stereotyping.

There was a lot of resentment from staff and even local residents. Change was never easy, but she saw the invisible line of segregation.

When Sharon retired, she recommended Maxine's promotion to program manager, which would make Maxine the first person of colour in a management role at Albatross. Sharon felt it only made sense since Maxine had been her protégé for years and was the best person to take over the seniors portfolio.

It was a flattering endorsement, and to Maxine, it seemed fair. The program director said they had to post the job externally as part of policy, since Albatross was government funded. Maxine had to apply for the position along with other qualified candidates. But naively, Maxine believed it was just a formality.

From what she had heard, there were four other people who were called for interviews. She had the itch to see them, to learn about their backgrounds, but it was kept very quiet; there was no talk about the other candidates.

She had to prepare a short presentation for her own interview and there was nothing really worrying about it. Some of her colleagues who were on the interview panel seemed nervous, and Maxine wondered if the other candidates were better, or if she was missing the mark entirely.

The final interview was with the executive director, Mara Novak. This time, she was nervous. Although Maxine had worked with Mara for years while Sharon was still around, she never felt completely comfortable around her. The way Mara's eyes watched her made her feel as if she were being judged or even scorned. During the interview, she found herself sitting on the edge of her seat, hands clasped in her lap, listening intently to every slow, icy word from the director's thin, pale lips.

Maxine knew about Mara. She knew that this was her way of being in complete control over her staff. She ruled with fear. Maxine often wondered how this cruel woman found herself a partner like Nancy, the kind-eyed, soft-spoken school teacher who sometimes came in to say hello when she was picking up Mara. Was she cruel to her partner at home? What kind of life did Mara lead when the doors were closed?

Finally, when the job offer was presented, with a decent compensation package, Maxine felt her body relax. She hadn't realized the stress had stiffened her because she was trying so very hard to remain composed. She was a strong woman and was good at her job, so there was no reason for the organization to hire someone externally and go through the process of training, not to mention introducing residents to a new face.

But deep down, she suspected that somewhere, in someone's mind, there was a need to preserve the traditional look of leadership. Maxine was all too familiar with stories from friends and family who were held in junior positions while younger, attractive Caucasians were catapulted into management.

Maxine hoped it was the beginning of a new era at Albatross. Perhaps the community organization would be a leader in progressive employment.

But now, as she watched the young, attractive woman walk out of her office, she felt a pang of uncertainty. What was it about this situation that worried her?

Sara stood cautiously in the doorway and knocked softly on the open door. Anna looked up from her desk and managed a smile, gesturing for Sara to come in and sit down. As soon as Sara sat down, Anna picked up her coffee cup, said, "I'll be back in a minute," and headed out of the office.

Sara placed her notebook on the desk. Strange. This woman seemed shifty somehow.

After about ten minutes, Anna rushed back into the office, placing a mug full of steaming coffee heavily on the desk.

"So, what is it that you wanted to know?" The direct look staring through the big glasses did not include a smile.

"Well, I wanted to find out about your role and responsibilities, so I can learn how the department works. And, of course, understand how my role fits with yours."

Anna looked away. "I work directly with the external organizations. I handle promotions with the community centre managers and help develop brochures and plan events with our partner organizations. I also work with them to deal with issues with the programs because we fund them."

Just when Sara thought she would be dismissed, Anna turned to a file and pulled out a few brochures and laid them proudly on her desk. Sara immediately picked up one of them and started leafing through it.

"Wow, I love the artwork. Who does the design?"

"We have a graphic designer who works from home who does all of our artwork." And then she quickly added, "I manage him."

"Okay, so if we need to create a new brochure, we call him? I just met with Maxine, who wants the Passing the Torch brochure updated." As soon as that last part came out of her mouth, Sara felt a mistake.

Anna's eyes widened. "Oh my God. Maxine wants her brochure changed? We just did that one last year!" Suddenly, there was life in her face. "Elizabeth and I worked with her on that brochure, and it took us weeks!" It was the first time that Anna had referred to the former public relations officer. No one had really mentioned her before or why she left.

"Maxine wants everything her way. She doesn't understand how to communicate with her audience. And she wanted to choose all the pictures. In the end, we just didn't show her the ones we picked. I think it looks great, so why does she want to change it? It's a waste of money!"

At that point, Sara knew that it would be a mistake to talk about the pictures and how they failed to reflect the targeted audience or the actual participants in the program. Somehow, this didn't appear to be a concern to Anna. Sara looked at the woman closely. Her eyes were pale blue, like a watercolour brush just lightly stroked the whites. Her hair, which was loose today instead of confined into its usual ponytail, appeared to be freshly coloured, lacking in dark roots. Blond, thin, wispy at the ends. Sara felt a little rise of compassion.

"Anyway, here is the folder with the contact information for the graphic designer. It's a good brochure, and the residents like it. I'm not sure it needs changing again." The voice was back to a stoic monotone.

Sara reached out, accepted the folder, and left the office, wondering what she was really supposed to do.

The weeks passed, and Sara found herself immersed in her new role. She usually stayed late, just because she was engrossed in a project and wasn't ready to shut down. Mara's car was usually still in the parking lot when she drove away, but Sara rarely saw her.

Although her office was across from Anna's, the two women didn't talk that much. In fact, some days passed without any exchange between them at all except for a polite "good morning." Anna was professional, however, and if Sara had a question, she would walk across the small hallway and quietly pose it to Anna.

She was grateful to be working on the new brochure with Maxine. When she first contacted the graphic designer to talk about new images for the brochure, there was a slight disconnect. At first, he wasn't sure why he was not working with Anna, and a few times, Sara had to repeat that she was new and was tasked with updating the brochure. Anna was in the loop, she finally told him, which seemed to put him at ease.

Then, he didn't understand when she asked for pictures of South Asians.

"Who are South Asians?" he said over the phone after a long pause.

"People who are from India, Pakistan, Sri Lanka."

"Oh, okay. You know that the brochure was just created, right? Did you talk to Anna about this?"

Sara felt annoyance circling her mind and took a deep breath before she answered.

"Yes, she is aware. I am working on the brochure now." And then a comment came out without her permission: "Is that okay?"

"Yeah, sure. So I will search some of the stock photography sites. We may have to purchase some of these pictures; is that okay?"

"I'll talk to Maxine and let you know." Sara was certain it would be fine with Maxine but was a little surprised that they didn't have such photos on file.

She mentioned this to Maxine when they were looking at the draft brochure copy. Maxine laughed and shook her head. "I don't know why you are so surprised!"

Working with Maxine was pleasant. Yes, she was tough, and she wanted her own way much of the time; Sara found herself biting her tongue every time Maxine changed a word here or there. But she was kind and encouraging to Sara.

Sara found herself wondering about this mysterious woman with minimalist style. She was from the islands, but where? Jamaica? Grenada? She wore no wedding band, and the photographs in her office showed her and an older Caucasian woman, with Maxine sporting a straight hair style. It wasn't as flattering as the afro, Sara thought.

There were some paintings, however. A few small pictures of what appeared to be scenes from the Caribbean—one with children running and playing in a schoolyard and another of a young girl getting her hair braided by an older woman. Her mother perhaps. The girl's face was wincing as if the plaits were being formed very tightly.

"It's great, isn't it?" Maxine's voice interrupted the daydream.

"The picture? Yes, it reminds me of the Caribbean."

"Yes, that's where I got them. I was visiting my grandparents, and I saw these pictures in the market. They were painted by a local artist, so I bought a few and got them framed. It's a good depiction of life in the villages."

"Yes, I went back a couple of times with my parents and remember seeing girls having their hair braided by their mothers while sitting on the front porch or sometimes in the yard. And the kids running around barefoot in the dirt. As we drove from one town to another, they stopped and stared. It was as if cars were a novelty, and we were outsiders. Even though I was born there, it seemed like a very different world. I wonder what it would have been like to grow up there."

"When did you visit last?"

"Oh, it was a few years ago. My parents go every now and again, but I am saving up for a trip to Europe. I've never been, and I really want to see Italy."

"I try to visit the Caribbean every couple of years. I love it over there. My grandparents have a home in the countryside, and I just find the pace of life much slower. I can actually feel my muscles relax the minute I get off the plane and take a whiff of the hot, tropical air."

"Yes, that's exactly the feeling! I remember stepping off the plane onto the runway, and it's so hot!"

"It's true; the heat just hits you like a wave." The two women smiled at each other, revelling in the mutual memory.

As they worked on the project, Maxine proved to be forthcoming, passionate, demanding, yes, but honest and fair. In the end, they had a brochure with pictures of elderly, smiling seniors of South Asian, Caucasian, and African descent talking to students from a variety of races. Sara had enjoyed the entire process, and Maxine seemed pleased.

Sara brought the brochure to Phillip for his approval. "Phillip, I wanted to show you the Passing the Torch brochure before it went to print." He took it from her hand and admired the cover.

"Great photos!" Leafing through it, he said, "Good job, Sara. I really like the layout, and the pictures do justice to the community. I'm sure the board will be thrilled. So how was it? Working with Maxine?"

"She was great." Sara smiled.

"Really?" He couldn't hide his surprise, but quickly said, "Well that's good. I figured you would be able to work together. Did you do a final proofread?"

"Yes, I've looked it over, and so has Maxine. Do you want to read it to make sure?"

"Nope, I'm good. As long as you're both fine with it then go ahead. Nice work!"

Handing it back to her, he turned back to his computer. Then suddenly, he looked at her again.

"Are you going to translate it into the top ten languages?"

Sara blinked—this was a step she forgot.

"Sure, we can do that. Do we have a list of languages? Who does the translation?"

Phillip looked at her seriously and said, "We have a translation company that does work for us. Anna will have the list of languages. Punjabi and Arabic are the top languages." He smiled knowingly at her when he said it.

She realized he thought she spoke Punjabi. What if he expected her to help with the translation? The thought sat over her head in a bubble for a moment as she waited, but he said nothing else.

"Okay, well that's great. I will talk to Anna about the list," she said and quickly walked out of the office. She was a little annoyed at herself for not thinking about translations. She wondered if she missed a perfect opportunity to tell him that she did not speak another language besides English. Or was it too soon?

Sara shifted her mind to Anna. She'd been hoping to get the brochure done without involving Anna again, but that was no longer possible.

As she walked back to her office, she held the brochure in the hand that was out of Anna's sight. She placed it in a folder and then walked across the hall. Anna looked up without a smile.

"Hi, Anna. Phillip said that you have a list of the top languages that we translate our copy into?"

Anna nodded. "Is this for Maxine's brochure?"

"Yep."

Anna's fingers tapped at her keyboard. She said nothing for about a minute, and then Sara heard the words, "I've just emailed it to you."

"Thanks," Sara turned and let her breath out.

The days melted into weeks, and soon three months changed anxiety into ease; Sara was starting to feel comfortable, growing accustomed to the paths within the large building and allowing herself to chat with the staff in the recreation areas. She worked on a couple of media releases that resulted in stories in the local and ethnic papers, and Phillip seemed pleased though he never said anything to her while she was in her office. His compliments came only on his side of the office, when she would stop to get approvals for projects. At least he was happy with her work.

One day, when the sun was high and the blue sky beckoned, Sara felt the urge to take a lunch break, so she ventured onto the patio that was situated just outside the lunchroom. Finding a seat wasn't always easy, since the office shared the lunchroom with the staff from the attached recreation centre. But as soon as she entered the area and the murmur of simultaneous conversations enveloped her, a staff member from the rec centre called her over. It was Cole, a middle-aged man who coached youth basketball, a soft-spoken gentleman with a young son and a wife who worked in finance. She was the head of the family, he would say proudly. He told Sara that he only worked part-time at Albatross because he had a computer repair business that he ran out of a workshop in his basement.

"Hey Sara, come join us!" His hand waved in the air.

She looked at the table. Cole, another guy in track pants and a hoody, and a woman dressed pretty much the same as the men sat together. Sara recognized the woman as one of the youth programs leads. It was a genuine invitation, so Sara walked over and took the empty seat.

"Sara, this is Chantal; she works with the youths in the after-school programs, and she's a bit of a troublemaker, so keep your distance."

Chantal kissed her teeth slightly at the jest and smiled at Sara, extending her hand. "Hey Sara, good to meet you."

"Great meeting you, Chantal. How long have you been with Albatross?"

"About three years now. Working with the teens."

"What kind of programs do you work on?" Sara took a sandwich out of her lunch bag and bit into the bun, tasting the simultaneous flavours of tomato and cheese.

"We teach some of these kids how to cook; sometimes we have chefs come in and teach. We also have guest speakers and workshops that provide life coaching and mentoring. Oh yeah, and the tutoring programs are relatively new."

"Kids learning to cook. That's kind of cool. Are they interested in being chefs?"

"Yeah, that can be one end goal. But it's mostly for kids of single parent homes. The cooking classes help them learn how to cook meals for themselves and younger siblings at home. A lot of kids' mothers work evenings, and they get home to an empty apartment. Lots of them end up hanging out in malls or around schools, and they can get themselves into all kinds of situations. So the cooking program brings them here, they learn to cook, and they can even bring younger siblings, and they get a warm meal."

"Oh, wow. I didn't realize that. It's a great idea. Who came up with that idea?"

"A cop, believe it or not." Chantal laughed. "A female cop told the school board that the kids needed to learn to cook for all those great reasons. So the board contacted us, and we got some funding and set up the partnership."

"And the kids like it?"

"Oh yeah. We have a waiting list. Now that's the problem. Too many kids want in, and we have no more space."

"Can you expand into other centres?"

"Yeah, that's what Albatross is supposed to be working on."

"You ask a lot of questions, Sara. Are you a reporter or something?" Cole's voice was filled with teases.

"Yes, actually. I used to be anyway."

"Oh yeah? For which paper?"

"The *Community Reporter*. I was a beat reporter for a couple of years. It was a lot of fun."

"So why are you at Albatross now? You could be a television reporter. I could see you on TV, reading the six o'clock news. Don't you see it, Chantal?"

"Yeah, I see it. She has the look."

Sara laughed and felt her face growing warm. There was no way she could be on television knowing that so many people would be watching her, judging her every word, every expression. It would surely result in flubs and stupid comments flying out of her mouth. Or worse, she would clam up and nothing would come out.

"Maybe. But I like working here."

"Yeah, you're new still girl."

"What does that mean?" She smiled as she looked at Cole, whose eyes flitted to Chantal.

"It means that you are still enchanted by the excitement. Albatross is a good place to work, but like everywhere, it's not perfect."

"Yeah, I can see that. I'm sure I'll figure it out."

The conversation shifted, and as the group joked around, Sara found herself enjoying the rare lunch break. As she laughed, her eyes flicked into the lunchroom, and she saw Anna looking directly at her. She was too far for Sara to see the expression in her eyes, and she quickly averted her gaze and went over to the vending machine.

"Hey, why so serious all of a sudden? You okay?" Cole asked.

"Yes, why? I am fine." She closed her lunch bag and crumpled the wrapping that had held her sandwich. "But I should get back to work."

"Okay then. Come join us anytime!" Chantal said and the rest of the table nodded.

As summer started to wind down, Phillip announced in one of the team meetings that Mara had agreed to the hiring of a community specialist to help with outreach to the diverse communities.

"We are looking for someone with lots of experience working with the South Asian community. Sara, you will be working closely with this new hire since their role will not necessarily be public relations but more community outreach."

Were they not happy with her work? According to Maxine, the brochure went over well with the community and the recreation staff, and she even heard that Mara and the board really liked it. So why someone new? She glanced over at Anna when Phillip shared the news. Her mouth was set into a straight, hard line. She said nothing.

When Anna got home, Rob knew something was wrong. She changed quickly into sweats and started preparing dinner without speaking to him. He knew better than to ask. So he simply sat at the kitchen table and read the paper as she pulled vegetables out of the fridge and washed them vigorously.

Finally, she spoke. "They're hiring another one."

"Another one?" he asked.

"Yes, another 'diversity person.'"

"Oh, what for?"

"To reach out to the South Asian community! Why do we need to keep hiring people because of the colour of their skin? We all work with them, and we have translators, so why does someone get a job because they are brown?"

Rob said nothing.

"Who knows what they will pay this person. A community liaison or outreach or something like that. I've been working there a long time, and they have never asked me if I wanted to do community outreach. I'm still planning lame anniversary parties!"

Rob kept quiet. His wife was ambitious. She'd been hired at Albatross as an intern when she completed her PR certificate only two years ago. But she was impatient, and when there was competition, all she cared about was defeating her competitor.

It wasn't completely her fault. Her parents had high expectations that their children would find professional success. Her brother owned an auto repair shop in town, and it was quite profitable. When Anna said she wanted to attend college, her parents were a little skeptical at first. Polish-born immigrants, they weren't educated themselves, and from their perspective, it would cost a lot of money.

It was hard for them to imagine their daughter attending classes with the elite, the people in town who went to the country club and golfed on Sundays. No one in their family had ever gone to university before. Surely she could get a job in an office without having to go to school? Maybe she could help her brother in the shop and handle the accounting?

But Anna wasn't interested in doing simple clerical work. She was determined to do something more, and so she convinced them that she would work and save up for tuition, if they would be willing to top up her contribution. They agreed and so she worked summers waitressing at the golf club, serving drinks to the parents of the kids she sat beside in class. Once in a while, one of her classmates would accompany their parents for brunch or even a golf game, and Anna would find herself placing drinks and plates of steaming, rich fare in front of them and cleaning up after they'd picked at their meals, leaving prime cuts of meat and buttery sides scattered untidily around their plates.

She learned to keep a straight face and not look them directly in the eye. In fact, they became blurry apparitions, so if she saw them at school or on the street, she wouldn't recognize them—not really anyway. If they recognized her, they never said.

When she graduated, her parents were in awe. They held a little dinner party at their home for family and friends with wine, cakes and pastries, lots of wonderfully rich fried Polish sausages, roast chicken, and plump, savory cabbage rolls. Anna had invited Rob and a few of her friends from high school.

She got the internship at Albatross the summer of her last year, and it was expected that she would stay on until her graduation in the fall. . But Phillip had liked her, and coincidentally, the full-time coordinator had decided to leave for another opportunity, so with the job open, Anna was moved into the role immediately.

Her parents were ecstatic. Not only did their daughter graduate from university, but she managed to secure a job right away, and it was in the city! They realized that Anna would be very successful. Visions of her moving up into a management role filled their minds, and they bragged to their friends and family that their daughter was a career-minded woman who would do them proud.

She married Rob shortly after, and soon Anna was on her way to having that perfect life. She would be just like the women from the country club, with their beautifully styled hair and sun-kissed skin, pushing strollers through the parks of their upscale neighbourhoods. Soon, she would be sitting at a table at the country club, where a student, putting herself through school as a waitress, would place a plate of prime rib and potatoes in front of her and then take it away with a few scraps scattered and superfluous on the plate.

Maybe she would take her parents to the club for dinner, so they could tell their friends and neighbours—who, like them, lived on the side of town where the weeds grew tall and the houses had siding and gravel driveways—that thanks to their daughter, they dined at the club on weekends.

The placement at Albatross was convenient, and she had taken the job to get some experience and then move on to something bigger. But two years had passed, and although she frequently perused job boards and dreamed of working in a glass building surrounded by bustling professionals, she never applied.

Fantasies about moving through the streets in a tapered power-suit to grab coffee in between meetings with clients were second to ones where children celebrated birthdays on summer days in the spacious backyard of a home that she owned with Rob.

Anna found herself more intrigued by baby clothes than fashions for herself. She often eyed rosy-faced mothers pushing strollers while donning designer sunglasses and heading towards the park near the office. She could see them from the window across the hall, in the office where Sara sat. Sometimes, she would go outside during her lunch break and see them talking and walking, and she'd imagine herself en route to the park near her home, coffee in one hand while the other guided the stroller gently.

Those days would soon come, she had thought. But when Sara was hired at Albatross and given the senior title and the office with the window, Anna felt something rising inside her, pushing up into her chest, and fighting to escape. She managed to keep it down, but in her mind, the race was on. The baby dreams forgotten for the moment.

9

The moon outside Mara's window was bright, round, and full. She rolled over and looked at Nancy sleeping soundly with her face in the pillow. Mara often wondered how she managed to breathe in that position. Her heart warmed, and she ran her hand gently over soft waves highlighted by rays from the moon.

She was lucky. She was smart enough to know that much. Nancy was her better half. So often, she felt unsure that she deserved this kind of happiness, to be loved by someone who gave more than she took.

Mara had come to terms with her own sexual orientation at an early age. She didn't tell her family, and when they tried to set her up with Jewish boys from the temple, she didn't fuss or resist. She simply tortured the boys with her cruel comments and criticisms until they walked away on their own. It worked well, and she suspected her parents finally figured it out when they stopped bringing boys around and asking her if she was dating.

It was in university that a sexual encounter with a woman presented itself, and Mara was ready. It was only sexual, and there was no emotional attachment, but the experience was satisfying, and she decided it would be fine to continue having brief, physical relationships with women. There was no need to make it more than it was.

The gay bar in the city where she went to school was a secret among the gay and lesbian community. Back then, being openly gay wasn't as accepted as it is today. You weren't as likely to march in a parade with your friends or wave a rainbow flag outside your dorm room window.

Mara was happy to keep it quiet. She was certain that her roommate suspected, though she never asked and Mara didn't tell. They shared a room but were never friends, and when Mara woke up to find big, sweaty football players lying face down in the opposite bed, she simply got up, got dressed quietly in the bathroom and left with her books. For the entire year, she didn't mention these mornings to her roommate and didn't let it bother her.

Sometimes after such an incident, the roommate would meet her eyes with hesitation and fear, as if waiting for words to come out in protest. But words were never exchanged. It didn't matter … the room was a place to sleep and keep her stuff. As long as they didn't touch her belongings and left her alone, she was not concerned.

Mara never brought women back to her room. She went to their apartments, or when the weather was nice, they walked to the woods and had sex in the dark. Once, in the winter, the woman she picked up couldn't go back to her apartment because her boyfriend was at home. So they went to the woods and kept their coats on while they slipped their hands under each other's pants, stroking until sighs of satisfaction prompted them to pull apart. Afterwards, Mara realized that the cold hadn't bothered her.

After a year, she moved out of the dorm and into a small room in a rooming house. It was easy to bring women home, but she didn't like it when they fell asleep and stayed. Mara would wake them up early and hand them their clothes, saying that she had a class to attend. There was never any resistance, and she never saw them again. It worked well.

When she met Nancy, it wasn't at a bar. At the start of her third year, Mara was exiting class one afternoon when her eyes found the delicate figure sitting on a bench under the fall sun. She appeared to be reading a book, and her curls spiraled down from her bent head, almost touching the pages. Something about the way she was crouched and the way the sun streamed softly through her curls made Mara move close, entranced. As she got within a few feet, Nancy flipped her head up, startled. Mara stepped back a bit, and the two looked at each other.

"Looks like a good book," Mara managed to say, despite the tornado inside her stomach.

"How can you tell?" A question to a question, from a soft voice. Mara smiled.

"Well you seem so engrossed in it. What is it?"

The beautiful girl turned the book over, so Mara could see the cover.

"Hm. I haven't heard of it. Fiction?"

"Yes."

"Not a fan of fiction really. I prefer non-fiction or memoirs myself."

"Oh really? What have you read lately?"

"Just started reading the one by K.D. Lang." It was a lie, but she wanted to test the waters.

"The singer?"

"Yep, that's her. She's pretty fascinating."

"I bet she is. That's interesting. Are you interested in country music?"

"No, not really, but I am interested in lesbian country singers who dress like men."

The words prompted a giggle from Nancy, and Mara saw dimples. "Yeah, me too." The curly haired girl was glowing, and as Mara sat beside her, she felt her insides tingling for the first time since she'd accepted her sexuality.

The courtship moved quickly. Within six months, the two were happily in love. Mara let her guard down slowly, but had trouble shaking some of her old defensive habits. She saw Nancy cringe at the occasional sharp criticism, and she always felt sorry afterward. She sometimes talked about other women who she'd been with, dropping words like hot and beautiful but never using those words to describe Nancy. Instead, she called her cute. She would watch as her girlfriend's face fell when she heard the compliments attached to Mara's former lovers. And Nancy would try harder to be pretty and keep Mara interested.

After they'd been living together for a few months, Nancy started feeling guilty about hiding their relationship from her parents. She had never told them about her sexual orientation, knowing they were safely tucked far away on the East Coast, though still connected to her by letters and care packages.

After she graduated, there was an expectation she'd return home and find a teaching job in the small town where they lived. After all, they had paid for her education with a sizable school fund they set up when she was a small child. So when they wrote to inquire about her return, wrinkles started to appear on her forehead and she began to toss in her sleep.

"Really, Nancy? Your parents shouldn't expect you to live with them. You're an adult!"

"Yes, I know. They don't think I will live with them in their house. Just close by because they are getting old, and there's only my brother, and he is busy with his wife and kids."

"It's a normal part of life. Fledglings leave the nest, and the parents do not expect them to return. Cut the cord, Nancy."

The conversation only made Nancy quiet. Mara would find her on the other side of the bed, turned away from her that night. Her heart softened, and she realized that if she didn't show Nancy her love, she would run the risk of losing her to the little East Coast town. So instead, she held her close and whispered that she understood.

"I know it's hard to be away from your family. It will take time to realize what you need to do. But I would be upset if you left me because I love you." And those words cemented Nancy's decision to stay and build a life with her.

So Nancy wrote a letter to her parents to let them know that she would not be returning home. Instead, she said, she was going to find a job in Toronto, where the schools needed teachers who were from across Canada. It wasn't entirely untrue. But the need for teachers at that time was growing.

Their response was surprising and even a little hurtful for Nancy. Her parents were thrilled that she was taking this bold step, and while they would miss her, they would be content with a visit soon. So that was that. Nancy's guilt faded and no longer did she worry about her parents while she was walking through the streets, holding hands with the woman she was deeply in love with.

So the couple found themselves an apartment on the third floor of an old Victorian in the Annex and set up their first home.

Over the years, Mara looked at other women and occasionally found them attractive. Usually the encounter was brief, at a work event or meeting, and her feelings quickly faded. But since the new, dark-skinned woman came to Albatross, Mara found her mind wandering more and more.

The bright moonlight fell across a sleeping Nancy, and as Mara stroked the curls of her love, she wondered how it was possible for another woman to hold her thoughts. She was a subordinate. It made little sense.

10

"So I hear your department is growing." Sara turned from the coffee machine to see Maxine's smile as she entered the kitchen.

"You mean the new community specialist?"

"Yes, that's the one. It's a good step in the right direction. I was in the interviews, and they have some good candidates. Phillip is going to announce their choice in today's meeting."

"Oh, really? Wow, that was fast. I thought the whole department would be in the interviews." She blurted out the last part and immediately regretted the whine.

Maxine paused for a moment before answering. "In a perfect scenario, it's a nice idea to have the entire staff meet the candidates. But sometimes they don't want a big panel. It's easier with a few people."

Sara wanted to ask if Anna had been in the interviews, but she didn't want to come across as insecure about this new hire.

That afternoon, Phillip announced that Venah, the new community relations officer, would start the following Monday.

Sara sneaked a look at Anna's face when the news was revealed. The straight line that was her mouth was intact, but this time, there was a flicker of annoyance in her eyes.

Good. Anna had not been a friend to her in the six months that she'd been with Albatross. She was abrupt and cold, and Sara suspected she complained to Phillip about her. So it would be good to have an ally—someone who was in their department who could see the way Anna acted and could perhaps provide some strength in numbers. Sara was looking forward to Monday.

Phillip walked into his office with his coffee and ten o'clock cheese Danish. The clock said 10:43 a.m. Staff meetings on Mondays always threw off the Danish routine by forty-five minutes, but then he'd push back lunch. It became a weekly routine on its own.

He was thinking about the look on Anna's face when he mentioned Venah. He was worried. Anna had long been aching for a promotion, but he wasn't sure she was ready. She'd talked to him about the senior role, Sara's job, but he knew that she wouldn't be a good fit. It meant working with program managers, and he'd had a few complaints about her abruptness. She needed some more time to grow and polish her image.

Even though he was her boss, he knew this was a conversation he was not prepared to initiate. How could he tell her to wear make-up and perhaps put on a skirt or a pair of high heels once in a while? It was sexist, really. He'd hoped that her competitive nature would prompt her to change her presentation when Sara started. The new woman's style was minimalistic and professional.

Lately, his concern about the dynamic between her and Sara had been growing. Anna had been in his office three times with complaints since Sara started. First, it was the brochure. Why did Sara and Maxine decide to redo the Pass the Torch brochure when Anna had finished it just a year ago? It made little sense, and it was a waste of money.

Phillip listened but didn't tell Anna that her brochure had not gone over well with the board of directors or Mara. It simply didn't reflect the community, and the content wasn't well written. Anna's writing was bland and failed to engage.

The other complaints were about Sara's knowledge, or what Anna believed was her lack of knowledge. She had asked when Albatross's anniversary was. She should have known that, Anna insisted. Why would she ask such a dumb question? Everyone knew the date of the fortieth anniversary that was coming up.

He did his best to listen and acknowledge her concerns even though he questioned her motivation. She firmly believed the job should have been hers. And she resented the fact that Sara was chosen for her ethnic background. Wasn't that reverse discrimination?

"Anna, you are a public relations professional. What is our first and foremost rule?"

"Understand the audience," Anna had mumbled.

"And our audience has a growing South Asian population. So it's imperative that our staff reflects this audience. It helps the audience identify with us and builds trust. And remember, we are only partially funded by the government. Some of our services are still paid for by the community. So we have to be competitive in the market."

As he spoke, he noticed the calmness returning on Anna's face. She was a smart woman, and she knew he was right. He thought that he'd won the round until she said, "Okay, I understand. But then why does her role need to be senior? She does the same work that I do. And besides, she's not even South Asian. She's from the Caribbean."

This little fact made no sense to Phillip. Sara was brown.

His response was calm. "Anna, the board wanted it this way. It will all work out. The organization is growing, and there will be many more opportunities for advancement."

The conversation troubled him. He knew Anna was ambitious, but he also knew she was not as experienced or as polished as Sara. From what he'd seen so far, it was clear that Sara had a lot of potential.

Phillip took a bite of his Danish and turned to his emails. There was one from Randi, his wife. He always got a little tickle in his stomach when he saw her name. Most of all, he loved opening her emails and scrolling down to her signature: Miranda Reynolds, LLB, Managing Partner, Hogarth, Reynolds, and Brown. He loved being married to someone who worked in a glass corner office and worked on high-profile cases that were featured in the news.

He first met Randi at a cocktail party in the city. He'd been invited by friends who owned a small advertising agency whose services he used as often as his budget permitted. He'd built the relationship up over the years and was always invited to their parties, which were held in their loft studio on King Street. It was a thirty-minute drive from where he lived in the west end. He'd have one, maybe two glasses of wine and by the time he was ready to leave, he'd be fine.

He heard Randi before he saw her. There was a circle of people standing near the work stations, and the loud, "listen to me" laugh came booming out from the inside of the circle. He slowly moved closer to see the source.

There she stood, five by what seemed like three. A beach ball in hot pink, glittering with gold jewellery and sharp, red nails. She looked at him for a minute, eyes hooded with blue and lips smashed with red as she took another gulp from her lsmeared glass. He looked at the others. All eyes were on her as she continued to chatter over the background noise of glasses clinking and heels clacking. He couldn't hear what she was saying, but was transfixed by the way the crowd stood around her, smiling and giggling as she led the conversation. She was a headliner.

He stood on the sidelines for a bit, hovering around the hors d'oeuvre table and nursing his wine. Although he was the public relations manager at Albatross and knew how to hold conversations, the sophistication of the city group and the confidence of the woman in pink held him back. What could he possibly add to the conversation?

"Phillip," he heard his friend David behind him and turned around. "Standing here all by yourself? Come, you have to meet Randi. She's one of the partners at the law firm that does some work for us."

Instantly, Phillip knew who Randi was, and he walked with David to the circle. As they joined the clique, Randi stopped talking and looked into his eyes. Then she shifted to David.

"Randi, I'd like you to meet Phillip. Phillip is the manager of public relations at Albatross Community Services and one of our best clients."

She grasped his hand firmly and said in her husky voice, "Pleased to meet you, Phillip. I'm Miranda, but everyone calls me Randi." And then she added with a coy wink, "For obvious reasons," drawing a laugh from the circle.

Then she turned back to her crowd and continued her show.

For the rest of the evening, Phillip stood at the edge of the circle and watched in awe. The roughness of her laugh was second only to her comments, which over time and wine, became more ribald. It excited him to see a woman captivate an audience the way she did.

And although Phillip would normally frown upon getting drunk at a work-related function, her boldness inspired him, and by the time he left the party, his knees were weak and his mind in a fog.

A sleepless night resulted in a dull, emotional hangover the next day, and he rose for work with one idea in his mind—forget that woman. And it worked for a few weeks. But then he got the call.

His mind was focussed on work when he picked up the phone and hastily said his name. The husky voice on the other end said, "Well, you sound like you're busy." He didn't recognize the voice and was a little annoyed.

"Can I help you?" he managed to say politely.

"Is this Phillip Williams?"

"Yes, how may I help you?"

"It's Randi. Randi Reynolds from Hogarth, Reynolds, and Brown."

The memory of that night jolted back and his stomach flipped.

"Hello, Randi. Nice to hear from you."

"Are you always this polite?"

"Um, well…"

The gruff laugh again and then, "Relax, I'm just kidding with you. Gosh, you seem so uptight! Listen, I didn't get much of a chance to talk to you the other night at the party, but I thought we could meet for a drink sometime."

The question was bold, and it took him a few seconds to absorb her judgemental description of him. A voice that he recognized as his own said, "Why yes, that would be great. When were you thinking?"

After going through Randi's tight schedule, they finally found a date the following week when she could "squeeze" him in. They would have to meet near her office however. It wouldn't be an issue, he said.

The courtship lasted a few months. It was the most exciting time of his life. Randi led him through her world of parties with celebrity guests, politicians, and CEOs of Fortune 500 companies. She was well connected and made a point to drop reminders here and there about the many suitors she had before him and the ones who were still eagerly waiting in line. But she chose to be with him, and he let her lead him into a quick romance and eventual engagement.

Of course, she wanted a large wedding. He'd managed to pull some money out of his savings account to give her the large, flashy engagement ring that she wanted, but his salary was not even close to hers. But if she wanted her nuptials to be grand, he would find a way, even if it meant taking on debt.

Ignoring the frowns from his parents, who flew in from Manitoba expecting a small ceremony and a modest backyard reception, he managed to give Randi her day in the spotlight at a large banquet hall in downtown Toronto.

He knew it was worth it when he watched her strut down the aisle of the large old church in her silk designer wedding gown. Randi wanted her gown to be flawless, and it was.

His parents didn't meet Randi until days before the wedding, and the only thing his father said to him about her was, "Will this make you happy?" The large, dreamy smile on his son's face didn't really convince him that happiness was the right word, but he patted his shoulder and nodded when Phillip said yes.

Three years later and Phillip was still high from being Randi's husband. The parties and work socials continued, and even the business trips she'd bring him on were extravagant. Five-star hotels and dinners in French restaurants, all paid for by her firm. It was the kind of life Phillip had always wanted.

Soon after they married, he sold his small home that was close to Albatross, and they purchased a sizeable condo in the downtown core. It meant a longer commute for him, but he didn't mind. He was pleased to tell his small-town colleagues that he lived downtown in a condo overlooking the lake. He was happy. He had made it.

Monday came and Sara was in the office early. She was curious to meet Venah, who would be sitting in the office at the end of the hall. It had been used as a smaller meeting room and a storage space, but they had cleaned it out to make room for the new hire.

At nine o'clock, Venah was escorted into the office by Phillip, whose red, glowing face greeted Sara as she sat behind her computer.

"Sara, I would like to introduce you to Venah, our new community relations officer."

Sara blinked at the woman donning a low bun at the back of her neck and wearing a dark purple *shalwar kameez*—the traditional long shirt and baggy pants that was a common sight around the community.

"Hi, Venah , nice to meet you." Sara managed a smile and extended her hand.

Sara glanced at Phillip whose red face shone as he watched the interaction between his two staff members.

"Sara is our senior public relations officer. She works on the promotional campaigns with the program managers, and she is responsible for ethnic media."

"Well, that is great to know. Very nice to meet you, Sara." Venah had a slight accent, and her beady eyes peered at Sara curiously. Her smile was one of amusement.

As Phillip took her to Anna's office, Sara tried to catch the look on Anna's face, but Phillip's large frame blocked her, and by the time he moved out of the way, all she saw was the familiar thin line across her face.

Venah spent the morning setting up her office, and Sara kept herself busy. Just before lunch, she saw purple at the corner of her eye.

"Sara. So how long have you been here, Sara?

"Since the spring actually. Just under a year."

"And how do you like it so far?" Sara felt uncomfortable as the woman's eyes bore into her.

"I really like it. The staff is great, and the organization is really innovative." It was a bureaucratic answer.

"Ah, well that's good to hear. So, your name is Sara?"

"Yes."

"Is it short for something else?"

Sara paused for a moment. It was a question she'd never been asked before. "Yes, actually. It's short for Saraswati."

"Okay, well I will call you Saraswati then."

"Actually, no, I prefer Sara, thank you." Her answer was firm.

"Why? You don't like your Indian name?"

Sara felt the tone pierce through her, and for a moment she was stunned into silence. She felt anger boiling up inside her, and heat rising to her face. A breath helped her regain her composure, and she answered calmly, factually. "My parents have always called me Sara. It's how I grew up."

"Well, I am sure that they named you Saraswati for a reason. You should embrace your Indian roots." Venah attempted an encouraging tone at the end of her interrogation. She turned and walked away, but not before throwing an authoritative look at Sara.

The comment stung. For the first time since she'd started at Albatross, Sara was angry. Who did this woman think she was to talk to her like that? Grabbing her purse, she decided it was a good day to get out and browse around the shopping mall, something she rarely allowed herself to do during lunch.

She thought about calling Richard. His calm demeanour would be reassuring. But it was too soon for him to see her this way. They had been on seven dates, and although it seemed like this could turn into a relationship, she didn't want to scare him off with a dramatic phone call that exposed her insecurities. A browse through a shoe store seemed an easy distraction.

Sara allowed herself to get lost among the shelves of neatly placed footwear, and as she wandered around the aisles, stroking soft leather and examining price tags, she forgot her anger for a moment and let herself fantasize about places these shoes could take her—places where work didn't exist.

A third trip through the aisles and her eyes focussed on a pair of red sling-back pumps on sale. The heels were high, and she didn't have an occasion to wear them, especially now that summer was gone for another year. She rarely wore high heels, preferring flats or loafers. But these were beckoning to her, whispering that happiness could be found if she slipped them on. As she slid her foot inside, the transformation into elegance and frivolity overtook her. She strutted down the aisle, confidence rising as she admired her foot arched in red. It was the lift she needed, and Sara clutched the pair tightly on the way to the cash register.

Satiated for the moment, Sara returned from the trip to see Phillip in Venah's office. Sara noticed a coy smile on the woman's face and was certain she'd been caught in her peripheral view. The woman laughed loudly and her head bobbed in an exaggerated nod as she listened to Phillip, eyes glistening as if the news he was relaying was wonderful. Sara couldn't hear what he was saying, but she felt worried as she walked into her office and sat down.

The high from the red sling-back purchase faded, and Sara spent the afternoon staring at words on her screen. She was supposed to be editing an article written by one of the recreation administrators, which on a regular day posed challenges. Today, she could barely make out what the words meant.

Her mind was flooded with thoughts about Venah. What exactly was Phillip's intent when he hired her? He said the board asked for a community relations person who could reach out and speak to the growing South Asian population. But how did her role interact with the others in the department? Did Venah have prior public relations experience or was her role completely different?

When Sara looked at the clock, it said 4:48 p.m., and she suddenly realized she hadn't done much work in the afternoon. Nervously, she glanced around, but the office was empty. It was time to go home. Grabbing her purse and putting on her coat, she left the office and allowed the tears to flow only when she was safely behind the wheel.

Sitting inside the car seemed secure. It was as though the windows were a shield that, despite their transparency, concealed all humanly actions being conducted inside. Sara often found herself turning away from people as they picked their noses while they drove. She recalled one horrid vision: a pretty young woman who popped her finding into her mouth.

But now, with tears melting her mascara, she wasn't worried about the people in the cars beside her. She didn't even look at them. When she turned onto her street, she wondered how she got there so quickly. The drive normally took thirty-five minutes in the evening from Albatross to her home in the southwest part of the city.

She searched for a parking spot among the parked cars on the side streets, which were already decorated with yellow leaves even though it was early October. Since she'd moved to the city, she'd become skilled at parallel parking and slipped into a spot easily. She walked down the block to the first-floor apartment that she rented in an old Victorian house.

At first, Sara wanted to get home as quickly as possible. But once the cool air entered her lungs and the leaves shuffled at her feet, she slowed her pace. She loved the fall and allowed herself to take in the moment between worlds: the tree canopy enclosed her and the brown office building was miles away. She closed her eyes and breathed. The smell of leaves was fresh and comforting as Sara's mind wandered to dinner. What would she have?

As she entered the tiny apartment, her mind was on the contents of the fridge. She had a fresh loaf of bread and cheese, the staples in her home. There were a few eggs as well and some apples, but she reached for the wedge of Gouda.

One bite of the crisp, buttery, gooey sandwich and the day's worries started to subside. Sara sat in front of the television in her flannel pajamas and savoured the sandwich with a glass of red wine.

The phone rang, and she leaned over to see the number. It was Richard. Normally, she would pick it up quickly but tonight, she wasn't sure she could contain the day's frustration. So she watched the screen until his name disappeared and the noise stopped. She would call him or text him later, when the wine took effect and her mind cleared.

Pouring herself another glass, Sara turned on her laptop and lay back on the couch. She logged onto the dating site where she met Richard and looked at his pictures. He was tall and so boyishly handsome. He was smart, but also a little passive. So when they went out, she did her best to contain her excitement and let him take the lead. If he suggested a restaurant, she agreed, as long as she was okay with the food. If he asked what she wanted to do, she smiled and asked him to surprise her.

The tactic seemed to work; so far he'd planned some good dates. Dinner, the movies. Once they went for a drive in the country to take in the fall colours. She was touched by that date. They drove north for a bit and had lunch at a tiny diner in the small town close to the agency where she used to work. The women in the office frequently lunched there on Fridays, and she'd heard them marvel at the quality of the home-style country fare. So when Richard asked where they could stop, she was eager to make the suggestion, and he turned the car in that direction.

He was indeed a find. She'd been on the dating site for almost a year and was at the point where she'd decided not to renew her membership. There were the consistent dead ends combined with the chore of finding new coffee shops for fear of staff watching her never-ending stream of first dates, gossiping and giggling as she struggled to find Mr. Right. Online dating was at best hard work and at worst degrading. But she'd never been good at meeting men in bars or through friends. Intriguing a guy through small talk, hair flips, and giggles was not her forte.

Then one day she received a message from a guy wearing sunglasses in a side-view picture that was relatively indistinct. Her first instinct was to ignore it, but instead she decided to read the profile and was impressed by the engaging writing style. Witty prose, void of spelling mistakes. Intrigued, she sent back a message, and it started a seamless, easy game of ping-pong chat that ended in an invitation for coffee.

It had only been a couple of months, but she was happy. Occasional feelings of doubt and anxiety would surface when she didn't hear from him for a few days, but then he would call and make plans. He texted often, but they were simple one-liners—enough to keep her engaged but not enough to make her feel really confident.

They met soon after she started working at Albatross, so when the topic of careers came up on the first date, she simply said that she worked in public relations for a non-profit organization. He didn't ask for elaboration, and she didn't offer more information. Sara was more interested in learning about his job as an elementary school teacher, and he was keen to provide details.

Finishing the last few sips of wine and browsing through his gallery of pictures, she suddenly realized that his profile was still active. Was he keeping his options open? They'd been spending a lot of time together, and he usually told her about his other plans with his friends, so where would he get the time, unless "friends" meant dates?

A ring tone interrupted her thoughts. She picked up her cellphone, reading the text.

"Hey, what are u up 2?"

She couldn't help but smile. There was no picture attached to his contact information since they had not yet connected on social media. The contact simply read "Richard."

Feeling the calm washing over her from the wine, she decided to text back right away. "Not much, just finished dinner. U?" She waited. Sometimes it took a few minutes or more for him to respond, so Sara got up and walked over to the window. She had a lovely view of the brick wall of the house next door. It wasn't exciting, but it was a relatively cheap, safe place to live, especially in this part of the city.

Her parents didn't see this reasoning. They lived in the suburbs and couldn't understand why their young daughter would choose to live in a small apartment on the ground floor of an old, creaky house in an old part of the city. They weren't certain of the safety, and her mother often called her on weekend nights to see if she was home.

The idea of leaving home was conceived a long time before it was born. There were many factors to consider and benefits to staying at home. She had always managed to avoid stoves by relying on her mother's culinary skills or going the sandwich route. But moving out meant having to face the iron beast or continuing the bread and filling diet. Dreaded visions of housekeeping were only allowed to surface briefly before they were shoved to the back of her mind. But it was a move that had to happen. She needed independence, and after allowing herself to get comfortable with the idea, she made the decision, quickly found the apartment, and announced the news.

It took less time than she anticipated, and it was mere weeks before Sara fell in love with the convenience and ease of city life. She learned countless new recipes for sandwiches with a variety of breads and fillings, and, of course, fruits needed no preparation. She rarely drove when she wasn't working because the subway was about a ten-minute walk from her place, and it took her downtown quickly. That's where Richard lived—five subway stops east in an area that was less residential and more eclectic than hers.

The chime called her back to the phone, and she read the next message, "Busy? Want to meet for a drink?"

A last-minute drink? He'd never suggested that before. Suddenly, anxiety gripped her, and she sat down on the couch, phone in hand. What was so urgent?

After the way the day had gone, Sara wasn't sure she could handle any more upsetting news. But then again, perhaps having it all come down on one day would allow her to move on and heal faster. She looked at the time. 7:22 p.m. It was still early.

She texted, "Sure, that sounds nice. Where do you want to meet?"

The answer came right away. "How about The Yellow Bird, near your place?"

Okay, he was coming to her. That meant a quick walk up the street to the local pub that served beer and various kinds of poutine—butter chicken, chicken parmesan, jerk pulled pork smothered over the melted cheese curds atop the crispy fries. The thought of the menu made her regret the grilled-cheese sandwich.

"Okay, what time?"

"8?"

"Sure, see you then."

Luckily, Sara had left her make-up on, so there was no need to re-apply. A quick change from flannels to jeans and a brushing of teeth and hair and she was ready. It was time to face all of the issues this day would bring, head on. A good night's sleep and then she could deal with a new path tomorrow.

As she walked down the street, Sara couldn't help but worry. He was going to break up with her, wasn't he? He had never asked her to meet him last minute on a weeknight, and since it was after dinner, the invitation meant that he wanted to talk, not dine.

When she first met him, the concern that he wouldn't consider a relationship with someone who was not Caucasian was in the forefront of her mind. Perhaps his parents would recoil at his choice of a woman with such dark skin, or maybe he would realize that he wanted kids who were blond haired and blue eyed.

She always knew that it would have to end at some point, so why not now? As she rolled the thoughts around, every step became easier, and the cold air through her lungs gave her energy. She was ready for it.

Richard's profile was visible through the glass as she approached the restaurant. He was sitting at a bar table, a glass of amber beer in front of him. It was half-full. Sara glanced at her phone—it was 7:57 p.m. So he'd arrived early to get a head start on the liquid courage. Why didn't he just tell her on the phone? They hadn't been dating for a very long time.. A text would be insulting, but a phone call would be okay.

As she approached, she saw Richard's face break into a toothy smile as their eyes connected through the glass. She was taken aback by what appeared to be genuine affection in his sky-blue eyes, and she couldn't help but mirror it with her own smile.

She opened the door and walked in. When she reached his table, he got up and kissed her on the mouth softly.

"Hey," he said.

"Hey ..." she glanced quickly at him and found herself looking away, feeling the smile wash away from her face. She ordered a draft, and he started chatting about his day. She heard something about a student who wrote a great story, another teacher who left, a new principal. She sipped her beer and listened, comforted by the sound of his quiet voice rather than the words.

"Sara?" His voice saying her name jolted her. "Are you okay? You look a little distracted ..."

"Oh, I'm okay, sorry. I'm listening."

"Is something going on at work?"

Sara hesitated. Asking him if he was going to break up with her would sound insecure. But he'd already read the worry on her face, and since he brought up work, her mind shifted.

"I'm okay. Work is fine, but there's this woman who's just started working in our department. She's South Asian, and she was hired to help reach out to the ethnic communities. But I don't get a good feeling from her. She questioned the use of my name ..."

"Your name?"

She couldn't stop. "Yes, she wants me to use my full name ..."

He smiled. "What's your full name?"

It was too late, so she said it. "Saraswati."

"The goddess of knowledge." It was not a question.

Her eyes jerked directly to his. "Yes, how did you know?"

He laughed at her surprise. "I took world religion in university as an elective. Plus, I like to read. And really, doesn't everyone know that?"

She blushed, a surge of warmth running through her. "Well, sure, I guess it's really common knowledge!"

"You don't like to use your full name?"

"No, my parents always shortened it to Sara because they believed it would be easier to have an Anglo-sounding name in Canada."

"That makes sense, but people need to recognize that this is a multicultural country. I'm sure the Aboriginals thought names like Jim and Mary were strange, but how many settlers started changing their names to be more native sounding?" he said, laughing.

The room seemed unstable for a minute, and Sara sat and tried to keep her balance. Warmth embraced her, or was it the beer? She wanted to reach over and kiss him, but she was frozen.

She managed an answer. "Yes, that's true. But I've always been called Sara, so I can't just change it now, just to make someone else more comfortable or to prove a point."

He laughed again. "Yes, that's true. So this woman thinks you need to use your full name in order to be more traditional? Or what's her reasoning?"

"I'm not sure. She just said that I should embrace my Indian roots. Perhaps she is not aware of the Indo-Caribbean community."

"But she's supposed to work with the ethnic communities?"

"Yeah. Many of the residents in the area are South Asian, African, Hispanic, or Caribbean. There are a lot of newcomers with varying cultural needs, and it's important that we make sure they receive the services they need without facing cultural barriers."

"Good message," he joked.

Sara blushed, "Sorry, I see this information all day, so it just sticks in my mind."

"It's okay. It makes sense the way you put it. So this new person thinks you should use your full name in order to appeal more to the ethnic community?"

"Maybe the South Asian community, perhaps. Maybe she just expects that all brown people should have ethnic-sounding names?"

"Yeah, maybe. She might be trying to deflect from her own lack of knowledge. One of the teachers that I work with is a bit like that. I suspect it stems from his own insecurities. He's a fairly smart guy, but for some reason he likes to put down others who are knowledgeable."

"I wonder if that's her issue," Sara replied. "She is supposed to be very experienced though."

"Where did she work before?"

"Mmm ... not sure. But she was an executive director of a non-profit organization somewhere downtown."

"Yeah, that's a fancy title for a manager."

Sara laughed in agreement. "Okay, well I will have to wait and see how it all plays out. Maybe I'm just not open enough to change. It's another person in the office that I have to work with, and it means an adjustment."

"Yep, every time a new teacher starts, the other teachers feel the same way. One person can change the dynamic of a work environment just by being there. It's about chemistry."

The words were wise, and she started feeling better about Venah . Maybe it would just take some time for them to get comfortable with one another.

Richard ordered another beer and asked if she wanted the same. Sara was only halfway through hers, and it was already making her head feel a little fuzzy. Perhaps she shouldn't have another one.

"You're not driving," Richard joked.

"I know, but I have to work tomorrow, and too much beer gives me a headache."

"Okay. You don't want to be hungover at work! I can have two or three, but that's my limit. The kids can give me headaches with or without beer."

"Do you like teaching?" Sara wanted to change the focus of the conversation away from her.

"Yes. I really do. I really like the kids too, don't get me wrong. But it's a challenging job simply because there is so much energy in the room all day. It took me some time to get used to it when I first started. I would go home and just crash."

"Yes, I can imagine how energetic a room filled with eight-year-olds would be. I am not sure I could be a teacher."

"You're great at what you do," he leaned towards her a little.

Sara leaned in and he put his lips to hers. The room twirled as they kissed. When they parted, she looked into his gleaming eyes and felt flushed. He was staring directly at her, and she wasn't sure what to do, so she pulled back and took a gulp of her drink. Richard leaned in again and took her hand. Wait, was this it?

"Sara, I was wondering ..." he paused and rubbed her fingers with his. "We've been seeing each other for a couple of months, and maybe it's a bit soon, but I was wondering ... well ... okay ... I was wondering how you were feeling about us."

"Feeling? About us ... you mean, if I'm happy with, um, us dating?"

A nervous laugh. "Yes."

"Well, I feel ... I mean ... I really enjoy your company. I like being with you, and we get along really well!"

He laughed again, softly. "Me too. I really like you. And I'm wondering if you want to date, just us and no one else."

"You mean exclusive?"

"Yeah."

She smiled. She felt like jumping out of her seat and throwing her arms around him. But instead, she looked right into his eyes and said, "Sure, I'd like that."

He laughed and kissed her again. So that was it. That was why he wanted to meet and talk. He wanted to be exclusive. This wonderfully handsome man who didn't care about race, religion, or her Hindu goddess name. He liked her.

"Want to come over?" she asked.

There was no hesitation in the answer. "I can get up early and take the subway home to change." It would be their first night together.

12

Venah stood in the middle of the tiny office after Phillip left. He'd proudly shown her this room at the end of the hall, tucked into a corner. It was a box with no windows. The desk was old fashioned, and the chair had a few blond hairs stuck to the headrest.

It was not the office she imagined when she was presented the job offer. Phillip had called her personally and told her how pleased they were that she had shown such interest in the role. He knew she could find another, more high-profile role elsewhere, given her credentials, and he was flattered that she chose to interview with Albatross. Would she consider taking their offer?

She had lots of community engagement experience plus she spoke Punjabi, understood a little Hindi, and knew many of the players in the South-Asian community. So she expressed her interest in the role but asked for a reconsideration of the salary. She threw out a more desirable number, and Phillip said he would take it to his superiors and get back to her. She noticed he didn't try to push back, agreeing to negotiate immediately. He knew what she was worth.

When he came back a few days later, the number jumped slightly, but not to the figure she'd put forward. Phillip reassured her that they would look at the salary after three months and reassess it, explaining that he needed to adhere to the HR guidelines. She hesitated at first and said she would think it over. She held off on calling him until after the weekend, but accepted under the condition that he kept his promise to review the salary in three months.

After they spoke, Venah put the phone down and felt her body ease into a calmness she hadn't felt in months.

She needed this job. Since being let go from her previous job as executive director of a small, non-profit organization downtown, she hadn't been able to land even one interview although she'd applied for dozens of jobs. Employment insurance paid some of the bills, but she had been forced to draw from her savings account, money that she'd been saving for her daughter's university tuition.

Rakesh had been in India, and although she knew better, she called him to ask for money. He finally called her back after a week, saying that he would be back home soon and would find a job. She'd heard that last part many times before. As usual, he was curt, and she could hear loud music and laughing in the background. She didn't even know what he was doing in India, only that he was staying with his mother and was working on a "business deal."

Venah never saw the fruits of these deals he always talked about, and she'd stopped asking questions long ago. The inquiries only made him defensive and prompted the booking of another flight, back to his mother and whatever else he was doing.

The thought of other women didn't affect her as much as the fact that he hadn't worked in over two years. He'd given up his job to move to Canada, and he seemed to simply lose interest in employment. So she carried the load of the expenses. Luckily, the mortgage rate on the house was very low. They had come to Canada with a sizeable sum of money, some of it given to her by her aunt, one of the wealthier members of her family, and some of it they had saved themselves.

So when they arrived a few years ago, they purchased a small townhouse in the suburbs. It wasn't the best area by Canadian standards, but compared to where she used to live in India, it was more than acceptable.

In fact, Venah was thrilled to have a place of her own. They'd been living in India with Rakesh's parents, and in typical Indian style, his mom ran the household and Venah complied with her requests.

So when the move to an old townhouse in a low-income area was presented, Venah welcomed the idea as a luxury. With most of the family still back home, they had little reason to entertain, so the furnishings they purchased were simple, cheap, and functional. The walls were faded beige, tired from years of tenants coming and going, and the parquet floors scratched. But Venah saw little need to spend funds on upgrades when she was the only inhabitant in the house most of the time.

When she wasn't in school, Amba was always at a friend's house or at the library. She ate meals at home but often left the house after dinner to study. "Why can't you study in your room?" Venah would croak. There were group projects, and they had to work as a team, Amba would explain.

"Well, bring your classmates here!" Amba would nod and say "sure," but it never happened.

After losing her job, Venah wasn't open to entertaining teenagers anyway. She had only met one of her daughter's friends, a loud South Asian girl who had picked up Amba one day before school. Venah heard the squeal of brakes and looked outside to see a big girl maneuvering out of the SUV, constrained in tight jeans. When Amba opened the door, the girl strolled into the foyer nonchalantly as she cracked her gum.

Venah made a comment about the girl's manners to Amba that evening, but her daughter just brushed it off and went into her room. Going in after her would have been futile. They weren't as close as a mother and daughter could be. Venah tried to get Amba involved in cultural activities, urging her to attend temple on Sundays, but she only agreed when it was a special occasion.

Getting Amba to wear a traditional outfit wasn't easy either. On their last trip to India, so many years ago, they spent a day in the market selecting colourful fabric from bolts of silk and taffeta and having their measurements taken by kneeling vendors as they sipped hot, sweet tea. It was a wonderful trip, and Venah was confident that it had allowed them to bond, which helped ease her anxiety over the increasing frequency of Rakesh's trips.

But when they returned and Amba was back in a Western environment with her friends and their social events, she became distant again. The outfits they bought together were placed in the back of her closet and only resurfaced when she made one of her rare trips to the temple.

What worried Venah the most was that Amba would soon be in university, and it was no secret that she was looking at schools out of the city and out of province. She wanted to move away, and there was the fear that she wouldn't come back. Or worse, return with a white man on her arm and a half-white child on her hip.

In truth, Venah could handle such a situation as long as Amba returned. It would be uncomfortable at the temple at first, but Venah knew how to play her cards, and besides it wouldn't be as shameful as having your husband leave you for months at a time. She stayed with her message that Rakesh was involved in a business venture in India but people were starting to get suspicious. There were whispers and quick changes of subject when she entered a room. Faces would suddenly morph, with great smiles for her and friendly chatter. She knew however, these faces would transform again once she turned her back.

One of the benefits of living with a manipulative mother-in-law was the skills acquired by watching the game in play. Venah knew that one way to shift the attention from herself was to redirect it onto another target. She'd tried it a few times at the temple, and it became quickly apparent how easily people were coerced into turning their attention onto someone else. Once the focus shifted, rumours about Venah's own dysfunctional life ceased. But attention spans were fickle at best, so when the Deosingh family arrived at the temple, Venah found a prime new bullseye.

They were new to the city, having emigrated from Guyana just a few months earlier. Devoted Hindus, as they called themselves, their need to find a place to worship and socialize led them to the temple, which was close to their new home.

When they arrived that first Sunday in the late summer, the service was half-empty because most of the congregation was on vacation. It was an ideal time for the family with two small children to ease comfortably into the new environment before services filled up with the regular crowd.

Venah didn't meet the Deosinghs until a few weeks after their first appearance. By then, the mother of the family, Chandra, was already making friends with the women in the kitchen and was helping prepare lunch when Venah walked in.

Chandra was pretty in a small village kind of way. Her skin was medium brown, and she wore no make-up except a reddish-brown lipstick that blended well with her complexion. Her curly black hair was pulled back into a ponytail, and an eager grin displayed a wide gap between her front teeth as she looked at Venah, who took the opportunity to display the judgemental look she reserved for new people.

"And who is this?" Venah said to the other women, while keeping her eyes on the doe-eyed newcomer.

"Oh, this is Chandra. Her family is new from Guyana," Pritti piped up quickly.

"I was hoping this new lady could answer the question."

"We just came from Guyana two months now," Chandra explained.

"And you know this is a temple of people from India."

"Yes … we realize that. But it's so close to our apartment," Chandra smiled as if she were not intimidated. It annoyed Venah.

"Well, the service is in Hindi. I hope you will be able to keep up."

"We don't speak Hindi, but the songs are the same ones we used to sing in the temple back home. And we know the words. It's a nice temple with very friendly people."

"Okay, well nice to see you," Venah turned her back and walked out of the kitchen, deciding in her mind that everyone needed to know that a non-Indian person did not belong in their temple, especially in the kitchen with the other women.

It didn't take long. All she had to do was enter the kitchen every time Chandra was around. Venah would stand and watch her closely making sure everyone could hear her criticisms.

"That's not the right way to do it," she said when Chandra was packaging sweets into bags. Venah stood beside her, barking directions and wagging her finger when a couple of sweets fumbled from Chandra's increasingly unsteady hands and dropped onto the floor.

When Chandra brought in fresh pink roses for the service, Venah eyed them scornfully and announced that they were not the right colour—flower offerings should always be orange or yellow because pink and red were for romance and not for spiritual events. Venah made sure the priest was not within earshot, knowing that no one would risk asking him to confirm the fact for fear of admitting ignorance. As Chandra's face turned red, Venah knew that, finally, this newcomer felt uncertain and out of place.

The strong woman attempted a few more gestures—fruit offerings instead of flowers, washing dishes instead of packaging sweets, but Venah's critical eye didn't waver and the nit-picking continued for a few months, until Chandra stopped volunteering. She came in with her family on Sundays, stayed for lunch after the service, and left. When Venah started gossiping about how Chandra and her family ate with their hands like low-caste villagers from India, the family started leaving the temple right after the service, saying that they had lunch at home.

Soon, the Deosingh family came to Sunday service once, maybe twice a month. When their visits ceased altogether, rumour had it that they found a new temple.

Venah felt a little pang of regret when temple members eyed her nervously during questions about the Deosinghs' departure, but shrugged it off. These Indian people from the Caribbean were not really Indians. They wanted so desperately to be Indian, and yet they insisted that English was their first language. They were phonies. Wannabe whites.

Now she had managed to secure a job in a reputable organization, and there it was again. Another Indian woman from the Caribbean who was supposed to be the public relations expert. The young woman named Saraswati seemed bright. Venah could tell just by the way she spoke. She was articulate and young and very pretty. No doubt, she'd swear that English was her first language, and yet she was Indian-looking enough that the community would relate well to her. And her senior title was a bit worrisome, especially since her own was simply community relations officer. She had tried to negotiate with Phillip, but he was firm that the title remain as it had been in the original job posting. Venah knew it was tied to the salary, another point that annoyed her because it meant that Sara was probably earning more.

13

Phillip looked around the room at his staff. It was ten o' clock on a Monday, and the staff meeting was just about to begin. He watched carefully as the employees chose their seats. Anna sat to his right, a few seats away, blinking through her glasses. Sara walked in and hesitated a bit before choosing her place to his left, coffee cup in one hand, notebook in the other. Venah came in afterwards and viewed the table for a minute. Her eyes went carefully from the chairs beside Sara to the chairs beside Anna. She walked around the table and chose a spot one seat away from Anna, close to the end of the table. Irene, Phillip's assistant, came in last, a little frazzled because she'd been dealing with a last minute call, and immediately sat in the chair closest to her.

He took a sip of his coffee and wondered about the dynamic of the team. Would it work? It was a lot of responsibility to build a team that worked well together and supported one another, and when he hired Venah, he was confident that she would be the magnet that could pull Anna and Sara together.

He looked at Sara and smiled a little. She was sharp and had lots of potential to be in a management role one day. It would be another accomplishment for him when she grew into a seasoned professional somewhere, though probably not at Albatross. No, Sara could learn here and then go elsewhere to advance her career.

His bigger concern was Anna. She was smart, but her insecurity was like a growth that she carried visibly on her back. If she saw Sara succeeding ahead of her, the relationship might never mesh. Mara had talked to him on a few occasions, asking that he work on Anna's approach and her presentation.

He thought it would be a good idea to take Anna to a nice restaurant for lunch to discuss her issues. She accepted the invitation to the trendy Italian restaurant without question. He would have to justify the cost to Mara, but if he had to pay for a portion out of his own pocket, he wouldn't mind. He needed to get her in the right mood for this type of conversation, in an environment where she could witness sophistication in action.

When they entered the quaint stone building that was once a house, they were greeted warmly by the hostess. Anna stared ahead, her mouth in the usual straight line, but her eyes slightly uncertain. When the waiter with the crisp white shirt held out her chair, she managed a nervous smile and slipped quickly into her seat.

He told her to order a glass of wine, but she declined and ordered a coke instead. He opted for a soda water and lime, and they made small talk until their drinks arrived. Anna immediately pulled her drink through the straw as if thirst had overtaken her.

He sipped his drink and smiled, leaning back.

"So, how are things?"

"Good."

"I was really pleased with the way you managed the event at the Bellwoods opening last week. Mara was really happy and so were the residents. Good coverage, happy client ... you're doing a great job!"

Anna smiled, but the look on her face told him that she knew he didn't ask her to lunch just to say she was doing a good job. So he continued.

"Mara wanted me to pass along the kudos."

Anna took a sip of her drink. "So why didn't she tell me herself?"

"You know that Mara doesn't offer compliments to staff. She prefers to stay within protocol, so she tells me because I am your supervisor."

"I guess." Anna pulled through the straw, which made a hollow, sucking sound in the empty glass.

"So how about you? How do you think the event went?"

"I thought it was good. Although the staff was kind of disorganized, and Mayree wasn't that helpful. It would have been better if Tina was there." Phillip knew that Anna preferred to deal with the executive directors of the recreation centres instead of the assistant EDs. But when she brought up Mayree's name, Phillip smiled.

"Well, Mayree thinks she is the ED."

"Yeah, she tries to take charge, but she's a bit full of herself."

Phillip laughed. "Yeah, and the English accent makes her sound snobby."

"But she's Indian."

"Yeah, she is Indian, but there are lots of them in England. I know that Mayree has been applying to become an ED, but Mara is not a fan of hers."

"Oh yeah? Why not?" Anna's question was direct, and Phillip wondered if he was on a slippery slope.

"I think that Mara is just not sure that Mayree is ready to be the head of a facility. She has lots of experience, but she doesn't have the leadership skills that Albatross needs."

"Yeah, I can see that."

"Well, Mara liked the event anyway, so you should be proud."

Anna smiled. "Thanks Phillip, I think it went well. I don't know that Mayree saw it that way though. She doesn't know the difference between a good event and a bad one. She just stands in the middle of the room trying to look important. At one point, she really annoyed me because she was barking orders, and she doesn't know anything about events."

Phillip took this as an opportunity to move into the real conversation. "Well, true, but we are the ones who set the tone of the events. Even if we are annoyed with someone's behaviour, it's up to us to take the high road and make sure the perception is positive."

He continued. "I know it's not easy to bite our tongues when we want to say something, but we need to try because honesty can come out the wrong way."

"Is that what Mayree said, or Mara?"

"No, it's not about what anyone said," he lied. "It's just about putting ourselves in the client's shoes, and sometimes that means being more diplomatic."

At that last word, she looked at the empty glass in front of her. He went on, "They don't see the mistakes that we do, and sometimes it's better that way. It makes them happier to believe the event is going well, and it makes us look like we have done a great job, which you did. They don't need to know the aggravation we feel when something is not perfect. When I attend events, I smile and nod a lot. You'll have to do this when you become a media spokesperson. You may have to smile and tell them what they want to hear, and I know it's not easy, especially if you are dealing with a difficult situation."

The phrase "media spokesperson" provoked her to smile as he anticipated. Anna wanted nothing more than to become a spokesperson.

"When we talk to the media we need to talk slow, wait, and think about the answer. And we need to be really diplomatic. Otherwise we run the risk of coming across emotional, and that can work against us," he continued.

"Also," he swallowed in preparation for the next point. "Perception is key. People resonate with the visual image more than the spoken word. So I try to wear suits and ties when I am on camera or at an event."

"Yeah, I can see that. It makes sense." Anna smiled and sat back as the waiter put a plate of steaming seafood linguini in front of her. The timing wasn't great. She became lost in the giant shrimp and lobster claws nested in creamy pasta.

The savoury smell of wine and mushrooms hit Phillip's senses, and his attention deviated to the plate of chicken Marsala that was placed under his nose.

"Great! Well I'm glad that you were happy with the event." His voice filled the background as the two picked up their forks and gave full attention to their lunch.

After his first succulent bite of chicken, Phillip assured himself that he'd done his duty and talked to her. She understood the point, he was sure of it.

Now, as he looked around the meeting room, he recalled the lunch meeting and his mind eased. Yes, there was a definite change in Anna, and he was certain that this team would work well. He could make it work. That's why Mara hired him in the first place.

"Well, good morning!" he almost bellowed and beamed at the faces around the table. "So this is our very first staff meeting with the entire team finally together. We have a lot to celebrate because we now have a public relations department where everyone brings their own unique set of skills and experience. I spent a long time looking for the right members who could take us forward, and I'm happy to say that Mara is really looking forward to the work we're going to do this year." His voice was strong as he recited the carefully rehearsed words.

"Are you going to talk about the work or the projects we are supposed to do?" Venah asked.

Anna shifted in her seat, and Sara looked over at her nervously.

"Yes, if you'll let me get to it," Phillip's tone was joking, slightly sarcastic, and got a smile and supportive nod from Irene.

"Okay, I just wanted to make sure," Venah retorted and smiled as if she had a little secret.

"So we have a big year ahead. As you know, we've been doing our best to increase publicity for Albatross, but our team was small, and we were stretched thin. For the past few years, it was only Anna, myself, and Irene, so naturally we haven't really been able to handle complete projects on our own. We've mostly been asking the staff at the centres to do the work upfront, and we review and execute the promotion. But now Mara has asked that we start taking on a little more. So this means we are finally going to be strategic public relations project managers."

As he emphasized the word *manager*, his eyes flicked to Anna, and he was certain he saw her sit up a little straighter. He moved his gaze slightly to Sara who was staring, doe eyed and intent, while Venah 's sharp eyes pushed him to avert his gaze to Irene.

His assistant's supportive smile was just what he needed to move on. Although he was often told that public speaking was his forte, he felt nerves creeping up from his stomach, filling his mouth and forcing him to recite his words carefully. He chaired this meeting every week, but today was the first time he was addressing this new group together.

He took a breath and continued, "This is a really big step for our department. We are growing, and this is a good opportunity for us to show what we can do for Albatross."

Venah inquired, "What kind of opportunities will this give us?" Her slight accent sounded more prominent in the meeting room.

He was starting to realize that Venah was not an easy person to deal with. He had suspected there would be challenges given the cultural differences, but figured it would just take some time to get used to them. She hadn't been the best candidate, not that he would ever reveal that to anyone.

But Venah had the necessary experience on paper. Her references were a bit muddy, which was somewhat suspicious, but when he spoke to Mara, she wasn't concerned.

"References are very subjective," she'd said nonchalantly. "The work will keep her happy and I have a feeling that she'll stay in the position for a long time. Just make sure she knows that it's an important role and that she will be the image of diversity who will help Albatross build bridges with the South Asian seniors."

Now, looking at the determination in her eyes as he spoke about the department, he wondered if those words had set expectations too high.

"We will have the opportunity to improve the profile of the department ... " he wasn't quite finished when she interrupted, "But what would it do for us? Each of us?"

"I haven't finished," he smiled and said the words sweetly, to which she nodded. "Being project leaders gives us the lead, which means we have more say in how Albatross is communicated to its clients and the community. We didn't have the resources before, so we let the program managers have too much say on the way we communicated and the events that we planned. Venah, you will be able to develop strategies to help us reach out to the communities which means you can guide the program managers in the best direction. They will need your insight into the communities"

Venah seemed satisfied with the answer. Phillip's knotted stomach relaxed, and he turned to Anna. "So Anna, do you have any questions?"

"So this means the program managers will now listen to us when we tell them how events need to be managed and how information needs to be written?"

"Yes, we will have more input now," he lied. Mara didn't say anything about the team having more input, but she did indicate that the team needed to take on more responsibilities. There would be more events to plan, and she wanted more reports and case studies published that would highlight Albatross as an expert in community services.

Anna was a good event planner, but she was not a strong writer, especially compared to Sara. Phillip came to the conclusion that even if she wasn't born in Canada, she was educated in the North American system, so that must have been where she got the training to write as well as she did.

He would assign Sara the majority of the reports and case studies, in addition to her role as the media lead, and Anna would take on most of the events. Venah would be responsible for attending committee meetings with the community centres and developing strategies for outreach programs. She would be a good consultant for the case studies and would attend the events to liaise with the community members and partners. Her role would entail working closely with both of the other women.

Anna would have to work with Sara but not very closely. Phillip would oversee all of the projects and give Anna a bit more attention, so she didn't feel the need to compete and win.

"Sara, any questions?" he smiled at her pleasing face, and she said quietly and a little nervously, "It sounds really great. I'm looking forward to the new projects."

She was still shy and uncertain, but this was fine with him. The other two had stronger personalities but were less polished. It was a good balance.

"Great! But you still have to work with Maxine," he teased.

Sara hoped her quick smile would hide her surprise, and she glanced at Anna who brightened at the comment.

"Um, well yes, Maxine and I worked together on the brochure for Passing the Torch and she seemed okay ..."

"There was nothing wrong with the first brochure," Anna interjected. "Maybe the pictures needed updating, but the wording was fine. Besides, she's always nice when you're new."

"Maxine likes to feel that she's in charge," Phillip added. "When Sharon left, Mara did not want to give Maxine that job. There was someone else who had a lot more experience with the community and the youths because he'd worked at one of the bigger centres, an assistant ED. But the board pushed her to hire Maxine."

Sara sat still and didn't say anything. It seemed unprofessional that he would be talking about Maxine in this manner in a staff meeting.

Anna chimed in again, "Maxine wouldn't have worked under him though."

"No, but then she could've left and found something else." Phillip shrugged. "But then the board would have been upset with Mara, and it wouldn't be worth it."

"She seems to know the community quite well." Sara heard the strength of her own words and looked at Phillip and Anna to see their reaction. Then she heard herself continue. "And the community seems to resonate with her quite well." It was a jab that stemmed from the anger rising inside her. They didn't know how to reach out to the community as well as Maxine.

"She thinks she knows more than she does. You haven't worked with her that long," Anna said flatly.

Phillip quickly jumped in, cutting Anna off. "So does anyone have other questions? I'm really happy to have the team together. Irene and I will be putting together a list of projects and allocating them to each of you. Then we can have another meeting and discuss how to move forward."

Anna grabbed her notebook and rushed out of the room. She always seemed to be in a rush. Venah walked straight over to Phillip as if she had something to talk to him about, and Sara went back to her desk.

Sara sat down in front of her computer and thought about the meeting. It was clear that they didn't like Maxine, and she wasn't sure why. From her own experience, Maxine was smart, knowledgeable, and actually quite friendly. Sure, she was strong and knew what she wanted, but she always listened and asked for Sara's opinion. So what was the problem? Was it simply that Phillip had wanted the other person to get the job? Monday had not started off well, and there were four more long days until the week ended. Sara sat back and realized she had not even been at Albatross a year.

Phillip walked into Sara's tiny office, shut the door with one hand, and sat down. He seemed awkward as usual, sitting on the edge of his seat.

"How are you doing, Sara?"

"I'm great, thanks. How about you?"

He chuckled nervously, his face reddening. She immediately started to worry. What was happening?

"So do you remember at our last team meeting, we discussed that Mara wanted us to take on more responsibility? Well, we will now have more opportunities to showcase our talents as a team and manage projects."

Sara waited for him to get to the point.

"There is a new retirement facility opening soon, and it will be host to the Pass the Torch program. For the official opening, we want you to take on the management of the event. You'd be working with the executive director and overseeing all of the publicity. We will need an event plan and a media component to ensure there will be lots of publicity for both the facility and the Passing the Torch program. Also, Mara wants us to invite the Minister of Children and Youth Services."

It was good news. So then why did he seem nervous?

"Wow, that sounds great, Phillip! I'm really happy to take on this project. The executive director is my main contact?"

"Yes, it will be Ruth Klein. She used to work at the Ministry of Children and Youth, and Mara really likes her. She can be tough, but she knows her stuff, and perhaps you get can some contacts from Minister Boland's office. You'll need to read about our protocol for dignitaries at events."

Sara realized that she had never seen anything about the protocol and made a mental note to look it up in the manual. This was important. She'd never dealt with a minister before, and, in fact, her involvement with politicians had been minimal. A city councillor attended a couple of events she'd worked on in the past, but she didn't really deal with him directly.

"Okay, sure, I can do that."

"Great!" Phillip got up quickly as if he were relieved to be leaving her office. As he walked out the door, he turned and said sharply, "I'll need to see the event plan by next Wednesday."

That gave Sara less than a week to develop the plan, which meant she had to contact Ruth today to find out the details. As she looked up Ruth's contact information in the directory, she felt herself getting excited. But suddenly a question entered her mind—wasn't Anna responsible for planning the events with the community partners? Then again, at their last meeting, Phillip had said their responsibilities would change somewhat. Sara decided not to worry about it. She loved planning events, and this was going to be a great one. She couldn't wait.

Ruth's office was decorated with prints of children playing in what looked like a village in the Caribbean, very similar to the ones in Maxine's office. Phillip's mention of Ruth Klein, who was admired by Mara, had brought visions of a stoic, pale-skinned, fair-haired woman. So as Sara stared at the pictures, she tried to formulate a reason the pictures were so proudly displayed on the office walls. Perhaps Ruth had visited one of the islands and fallen in love with the scenes of dark-skinned children in school uniforms, schoolbooks at their sides and pigtails adorned with ribbons.

As Sara studied a photo of an older Caucasian woman hugging a tiny black girl in a neat frock, a movement behind her made her jerk around, and the woman in the photograph materialized and sat down at the desk. She looked directly at Sara and held out her hand. Caucasian yes, stoic—not really.

"Hello, I'm Ruth Klein," she said with a slight Jamaican accent. Her eyes were green and twinkly.

Sara couldn't help but smile. So this is why Phillip wanted her to work on this event?

"Nice to meet you, Ruth. I'm Sara."

"Hi, Sara ... and you have a last name?"

"Oh yes, Ramnarine." She'd gotten used to saying only her first name when introducing herself because at the sound of her last name, people's foreheads wrinkled, and she always had to repeat it.

"Sara, I'm really glad you'll be working with me on this project. When I heard that Albatross was finally smart enough to hire someone from the Caribbean community, I called Phillip and said that you were the right person to help with this project since many of the residents and their families are from the Caribbean. We need someone who can understand the culture, besides myself."

"You're ... Jamaican?"

"Yes, you can tell by the accent?"

"Yes, mostly. And I noticed the prints ..."

"Oh yes, I brought those from home the last time I visited."

Home. It was a word that many of her family members used when referring to their birthplace.

"I moved here when I was in my early twenties, but I still think of it as home." Ruth seemed to have read her thoughts. "So, do you mind if we get started? I have another meeting in an hour. What do you need from me in order to plan this event and make it successful?"

Sara liked her no-nonsense attitude, which was so similar to her mother's. She pulled out her notes, and they spent about an hour discussing the event: possible dates for the launch, the list of speakers, and the protocol for inviting the minister, whom Ruth had worked with in the past. Ruth was happy to contact her if necessary, but she thought Sara should reach out to the chief of staff first.

"I'm here to help in any way that I can, but I'm sure you will be able to handle it. The minister loves these kinds of events because there will be a photo-op, and if it involves a new facility for the community, especially one with a great program like Pass the Torch, then it will make her look good."

Sara wasn't sure if she should laugh or not. But Ruth chuckled, so she smiled and nodded as she took notes.

As she drove back to the office, creative ideas about the event started to bubble in Sara's mind. She couldn't wait to get back to her desk to start writing the event plan and contact the minister's office.

When she walked into Albatross, Phillip was in Anna's office. They both stopped talking. Phillip didn't turn around and said something in a hushed voice to Anna. When he turned, his face was red again, and he walked away quickly.

Anna picked up her coffee cup and stomped out of her office. Sara guessed that Phillip had told her about the event.

Suddenly, the high she was feeling after her meeting with Ruth started to fade. Apprehension set in, and Sara wondered what would happen next. It was clear that Anna already disliked her, and now she had been given a big project that Anna perhaps felt belonged to her. But Ruth had requested her, so Phillip didn't have much choice.

It was a good half an hour before Anna returned to her desk, coffee cup in hand, steam indicating it was full. She looked in Sara's direction and managed a pursed smile. Sara relaxed a little and figured her colleague took the time to cool off.

But instead of sitting down at her desk, Anna placed her coffee cup down, picked up a folder, and headed towards Sara.

"Sara," Anna said in her abrupt manner, "Phillip wanted me to give you this file on event protocols. He said you would be working on the Passing the Torch anniversary event. Let me know if you need any more information." She dropped the file in front of Sara, turned, and walked back to her office with an air of prickly indifference.

"Thanks, Anna."

Sara felt her stomach drop a little. Was Anna aware that Ruth had asked for her?

She opened the folder and started leafing through the information. It was filled with printed emails between Anna and Phillip suggesting dates and times for the launch, a list of caterers for refreshments, and an email forwarded by Phillip from Mara indicating that the launch must get media coverage.

Sara spent time reviewing the information in the folder because she knew Anna would be watching. She then placed it at the front of her file organizer and started crafting an email to the minister's office.

15

Phillip knew that Anna would be upset when he told her the news about the event. He had begun planning the event with Anna when Ruth called Mara and asked for Sara to be put on as event lead. She'd never met Sara before, but Ruth had always insisted that Anna was just not warm enough and didn't seem comfortable around the ethnic families. She needed to learn diplomacy and patience, Ruth had said.

He tried to probe Mara for more information, hoping he could get more details about the conversation, but all she would say is that Ruth asked for the new girl with the Caribbean background because many of the families in that area were also from the Caribbean.

Phillip was puzzled. Anna had mentioned something like this before, but he wasn't sure how Sara could be from the Caribbean. Was she half-black? That would account for the dark skin, but he was so certain she was South Asian. Her last name sounded that way, and her hair was very straight.

Maybe Ruth was just mixed up herself. She saw the skin colour and thought it would look good to have someone who looked ethnic at the event. Visibility was important, and Phillip understood this as well as anyone. Sara would work with Ruth and be visible at the event, so the media and attendees would be confident that Albatross was open to diversity among its staff.

He decided not to tell Sara that Ruth had asked for her. He knew she would be excited about inviting the minister and being the lead on the event, and he didn't need her head to swell.

Telling Anna would not be as easy. She was already looking into the refreshments and the setup of the room. Anna was good at logistical things like that, but she didn't think about the big picture. She wouldn't consider a creative menu that appealed to the ethnic families, nor would she position the event in a way that showcased Albatross's diversity mandate.

Anna did not believe in doing anything special for an ethnic audience. She never said this out loud to him, but he noticed the way her face pinched and her mouth pursed when he talked about community outreach and translating some of their materials into different languages. She never chose pictures that included ethnic faces. In fact, she seemed determined to keep Caucasian faces in all of their materials.

That was what got her in trouble with Maxine.

He'd had a conversation with her to discuss how their materials needed to reflect the audiences, but she insisted that the pictures clearly depicted the program—seniors talking to youths. There was no need to highlight one particular audience over another. Weren't there Caucasian seniors and youths in the programs? Phillip knew it made little sense to argue with her. When she held onto something, only time could ease it from her grip.

When he hired Sara, she felt he was compromising quality by purposely looking for someone ethnic, and she was certain there were equally good, if not better, candidates who were Caucasian. Italian or Portuguese even! When Venah was hired as well, Phillip knew Anna would be angry, but also realized she was worried about being pushed out. It would be two against one.

And he had no intention of letting her slip away. She might not be the most talented worker, but she would be happy as long as she was given a certain amount of responsibility and perhaps a promotion at some point. She would be loyal as his second in command. And as far as he was concerned, she held this title, even if it wasn't official.

He'd waited until Sara was out of the office to talk to Anna about the Passing the Torch anniversary.

"It's just for this event," he assured her.

"It's a big event, and she is still new. Can she handle all the details?"

"Well, that's why she will need your help. It's a good way to learn how to manage staff."

Anna seemed to relax at the last statement. But he regretted it at once. She would not be managing Sara. He was certain that Sara could manage the event on her own. Now he would have to talk to her about working with Anna. Maybe he would suggest a meeting, so Anna could inform her about the event protocols at Albatross.

"Okay, I'll help her."

"Great! So walk her through the event protocols and make sure she knows what to do. Check in with her from time to time but don't micromanage. You need to give her space, and if she makes a mistake, it's on her. But she needs to learn."

"Sure." Anna's voice was more cheerful again. He sighed with relief.

"It will work out fine. A good leader is a team player, remember?" He leaned over and said this to Anna in a lowered voice. Then he walked out the door, averting his eyes from the direction of Sara's office.

Phillip announced the Passing the Torch anniversary event at Monday's team meeting, and in true Phillip fashion, boasted about the fact that the Minister of Children and Youth Services would be sure to attend because the program was renowned.

He explained that Mara was keen on having his department work on the event, and that Maxine wanted to be part of it—perhaps lead the entire event since she felt she owned the entire program because of her manager's title.

As Phillip talked, he exchanged knowing looks with Anna while Sara sat quietly.

Finally, Phillip hit the note that sent the room spinning. "And this project launch will be coordinated by Sara."

He had a big smile on his face, almost genuine. Then Venah 's energy intruded.

"Oh, so Sara will be looking after this very high-profile project? What about the diversity component? There are ethnic families in this retirement home, correct?"

"Oh yes, there are. Sara will be working with Ruth on some strategies to make these families feel comfortable."

"What kind of strategies?"

"Sara?"

She sat stunned for a minute. The only strategies she was developing were related to the actual launch of the event. The logistics of the day, the refreshments, the media release, the guest list, and the speeches. There was nothing that was culturally specific.

"Well, the refreshments will be culturally sensitive ... just making sure there are vegetarian options and non-dairy options and, of course, there will be accommodations if necessary, and we will have translators if necessary ..."

"What do you mean if necessary?" Venah barked.

"Most of the families are Caribbean, so their first language is English. I am not sure how many of the families speak another language, but I will work with Ruth on this."

"There are people from the Caribbean who speak another language. Some speak Hindi."

"Maybe, but not many as a first language."

"Well, you don't know. You are not the diversity expert. Phillip, I should have some input into this event."

Phillip paused for a moment. "Sure, if you think there is an opportunity to do some community outreach, then you should attend. Anna should be there as well. Our team should be present at all events to help make sure things run smoothly. Mara would want that."

Sara was disappointed. She had hoped that there would be little interference. She was building a good rapport with Ruth and was looking forward to working under her direction. Adding more people who wanted to control the situation would make it more complex and difficult to manage. She wasn't good at conflict, and Venah made her nervous.

"Good, well I will definitely be there. And for you Sara, there may be more need for cultural accommodation besides food." She actually pointed her finger when she said this.

The silence was overpowering. Suddenly, Phillip changed the subject. He shifted the conversation to an anecdote about his son coming home from school worried after he was questioned about his "culture," and so Phillip had to explain that he was adopted ... Sara tuned out, worried again.

The right thing to do was stand up to Venah, but she didn't have the right words. Nor did she want to be as harsh as Venah. It was not professional. The rest of the meeting was a blur, and when it ended, she got up and walked out, drained.

16

Anna walked back to her office and started checking her emails. The meeting was weird. Sara looked a little upset, and Venah was kind of aggressive. When it was just her, Phillip, and Irene, the meetings were fun. None of this infighting went on.

She didn't like Sara, but so far she'd managed to tolerate her. But Anna wasn't sure what to make of Venah. Phillip said she had a lot of experience in community relations and would be instrumental in helping to reach out to the ethnic communities. Still, Anna wasn't sure what Venah did exactly.

The whole diversity initiative was puzzling to Anna. Everyone had someone in their family who spoke English. And for the ones who didn't, there were staff members who spoke their language. There was nothing for a public relations team to do for them. Perhaps some samosas as refreshments, but they didn't need Venah to tell them that.

She sighed and decided it was not worth the effort to continue to be annoyed at this. Mara wanted Venah and Sara because the board of directors insisted that they have staff who reflected the community—brown people. Hiring people because of their skin colour was discrimination plain and simple. Everyone knew it.

Anna had to play the game and wait it out, but something was puzzling her. Based on the meeting this morning, she guessed that Venah didn't like Sara or something ... Anna wasn't sure what it really was. Even Phillip seemed confused.

Funny enough, when Venah was hired, Anna was concerned that she would be outnumbered. If Albatross was hiring more and more brown people, she would suddenly be the minority, ironic as it seemed.

As she sat in front of her computer, Anna thought back to her days in college. She had attended a community college in the north end of Toronto, just east of Albatross. Back then, only a quarter of the student body were people of colour.

The cliques formed accordingly—browns with the browns, blacks with each other, and the few Asians hung out together, speaking a language other than English.

The brown kids seemed obnoxious to her. The guys were loud, and when she passed a group of them, the smell of curry wafted under her nose. She'd heard that the spices they cooked with were so strong that the odour emanated from their pores. There were a few brown girls in her classes who she chatted with sometimes. But it was always about class-related stuff.

There was that one time in the coffee shop, though, that Anna remembered vividly. It was a blistery, snowy day, and she'd decided to visit the Starbucks on campus. She rarely went to this place because it was always filled with loud students, most of whom were brown. But this time, she needed a coffee and didn't want to go across the street to the Tim Horton's like she usually did. As she walked in, their obnoxious laughter engulfed her, and she felt suddenly very self-conscious. She had looked around nervously and spotted a seat at the back, near the window. The lineup was long, and she considered putting down her coat at the table to secure it, but then she'd lose her spot in line.

The line seemed to take forever, and when the cheery girl asked for her order, she felt irritated, especially when she had to repeat it. These kids working in coffee shops were never very quick.

Luckily, when she finally got her coffee and glanced over at the table, it was still empty. Quickly she grabbed sugar and cream and bolted towards the back, but too late. Halfway there, a brown couple slipped into the seats. The girl's shiny black hair gleamed as she sat with her back to Anna, giggling at her companion in the typical black leather jacket.

So now what? All of the other tables were taken as she stood in the middle of the crowded shop, hot coffee in hand and not sure where to turn. Suddenly, she heard her name and looked for the source.

There, sitting at a table not too far from where she stood, were two of the girls from her media class. The table was filled with brown kids, mostly girls but a couple of boys. She suspected they were the ones responsible for the loud laughter when she walked in.

"Hey Anna, there's a seat over here," the one girl whose name was Sarjit or something like that motioned for her to come over. Anna hesitated. Yes, there was an empty seat, but she didn't know any of those people. Sarjit and the other girl from her class, whose name she could not remember, were smiling broadly. She decided to take the seat.

As she sat down, brown faces looked at her. A few people held out their hands and introduced themselves. The babbling of strange names overwhelmed her. She smiled, shook a few hands, and removed the lid of her coffee to let it cool down a little bit before she took a sip.

"So Anna, how do you know these crazy girls?" one of the guys asked. His boyish face was dark brown, and his black hair looked a little greasy. She could detect a slight accent, an awkward pronunciation of r's.

"Shut up, Amit—you're the one who's crazy," Sarjit waved off the jokester and looked at Anna, who managed to reply, "We sit together in media class." She smiled and sat up straight. Her voice must have been loud because the table got quiet, all eyes on her; Amit smiled and nodded as if the answer was sufficient. After a slight pause, the conversation resumed. She sat on the edge of her seat, coat tightly around her, bag on the floor between her feet, and sipped her coffee.

Sarjit, who seemed to be staring at her, smiled. "So, I don't usually see you in here."

"No, I usually go to Tim's across the street, but I didn't want to run over in this weather."

"Yeah, I hear you. We usually hang out here. I haven't been across to Tim's in a while." Sarjit was smiling directly at her, sitting a bit too close. "So, what did you think of the last test?"

"Oh, it was okay. What did you think?"

"I did okay as well. I really like the class, but the teacher is a little strange. He used to be a reporter, right?"

"I think so."

"I heard that reporters can be odd." She looked at Anna eagerly for a response.

Anna thought about their media teacher. A small, thin man with curly hair and a goatee. He used to write for one of the big papers but got laid off a couple of years ago. So he taught media at the college and said he was also "freelancing."

"Oh yeah? I don't know many other reporters. In fact, I wouldn't watch the news if it wasn't a requirement for media class."

"Oh yeah, the news can be depressing, but my parents force me to watch it. They say I need to keep up with current events. Between them and the teacher, I make it a point to be in front of the TV at six every night just before dinner."

Visions of an Indian family sitting around a table, eating with their hands, flashed into Anna's mind. She saw the man wearing a turban, and the woman in a sari, scolding her daughter and pointing one finger in her face, like she had witnessed once in a mall. Anna wasn't sure what to say. She didn't want to make a joke because she was afraid to sound racist at this table filled with Indians. So she just smiled.

"Your parents aren't on your case about watching the news?" Sarjit wouldn't let up, and Anna was feeling more uncomfortable.

"Not really."

Sarjit looked at her curiously for a moment and then shifted to another girl to her left. Anna stared straight ahead and gulped her coffee. The conversation at the table continued.

The buzz in the room swirled around her, and she felt like she was sitting in a glass tube, alone, unable to interact with the others around her. It made her feel secure as she drank her coffee, looking around at the faces and smiling every once in a while as a formality.

Suddenly, she realized that she could go to the library. The idea jolted her out of her seat.

"Anna, what's up?" Sarjit looked concerned.

"Oh, I just realized that I have to go to the library to get a book." She picked up her bag. "Thanks for the seat, see you in class." She hurried off, not looking back.

The next time she saw the girls in media class, they smiled but didn't engage her in conversation. Luckily, the weather permitted her to cross the street for her Tim's coffee; she didn't go back to the campus Starbucks for a long time.

As she recalled the memory, she thought about the bond the students seemed to share. And yet, this morning, she didn't see the same bond between her two colleagues. In fact, since Venah started, she noticed little interaction between her and Sara. They always sat on opposite sides of the table, and it was clear that Venah thought very little of Sara's ability to run an event, a perspective Anna shared.

Anna didn't think much of the older woman and her harsh comments, but at least it was reassuring to know that the two brown people wouldn't gang up against her. The anxiety she'd been feeling since they were hired was now slipping away and being replaced by confidence. She felt strong again, and the little smile on her lips while she worked was something she could not help.

17

Sara took a sip of the foam that skimmed the top of her glass. He wasn't due for another fifteen minutes, but she wanted to calm her nerves before he showed up. She didn't want to keep talking about her work issues with Richard, and after the last time, when he could tell she was upset, she wanted to make sure the alcohol seeped into her bloodstream, softening her worry.

He often told her about his issues at work. Sometimes she marvelled at his honesty, the openness and vulnerability it took to reveal the conflicts he had with other teachers. She listened intently, hoping to learn from these second-hand interactions, avoided sharing her own issues. Her mother always told her that men liked women who supported, not complained. And it was one of the few bits of advice she chose to accept.

The other was career advice, and the angle was similar—don't complain.

"You must remember, Sara, that you are a brown girl."

"But I grew up here," she protested the time she'd complained about feeling ostracized at the agency.

"Yes, you did. But some people don't see it that way. You are dark skinned, and therefore not in the privileged category. We need to recognize that ethnicity is one strike against us in this country. If you speak up and become too defiant, you will have two strikes. Keep your complaints to yourself at work. You don't want to lose good opportunities because you are considered too much of a wild card."

The term *wild card* made Sara laugh out loud. Surely, she was not a wild card, but her mother had a good point. It was the very reason she stayed quiet when Violet boycotted her birthday, and the reason she would keep her emotions in check at Albatross, and with Richard.

She regretted telling him the story about Venah and hadn't brought it up again, hoping it would fade into the background. She didn't want him to find out that the only other brown person in the department didn't like her for fear that he would question her character and wonder what lay beneath her exterior that caused another person to feel this way.

A third of the glass was empty as the alcohol tickled her senses, and soon she was feeling relaxed. This is why people drank when they were upset, she thought. It numbed the pain and made the world seem fuzzy and surreal. She wasn't at that stage yet, but knew that two more of these golden drinks would turn the world into a Dalí melted-clock painting.

Even Phillip's announcement about Venah being the "diversity" representative for her event started to seem reasonable. Why shouldn't she handle the cultural needs of the families? Isn't that why she was hired? It wasn't an area that she, Sara, should be involved with anyway. Her job was to organize the event and ensure Minister Boland was able to attend, speak to the crowd, and cut the red ribbon. The media would show up, take a few pictures, and the event would be publicized in the local paper, making everyone happy.

She took a big gulp of the warming beer, which caused a wide smile on her face, as Richard arrived.

"What's so amusing?" he asked.

"Oh, nothing ... just thinking about something ..."

"So, care to share?" He leaned over and kissed her softly on the mouth.

"Mmmm nothing important ... how are you? Good day at work?"

"Yes, it was a great day! The kids and I are working on a new project, and I'm feeling the energy."

"Oh yeah? Tell me about it."

Richard gestured to the waitress and settled into his seat, jumping right into the story as if it were sitting on his tongue, waiting for his teeth to open the gates. "It's a history, political-science type project, and it's meant to demonstrate privilege and inequity to the students."

It wasn't a topic that Sara was expecting, but it seemed interesting.

"The kids are divided into groups that consist of two aboriginal groups, one group of settlers, and one group that is the Canadian government in the 1700s, in the days of New France."

Sara watched his face, the way his eyes changed and he seemed to go back in time as he spoke.

"The project focuses on the French making trades with the Aboriginals, the issues that surfaced, and then the British involvement. It will examine the Aboriginal way of life, their own forms of government, and also the European ways of the French and British."

"So you want to re-enact the days of early Canada, when the Aboriginals'

86

way of life was changed?"

"The way they were pushed out." His voice became suddenly passionate. "The other day, one of the teachers was talking in the lunchroom and complaining about how we have to accommodate all of these newcomers. There is a boy in one of his classes who wears a turban, and his parents are trying to get the school to let him wear his traditional kirpan under his clothes. The teacher is a bit of a redneck and keeps talking about the way newcomers want to change our laws and our way of life. A lot of other teachers agreed with him, but all I could think about was that early European settlers did the same thing. Aboriginals were living in Canada for over ten thousand years. And we have only been here for five hundred."

Sara was a little stunned. She often heard comments about newcomers wanting Canadians to change their laws and alter their way of life. Truthfully, she didn't know who was complaining, since her family and all of her friends who were brown and black didn't complain. Not that she'd heard anyway.

But she did know about the kirpan, the traditional dagger that all Sikh boys and men were supposed to wear, along with a turban, as part of their religion. It was against the law to carry a concealed weapon and technically, the kirpan was a weapon. But some Sikh parents felt it was necessary for their children to wear it all the time. It was a real controversy in schools, and she didn't know how to react when the topic came up. Frankly, she didn't understand why the dagger was necessary to show devotion to one's religion, but perhaps it was important for some Sikh families. In any case, she never offered an opinion on the topic.

As she listened to Richard go on about the injustice that the Aboriginals faced, Sara remembered Grace, the only Aboriginal person she knew when she was growing up. Back in the nineties, there were very few Aboriginal families living in Toronto, and even fewer who were open to admitting it. But in grade three, everyone knew that Grace was different. She had light brown skin, and her face was slightly broader than everyone else's. Grace, Sara, a boy from India named Dev, and two black kids—Sharon and Colin—were the only visible minorities in their class. Sara hung out mostly with Sharon, who was Jamaican, and one other girl named Becky, who had red hair and freckles. Becky was a sweet, simple girl who talked to everyone and was always inviting Sara and Sharon to her house after school. But Sara's mom wanted her home right after school. Loitering at someone's house was not a good idea, and she could invite Becky and Sharon over on the weekend.

The three girls sat together in class and spent lunches and recesses chatting about TV shows and boys who caught their fancy. Sometimes they would walk over to their special spot behind the school in the grassy area close to the park, away from the buzzing of kids' voices.

It was a comfortable trio, and the differences in ethnicity made little difference to them. Not like a small clique of girls in their class, to whom it did matter. Back then, they were the cliché popular girls. The ones with the fair, silky hair and magazine wardrobes. The ones whose parents dropped them off in the mornings in their Volvos and BMWs.

They had called her Paki before. She knew what it meant but was surprised that kids were still using the term. Not only was it inaccurate, since she was not from Pakistan, it spewed such hate and ridicule that it stunned her into not being able to think of a comeback. She always just looked away and pretended not to hear, wondering what kind of effect it had on someone who really was from Pakistan.

They had called Sharon a blackie once too, and then they took to labelling Becky as a "blackie-lover, Paki-lover." The sting of humiliation would affect Becky, and sometimes Sara could see a questioning in her eyes. The girls never used the N-word though. Perhaps it had become so taboo over the years that they knew it was forbidden—more so than Paki, a word they seemed to find funny.

It was Grace however, that these girls tormented the most. They always sneered at her clothes, which were limited to a sparse selection, simple and faded sometimes. Or they would make fun of her lunch bag, which was usually a plastic grocery bag.

Grace didn't seem to let the comments bother her because she never responded with comebacks or emotions. She was always very quiet in class and mostly kept to herself. One day, her class had been learning about Canadian citizenship and immigration. The teacher pointed out the fact that many Canadians were immigrants. "Who is truly Canadian?" she asked. Did anyone know?

She asked the class to stand up and come to the front of the room. Now, she wanted the students who were not born in Canada to stand on the left side of the room. The ones who were born in Canada had to go to the right side.

Sharon and a few others moved over to the left side, while the popular clique marched to the right, where Sara and Grace also stood.

"What are you doing here?" hissed Madison under her breath. Sara looked away and didn't budge. Grace didn't respond and didn't look at the girl.

"Now, whose parents or grandparents or great grandparents came from another country?"

The popular girls looked at each other and put their hands up, along with Sara and a few other kids.

"Okay, so you move to the group on the left." The teacher pointed.

The only person left on the right was Grace.

Madison and her gang snickered as the teacher turned her back. "Why is she still over there? She's not Canadian."

But the teacher heard. She turned around and looked at Madison. "Actually, Grace is the only one here who is the true Canadian. She was born here, and so were her parents, grandparents, great grandparents and their parents. Madison, you were born here, but your parents are from England. Emma, your grandparents are Ukrainian?" Emma nodded.

"So I wanted everyone to see that we are mostly a group of immigrants. Grace is the only true Canadian in the room because she is Aboriginal."

Being labelled an immigrant didn't sit well with Madison and her group of girls. They bullied Grace at recess and took away her hat, putting it in a pile of slush and stomping on it. "If you're the only Canadian, then you don't need a hat to keep you warm! Eskimo! Go live in an igloo, Eskimo!"

Grace didn't tell anyone, and Sara saw her walking home after school with the wet, tattered hat in her hand, her head bare.

The memory stung. Sara had wanted to befriend Grace after that but fear of being bullied made her stay away. It was a regrettable action.

"So what do you think?" Richard's voice interrupted her thoughts. Yikes, she hadn't heard what he was saying.

"I think it's really a great idea," she ventured. "What do you think?"

Luckily, he didn't seem to notice that her mind had wandered for a few minutes. She shook the painful memory from her mind and directed her full attention to Richard.

"I'm hoping it will make a difference. I want these kids to understand the reality of the true history. My grandmother was Aboriginal and faced discrimination herself, and I remember my mom saying how hard it was for her—the memories of what happened to her own father, the alcoholism that nearly destroyed her home, and the way they were treated."

"Where did she grow up?"

"Manitoba. She came to Toronto after she married my grandfather. At that point, she had pretty much adopted a modern Canadian lifestyle, but she remembered the injustice that her parents faced."

"Your grandfather was not Aboriginal?"

"No, he worked in the town just outside the reserve where my grandmothers' parents lived."

"Really? That's an interesting story. How did they meet?"

"My grandmother told me the story. She was eighteen, and her mother had sent her into town to pick up a few items from the store. She bumped into my grandfather, and I guess it was love at first sight. He started talking to her, and then they continued to see each other in town. Apparently she was very beautiful, and he was instantly smitten."

The details were sparse, but Sara realized that men were often big picture when it came to romance. Descriptions of his grandmother's attire or the way his grandfather felt when their eyes met were tiny pieces of information that she craved.

"Did anyone have an issue with the marriage? I mean, back then it was a mixed marriage, wasn't it?"

"Back in those days, I'm not sure how they viewed marriages between Aboriginals and Caucasians. There could have been some resistance. But it was a small town, and my grandmother's father held a good position among the people on the reserve, so I believe they were well respected in the main town. My grandmother didn't talk much about the townspeople. Her stories were about facing discrimination when they moved to Ontario and lived outside a reserve. She had a native status card and people used to treat her differently when she presented it at stores."

So there it was. Richard had an Aboriginal background. Sara looked closely at him, looking for some kind of evidence of this, but she couldn't tell. His features were bold, his skin was pale, and his eyes resembled the sky on a clear day.

But Aboriginal blood ran through his veins. Something about this story, his passion and even his pain about the way his family had been treated, made her feel closer to him, more comfortable. He knew the pain of discrimination.

18

Venah stood outside Phillip's office, waiting. She knew he saw her as he continued his phone call and felt annoyed that he didn't gesture for her to step inside and wait. But she was determined to talk to him today, and so she waited, staring directly at him so he knew it was important.

She was irritated about the upcoming event. Why did he assign Sara to be the manager? And why was she only pulled into the event when she stood up and insisted during a staff meeting? What if she hadn't said anything—would he have asked for her input at all? Would she have even been invited?

She would attend, but Phillip needed to understand that she was not to be an afterthought, nor was she taking orders from the young girl. Finally, Phillip hung up the phone and looked up, ruddiness creeping up his cheeks.

Venah walked into his office and sat down in front of him.

He managed a smile and said, "Hi, Venah, how are you doing?"

"I am not doing well." Her strong voice reeked of disapproval, urging him to ask the next question.

"Oh, well, what's wrong?" Phillip knew he had to ask but realized he was being led down a dead-end road.

"The event with the minister. Sara is the manager?" It was an accusation.

Phillip thought about his words carefully. "She is coordinating the event."

"So she is not the manager?"

"Sara is working with Ruth, the executive director of the retirement home. We have no managers in the department."

"Okay, she is *leading* it."

"Venah, you are getting hung up on titles. Sara has been assigned to do what her job is—work with the senior staff of our partners to make sure the event runs smoothly and support them on whatever they need."

The words seemed to calm Venah somewhat.

"But what about the diversity and community outreach?"

"Yes, I said you would be working on that."

"But you didn't tell me about it before."

"I told you about it in the meeting. I wanted to bring it up in front of the staff, so everyone would know you would be handing the community relations part of the event."

The answer satisfied Venah .

"Okay, so I will be handling that part of it. And Sara is aware?"

"Yes, she is aware."

"Okay then. I need to make sure there are culturally appropriate accommodations for the families." With her nose slightly in the air, Venah looked satisfied.

"Yes." Phillip smiled and relaxed.

Reassured, Venah got up. So Phillip understood her concerns, and she would be overseeing the community aspect of the event. She wondered if she needed to talk to Sara to make sure this was clear. As she walked by the young woman's office, she slowed and looked in. Sara glanced up, and Venah picked up her pace and walked to her office. Phillip already said that Sara was aware.

Sara watched as Venah paused in front of her office. Venah's eyes lingered on Sara for a moment before she quickly walked away. Sara was certain that she wanted to engage in a conversation, but instead, she continued on, so Sara resumed her work.

So far, the minister's staff was responding quickly. They were checking her schedule and would be getting back to her on the minister's availability.

Sara refreshed her email. There was one from Phillip. He had forwarded an email from Mara and his comments were short: "Sara, see Mara's email. Do you know how many board members are attending the event?"

Anxiety. Was she supposed to invite the board? She'd thought Phillip would do that. The plan included the board chair speaking, and she had touched base with her to say the speaking notes would be coming soon. But no one told her that it was her responsibility to invite all the board members.

She still had time. The event was not for another three weeks, and Minister Boland had not yet confirmed, so she wrote back, "Not yet Phillip, I was hoping to confirm the minister's attendance before I let the entire board know. But I realize time is running out, so I can send the invitation to the board and let them know that the minister's attendance is yet to be confirmed. Does that work?"

Phillip's response was immediate. "Sure. Send the invitation to Irene, and she'll forward it on to the board."

Whew.

Irene responded just as quickly and said she'd collect RSVPs from the board and pass them along to Sara. Sara pulled up the event plan again and looked at the timelines in a panic. What else did she miss? She decided to print it out and review it again, so she could identify any small details that were missed.

"Sara, did you invite the board members to the event?" Anna's voice was loud. Sara hadn't noticed her standing in the doorway.

"Yes, Irene is taking the RSVPs."

"Because I was just talking to Derek, who's on the board, and he didn't know about the event."

"Irene only sent the invitation this morning. He may not have checked his email yet."

"Why was it only sent this morning?"

Sara didn't think she needed to explain herself to Anna, but the woman's tone was so harsh, so accusing, that it made Sara get defensive and a little nervous.

"I was waiting for the minister to confirm before the board was invited."

"The board needs notice."

"Yes, I realize that. But we still have three weeks before the launch."

"That's not enough time ..." Anna huffed away.

Sara wondered if this was true. But three weeks is more than enough time to put an event in someone's calendar.

She got up and went into the coffee room, cup in hand, her eyes avoiding Anna's office.

Maxine was making a new pot of coffee and greeted her as she walked in. Sara managed a smile.

"Everything okay?"

"Sure, yes ...do I not seem okay?"

"You look a little upset."

"Oh, well, you know. The usual work stuff."

Maxine smiled, poured some fresh coffee into Sara's mug, and said, "Come into my office for a minute."

Sara felt a pang of gratitude. She wanted to talk but she would never start the conversation. She knew that there were eyes and ears and frankly, she was still uncertain whom she could trust.

But she followed Maxine into her office and sat down as the door was shut.

"How are things going over there?"

"Things are okay."

Maxine laughed a little. "I know you don't want to say much. Talk travels fast around here, so I don't blame you. You're ahead of the game already, but I've worked with that team for a long time. For the longest time, there were just two people who ran the show and did whatever they wanted. The executive director allowed it because she is friends with Phillip. So when the board wanted more diversity in the department, I know they resented being told that they had to change the staffing a bit. But you need to stay strong and do your job. They will be looking for mistakes."

Talk travels fast? Looking for mistakes? They resented having to hire her? What was going on ... what kind of place was this? "I don't understand Maxine. What did you hear?"

"Well, I heard that you are doing a great job." Maxine's voice was soft. "You're a rising star, Sara, and not everyone admires the light from that star. Look, I don't want to do 'he said, she said,' and I don't want you to worry. But just keep your head up. There are always people who want to pull you down so they can climb higher. And Sara, remember that people like you and me have to work harder than everyone else."

Sara didn't ask for elaboration. "Okay, I understand what you're saying." It was her mother's advice again.

"If you need to talk, you can call me. I have been here a long time, and I had to fight to keep myself here. Some days, I still do." Maxine's eyes rolled a bit, but she got up and smiled. The conversation was over.

Sara rose and nodded, still silent because she feared she might cry if she spoke and, really, she didn't know what to say. Maintaining her composure as a professional was important.

As she walked out of Maxine's office, she wondered if she should talk to Phillip. Perhaps he could give her the reassurance she needed. He had always been nice to her. As she passed the hallway that led to his office, she decided to wait. There was nothing to talk to him about, really.

"Sara, heads up." The executive director stood in front of Sara, who had been so deep in thought that she nearly ran right into her.

"Oh ... hello, Mara. Sorry, I was thinking about something."

"The Passing the Torch anniversary launch no doubt."

"Um, yes, I was thinking about that."

"How are the arrangements coming along?" The executive director sounded friendly.

"So far, so good. The minister has not confirmed attendance yet." Sara didn't realize she had blurted that comment until it was out in the air. She waited for the fallout.

"Yes, well that's normal. She has a busy schedule and won't confirm until closer to the day. Talk to Ruth, she worked with her, so she'll be able to give you a better idea of how to proceed."

Mara walked away as she said the last words, quickly ending the conversation. Wow. Sara breathed deeply and wondered if perhaps she was worrying unnecessarily.

Okay, so she would ask Ruth. She hurried back to her office to call her when she noticed Phillip sitting in Venah 's office at the end of the hall. Anna was there as well. As she walked to her own open door, the voices lowered.

She slipped into her office and looked up Ruth's number. Ruth answered on the second ring. "Ruth Klein."

"Hi, Ruth. It's Sara."

"Sara! Hello, my dear. How are you doing?"

"I'm fine, Ruth. How are you?"

"I'm good. Busy as usual but doing well."

"Ruth, I've contacted the minister's office to invite her to the event. I asked if she would say a few words that night, but they have not confirmed her attendance yet."

"Did they get back to you?"

"Oh, yes. The staff has been great. But they said she has a very busy schedule, and they cannot confirm just yet."

"That is pretty typical. Minister Boland is probably one of the busiest of all the ministers in the province. Now that there is a push for more funding, she'll have many requests to visit more centres. So you won't hear anything until a few days before the launch, unfortunately."

"A few days? So how do I plan this?"

Ruth laughed. "Just go ahead and plan it with her attending. But have a back up to take her place, just in case."

"Okay, someone like the board chair?"

"No, perhaps an MPP. Who are the MPPs that are coming?"

"I haven't heard back yet." Sara fished around in her mind to recall if she sent the invites to the MPPs yet.

"Okay, so look at the list of MPPs and contact the one who would be the most appropriate to speak if the minister can't make it. In the meantime, I will send her an email and ask her myself."

"Oh, that would be great!"

Ruth laughed again. "Sure, I'm happy to do it. Although, I don't have much influence on her schedule. But hopefully she will remember the times I saved her ..."

Sara felt better after the call. But now she needed a backup. She would not ask Phillip who he would recommend to stand in for the minister. She would choose someone herself. She found the email asking the MPPs to attend the event. No responses to date, so she decided to send a reminder.

Then she looked up each MPP to see their portfolio. The local MPP was on the list, and so Sara figured he would be the best stand in. She still didn't want to ask Phillip, so she picked up the phone to check with Maxine.

"Hi, Maxine. It's Sara."

"Well, that was quick! What's up?"

"Maxine, is there a particular MPP that has worked with Albatross in the past?"

"Yes, James McCrae. He has come to most of our events. And I know Mara knows him well. Why?"

"I need someone as a back-up in case the minister can't make it. You know, someone to say a few words and cut the ribbon."

"Oh yes, he's a good choice."

What would she do without Maxine?

19

Phillip sat in his office and sipped on his coffee. He took a bite of his cheese Danish and realized it had been sitting there all morning, and it was already past lunchtime. He sighed. The meeting with Venah and Anna had worried him. They both wanted, well, no, demanded that they have a part in the Passing the Torch event.

Both were convinced that Sara was not going to manage the event properly and would embarrass them. He didn't agree, but he didn't tell them that. What he'd seen from Sara since she started was impressive. She was very organized and professional, and she was a hard worker. Besides, with Ruth behind her, she couldn't fail.

In fact, Ruth had called him after she met with Sara to declare how pleased she was to be working with the new public relations officer. She had asked the right questions, Ruth explained, and she was very polished and well spoken. Sara would have the support she needed to make the event successful.

But Anna was upset, and so was Venah. And he didn't know how to handle it.

Venah was insisting that she take over the community relations aspect of the event. She wanted direct access to Ruth. But Ruth already had plenty of staff who understood the families and their needs. Asking her to take directions from Venah would be insulting. Besides, he was not comfortable letting Venah have direct access to Ruth, who would not appreciate her brash, pushy manner.

Anna complained that Sara was not keeping her in the loop and that she had not even invited the board members yet!

Phillip assured both of them that the event plans were fine, but he ended up agreeing to a team meeting to review everyone's roles. He hadn't told Sara yet and feared he would end up moderating a heated discussion.

So he picked up the phone and dialed Randi. As usual, her voicemail kicked in. "Hi there, this is Randi. Leave a message." He didn't. She would see his number and call him back, hopefully. He decided to send her a text anyway. "Honey, give me a call when you have a minute. Work crisis."

His wife was his go-to advisor when employee situations like this one presented themselves because she knew how to handle people and always had clever tactics to get what she wanted.

He stared at his phone for a few minutes and decided to grab some lunch. A vision of a burger formed in his mind, and he grabbed his jacket. The burger place was just a few blocks away, and his stomach grumbled at the thought of the handmade cheeseburgers dripping with sauce. This particular joint formed the burger with cheese in the middle so when you took a bite, it oozed out. The thought grew in his mind, and as he started his car, he became impatient to get there.

As he parked his car in the tiny lot, he saw through the glass that the lineup was long, as usual. This was the only homemade burger place in the northwest end of the city. Owned by a local couple, it was a landmark, famous for its gourmet fast food.

His stomach nagged him, but he knew it would be worth the wait. As if she'd read his mind, Randi called back while he was waiting in line.

"Hey, lover. What's up?" He loved when she called him that name.

"Hey, beautiful. Thanks for calling back so quickly. You busy?"

"Yep, just got out of a meeting with a new client. Big case, big client. They heard about my last case and said they wouldn't want anyone else to represent them."

"That's great. You have a reputation for sure."

"Yes, they need a pit bull ..." her rough, sexy cackle gave her a wild edge.

"That's you!"

"Yeah, well at first Bill wanted to put Janet on it, but I pulled him aside and told him that her straight-line walking wouldn't get the results this client wanted. "

"Good."

"Not sure why he thought of her first, though. I'm sure the client asked for me. It's a big case, but I can't say too much right now."

Phillip waited for her to finish, adhering to the agreement they'd made before Adam.

When he first brought up the idea of a baby, Randi dismissed it. Just two years into their marriage, and she was rarely home. Some days he felt like her personal assistant, shopping for her clothes at high-end stores, stopping after work to pick up her endless hangers of dry cleaning, and eating dinner alone most nights of the week in front of the TV.

She was a busy lawyer with demanding clients, she explained. He knew this when he married her.

Perhaps a baby would prompt a change. Her first reaction was close to horror, eyes widened, black dots in the middle of thick, green borders. But immediately, true to her training, she assumed a poker face and shrugged. "Let me get back to you on that." The idea already dismissed.

Usually, Phillip didn't challenge Randi on her decisions. But this was his life, and he wanted a child. So he let a few weeks go by and slipped the idea back into a conversation over dinner at one of their favourite upscale restaurants down by the water.

"So did you think about what we talked about?" He didn't provide details, but he knew his wife; she was sharp.

"I've thought about it. I'm not sure I have time to raise a child, Phillip. I mean, look at my schedule."

"You don't want to have kids?"

"I didn't say that. I just said that I am not sure I can commit the time."

"I know. You have a really busy career, but mine is not as hectic."

She paused to spread a thick layer of caviar over a buttery cracker and opened her scarlet lips to let her pearly teeth take a bite. Then she responded.

"What are you saying?"

"I'm saying that I can be the primary caregiver, and I would take paternity leave. That way you can continue to build your career." He said the words carefully, as only a skilled spin master could.

"It still means carrying the child for nine months. Can you see me in court with a beach-ball belly? Now that would change the perception of me as a pit bull somewhat."

The image made Phillip smile. Pit bulls had babies too.

"Well, I have looked into adoption," he said.

Randi turned her attention away from her love affair with the Russian caviar and looked directly at her husband with granite eyes.

"You've looked into it? How long have you been looking into adoption?"

Phillip swallowed. Was she upset about the idea of adoption or the fact that he looked into it without talking to her first? He paused to let his mind work.

"A while now. I wanted to have all the facts before I approached you about it. I know how important your career is, and I thought this could be a way for us to have a child without putting additional pressure on you."

She sat back and turned to the caviar once again. After putting a cracker past her lips, she said in between small chews, "Okay, that makes some sense. So what did you find out?"

Phillip felt himself relaxing slightly but knew he had to provide solid facts, or she would just roll her eyes and not take him seriously. He'd been researching and preparing for weeks. "It could take as little as a year to get a baby, less time if we wanted a toddler or an older child," Phillip recited the words that he'd run through his mind time and time again.

As he spoke, she took in all of the information, her eyes flicking back and forth from her bowl of shiny black caviar to his eyes. He knew that she was trained to look at a person's eyes as they talked.

He finished with confidence, smiled at her, and picked up his fork and speared his salad.

She took a moment to contemplate what he had said. When a small pool of oil and herbs became visible on his plate, and the last bite of green was safely in his mouth, he heard her voice.

"Okay, I will think it over and get back to you." Her green eyes were softer, less harsh, like a cat who was no longer threatened.

"Great," he smiled at her and knew that it would be just a matter of time before they were parents.

The line was moving, and he held the phone with one hand as he fished for his wallet with the other.

"Honey ..." he waited until there was a slight pause but caught her in a word.

"Yep, oh you called me," she said suddenly. She was always so considerate.

"Yes, it's about the event with the minister."

"Uh huh."

"You know I assigned Sara to manage it because the executive director of the home requested her. But now the other girls are upset. They want bigger roles in the event, and they want me to hold a meeting to discuss ..." He didn't have to elaborate or finish. Randi was already advising.

"Oh yeah, well, women are competitive. You know that. They want to be acknowledged, but you already assigned it to someone. It's going to be the same way with Janet. But I told Bill that this case can't be won unless I'm on it. He is going to have to stand his ground if she says anything."

"So you don't think I should hold a meeting and assign larger roles to the others?"

"Hold the meeting but stand your ground. The other girls can have a role, but there is one lead."

It wasn't the answer he wanted to hear, but it gave him some strength.

"Okay, thanks. It's just what I needed to hear."

"Great! Okay, gotta run. Haven't even had lunch yet." And then he heard the click. She was always on the run.

He was at the front of the line, and by the end of the call, he'd been distracted by the waft of the grilled meat and fried potatoes. He ordered quickly.

Driving quickly, Phillip resisted the urge to open the bag with one hand and take a bite. No, he needed to wait until he got back to his office. He would close the door and enjoy the food slowly.

As he was rushing into his office, Mara came barrelling in. She must have been waiting for him.

"Phillip, have the board members been invited to the event? I just talked to Joan, and she didn't know about it!"

"Yes, Irene sent the invitation today or yesterday. Sara was waiting for the minister to confirm."

"Well, we can't wait. The minister won't confirm until a few days before. Perhaps I need to review the plan with Sara. I haven't seen the final version."

Phillip's mind spun. Did he show Mara the final version of the plan? He couldn't remember. His burger was getting cold.

"I'll check with her."

"Fine." Mara walked back to her office.

Phillip sighed. He shut his door and put the bag on his desk. He sat down and pulled out the warm burger, grabbing a few fries on the way up. As he peeled back the wrapping, his teeth cut a large bite, cheese dripped onto his bottom lip, and sauce leaked down his hands. He sighed and leaned back in his chair.

20

Mara walked into Phillip's office and sat across from him. Phillip looked at her face and realized something was wrong. She placed the event plan on his desk in front of him.

"So I reviewed this."

"Great! What did you think?" He was doing his best to sound positive, but inside he was waiting, waiting for the fallout.

"Well, I've made some edits. You'll see them here."

Phillip waited.

"But it's not bad. Concise, well thought out. I like it."

He felt the air escape from his lungs and his stomach settled slightly.

"Next time though, I need to see the final copy at least three weeks before the event happens. And, the board members must know about it sooner."

As Phillip started to say something, she stopped him with her hand. "I know, there is time, but I don't want to get calls from board members about an event they've heard about but not yet been invited to."

With those words, Mara got up and walked out.

As soon as her figure disappeared around the corner, Phillip grabbed the document and leafed through it. A few edits here and there … she wasn't kidding. He smiled. When there was nothing to correct, she would make minor changes to the language. So she couldn't find any significant problems with the plan. He giggled to himself. She liked it. This was a first.

As he picked up the plan with excitement to take it to Sara, a sudden thought hit him. Mara liked Sara's plan. Mara, the executive director, who was being pressured by the board of directors to hire staff with awareness about the diverse community. He was not a member of this community and his awareness was limited, but Sara was.

He picked up his phone and Sara's extension. She answered. Her voice was quiet, uncertain.

"Sara, it's Phillip."

"Hi ..."

"Can I see you in my office please?"

"Sure. I'll be there in a minute."

He hung up the phone and sat back in his chair. She arrived within two minutes, as he knew she would. Her hand held a notebook and pen, and she knocked softly on his door, even though it was open.

"Come in." He smiled.

Her face was sombre. "So Mara has reviewed the plan."

"Okay, that's good, right?"

"She was a little unsure why the board wasn't invited earlier. When a board member calls her and asks about an event they've heard about but have not yet received an invitation to, it looks as if they have not been included."

"I know, but I was waiting for confirmation from the minister's office ..."

He continued as if he had not heard her, "... and this board needs to be included. They are the governors of Albatross, and Mara reports to them."

"Yes, I understand."

The last answer was defeat, and her fearful face caused him to soften a little. He leaned in slightly. "Now I know you were waiting for the minister's confirmation. But perhaps next time, just check with me first."

"Sure. I'll do that."

"Also, you should always send Mara a final copy to review at least three weeks before the event."

Sara looked directly at him. Three weeks was a lot of lead time, and the details hadn't come together until recently. Besides, he was supposed to send the plan to Mara. That was the agreement. She opened her mouth to explain, but his eyes were direct and his mouth was a hard line against his red face.

"Okay, I'll factor that into the plan."

Phillip reached over and placed the event plan in front of her. "Mara has made some changes. But the plan seems fine. So please proceed. Have you confirmed with the minister yet?"

Sara felt her body relax. "Not yet. But the MPP James McCrae will be attending, and he can speak if the minister does not attend."

Phillip considered this for a moment. "Okay, that works. Fine then." He stood up and walked around his desk, which was the cue for her to leave his office.

"Thanks, Phillip."

He chuckled a little nervously. "You're welcome."

Phillip brought up the event again at the Monday morning meeting. He said that all staff would be in attendance. Anna would be there since she had worked with the retirement homes in the past, and Venah had experience with the community. But he didn't clarify their roles or assign them specific tasks.

At first, Sara was confused. She waited for the others to protest, to ask what their roles were, to even volunteer to oversee certain tasks, but no one said anything.

When they adjourned, Sara walked back to her office, pleased. Perhaps the storm was over. Perhaps both women just decided that they had to step back and be supportive. As she smiled and allowed herself to relax, a quick check of her email revealed the confirmation she was looking for. The minister would be attending the event!

Sara felt giddy and let out a sigh of relief. Now to tell Phillip. She wanted to run into his office and reveal the news, but he might not appreciate that. So instead, she sent him an email and copied Mara. Then she picked up the phone and called Ruth, who was pleased in a quiet way that made Sara think that she'd had a hand in securing the minister's attendance.

Maxine was the next person she called, and she didn't disappoint, seeming to be as excited as Sara was.

Phillip's response to her email was curt, though he used an exclamation mark after the words "Great news!" Mara did not respond.

Sara's high fuelled her for the rest of the day. The event was a week away, and she still had to get everything else organized. As she looked up, Anna was staring at her again. Sara smiled and looked away, not waiting for her colleague to reciprocate.

The week passed quickly, and Sara kept herself busy with the logistics of the event. She visited Ruth a couple of times to view the event space and conduct a quick dry run with the staff.

She was flying high. The notes were finished for the board chair and for Mara, the information about the event was provided to the minister's office—it was all finished with less than a week to go. Phillip was in a good mood and even gave her what looked like a genuine smile a few times when she passed him in the office. But he never came into her office to chat the way he did with Anna. One time, she noticed he was sitting in Venah's office, and the two of them were laughing. Venah had looked at Sara and smiled smugly. Perhaps he knew she was busy and didn't want to bother her; she quickly dismissed any negative thoughts that threatened to sway her mood.

The day before the event, Sara got into the office at seven thirty to go over everything for the next day. She'd also been staying late the past week, just finalizing details. Plus there were other projects she had to stay on top of. Phillip had not reduced her workload and she wanted to demonstrate that she was capable. Asking Anna for help wasn't an option as far as she was concerned. Her aloof demeanour indicated it was best not to approach her unless necessary.

But on this morning, the day before the event, Anna came in early as well. After getting her coffee, she walked over to Sara's office and stood in the doorway.

"Morning, Anna," Sara said.

"Morning. So are you all ready for tomorrow's event?" Anna's tone was authoritative.

"Yes, I think so. I'm just going to go over the list again today to make sure everything is on track."

"Okay, let me know if there is anything I can do to help."

Sara was a little stunned and didn't get her voice until Anna's back was turned. "You'll be there tomorrow?"

"Yes."

"Okay, well thanks, Anna. I appreciate the support."

A mumbled "no problem" emanated from Anna's back as she returned to her office.

Sara stared at her screen for a couple of minutes. Anna was offering to help? What had Phillip said that made her so cooperative?

Then, at around nine, Venah followed suit.

"Sara, how do you need my help tomorrow?" Venah peered at her with narrowed eyes as if she were presenting a challenge.

"I think it's all under control. You will be on site tomorrow to engage with the families?"

"Yes, I will." Venah's accent was clear.

"Okay, well thanks. Ruth will be able to tell you which families will need the most support."

"Are there vegetarian options?"

"Yes."

"Will there be translators?"

"There are some staff members who speak other languages."

"We don't have translators?"

"Ruth felt it wasn't necessary to hire external translators because she has staff that can help if necessary." In fact, Ruth said that the vast majority of the seniors spoke English and translators were not necessary.

Venah's smile turned sour. Anger sparked in her eyes, and she opened her mouth but nothing came out. As if she changed her mind, her mouth closed, and she walked away.

Sara inhaled deeply and closed her eyes for a minute.

Venah was annoyed. Not only did Phillip ignore her request to have a lead role in the event, but now Sara hadn't even considered the needs of the diverse audience. Phillip should have allowed her to manage the community part of the event. After the Monday meeting, she had stormed into his office and closed the door. She told him that she was not pleased that he didn't tell Sara that she would be handling the diversity piece.

He listened to her and then said, "Venah, I was clear in the meeting that you and Anna would be attending the event and lending your support. You have been hired for your experience in community outreach. Sara knows this, but she is also working with Ruth, and Ruth is the one who is overseeing the event."

"But …"

He leaned over at that point and said softly, "Venah, you have an important role. Don't worry."

His calming voice had an effect on her. She also realized that he was not going to take a stand and make Sara let go of the reins. So it was up to her to take control on the day of the event.

"Why don't you ask Sara what needs to be done?"

"I do not report to Sara."

"Well, she is coordinating the event, and you can simply ask her what you can do, but bear in mind, Ruth likes to have things her way. So Sara is really only carrying out what Ruth wants."

The last point made Venah realize that she should be talking to Ruth. Sara was irrelevant.

"Okay, thanks." She stood up and walked out of his office.

Phillip held his coffee cup in one hand as he propelled himself though the office. He decided it would be a good idea to visit the staff and gauge the environment. The event was tomorrow, and based on his conversation with Ruth, it seemed to be under control.

So the only issue left to deal with was Venah and Anna. Anna had not said anything to him since Monday's meeting, but Venah had been forceful in her dissatisfaction. He couldn't divide the management of the event into several pieces. It would simply not work.

In the short time she'd been at Albatross, he'd watched her become brasher in her tone than she'd been in her interview, and he was starting to realize that she was not as experienced as she'd bragged. She had an air about her that spoke of arrogance, and yet he suspected that her knowledge of diverse communities was actually limited. She knew a lot about her own traditions but didn't seem to have an open mind when it came to other cultures. What was worse was that she didn't admit her weakness but projected it onto Sara, insisting that the young woman was not knowledgeable enough to handle the role she'd been given. That concerned him, but more importantly, it surprised him. He was so sure they would work well together.

He'd hoped that the event would help them bond. However, he noticed that Sara did not approach Venah or Anna to bring them into the loop. She was working in a silo, which was not a good method. But for now, he would watch, and while on site, he would take control of the event. It was easier that way.

"Morning, Sara!" his voice boomed, and his face stretched upwards.

"Morning, Phillip."

He sat down in her office and actually leaned back this time. He took a sip of his coffee and looked at her, continuing to grin.

"So, everything on track for tomorrow?"

"Yes, I'm just going over the plan and checklist today."

"Minister all confirmed? Board chair and Mara have their notes?"

"Yes."

"Great!" He turned slightly and said loudly, "Anna, Venah, can we chat for a minute?"

Anna looked up, and he realized that Venah may not have heard. He stood up and looked down the hallway, gesturing towards the office at the end. Then he sat back down as the two women approached and stood in Sara's doorway.

"So tomorrow is the big event! I don't have to tell you that we are very excited that this program is now entering its second year. And with the new funding from the ministry, it has the potential to be a model for other homes. Mara is watching our department to see how we manage this event. So Anna and Venah, you will both be on site to support the event. We will also need to be mindful of what Ruth wants tomorrow. She is the client, and we need the client to be happy. Right?" He looked around at all the faces. There were nods.

"What time do we need to be there?" Venah 's question pierced Sara's ears.

"I would be there as early as possible. The event starts at—Sara, it starts at ten?"

"The minister speaks at ten. But families will be arriving at around nine."

"So then we should be there by eight, just to make sure everything is ready."

He smiled at his staff and stood up, with both Anna and Venah taking the cue to walk away. The pep talk was over.

Richard wanted to spend the night, but she couldn't let him see her in worry mode. She had told him about the event but downplayed it. No big deal, she said. Anyway, Sara was sure he just wanted to spend the night because it meant sex, and she was in no mood for that.

So she opted for a telephone call instead, and after hanging up, poured herself a big glass of wine, slipped into PJs, and sat in front of the television. She wasn't certain what show she was watching but at some point, woke up in the middle of the night with the TV still on and her glass empty. It was two thirty in the morning, and that's when panic struck. Sara knew, from experience, that she would not be able to get back to sleep easily. So she got up and went to the washroom and took an allergy pill, the kind that makes you drowsy, and then she got into her bed.

A bell was ringing in her dream when suddenly consciousness took over and Sara opened her eyes, realizing that it was six o'clock and her alarm was chiming. Throwing back the covers, she headed to the shower to start the day.

22

Ruth was already at the centre when Sara arrived. It was 7:52 a.m., and she managed to get a parking spot close to the front doors. Great, she had lots of items to unload. Thank goodness for her IKEA dolly, onto which she could pile box on box so her hands were free to carry the pull-up displays, neatly rolled in their cases.

Although the parking lot was quiet, the main foyer, where the event would be held, was already buzzing with staff milling around. Ruth was in the centre, directing the caretaker where to place the podium. She saw Sara and beckoned for her to approach.

"Do you think the chairs are in the right place?" she asked. Sara put the displays on the registration table at the front of the room and looked around. The chairs were facing the right side of the room as one entered, and the podium was on the far right. As people came in, they could see the audience facing the podium, but they would not distract the speaker. It was well situated.

"It looks great!" she smiled and started setting up the registration table. As she was unzipping the first display, she heard a voice behind her. "I'll set up the table." Anna had picked up one of the boxes and was pulling out brochures and sign-in sheets.

"Morning, Anna. Thanks."

They worked in silence, and soon the smell of warm cinnamon buns wafted through the air. Sara realized that she had not yet had breakfast or her morning coffee, and the sweet aroma poked her stomach, which started to growl.

"I'm going to get a coffee, do you want one?" she asked Anna.

Without looking at her, Anna gruffly replied, "Sure," and they made their way to the refreshment table.

"So how do you think it looks?" Sara dared pose the question.

"Who did the set-up?"

"Ruth had the caretakers set it up."

"The podium should be at the back, so when people walk in, it's the first thing they see." She looked straight ahead as she marched quickly across the room.

Sara quickened her pace to keep up with Anna's stride. "Oh, really? I thought this way would be less distracting to the speakers."

"They don't get distracted. They're used to it."

Sara suddenly felt stupid. Of course, they were professionals; they wouldn't get distracted. So now what? Would Phillip and Mara frown at the set-up?

She picked up an empty coffee cup and was surveying the podium again when Ruth appeared.

"Good morning, Anna! You're here early to help Sara?"

"Hi, Ruth."

"Everything looks great, Ruth. I love these cinnamon buns!" Sara answered quickly, hoping Anna would not bring up the podium location. It was too late to change anything at this point.

"Well, you're welcome. I thought they would be a nice touch in addition to the samosas and fruit trays. All vegetarian options! So what time will the minister be arriving?"

"Her office said she would arrive fifteen minutes before her speech, which is at ten. So we still have about forty-five minutes before she's here."

"Oh, Sara, before I forget, there are a couple of seniors and students who have agreed to talk to the media. But the family case worker just wants to ask you a few questions first. Can you come with me?"

"Sure. Anna, would you mind looking after the registration table?" Her eyes met Anna's, and once she saw the nod, she followed Ruth into the administrative area.

When Sara returned, she found Venah was standing at the registration table with Anna.

"Hello, Sara. Are you ready for this event?" said Venah with a coy smile. She was wearing a dark green *shalwar kameez*. The long shirt had embroidered patterns on the front in gold. The pants were very tight around her thin legs, and she wore gold mules. Her hair was pulled back into a tight bun at the nape of her neck, and she had red lipstick on. It was the first time Sara had seen make-up on Venah .

She saw Venah 's eyes run up and down her frame, taking in the grey suit and yellow blouse she'd carefully selected for the day, and busied herself at the table, hoping to avoid conversation.

"Hey, Sara. How's it going?" Don Porter from the local paper looked up at her with his usual serious face as he wrote down his name on the media sign-in sheet.

"Hey, Don. How are you doing?" She leaned in for his quick embrace. They had both worked in the same office, back in her beat reporter days, and she knew he would show up to support her event.

"I'm good. The usual. How are you enjoying the dark side?"

"Ha ha, yeah, we publicists say the same thing about reporting. I've left the dark side."

When two other reporters strolled in, one from the South Asian paper and the other from one of the dailies, Sara felt the excitement rising in her throat and closed her mouth for fear it would escape in a little shout.

"Sara." The voice stifled Sara's excitement.

"Yes," she turned and smiled at Venah.

"None of the materials are translated into other languages."

"No, we didn't do any translations this time. Maxine and Ruth didn't think it was necessary for this event since all of the families are already aware of the value of the Passing the Torch program."

"Still, we should be translating into other languages. Some of the seniors do not speak English!"

"Well, the attendees today speak English. That's what Ruth said."

"Well, for your information and Ruth's too, there are many here who need information in their own language."

Her mouth opened but nothing came out. Thankfully Maxine's voice broke the tension.

"Hey, Sara, it looks great!" Maxine gestured to the foyer filling up with people.

"Thanks. Ruth and her staff did the set-up."

"Yes, but you managed the entire event. And getting the minister here is a great bonus!"

"The minister comes to all of these events," Venah interjected. "When I was executive director at the Rajasthan Centre, she came all the time. All I had to do was pick up the phone and talk to her."

Maxine shot Sara a reassuring smile and patted her arm. "I'm going to say hello to Ruth. I'll see you in a bit. And congratulations again!"

Sara tidied the table again, and when she gained the courage to look beside her, Venah was gone. Anna was refreshing her coffee cup. Suddenly, there was a small crowd at the front door. Two young, fair-haired women walked in and introduced themselves as the minister's staff. The one named Brittany asked to see the podium and the set-up, while Lauren surveyed the refreshment table.

Sara glanced over at the registration table and saw Anna scrambling to hand out information and answer questions. There was a flood of people walking in, and she quickly shifted a few steps to where Venah stood and asked softly, "Can you give Anna a hand over at the registration table? I am helping the minister's staff with their set-up."

Venah wagged her finger and said, "Oh, no, that is not my job."

Suddenly, there was a buzz at the front entrance. Sara turned and saw the entourage and then the middle-aged, heavyset woman with short, dark hair walking through the door, an air of celebrity surrounding her. She'd met Ontario's Minister of Children and Youth Services once, back in her beat reporter days, but she realized that reporters' faces were unrecognizable to someone who spent her days meeting vast groups of people, so she stood aside and watched the scene unfold.

MPPs walked over and shook hands. Albatross's board chair smiling and grabbing hands. Mara and Phillip in the mix, eager faces and matching hands. Cameras were flashing and photographers moving around to get different angles. Sara stood by and watched as Minister Boland made her way through the crowd, shaking hands and talking to community members. She approached the podium and looked out at the crowd. The event was about to begin.

Sara watched as speeches were delivered, and guests listened intently as they sipped coffee, balancing paper plates filled with bits of cinnamon bun and samosa crumbs on their laps. The entire program took forty-five minutes, and when the last speaker thanked the crowd and encouraged another visit to the refreshment table, Sara allowed herself to exhale.

"Hey, Sara, can I talk to your board chair?" Don was standing beside her, phone in hand, his crooked grin and ruffled hair prompting her to smile.

"Sure, I'll get her." Sara went in search of Joan Rodriguez, the board chair who worked as a mortgage broker during the day and the chair of a community organization at night. It was a strange pairing. But she was rumoured to have many contacts within the community and within the various levels of government.

She found Joan chatting with Phillip, and she approached, feeling the sting of perfume as it entered her nostrils.

Phillip stopped talking and acknowledged her politely. "Sara, how are you doing?"

"I'm good, thanks. The reporter from the local paper wants to interview Joan, if that's okay?"

Perhaps Phillip should introduce her to Joan? Or maybe she should extend her hand ... Sara's nerves kept her still as Joan smiled and sized her up with cognac eyes, widened with black eye make-up.

"Yes, that's fine. Where?" Her voice was strong and direct, emanating from hot-pink lips.

"I'll get him. Do you want to speak over there where it's quiet?" Sara indicated two chairs in the back corner of the foyer.

"Sure, that looks good. Phillip, did you want to come along in case he has other questions, or to make sure I stay on message?" She smirked and he blushed as his chest puffed out just a bit.

On her way back from leading Joan to Don, Sara noticed Venah standing behind the registration table, hands clasped behind her back, staring into the room. Wasn't she supposed to be engaging with the members of this diverse community? Strange ... perhaps Venah had been out talking to families, and she didn't notice with everything else going on.

Oh well, maybe it didn't matter.

The clock said 11:53 a.m., and the crowd was thinning. The minister and her staff were long gone, and only a few families and staff members milled around. Anna helped Sara pack up, and the two women headed out to the parking lot.

"Thanks for your help, Anna." Sara said as they placed the items in her trunk.

"Sure." Anna actually smiled as she walked to her own car. "See you at the office," she said over her shoulder.

As she drove to the office, Sara was euphoric. Her first event at Albatross and it went really well. She couldn't wait to tell Richard.

Sara unloaded the boxes onto the dolly, slung the display case over her shoulder, and walked into the office building, a smile on her face.

Venah was angry. As she pulled into the parking lot, her mind was racing. The event went well, but she had little part in it. Sara was running around dealing with the families and the media, and yet she didn't ask for her expertise. She could have introduced her to the media as the community specialist and diversity expert, and they could have interviewed her. She had done a couple of interviews in her days as an executive director, so she was well experienced in this area.

Standing behind the registration table made her look as if she were doing nothing. She didn't want Phillip or Mara to see her standing there handing out brochures. Anyone could do that. Anna was doing that, in fact, because that was her job.

And then Sara asked for her assistance. She wasn't there to assist Sara … who did that young girl think she was? Venah was asked to be at the event to supervise, to make sure the cultural accommodations were taken into consideration. And no one even introduced her to the minister!

She had ended up going into the office to ensure the staff had what they needed to support the event. They were very pleased to have a representative from Albatross there. Perhaps the next time around they would request her attendance at all events. In fact, she should meet with Ruth to discuss the cultural needs of the seniors and their families. There were a few families wearing traditional clothing, and yet Venah wasn't brought over to talk to them.

She wasn't even sure that Phillip or Mara saw her in the office. So it was important that she remind him about the reason he hired her. He needed to know her value. As she walked into the building, she made a mental note to talk to him soon.

Phillip was sitting in Anna's office as she passed, so she slowed her pace and tried to hear what they were saying. But they were speaking too quietly—what if they were talking about her? What if Anna was complaining that she didn't help her at the registration desk?

Panic ran through Venah's body. She went to her desk and sat down quickly. As her computer booted up, Venah rolled thoughts over in her mind. If Phillip thought she didn't help Anna, then there could be trouble. It was obvious that Phillip favoured Anna. The two of them had worked together for a long time, and the blond woman definitely had Phillip's ear and support.

So what she needed was a strategy to make sure that Anna was on her side. It wouldn't be that difficult. She'd done this before.

Phillip walked out of Anna's office and ran into Sara on her way in.

"Hi." Sara's face was beaming. She was pushing a dolly and had the display case over one shoulder. Phillip frowned slightly. Didn't the other girls offer to help bring the stuff back to the office?

"Sara. How are you? So how do you feel about the event?"

"I think it went well. Ruth said the minister was happy." Sara blurted this out because she was certain that Phillip would be as excited as she was. But he looked taken aback, and his smile was forced.

"I thought it went well too. Congratulations ... good job." He walked away as he spoke, and Sara stood in the hallway for a moment, slightly puzzled.

When she reached her office, she almost dropped the display. It wasn't really heavy but having to carry it from the back end of the parking lot into the building made her shoulder sore.

As she fired up the computer, her mind was still focussed on Phillip and the strange way he behaved. Something was up. When she told him about Minister Boland's reaction to the event, he didn't seem pleased. She was hoping for the same elation she felt when Ruth told her the news but Phillip seemed uncomfortable.

Perhaps he had heard differently. Yes, that must be it. Perhaps the minister told Mara that she wasn't happy with the event. Maybe there was not enough media there. Maybe the staff didn't like the way Sara handled the logistics of the event. Was she supposed to have been mingling with the minister's staff instead of the media?

Sara's forehead creased in worry and the bubble she'd been floating in since she left the retirement facility suddenly popped; she was once again the person whom neither Anna nor Venah liked. Her glory was gone as soon as it had appeared.

She sighed and looked at the unread emails in her inbox. It was way after noon, and she hadn't eaten lunch yet. She forgot to pick something up on the way back and realized that she didn't bring anything from home, not even a snack.

Hunger filled her body, and she felt weak and drained. Now she would have to go back out and get something to eat. Luckily, there was a small family-owned diner just around the corner that always had soup and fresh bread and soft cookies.

Putting her coat back on, Sara picked up her purse and headed out to lunch. The cold air was delicious on her hot face as she walked down the street.

The smell of stale gravy, bleached dishtowels, and coffee wafted through the air as she stepped inside. Agnes and Sam, the couple who owned the place, had lived in the area for their entire lives and had opened Sam's Diner about twenty years ago. It was a shabby, homey place where older locals sat around all day and drank coffee. The tablecloths were plastic with blue and white checkers and the coffee pots were stained brown.

An older woman sat at a table facing the door, a cup in her hand. Beside her was a shopping cart, the kind that had a string to close the opening. It had red and white stripes and was overflowing with what looked like plastic shopping bags. Sara didn't look long enough to see what was inside the bags. But it didn't take much peering to notice the grey wig that perched on top of the woman's head. It was slightly askew so the middle part was slanted on her head. The woman stared at her as she sipped from the cup, refusing to look away; Sara was an unfamiliar sight to her. Sara's eyes flicked to the menu behind the counter.

Sam's Diner wasn't fancy, but they had sinful, greasy bacon-and-egg breakfast sandwiches. Sara considered ordering one as the thought of salty, crisp bacon combined with soft egg yolks got her stomach rumbling, but instead, she ordered a bowl of homemade soup and a fresh bun. Two fresh-baked chocolate chip cookies were the only sin she committed, and a carton of milk completed her lunch. The simple meal would suffice; she didn't need extra calories now that Richard was seeing her without clothes. The thought of Richard made her suddenly cheerful as she walked back down the street to the Albatross building.

Mara watched Sara as she walked up the pathway into the main entrance of the building. She turned and faced her computer, not wanting to meet the young woman's eyes.

Sara had done a good job with the event today. The minister seemed pleased as she thanked her, and so did Joan. Mara was well aware that this made Sara look really good. So now what?

On some level, she'd hoped the young woman would fail, so she could exercise her authority as executive director and haul her into the office for a talk. Perhaps she should be satisfied. Nancy was always telling her that if someone else did a good job, she should just learn to let them have it. But it was too soon to let this young woman feel that confident. Not just yet.

Mara sat back in her chair and thought.

Maybe she needed to work with Sara on a project one-on-one. But could she deal with it herself? She'd finally admitted to herself that this young woman was attractive, and sometimes she allowed her lustful thoughts to carry themselves into a fantasy that fuelled her lovemaking with Nancy. At first, she felt guilty, but what Nancy didn't know wouldn't hurt her. Besides, couples fantasized about other people all the time. Thinking wasn't cheating.

Last week, she'd let her thoughts wander during work and left a flirty phone message to Nancy; when she got home, a wonderful meal was waiting and so was Nancy, in a sheer nightie. The sight of her lover in a sexy, lacy negligee drove her to push Nancy into the bedroom and onto the bed even before she removed her coat. Mara loved the smell of Nancy's body—a woman's body, strong with a musky scent and the salty taste of the ocean. They spent that evening making love, lustful and exciting, something they hadn't done in a long time. Afterwards, as they refuelled with the reheated meal, Nancy asked what had lit her wife's fire that way.

Mara just smiled, placed her hand on Nancy's, and said that she had been so busy with work that she just realized what she'd been missing at home.

Nancy had no reason to question Mara's fib. They left the dirty dishes on the table and headed back into the bedroom.

So what project would be suitable? There was the diabetes awareness program at Raleigh. It wasn't new, but the families living in the area had changed. The young, Caucasian families had moved farther north, leaving the Caucasian seniors, refusing to budge from their long-time homes, to get used to newcomers. New immigrants from India had high levels of diabetes and many of them brought aging parents who had never had access to such health programs before. So they took full advantage, and the programs were filling up quickly.

Yes, perhaps that was the best project to work on with Sara. She would mention it to Phillip and see what he said.

Venah waited until Sara left her office to approach Anna. She walked into her office with a smile and sat down without waiting for an invitation.

"So Anna, how did you like the event?"

"I thought it was okay. I didn't like the set-up of the room though. The podium should have been opposite to the front entrance. That way, people would see the speakers as soon as they walked in."

"Yes, yes, I noticed that too. Who did the set-up?"

"Not sure. I guess Sara worked with Ruth on it."

"Okay, well she should have asked for your opinion. Didn't you work on all of the events at the centres in the past?"

"Yeah, I used to do them before."

"So what changed?"

"Not sure. Phillip said Mara wanted to spread out the duties a bit. Sara hadn't done an event before, and they probably wanted to see if she could do it."

"Well, that is a big event to give to someone so junior."

"I don't know that she's junior. But it was her first event." Anna heard herself defending her colleague, to her own surprise.

"Well, when I say 'junior,' I mean junior to you. You have more experience in the events than she does. I was supposed to help with the families, but the staff in the office were busy and asked for my support. They were putting together information about the new families who joined, and they needed my help with the names and understanding more about the South Asian community." Venah came up with the lie quickly.

"Oh, really? Yeah, I guess that would be helpful."

"That's why I didn't stay at the registration table. I know Phillip would have wanted me to help the staff. They need to understand the culture."

"Yeah, sure, that makes sense."

"Well, I think you did a great job today."

When she was gone, Anna thought about Venah's comments. Perhaps the staff really needed her help with the names and the new families. Who knows? Anna knew by now that Venah did not like Sara. It was probably because the young brown woman was modern, and according to their traditions, she should be listening to and working under Venah, not the other way around. But it didn't matter to Anna, not one bit. If the two of them didn't get along, it would only help her get better projects if she could work with Venah.

She smiled as she pulled out her lunch bag and fished for her glass container filled with pasta and meat sauce. It was time to eat, so she headed to the lunchroom to warm up the food.

Pizza was comfort food for Phillip, and as he bit into the gooey slice, the sweet tomato sauce combined with savory, salty pepperoni engulfed his taste buds. He sat in the pizza parlour by himself, completely ignorant to the people who filled the tables, chattering and eating their hot Italian lunches. He didn't come here very often, but today he hadn't brought lunch, anticipating that Ruth would have had more than finger foods. He'd had some cheese and crackers, but it wasn't enough to satisfy his appetite, and so he headed over to the pizza place after chatting briefly with Anna. He also wanted to avoid Venah. He'd seen her face as she glared at Sara from the safety of the small office outside the room where the event was held. He knew immediately that she was not happy. Sara was busy running from one place to the next, and Anna was behind the registration desk, taking note of all the mistakes and things that needed improvement.

Venah was supposed to have been walking around, talking to the families. Or she could have stood behind the registration table and greeted the ethnic families as they came in. Either way, she was not supposed to be helping the receptionist. But he didn't intervene, even though he knew she would be barrelling her way into his office at some point in the afternoon to complain that she didn't have a more prominent role.

Anna had already provided her dollar worth of whining. He sighed and bit off another large piece of pizza. It was heaven. He had bought two pieces and a chicken parmesan sandwich for later.

As he picked up slice number two, anticipating the taste of the Italian sausage and onion, he felt the buzz of his phone. The point broken and in his mouth, he fished in his jacket pocket with his empty hand so he could view the number on the iPhone. It was Mara. Crap. What did she want? He had a right to eat lunch. He stared at the phone and felt the vibration in his hand for a moment … and decided not to answer it. He'd call her back or pop into her office on his way in.

What could Mara want? The event had gone really well. He had to admit, he hadn't been expecting Sara to pull it off as well as she did. The speeches were great, there were no logistical problems, and most importantly, Ruth was really pleased. And when Ruth was happy, she used all of her power to provide the best support—which she gave to Sara.

It troubled Phillip. The minister was thrilled, according to Sara. He wondered if Mara knew about this. She didn't like anyone to be too comfortable or confident. In her mind, this took away some of her power over them. If she knew that the minister was pleased, Sara would be in for a difficult time. Should he let Sara know that she shouldn't tell Mara? And how could he? This was a tricky one.

Sara was so eager, her face so bright and glowing when she told him. She had no idea that it was not a boon to do so well, so quickly.

Anna was already trying to tear her down. She talked to him about the poor room set-up and blurted out a list petty details: Sara didn't spend enough time at the registration table, she let the minister's staff do their own thing instead of taking charge, and oh, how could she have asked Anna the date that the Passing the Torch event was taken to the board for approval? That was a detail she should have known off the top of her head. It was her job to KNOW this. She clearly was not capable of being the lead on this kind of high-profile event.

Phillip had listened and nodded. He thanked Anna for her concerns and said he'd talk to Sara. But he knew there was nothing to talk to her about. She'd done a good job and those small details didn't make any difference in the execution of the event.

Now he would have to deal with Venah. He sighed and popped the last bite of crust into his mouth and finished the last bit of Coke. It was a satisfying lunch. Pulling on his coat, he grabbed his paper bag and headed back to his car to make the drive to the office. He glanced at the clock on the wall before exiting the parlour—it said 2:15 p.m. Sigh. Too early to go home. He would have to face the women and alleviate their insecurities.

The evening air was cool again and made for a rejuvenating walk to the subway. When the wind was minimal, Sara could stand the cold, even enjoyed it. She was still high after the success of the launch, and she couldn't wait to tell Richard about it. It was Thursday night, the evening to find a table in the corner of the pub that hosted an open-mic night every week. Young, artsy musicians lined up for the chance to showcase their raw, gifted voices and musical abilities. Some were really great, others not so much, but it was always a fun evening.

If Richard had his way, they would go every Thursday, but Sara wanted to keep her late weeknight outings to a minimum, and so they agreed to go a couple times a month at most. She wasn't sure how Richard could chug back a few beers and then get up at six the next morning to lead a group of elementary students all day. Tonight though, a celebration was necessary, so when he texted in the afternoon to see if she was up for it, she didn't hesitate.

It took five subway stops to get to the pub, which was one street north of Bloor and walking distance from Richard's apartment. It was just before eight o' clock and the work crowd was long gone, leaving the train relatively empty. Sara found a seat across from a group of three girls chatting. She looked at them. An advertisement for GAP or maybe Ralph Lauren? No, perhaps Canada Goose since all of their coats boasted the round red-and-white emblem on the right shoulder. Sara knew about those controversial coats. Six hundred dollars for real Canada goose down and hoods lined with coyote fur, stolen from trapped animals who were rumoured to spend days struggling to free themselves from the steel traps.

As she eyed the girls, she imagined the fur framing the pretty faces with creamy white, unblemished skin, and the long, straight, silky locks spilling out from under the hoods and onto their shoulders. Two wore Hunter boots, and the other was radical in Sorrels. Sara knew who these girls were. Wasps. As she watched them, visions of homes behind aging trees on Ellis Avenue in High Park developed in her mind. She imagined the inside of the homes—warm, tidy, odourless, and decorated in a French-country style like she saw once while flipping through a *Homes and Gardens* magazine in a doctor's waiting room. Furniture from De Boers, accented with a dancing Shiva from Pottery Barn, said the photo credit—purchased at full price with platinum credit cards by blond mothers who went to yoga class and drank martinis for dinner.

What would it have been like to grow up in such a home? How would it have felt to be part of a ski club and spend Christmases sitting in front of a fireplace with other families whose fathers worked on Bay Street?

The girls were clearly from that class. They sat together and talked, but were not loud or rowdy. Their quiet decorum told of breeding that would have started, generations ago, in finishing school. Their body language shut the world out, encasing them in a tight, upscale bubble that sheltered them from the communities that trolled the subways of diverse Toronto.

White privilege was something as foreign to Sara as she was to them. Perhaps they went to private school. Then she wondered what they were doing on this subway line at this time of the night on a school night. Strange. Where were these rebel girls headed? They didn't look old enough to be going to the pub, nor did she expect to see a circle of them sitting inside the dark, musty place amid aspiring artists donning loose dreadlocks or lanky blond tresses hanging out from under shabby toques.

No, they were probably heading downtown into Yorkville or the Annex. Perhaps that's where they lived, and they were simply going home from whatever outing took them to the west end of the city. One of the group fished in her Lululemon tote bag and brought out a bottle of water which she offered to her companions. Always prepared. Perhaps a few granola bars were stored alongside the drink.

As she stared at them, Sara imagined how it would feel to sail through life without worrying about money. How easy would it be to have funds for university and have your pick of any guy on his way to success who was looking for a suitable wife, mother, and hostess. What struggles would these girls have in life?

She felt a rising stab of envy, as she often did when she was around white privilege. They were fascinating and yet, so out of her own reality that the three sitting together seemed like they were in a scene from a movie.

She thought about her own friendships with Catherine and Giselle. Did they look like that? Hipster Catherine with her eclectic, mismatched wardrobe pulled carelessly over her stocky frame, Korean eyes animated without reservation. Giselle, tall and watchful, her Roman nose sniffing for weakness when her piercing dark eyes found their subject.

These fair girls resembled one another. Shortbread cookies, created with the same cutter. Most likely, they had similar backgrounds, so identifying with one another would be seamless. Perhaps their mothers ate cucumber sandwiches together at lunch, and their fathers belonged to the same golf clubs.

Sara's parents never had lunch with Giselle's or Catherine's parents. In fact, the relationship between their families had always been polite acknowledgement from afar, perhaps a hello when forced closer.

Sara's high school friends were all from various backgrounds but most were first-generation immigrants whose parents struggled to make ends meet and were just on their way to comfortable lifestyles. None were accustomed to privilege and most had to apply for loans to attend university. Some of her friends worked summers to save for their post-secondary education, and all of them understood the value of a dollar.

But they had good times and spent afternoons at the mall or at each other's homes, watching movies and ordering pizza. Sara enjoyed her high school friendships but didn't have a bond with other girls in her group the way these beautiful creatures seemed to. Sara was kind of in between cultures and didn't have a person in her group who really identified with her background. She was South Asian in looks, but Caribbean in culture.

Her first language was English, and although her parents went to the temple on occasion, their practice of Hinduism was "islandized." When South Asians were brought over to the islands as labourers, they held onto whatever customs they could. Mixing with the African slaves and Chinese labourers under the rule of the British then French then British again, the mix of cultures amalgamated into one.

So she went to the homes of her female South Asian friends, but the food was always highly spiced, and she was embarrassed when her cough and sputter provoked raised eyebrows from their parents. Her white European friends looked different, but she also felt the same polite discomfort around them as she did with the South Asians. There was Roxanne, who was Jamaican and with whom Sara identified with the most, but eventually, Roxanne changed crowds, hanging out with the Jamaicans in the last year of high school, leaving Sara on the peripheral.

She often watched the white crowd as they sat together in the cafeteria, joking with one another and planning cottage weekends. They were the same as these girls on the subway. The same social status and the lasting bond of friendships that would take them to their wedding days and beyond.

Suddenly she wondered, what group was Richard part of?

The jerk of the train jolted Sara out of her thoughts, and she realized she was at her stop. The train slowed, and she bounced up, averting her eyes from the wasps in case they gave her the once over. She needed to keep her confidence up to meet Richard.

He was waiting at a table in the corner. It wasn't the table they usually preferred, but it was fine. The place was already filling up with a random crowd of characters.

"Hey." He leaned over and kissed her on the mouth softly. "I ordered your favourite German beer."

"Thanks." She couldn't help but blush. He was so thoughtful.

"How was your day?"

"It was great. The launch was today, and I think it went really well. Ruth said the minister was very happy."

"The minister? Hey, that's great. Did you have to work with the new woman? The diversity coordinator?"

"Yeah, she was there, but she was doing her own thing. She was supposed to be helping me, and when I asked her to, she said it wasn't her job. I don't know what her issue is."

"Wow, really? She's not a team player, is she? Sounds kind of toxic. Maybe you should talk to your boss about it?"

"I don't know … maybe. How was your day?"

"It was okay. The kids were pretty hyper today. And the principal was not in a good mood. Overall, I would say that I'm glad to be out and having a drink."

He was just finishing his first draft as the waitress put down another in front of him and one in front of Sara. She took a sip and tasted the slightly spicy, rich flavour of the dark German wheat beer that she favoured. The taste of cloves made it subtly sweet. It reminded her of Christmas, even though she never drank beer with her family at Christmas.

Richard always drank Canadian beer, but he'd have wine on occasion when they went for dinner. Otherwise, his staple was the popular light beer that was a familiar sight in front of the men at most of the tables in the pub.

Sara sipped her beer, and Richard chatted about the school, the kids, and the principal. It surprised her to hear that there were politics in a school environment. How could teachers and principals struggle for power when their goal was to educate children?

But she liked hearing his stories because they allowed her to draw comparisons to her own work environment. His principal sounded like Mara, his colleagues like Phillip, but no one seemed to be similar to Anna or Venah. He talked a lot about the other teachers who had their quirks but avoided conflict. And he never said anything that was too negative. The principal could be a dictator, but when he spoke about her, it was more about the decisions she made and never criticism about her personality.

"... she won't let us talk to parents on our own. The other day, Frieda, the head of the math department set up a meeting to talk to the parents of this one boy who is just a consistent disruption in her class. But Mila was just adamant that the meeting happen in her office while she was present. I think she just likes to control the situation. But then again, it takes the pressure off us. That's how Frieda took it."

Sara thought about Mara meeting with families of clients or even board members. Phillip said that she had strict rules about us interacting with the board or clients and their families.

"Have you ever met with parents before?"

"Yeah, sure, sometimes. We always do at parent-teacher night, but one-on-one, when there's an issue, Mila is always involved."

Sara wanted to ask him about his other colleagues. Did any of them dislike him? Did they make snide comments the way Venah did? Did they make him feel uncomfortable about his knowledge or cultural background? He worked in a very ethnic neighbourhood, so many of the kids were from visible minority, mostly newcomer families. Perhaps he was told by a teacher or two that he wasn't qualified to deal with ethnic families?

But she ran the risk of sounding like a whiner—pulling the race card. She couldn't be a victim of racism because Venah was South Asian. And Anna, well she was just cold and, frankly, insecure.

A few more sips of the flavourful drink, and the fuzziness flowed through Sara's body. She shook the negative thoughts from her mind and concentrated on Richard's mouth as he spoke. He was almost finished his second beer, and she knew he would order a third. But that was usually his limit when he had an early start in the morning.

"Hey, it's really busy here tonight." She looked around and saw that there was standing room only. Thursdays were always busy but not this packed.

"It's a PD day tomorrow. Maybe there are lots of other teachers here!"

"Oh? I didn't know that." She realized the three-beer limit would probably not apply tonight as she watched him down the last mouthful and motion to the waitress.

Flannigan's was owned by a middle-aged Irish immigrant couple. They boasted about being the last of the "good hippies," and their appearances backed up the title. Finn was tall and lanky with grey hair pulled back into a long braid that fell down his back. He had a scruffy beard, and Sara guessed that he didn't shower very often, just based on his general shabbiness and the greasy strands of loose hair that escaped from his braid.

His wife, Maeve, had a head of red coils that never seemed to sit still. She was plump and much shorter than Finn and had a personality that matched her curls as she bounced from patron to patron to chat and flirt. Some nights she was behind the bar, other nights she served. Finn just sat at the far end of the bar with a pint in front of him, observing.

Richard always spoke with Maeve, who directed her flirty comment at him, but with one sly eye on Sara. Occasionally, she would turn to smile at his girlfriend but never invited a conversation. Sara knew she wasn't Richard's type, so the mild flirting didn't ruffle her as much as the words that flew out of her mouth, which bordered on uncouth. It was better to keep quiet and observe when Maeve was around instead of encouraging her.

Tonight she was especially jovial. Bouncing from one end of the bar to another, she was sporting a new hairstyle in a more fiery shade than usual, and Richard was giving her his full attention.

"Hey, Maeve, nice haircut. You look like you're on fire!" Richard called out as she sashayed past him.

"That's the idea, darling!" And she threw a glance at Sara.

Suddenly, Sara heard her own voice, "I wish I had curls like that."

Maeve giggled. "Yeah, I think your guy likes redheads!"

Richard laughed. "Yep. Redheads are the best."

Sara's eyes flicked and met Maeve's amused green marbles. She struggled to keep the smile on her face, but it melted as she blushed. She glanced around the room, aimlessly, letting the comment swirl around in her mind.

Did Richard prefer redheads? If so, what was he doing with her? She didn't have red hair, nor did she have curls. Her hand slowly went up to feel the stick-straight hair that was the result of her own, ethnic DNA.

Her eyes shifted to Maeve, who was still flitting around the room, her tight jeans hugging her round bottom, her large breasts struggling to escape her fitted t-shirt, black in contrast to her alabaster skin.

"Sara?" The voice jolted her eyes towards Richard's crinkled face. "Are you okay?"

"Yeah, sure. Why?"

"You look upset, and I said your name three times."

"I'm good."

"You don't seem good."

"I have to use the bathroom." Her body pushed her up and out of the chair, and she felt herself being propelled towards the back of the room to the steep staircase that led to the washrooms in the basement.

Safely inside the dark stall, Sara breathed and closed her eyes and let her thoughts ping-pong from irrational to rational. Why would he say something that insensitive when she was right there? It was just harmless flirting. He didn't mean it. Did he really prefer redheads? What was he doing with her then? It was the alcohol. He wouldn't remember tomorrow. But wasn't alcohol a truth serum?

"Hey, are you done in there?" The voice was liquor laced. Sara realized that she was sitting on the toilet, pants around her ankles. Flushing, she exited the stall to see a lineup of annoyed women. She quickly washed her hands and slipped out of the small space, head down, distracted from Richard for a minute.

Her anxiety dissipated with each stair, and by the time Sara reached the top, one deep breath urged her to relax and let it go. Nothing was amiss.

The crowd was thicker now, and she couldn't see Richard from the stairwell, but as she maneuvered through the spaces in between elbows, she finally caught a glimpse of him, Maeve, and another, younger, redhead, sitting in her chair.

Sara's pace came to a halt with the shock of the vision. The young redhead was laughing, leaning in toward Richard whose face was visibly flushed, his hair seemingly ruffled; he was clearly enjoying himself. Maeve was standing beside the table, a twinkly-eyed cupid with bouncing curls. As if by instinct, her eyes looked up and met the young man's girlfriend, who saw the shimmering green and the saucy smirk of her red-painted mouth.

Meeting Maeve's eyes, Sara felt her stomach swirl for a second. But the challenge that stared back at her was fuel, and she moved herself forward. Once beside the table, Sara smiled directly at the young redhead, whose narrow, glassy eyes indicated she'd been drinking for a while.

"Hi, there. I think that's my seat."

Eyes widened at the comment, and the girl jumped out of the chair.

"Relax, honey, she was just keeping it warm for you." Maeve's tone poked at Sara's anger.

"Well, I'm back now." Sara was surprised at her own voice, and even Richard looked up. Maeve took the cue, nodded slightly, and walked away from the table as the girl disappeared into the crowd.

Slipping into her seat, Sara picked up the glass in front of her. The amber liquid still filled a third of the glass, but somehow, she didn't want to drink it. "I need another drink."

"There's still some left." Richard's voice was soft.

"Yeah, but I'm not sure if that girl drank out of it. She looked pretty drunk." Her eyes moved to Richard's, and she saw confusion.

"She didn't drink out of it." This time his voice was defensive.

"I'll get another one. Or I may just go home. I have a bit of a headache."

"The bands haven't even started yet!"

"Yeah, but I'm not really feeling up to it tonight. Maybe your new friend will join you. And Maeve."

"Sara, get over it; we were just talking."

Her eyes snapped up to stare at his face. He was annoyed, maybe even angry. "She seemed like she was hitting on you. Or vice versa?"

"Are you serious? You think I'm going to hit on someone while I'm out with my girlfriend?"

"Well, you said you preferred redheads."

"I was joking!"

The room became blurry, and Sara realized that her eyes were watering. She lowered her head so Richard couldn't see her face and then turned to look in the opposite direction, breathing deeply, willing the tears to recede back into her sockets. She got up.

"Where are you going?"

"To get a drink."

"The waitress is right there, just order it from her."

"Why, you don't want me to get it from Maeve?"

"Oh my god. Sara, seriously? You think I'm interested in Maeve?"

"Well, you're always flirting with her."

"Maeve flirts with everyone."

It was true. Maeve flirted with all the men and was catty to the women. "Okay, fine." Sara wanted the conversation to stop. Flagging the waitress, she ordered another draft and smiled at Richard, which seemed to appease him for the moment.

"The first singer is on," Richard's voice drew her attention to the front of the room as a young woman with curly dark hair and an acoustic guitar adjusted the microphone. Sara accepted her drink from the waitress, took a big gulp, and relaxed as the strings released a tune, and the soft, raw voice of an untrained singer filled the room.

26

Phillip walked to Mara's office and knocked on the open door. She motioned him in and got up to shut the door.

He sat down opposite her and tried to look casual by leaning back.

"So, the event went well yesterday, don't you think?"

He paused and thought for a moment before answering. "Yes, it seemed to go smoothly."

"Did you talk to the minister?"

"No, I didn't."

"I talked to her for a few minutes. She seemed pleased. Ruth was happy as well."

"How did Joan like the event?"

"Joan seemed fine. I wasn't too thrilled with my speaking notes though. They sounded like I was making a high school graduation speech. So simple and banal, really."

Ah, so there it was. One less than perfect detail. Phillip felt himself relax slightly.

"Okay. Did you give feedback to Sara?"

"No. She doesn't report to me. I'm hoping you will pass along the comments. Joan wasn't so keen on hers either."

Phillip said nothing. Joan had recited the speech word for word and complimented his team on it afterward.

"Did she mention anything to Sara at the event?"

"I'm not sure. She's not supposed to. You know the board isn't supposed to talk to staff. So I'm passing along the comments to you."

"Well, I reviewed the speaking notes. I had Joan send them to me, and I agree, they were too basic. They needed more passion. She needs to know Joan's voice."

Phillip heard himself lie. He had reviewed the notes before they went to Joan and Mara, and they were surprisingly good. Sara was a talented writer, and now the board chair, the head of the organization, who was also brown, was aware of this talent. He had watched Ruth and Maxine complimenting Sara and saw her hug the reporter.

She could be a leader someday.

He wondered if Mara should meet with the young woman. One meeting behind closed doors with the condescending ED would serve up confusion and hijack her confidence. Maybe it was exactly what was required.

"Okay, well how about if you worked with Sara? I'd be okay with that. She could get to know you better and that would help her understand your writing style."

"Hmmm ... I could do that." Mara's eyes sparkled. "She could also use some coaching on her writing. I can help with that."

Mara was a terrible writer, but he managed to smile as he nodded and said, "That would be great!"

"Okay, well, can you set that up then? Have her contact Natasha for my schedule, and we can meet next week."

"Okay, will do. Anything else?"

"No, that's all, thanks."

Phillip got up and left Mara's office. He did his best to please Mara. He invited her and Nancy to parties, and she got along well with Randi. He gave her an expensive bottle of wine every Christmas, and he never refused an invitation to her home.

But he didn't particularly like her. She was a mean lady, and he knew it stemmed from her deep-rooted insecurity. He understood it a little. How difficult it must have been for her to grow up with very conservative Jewish parents while hiding the secret of her sexuality.

But now he had given her permission to unleash her nastiness on Sara. The young woman was already gaining a following of haters; he felt a pang of guilt rise up in his chest. Was it really a good idea?

He needed another cup of coffee. He already choked one down before he met with Mara. He had hoped the meeting would be scheduled for later in the day. But no, Natasha said Mara was only available first thing in the morning. It was important.

The smell of the coffee brought him comfort. He added cream and two sugars and walked back to his office. He opened the paper bag that held his Danish and took a large bite of it and then a sip of the coffee. Phillip let the taste sensations flow through his body and sat back in his chair as sweetness dominated negative thoughts.

The email came to Sara at the end of the day on Friday, which seemed to take forever to arrive. She'd stayed with Richard at the pub for longer than she'd planned because she felt guilty about expressing jealousy about Maeve and the redheaded girl and muffled her feelings with a few more beers. So by the time she was ready to go home, they were both fairly drunk. Since the next day was a PD day, Richard didn't have to get up early, so he stayed over and they both passed out as soon as their heads hit the pillows.

The next morning, she woke up and turned to see him lying on his side in a fetal position, mouth open and hair standing straight up. He looked like a Muppet, and she stifled a laugh so as not to wake him up. Then she recalled the night before. Maeve and her manipulation, introducing Richard to the girl when she was in the washroom.

Thoughts ran through her mind while she showered. She stopped for a moment to stare at the stark contrast of the ivory soap against her dark skin. Is that how their skin was? White and smooth and silky to the touch? While hers was dark with small black hairs visible if you looked closely.

Two painkillers washed down with a glass of orange juice was breakfast, and, as she drove to work, Sara prepared herself for the seven hours that were necessary to endure until her weekend started. She planned to slip out the door early and hoped Anna would do the same.

But as she stared at the email, she realized it was already four thirty and both Venah and Anna had left. At first, Sara wasn't sure she'd read it correctly and figured she was only seeing the negative. So she closed it and tidied her desk. Then she went to the washroom, and upon her return, she opened it again. Yes, she had seen only the negative in her first look, and now she could see that it was a simple email that provided feedback on the speeches for the event.

The board chair and Mara felt her speeches needed some work in order to represent Albatross effectively, and Mara was happy to work with her on developing her style.

The email went on to say that working closely with the executive director was a great opportunity to learn and that many speechwriters never get the chance to work with the people they write for. She should take this as a wonderful learning boon.

As she read the words, each line made sense on its own, but for some reason the message made her queasy, and she wondered if the sick feeling was from the alcohol or something else.

When Anna wanted something, she held fast. Phillip had learned this over the years and knew that it was best to let her know right up front if she could have what she wanted or not. This time, the request was doable, but he was not sure how it would go over in the department.

She had done her research and sent him the request via email, outlining the benefits of hiring a student that she could train and mentor. He knew exactly where she was going with this. He sighed.

Phillip always knew that he would have to deal with competition among the staff at some point, but it scared him. Anna was very ambitious, and she wanted to move into a role where her title was manager at the very least. She wanted to be in charge of people. Her tactics were aggressive, and she would undercut anyone who dared get in her way. This was her issue with Sara.

She was always finding fault in her colleague's work. Sara didn't manage the set-up of the podium properly, she wasn't assertive enough to deal with Ruth, she was talking to Maxine about their department and who knows what she was saying?

Just thinking about it made Phillip tired. He knew competitiveness could arise, but he didn't expect it to be this obvious. And he assumed he would only have to deal with Anna, not Venah. Phillip fully believed that Venah and Sara would bond. Sara looked like Venah, and he assumed they shared some similar traditions. Only after he hired Sara did he learn about her Caribbean background. But she was still of South Asian origin. Besides, Venah was much older and could be a good mentor to the young woman.

But it wasn't working out that way. Venah was consistently trying to point out the fact that Sara did not have the experience to deal with diverse communities. She did not speak any languages besides English, and she didn't acknowledge her cultural background. Venah was certain Sara was ashamed and "trying to be white."

Phillip hadn't considered this thought until Venah mentioned it and wondered if Sara was shy about her own cultural background. Saying she was "West Indian" could be her way of Westernizing herself. He made a mental note to try and bring out her culture and encourage her to be more open. She was still young after all, and perhaps she had never worked in an inclusive, accepting environment before.

Still, he was pleased there was no overconfidence to her, despite the fact that she was very smart and quite attractive. It was a little puzzling to him. He rarely met women who were pretty and didn't seem to be aware of it. Sara was that person. She wore no make-up on her unblemished dark skin and her straight black hair framed her face like a veil. Some days, the ponytail she wore emphasized her youthfulness and her big doe eyes.

He could understand why small-town Anna, plump and plain, would be jealous. And even Venah, who had lost her youth to a wrinkled and tired face, probably saw Sara as a reminder of what she no longer was.

It was going to take some work to manage the staff situation, but Phillip knew that Randi would provide some good advice. She worked with attractive female lawyers every day, mentoring interns and choosing the best ones to hire. Many of these women were stunningly beautiful and used their looks to intimidate. Aggressive, competitive female lawyers were in a different league than Anna and Venah, so he was sure that a bit of sound advice from his wonderful wife would get him over this little hill.

He decided to wait before he responded to Anna's email. She needed to sweat for a day or two perhaps. If he agreed too quickly, he would appear too easy, too much of a pushover. But she would get her student intern. It would allow her to feel a sense of authority, and perhaps this would take her attention away from Sara.

He looked at the time and realized it was close to lunch. His thoughts suddenly went to the chicken sandwich he had the other day, and he decided that's what he would have again. He grabbed his coat and walked out to the parking lot.

Sara sat on the edge of the chair, just outside the closed door to Mara's office. Natasha said Mara was on a conference call and would be with her soon. The meeting to discuss the speaking notes from the event was scheduled for 12:15 p.m., but it was now 12:30 p.m. Sara's stomach rumbled, and although she had a few almonds before the meeting, she wished she had eaten the sandwich that was sitting in her lunch bag on her desk.

Did Mara not have lunch? Why would she schedule a meeting during the lunch hour?

Gripping her notebook in her hands, Sara ran over how this conversation would go in her mind. Mara would go through the speaking notes, line by line, and she needed to make sure she had the right answers. Why did she choose the introduction that she did? Well, she wanted it to be engaging and welcoming. The body was composed of details about the mentoring program, its development over the past year, and the funding from the Ministry that made it all possible. The language was clear, but not overly descriptive, since Phillip indicated that speaking notes were simply a guide filled with facts. She was not supposed to read the speaker's mind. The speaker would use the facts and make the speech their own.

That advice made Sara feel more confident. Phillip had worked with Mara for a long time, so he knew her well. There was no reason for him to have steered her in the wrong direction. She sat quietly and listened to Natasha's typing.

Suddenly, the door swung open and Mara bustled out. She looked quickly at Sara and then walked over to Natasha's desk and asked her to send the emails that were in the draft folder. Natasha nodded without smiling and went to work.

Mara then turned and looked down at Sara. "Come in, please," she motioned to the open door.

Her office was large with a mahogany desk at the far end and a round table with chairs near the window. She gestured for Sara to sit at the table and closed the door before she sat across from her. Sara looked at the executive director as if she were seeing her for the first time. It was the first time that she'd met with her one-on-one.

"So Sara, as you know, I scheduled this meeting so we could discuss the speaking notes you prepared for the Passing the Torch anniversary event." Mara's voice was stern, commanding, and Sara's nerves kicked in.

"Yes, I brought them."

Mara put her head back slightly and laughed, "Well, I hope you brought them. We can't discuss them unless you have them in front of you." The mocking tone heated Sara's face as she opened her folder and took out the notes, hoping her hands would not shake.

Mara opened her own folder to reveal red marks all over her copy. The bright colour looked harsh, accusing, against the white sheet and black text. There were lines crossing out sentences, and Sara saw a few exclamation marks. She realized she was staring at the notes and quickly looked at Mara, who was watching her, looking somewhat amused.

"So, as you can see, I've made some changes. I realize this was your first event, but it's important to know, right away, what kind of notes I prefer for my presentations."

Sara nodded.

"You probably noticed that I used some of my own notes for the event." Dark, narrow eyes peered at Sara, who nodded again.

"So let's start at the beginning. What was your intent for the introduction?"

Sara stared at the speaking notes in front of her. Wasn't it obvious? The first few sentences had Mara introducing herself and then thanking the minister and Ruth. She hesitated for a minute, not sure what to say.

"Well, it allowed you to introduce yourself and then the minister, and then thank the Ministry for the funding and Ruth for leading the anniversary event." Sara's voice was firm.

"Well, it's not my style to say, 'Hello, I'm Mara Novak ...' It sounds informal, almost gauche, really. I would change it to read, 'Hello, as executive director of Albatross, I'm pleased to be here today with the Honourable Minister Boland ...' People know who I am; I don't need to say it out loud."

Sara nodded even though she didn't agree. No one knew who she was. Most of the families that were there had never met Mara before and didn't even know what Albatross was. They only knew about the mentoring program itself.

"Next, the minister should be introduced, yes, okay, that's okay. And then Ruth—it's fine, but the words are so basic. What about putting in some more sophisticated language? See here, look at what I've written." She showed the sentence to Sara, who read it quietly. Bureaucratic clichés. It was language that no one would relate to, but there was little benefit in arguing, and she was still embarrassed from her last bold statement. She needed to back down, even though she feared that she would never be able to concoct such language. She would fail.

"See how I've used phrases like 'mutually respectful' when referring to our relationship with the Ministry? Families need to know how closely we work with the Ministry. It gives us credibility."

As she spoke, Sara took notes and listened intently. But her concern was growing. This was not the correct way to communicate with seniors and their families, especially the newcomers.

"So, does this make sense?"

"Um, yes, I understand, but I was thinking that maybe the newcomers would identify with simpler language. Maybe some of the words are a bit complicated."

"Well, Sara, I certainly cannot get up there and recite kindergarten nursery rhymes. The speech you wrote for me was quite banal and, frankly, a little unsophisticated."

Sara said nothing.

"Can you understand what I'm saying?"

"Yes, of course."

"Well good, because I won't have this kind of time to help you every time I need a speech. This is why you were hired. You really should have caught on by now. You've been here for what, nearly a year?"

"Yes, almost a year."

"Well, then this should be simple. I am doing you a favour by helping you with this. Most speechwriters are quick to pick up the leader's style and emulate it easily. I think you'll need to pay more attention when I speak so you can learn how to write a speech that can be delivered to maintain Albatross's reputation."

Sara felt the slow crack of her spirit. Her brain seemed heavy, foggy, but she managed to nod and agree. It would not be easy to write such jargon, but somehow she would have to try her best. She thanked Mara for her help, picked up the red-lined notes, and walked out of the office.

Sara walked to her desk and put the folder in the top drawer. She may as well eat—perhaps that would make her headache go away. She turned to face the window and bit into the crusty bread and sighed, fighting back the tears trying to well up in her eyes. There was nothing to cry about. She always believed that writing was one of her strongest skills. Perhaps she was wrong. She couldn't think anymore and continued taking bites and chewing sawdust.

28

Mara knew she'd been a little harsher than usual. But it was necessary. The young woman needed to know who was in charge and who had final say. She didn't tell Sara that the board chair had no issues with the speaking notes— liked them in fact. This little bit of truth would serve only to inflate her ego and then she, Mara, would lose control over the situation. Keep them guessing and all would work out.

She even used this tactic with Nancy. Like the time that Nancy had prepared Mara's favourite dish, beef bourguignon, for her birthday. It was far better than any dish she'd had in the finest French restaurants. Nancy had spent all day in the kitchen preparing and fussing over the ingredients to make sure it was just perfect. And it was. But Mara didn't tell this to her. She ate the dinner slowly as the tender pieces of meat, steeped in wine and mushrooms, melted in her mouth, and as she savoured it, she thanked Nancy but never told her how delicious it was. She smiled once at Nancy, who sat in front of her, wide eyed and uncertain.

Later, she felt a little badly, but she couldn't admit the truth. It wasn't like she had lied, she convinced herself. She just didn't give Nancy the accolades she wanted because she could not let her confidence start to soar to the point where she would meet someone else. Someone better.

So when she saw the wide, childlike look on Sara's face, Mara knew that her tactic had worked. Sara would go back to her office and work harder on the notes and continue to try to please her because she feared for her job. She would want to reach that peak—the point where the notes were perfect. But she'd never get there. Mara would always make sure that there was some detail, a tiny nuance that kept perfection out of her reach.

The thought of the eager way the girl wrote down her instructions made her smile. She remembered the soft, timid voice thanking her politely before disappearing through the office door. The satisfaction she felt helped ease her own nerves; it wasn't easy to sit so close to the young woman who smelled faintly of fruit, strawberry perhaps. She must have been wearing a body cream of some kind or maybe one of those fragrances from The Body Shop. It wasn't perfume, though, and fittingly so. Perfume was heavy, ideal only for evenings and more fitting for older women. A soft, fresh, fruity scent was appealing and, somehow, innocent.

But Mara made sure not to maintain eye contact with Sara, and she was careful not to sit too close or to let her hand brush hers. The early feelings of attraction were under control. Yes, she felt a stir when Sara was close, and she'd watched longingly as the young woman walked out of her office, her pants fitting around her round bottom as she skitted quickly around the corner. But Mara had met many women like this before, and she knew how to control her desire.

She opened her email and began crafting a message to Phillip. It was very important that he was aware of her "concerns"—it would also keep him on his toes. Phillip avoided confrontation when he could. He was the typical family man who wanted a cushy job, and he was very good at playing political games. He managed "up" and let Mara pull his strings easily because he knew she valued someone who she could trust and, more importantly, control.

The relationship had taken a long time to develop. At first, Mara wasn't sure he would do as she asked. So she tested him. She made small, petty changes to his work, she picked on tiny details, she made him work unreasonably long hours. And he did all of it without complaining. He also became her informant. The first time it happened, he walked right into her office, sat down across from her, and said, "Mara, I overheard something that concerns me."

"Really? What is it?"

"I heard Isabella telling Natasha that she was looking for another job because she felt you didn't like her."

"Oh? Where were they talking?"

"It was in the kitchen. They stopped when I walked in, but I heard that much."

Isabella was a director who worked closely with the Ministry to allocate operational funds for community centres. She was very creative, efficient, and well-liked by the board, partly because she was Hispanic, Mara suspected.

"Hmm … well, that's interesting. Thank you for telling me." And with that cue, Phillip left her office.

Mara was annoyed at the second-hand news. She never liked Isabella, who thought too highly of herself, and resented her saying that she was thinking about leaving because of her!

Mara had longed to get rid of the woman, but couldn't find a way to justify it to the board, and really, herself. Isabella did a good job, but Mara simply did not like her.

But when she received this tidbit from Phillip, it was too much. Although she wanted Isabella to leave, she knew that if she quit, it would reflect badly on Albatross.

So, Mara put Isabella on a committee to work on a project. She was invited to the first meeting, but not the second or the third. At the fourth meeting, she asked Isabella for the report that was discussed at the second meeting. Isabella looked at her wide eyed and said she wasn't aware that she was supposed to do a report.

"Well, if you could not attend the previous meetings, it was your responsibility to find out what action items needed to be prepared."

"I didn't get an invitation to or an agenda for the past meetings." Isabella tried to explain, but Mara, showing her disappointment, dismissed her and said she would have to get it to her by the end of the day for distribution to the committee.

Finally, she took all of this information back to the board chair, saying that Isabella was not a good fit anymore and that they should find someone else who was more committed to the role. Then, she let her go.

She remembered the confused look on Isabella's face as she told her the news. She was stunned and sat there with her mouth open, saying nothing. She gave her a small but fair settlement packaged, knowing that Isabella would challenge her. Mara instructed her lawyer to drag out the case for months, hoping that the opponent's lawyer's fees would add up.

It worked. They got by with a small settlement and a reference letter, and she was rid of the director who had threatened to quit.

Mara never talked to Phillip directly about the situation, but she knew that he was aware of his role in Isabella's dismissal. At first, he seemed concerned and tried to question the decision. But she brushed off the conversation, and promoted him to manager of public relations. She didn't need the board's permission to change his title and give him a few thousand dollars more. Once she told him, in the privacy of her office, she knew that he realized that keeping her in the loop was of great value not only to her, but to him as well.

The move secured Phillip's loyalty, and he soon made a point of telling her everything that he heard and saw. And he always took her side if there was a situation where she was being challenged, even when she was wrong.

Mara saw that Sara was young and inexperienced enough to be easily malleable as long as she was always kept on the edge of her seat. She could be used as a pawn if necessary. For now, Mara and Phillip would need to keep her in line.

29

Anna couldn't wait until the Monday staff meeting. Phillip had agreed to her request for a student, and now she would have a staff member of her own. This would help her get the management experience she was looking for. She had spent most of the day checking out the different college PR programs and deciding which one was the best to recruit her student from.

It had been a long night. She'd sent the email request to Phillip on Thursday morning, having pondered over it for a week. Although she saw him during the day, he didn't mention it. She kept a watchful eye on her emails, but by late Thursday afternoon, there was still no response. At home, she kept her Blackberry close and checked it frequently; Rob laughed at her, asking if she had some kind of big project going on or if she was waiting to hear about a promotion at work. The comment set her off, and she snapped at him, spending the rest of the evening in the den in front of her computer.

By 7:30 a.m. Friday, there was still no response, and she started to worry. She'd mentioned the student in the past, and he'd been receptive, but this was before Sara.

As she was driving into the office, Anna's mind was focussed on the new girl who was hired simply because she was brown. So now she was the star? Perhaps Phillip had promised Sara that she would get a student. How could someone just waltz into Albatross and, less than a year into the job, get whatever she wanted?

As she parked her car, Anna was seething. So perhaps Phillip was going to tell her in person. He wouldn't put something like this in an email. He would call her into his office and tell her in his non-committal way. He'd say that right now she couldn't get a student, but it would happen soon, and that the board wanted Sara to work with someone. He would try to use a manipulation tactic to make her feel like she was still in charge of something. Phillip was really great at spin.

She could hear him saying that he needed her to watch Sara, to make sure she was managing effectively and then report back to him. But she wouldn't fall for that again.

Or maybe he would say that the student would be hired but would be a shared resource between the two women. Anna rolled the various scenarios over in her mind. She would sit and listen quietly. She wouldn't get angry or upset, but instead, she would ask him whose decision it was, and then she would remind him that she has been at Albatross longer and that she was still teaching Sara the job.

He would try and say that Sara was in a higher position, but what sense did that make, if Anna had to train her? Phillip would be stumped then, for sure. What could he say? She had been at Albatross longer, and she deserved to be a manager, even if it was just to manage a student.

By the time she got into her office, the strategy was all mapped out in Anna's mind. She was ready. She would get her coffee, start her work, and wait for Phillip to call her into his office for the discussion.

She only hoped he didn't drag it out over the weekend. Waiting three more days would be torture. And Rob would suffer all weekend.

Anna walked to the kitchen to make her coffee and thought about the way she had snapped at Rob last night. Poor guy. He was really a gem, a simple guy who wanted nothing more than a solid family life and a good home. He was happy to let her take the reins as the strong partner in the relationship, and she knew it was because he loved her.

She would pick up something special for dinner this evening, something that he liked. That would make him happy.

Returning to her desk, Anna set the steaming cup down and glanced at her email. A response from Phillip. So he was doing this by email? Or perhaps it was just an invitation to talk in his office. She stared at the unread email for a minute and then took a sip of coffee. She breathed and double clicked:

Hi Anna, this sounds like a great idea. Please go ahead and look into it and get back to me with the details. Thanks, Phillip.

That was all. No mention of Sara. Anna blinked and read it again. She closed the email and took another sip of her coffee. Then she read her other emails, and when the coffee was finished, she reopened Phillip's email and read it again. A smile made its way to her lips. She was going to be a manager.

30

Phillip was dreading the Monday morning meeting. Not just because he hated Mondays like most people, but because he knew that Anna was going to talk about her student intern. He knew this announcement would flare Venah and could make Sara feel slighted.

Lately, managing this new dynamic was getting on his nerves. He knew it was part of his job, but somehow the group was not meshing the way he had anticipated. But Anna deserved a student. She had been reminding him that she'd put in her time and that when she was hired, he promised that she could grow her career at Albatross. His plan was to promote her to his second in command and mentoring a student would strengthen her credentials.

He anticipated that Venah would now want her own student as well. Maybe there was no avoiding this, but in any case, what harm would it do? A student worked for an honorarium, and he could pull that out of his budget easily. Mara didn't need to sign off on decisions like this. And a diversity intern would only improve their reputation with the community. Yes, letting Venah hire a young, ethnic student who could be at events and connect with people would really help with Albatross's image.

The highway was moving slowly. Phillip hated the drive from downtown Toronto to the office. It took about one hour in the morning and an extra half an hour in the evening. He was also pretty tired from the weekend.

One of Randi's colleagues had invited them to a cocktail party in the Bayview area. The couple were both lawyers who owned a beautiful stone house with a large backyard that housed a hot tub on the deck. Phillip purposely didn't bring his swimming trunks, but that didn't stop Randi, who spent most of the evening in her hot-pink bathing suit, wedged between three men under a bubbling mass of heated water.

Phillip watched amusingly as her red lips moved about, stopping only for a swig of champagne or a bite of jumbo shrimp. Women eyed each other, but he knew it was only jealousy. Randi was not the typical model-thin waif, but she. knew how to use her body and her energy to create a presence, and it excited him. He was certain it excited other men too, and he liked to watch when she flirted, always staying close in case she needed anything. He loved to watch her entertain because when the event faded, she would be going home to his bed. And that's when his reward for loyalty would begin.

They had stayed particularly late on Saturday night, and when the cab finally pulled up in front of the stone walkway, he had to hold Randi firmly by her left arm to make sure she didn't twist her ankle in her four-inch stiletto boots. She laughed as he delicately pushed her into the backseat and climbed in after, directing the cab driver to their home.

Once the cab started moving, she rested her head on his shoulder and leaned against him. The familiar smell of Dior wafted up to him, and he closed his eyes and relished the curls against his chin. Some days, like Saturday night, he wondered how he'd gotten so lucky.

She was in pretty rough shape the next day, so he didn't bother her with questions about his work situation until late Sunday evening. They were sitting in bed watching television, and he told her about Anna's student.

"Well, you said you were training Anna to be the supervisor of the department at some point, so this is good experience," Randi had reassured him.

"Yes, but I'm concerned the other girls will take issue with this. I know Venah will be upset."

"So, why not let her have a student as well? What's the harm?"

"Yes, I thought about that. What about Sara?"

"What about her?"

"She is senior to Anna, so she may question why she can't get help. She really has a bigger workload than the other two."

"Yeah, you have to decide if the student should work exclusively for Anna or if she will help Sara too. Perhaps Anna can still manage the student but allocate some of her time to Sara if necessary."

"Yeah, that's a good idea."

"I don't know why you worry about these things. You have to do what you have to do. The feelings of the staff shouldn't be the basis for management decisions. It's about good business. I know, I know ... you have to take their concerns into consideration, but at the end of the day, you are the boss, and you need to do what makes sense for the bottom line."

Randi had a point, though the critical tone of her advice ruffled Phillip a little.

"How do you know that Sara won't ask for management training?" Her voice was softer now.

"I don't think she will say anything. She seems happy with the projects that I've given her. She'll be fine for another year or two, and then she can get a senior job at another organization or just work under Anna." Phillip had cemented this plan in his mind, and there would be no deviation.

"Good, you've made that decision, so then just deal with it." Randi's tone indicated that the conversation was over, and she focussed her attention on her laptop as she continued to check her emails, a Sunday evening routine.

The traffic was moving again, and Phillip hit the accelerator to take advantage. He changed lanes, moving in and out of traffic until he managed to get ahead of the clog. Soon, he was bolting up the highway that would take him to Albatross.

After exiting the highway, Phillip pulled up to the Tim Horton's drive-through. He would order two Danishes—one to eat now and one for after the meeting. His large coffee would get him through the meeting at least.

When he finally pulled into the Albatross parking lot, he was ready for the meeting.

Anna arrived at the meeting before everyone else. She'd spent all weekend writing up a job description and came in early to send it off to two colleges so they could post it on their student intranets. As she sat in the meeting room sipping coffee and waiting for the other staff members to arrive, she rehearsed her announcement in her head. She'd already called her parents to tell them the good news.

She was looking forward to interviewing and hiring her assistant. She still needed to talk to Phillip about finding a place in the office with a desk for the intern. She would prefer if they sat close to her. In fact, there was room just outside her office for a small desk; she would propose this idea to Phillip.

"Well, you look happy for a Monday morning!" Venah's sharp, accented voice cut through Anna's thoughts. She realized she was smiling subconsciously.

"I had a good weekend," she blurted the excuse out quickly.

"Good for you." Venah smiled at her and set herself in her usual seat across from Anna. "What did you do for the weekend?" she said after a short awkward pause.

"Oh, we just went out with friends. Had a good time … lots of laughs." The lie came easily to Anna, who had told it on many occasions. Truthfully, she and Rob rarely went out on weekends, and when they did, it was usually with one of his cousins and their spouse. She didn't have many girlfriends who were more than lunch acquaintances, and she didn't want to reveal that her typical Saturday night with Rob was sitting in front of the television, eating Doritos and watching the hockey game.

"That sounds like fun. I was out with friends too," Venah offered the information, even though it wasn't accurate either. Her weekends were spent reading or watching television. Amba was always out with her friends and sometimes spent the night at their homes, leaving the house empty and quiet. Her weekend highlight was always Sunday morning temple service, where she could be adorned in her best outfits and spend the day improving her status among other members of the temple.

Soon, she would be as respected at Albatross as she was at the temple. She just needed time to demonstrate her leadership skills.

"Good morning!" A cheery greeting from Phillip as he strolled into the meeting room accompanied by Irene changed the uneasy mood in the room. He squished into the chair at the head of the table and looked around the room at his employees, smiling at each one purposefully.

"Happy Monday morning everyone. Good weekends, I hope?"

Soft mumbles of yes. Phillip quickly moved into his next message.

"So, we're now starting to get busier. There are a couple of big events coming up, and I'll be assigning projects accordingly over the next week. Every one of you will be getting the chance to lead an event, and we are going to start using a new event protocol so that all events will now be consistent."

Sara listened as Phillip talked about the new direction Mara wanted for the public relations department. She sneaked glances at Anna and Venah, who appeared to be listening intently. Anna's face was glowing, a slight smile on her lips instead of her usual concrete look. She had something to tell everyone, Sara realized. Something new was about to be revealed, and Anna was about to burst if she didn't speak soon.

Finally, Phillip asked for the updates. And he started with Sara.

Sara talked about the good news story that was a spin off from the Passing the Torch event. A senior who had been a highly respected criminal lawyer had mentored a young, black male student when he was in high school. The two had struck up a friendship that lasted through the student's time at law school, and his mentor made it to his graduation, in a wheelchair, just out of the hospital.

The local media had done a fantastic job of telling the story, and the best part? A daily paper in Toronto wanted the story as well and was in the process of interviewing both the senior and student.

Once she was finished, she looked around for affirmation. Phillip and Irene were both smiling. Anna was staring at her notebook, and Venah's mouth was pursed, her eyes narrowed.

"Is this senior from an ethnic background?" Venah demanded.

"No, but the student is of African descent." Sara's voice was small.

"We should have found a senior from the South Asian community."

Sara looked at Phillip, who gave a nervous laugh and answered quickly: "It is always ideal if we can find someone from the South Asian community. But in this case, the focus was on the mentorship and the success of the student."

"We didn't really find a compelling story among the seniors of ethnic origin," Sara's words hung in the air.

Both Phillip and Anna looked at Sara, mouths slightly open—they had never heard her speak up in that manner.

"You did not look hard enough." Venah held her accusing finger up.

"I am sure Ruth did her best to find the most suitable mentor and mentee to speak to the press." Phillip cut in quickly, stopping any other words from flying out.

Sara stared at her notebook and realized she was shaking. Anger filled her mind, and she had to take a deep breath. Venah had no idea about public relations or media. They couldn't simply feature a mentor in the news just because they were ethnic. There had to be a good story that was newsworthy.

Phillip asked Venah to talk about her projects next; Sara heard Venah's voice, but the words sounded like a string of notes. She needed to calm herself or she feared she would cry.

When she finally looked up, Phillip was staring at Venah, his face very red and sweaty. Anna's smile had dissipated, and her face was hard once again. Sara forced her lips to turn up slightly, and she held her head up. She would not show her emotions.

Finally, it was Anna's turn. Her words spilled out quickly, as though they couldn't be held back any longer,

"Phillip has approved the hiring of a student intern. I have contacted the colleges with public relations programs and sent a job posting, and I hope to hire a student by the end of June to help me during the summer."

Phillip smiled, but he jumped in to clarify. "Anna has been asking for a student for a while now. The student will assist the entire department on projects and, in turn, gain good work experience. The student is free to help everyone with their projects, but she or he will report directly to Anna."

Once his voice stopped, there was no sound in the room. The silence was finally broken by Irene, whose motherly tone attempted to ease the rising tension: "Well, that's just great news. We have been so busy, the extra pair of hands will be welcome."

Sara blinked, and Venah stared.

"Well, then I should tell you now, Phillip, that I am putting in a request for a student as well," Venah said.

Phillip gave a nervous little laugh and said, "Okay," and tried to move on, looking to Irene for her update. But she continued, "And my student will be able to speak Hindi." She looked directly at Sara, who, at first, didn't realize the comment was directed at her. "Because Sara says she cannot speak Hindi or Punjabi."

All eyes were focussed on Sara as Phillip tried to smile his way through this. "Maybe not, but Sara can wear a sari to the next event, and then we can really be a diverse team," he said, looking directly at Sara with a satisfied expression.

"Yes, that is a good idea, and it's the least she can do if she cannot speak another language." Venah 's eyes were glowing as she looked at Sara, who suddenly felt as if she were very far away, sitting alone at one end of the table. Heat on her face, coldness in her palms as she looked at Phillip in disbelief. He was smiling as if he was pleased with his joke, not realizing that the only person laughing was Venah.

Irene quickly piped in again and broke the silence, and as she gave her update, Sara breathed deeply.

Finally, Phillip dismissed the group. Sara bolted out the door and whisked into the washroom. For the first time since she'd arrived at Albatross, she wondered if she had made a big mistake by leaving the small-town agency.

Ashleigh locked the car doors and proceeded to jaunt to the building, but turned back to view her new vehicle. Her parents had gifted it to her when she received the internship at Albatross, and while it was two years old, it was still a shiny, red Volkswagen Beetle. Her car of choice.

Filled with sudden confidence, she held up her head and marched through the parking lot. It was the first day of her internship at the non-profit organization that had been her first choice among the places she applied to. And out of all the students in her program, they picked her. It was what all the students wanted—the chance to work in the public relations department of a recognized organization. She had been worried that her friend Soo-Lynn would get it because her grades were the highest in the class and the teacher had put her forward, but the offer was presented to her, apparently because she had the best resume.

As she approached the glass door, her eyes caught her reflection, and she slowed her pace. The bob was a new cut, and the sun picked up the blond streaks that waved through her chestnut mane. Her hand instinctively went up and patted down a flyaway, but she was pleased with the look. It was a good style.

As she flung open the glass door, the receptionist raised her head and smiled encouragingly. Already, Ashleigh had a good feeling.

Sara wanted to call in sick. She reached for her phone and checked the time. It was 7:38 a.m.; she'd overslept again, exhausted from not getting enough sleep.

Since the staff meeting last Monday, she found herself waking up in the middle of the night and looking at her phone, which usually displayed a time around 2:30 a.m. After changing from side to side in repeated attempts to find a comfortable position, she'd turn onto her back and stare at the ceiling until the sky started to lighten, only to find herself jolting up to an alarm that had been nagging since seven.

After that meeting, she'd kept to herself and stayed in her office. It wasn't much different from her usual behaviour, but she now felt separated from the department. Phillip made his usual rounds through their area, stopping briefly at her office while he was on his way to chat with Venah. He'd usually end up sitting in Anna's office chatting for at least fifteen minutes. He never sat with Sara and never said much more than one or two contrived lines of greetings and acknowledgements.

Sara did her best to look up and smile when he breezed by, hoping he wouldn't see how confused she was.

She had replayed the conversation over and over in her mind and still couldn't find an answer to her question—why would he say that she needed to wear a sari? To work? She didn't even own a sari. When she went to family weddings, which was rare, she wore a nice dress, and so did her mother and sister. In fact, her aunts and cousins only recently jumped on the Bollywood bandwagon along with the rest of the Western world when it became trendy to wear saris and Indian outfits, as her mother called them. And while she had been planning to purchase one, it just wasn't on her priority list; she was waiting until an occasion like a wedding presented itself.

And of course, Venah had to pipe in and criticize her for not speaking Hindi, in her usual condescending manner. Venah had no idea about the difference between West Indians and South Asians, which was ironic since she was hired for her "diversity and community expertise."

The incident took Sara back twenty years to elementary school in a lower-middle class neighbourhood in Toronto. Her parents had moved into an apartment in the neighbourhood after arriving from the Caribbean, and it was where she and her sister Maya were born. When Sara was still young and Maya was a baby, they managed to move up into a townhouse in the same neighbourhood. There were lots of newcomers in the community, with a wide range of backgrounds from Caribbean to European. There were a few South Asian families, but they spoke their own language, and the women wore traditional clothing.

Just a few days after Sara's family had moved into the townhouse, boxes still piled high in the hallway, there was a knock on their door. Her mother opened it to find one of the South Asian women smiling at her. At first, the woman spoke in an unfamiliar language, and when her mother didn't answer, she switched to a heavily accented English and asked if they were from India. Sara's mother smiled and shook her head, and the woman frowned, turned, and left. She was never friendly afterwards.

At school, some of the teachers, who were mostly Caucasian, would ask

Sara what language she spoke at home, only to frown in disbelief at her answer. Maybe she was shy or embarrassed to speak her mother tongue, she'd overheard them say to one another.

But the toughest part of her childhood was the names she was called. "Paki, Paki," from some of the tough white boys whose families lived in the apartment buildings. The first time she was called this name, Sara didn't understand it, but the hated and derision it was delivered with made her realize it was not a compliment.

She had run home and cried to her mother, who hugged her and said it was just a silly way kids made fun of other kids. She never explained to her that Paki was a racist term for people from Pakistan, and even India. Sara found out from the one Pakistani girl in another class whose red face would hang down when the label was hurled in her direction.

Sara and her family lived in that old Toronto neighbourhood until she was twelve and Maya was ten, until her parents' savings rendered the faded townhouse antiquated. Her family moved to a bungalow in north Toronto in a predominately Caucasian community with a sprinkling of Italian, Portuguese, a couple of South Asian families, and one black family from St. Kitts.

Sara entered her new school in seventh grade, and that's where she met Peter.

He was tall for his age and lanky with straight blond hair that hung loosely around his face, in true skateboarder style. He was cute, as determined by many of the girls in her class, and he was cool.

Sara admired him from afar, but held no expectation that he would reciprocate. There were so many girls in her class with straight, lanky Avril Lavigne locks, whose torn jeans and sneakers matched Peter's style. Her own straight and smooth hair was jet black, and her mother would never let her out of the house in a pair of jeans that exposed knees through ragged strings. But she managed to get a pair of black sneakers with blue laces and wore them every day. At least this way she wouldn't look like one of the preppy girls, with their blond ponytails and crisp white sneakers.

From afar, she adored Peter and watched with some detached envy as the blondes giggled circles around him. Then one day after school, she found herself walking behind him as the crowds pushed their way outside. As she approached the door, he turned, grinned, and held the door open, waiting as she passed through it. Sara felt her face flush as she managed to mumble, "Thanks."

"Hi," he smiled back as his own complexion pinked, to her surprise. "You're in my class. Sara, right?"

The words seemed to catch in her throat. "Um, yes. You're Peter?"

"Yep, that's me." His grin revealed straight, white teeth. "So are you walking home?"

"No, I'm taking the bus."

"Okay, I'll walk you to the bus stop. Where do you live?"

"I'm up at Martin Grove and Eglinton."

"Oh, yeah? I go up that way. I'm just one street south of Eglinton. I usually walk though. Come on, let's walk. It's only about twenty minutes."

Sara hesitated. She would get home a bit later than usual, so what would she tell her parents?

"Oh, look, you already missed the bus. There it goes." He pointed to the red rocket bolting quickly past the front of the school. There would be another one along in ten minutes, but she found herself already walking through the football field with Peter.

"Do you take the bus in the morning too?" he asked.

"Yes, usually. They get me home in about ten minutes."

"Yeah, that's true, but if you walk, you get exercise and you save on the bus fare."

"Yes, that's true, too."

They walked in silence for a bit, and then he reached over and grabbed her backpack.

"That looks heavy. Let me carry it for you."

Sara let him slip the strap from her shoulder, and she watched as he slung it over his own backpack.

"Don't you usually skateboard to school?"

He grinned again. "Yeah, usually. But my deck cracked, and I haven't got a new one yet."

"Oh, what happened?"

"Ah, nothing ... just at the skate park last weekend. I'm getting another one this weekend."

She was quiet.

"You're a quiet one, Sara." He poked her arm, and she smiled at him. His eyes were twinkly as they peeked out from between dirty blond locks.

"Sometimes," she said shyly.

"That's okay. I like quiet girls. Some of those girls in our class are so annoying. Always giggling and gossiping. I don't know why they don't mind their own business sometimes."

The comments surprised Sara. She didn't know what to say but found herself laughing.

"Oh yeah, I know what you mean. Some of the girls in my classes are always joking around."

"Too much. But you're not like that, right? So how come you're walking alone? None of your friends live out your way?"

"Not really. My friend Ciara goes to the Catholic school."

Ciara's family lived three houses away from Sara's new home, and the two girls met as Sara was trying to navigate her way to the corner store for a pint of milk. Ciara had seen the new girl wandering down the street, obviously unsure of her location, and decided to step in and provide some assistance. The two ended up walking together to the Mac's Milk, chatting furiously, and as their journey ended, with Sara's arms heavy with milk bags, they exchanged numbers and agreed to meet again.

"Yeah, lots of my friends go there. My parents wanted me to go there, but I didn't want to wear a uniform every day," Peter said.

"I can't see you wearing a uniform," Sara laughed, starting to feel comfortable as they synchronized steps. He pointed out his house as they walked past it and brought her to her front door. Nervous that her parents would see from the window, she quickly grabbed her backpack from him and thanked him, edging to get inside.

"Nice house," he said, and she turned to look at the green door that acted as a beautiful backdrop for the multi-coloured tulips in her front yard.

"Thanks. My mom's flowers."

"Yeah, my mom's a gardener herself. Sometimes I go out and help her pull weeds. So hey, nice walking with you, Sara. Maybe we can do this again sometime?"

"I usually take the bus, but maybe I can walk."

"Cool, let's meet in front of my house tomorrow morning at 8:15 a.m."

"Okay, that sounds good. See you tomorrow." She turned and bolted inside, her heart racing.

Strangely enough for Sara, he began to pay more attention to her during school, walking with her to classes and even sitting with her at lunch. They fell into a comfortable friendship, and she didn't really think much of it beyond that.

But she noticed the looks from the other girls, and once or twice heard comments behind her back—comments like "Why does he like the brown girl?"

Sara wasn't entirely offended by the comments because the very same thoughts entered her own mind. Even when he kissed her for the first time, one day at lunch when they'd gone for a walk outside, she was caught off guard.

His lips were softer than she'd imagined, but then again, she had never kissed a boy before, so she had nothing to compare them to. When he slipped his tongue into her mouth, she felt herself pulling back a little—and looked into his smiling eyes. Was he laughing at her—no, he was smiling with her. And so she closed her eyes and returned the wet, sloppy teenage kisses until it was time to go back to school for the afternoon.

They continued to spend time together until school ended, but when the summer began, his calls started to dwindle. Soon, it was apparent that they were not seeing each other anymore. She didn't know how to ask him what had happened. After all, there was never any declaration that they were more than friends who kissed. He never visited her home, and she had not met his family. Their interaction was limited to walking and lunchtime kissing.

But still, they lived one block away from one another, and Sara would find herself looking around the neighbourhood during the long, hot days of summer, wondering if his lean shape, balanced on his skateboard, would whizz down the street. But for some reason, this never happened.

Finally, when the school year started in September, she spied him during lunch, strolling in the direction of their park with one of the blondes, transformed from her preppy image to that of a lanky-haired skater girl.

Sara knew she was looking directly at him but couldn't avert her eyes, and when their gazes connected, he half smiled and nodded, and she smiled back. That was it. Although they would acknowledge each other from time to time, she resumed taking the bus to and from school and watched his figure disappear as it passed on his skateboard. The following year, she heard that his family moved, and she never saw him again.

Looking back, she realized that he was her first boyfriend. And although it was never official and never went further than a few kisses here and there, he had set the tone for her romantic preferences for the future. The only guys she ever seemed to date were Caucasian. It was as if she was simply drawn in that direction, without thinking about it or needing a reason.

And there was reciprocation. There were a couple of other guys since Peter but none that seemed to fit the title of serious boyfriend like Richard. And although they were both keenly aware of the difference in skin colour, Sara always felt safe and comfortable. But now, as she sat in her office, staring at the words on her screen, she couldn't help but wonder if Richard pictured her in a sari when she was with her family.

Phillip loved Ashleigh. That much was clear. He was spending much more time around Anna's office, stopping at the intern's desk to ask how she was doing. He would often bring Anna into the conversation, and Sara would watch as the trio giggled and joked, just outside Anna's office and right in front of her own door.

At first, she felt herself longing to join and once made an attempt, standing up and laughing at a joke. Anna turned toward Sara, and when their eyes met, she turned back to rejoin the clique. Sara sat back down in her chair and decided not to try again.

Sometimes Venah would walk by and push herself into the mix, and Phillip would say something to her, but the circle never parted to make way for her to enter. So she would resume walking as if nothing had happened.

Ashleigh was a smart intern. She was quick and eager to learn and also very observant. She had already realized who held the power in the department. Increasingly confident, she took the liberty to walk into Sara's office and point things out that "could be done better." At first, Sara was annoyed but would find a way to laugh it off, nod her head, and say, "Okay, that's an idea."

One time, Sara had come back from lunch to find Phillip at Ashleigh's desk, the Passing the Torch brochure spread out in front of her. Ashleigh was pointing something out, and Phillip was nodding. When he noticed Sara's arrival, he picked up the brochure and walked into her office.

"Sara, Ashleigh noticed something in this brochure, and I think she has a good point."

The stomach flip was instant, and Sara did her best to hide her annoyance.

"Okay," she said softly.

"The colours could be a little softer, maybe some more orange in it. Ashleigh said that in her visual communications class, she learned that orange is one of the most appealing colours to use in design. The brochure has a lot of blues and greens in it, and blue is a pretty cold colour."

Sara just blinked. He had approved the colours. In fact, he wanted to use Albatross colours which were blue, green and yellow. Orange would be completely out of their visual identity guidelines.

"Yes, that's a good idea. But we don't have orange in our visual identity colour scheme for Albatross."

"Perhaps, but we need to be more creative if we want people in this community to take notice. I think Ashleigh has brought a fresh perspective here."

He placed the brochure on her desk. "The next time you and Maxine are going to update the brochure, you may want to suggest a different colour scheme. Perhaps Ashleigh can help with that."

Sara looked over at the young girl's face to see rosy cheeks and a bright smile as she sat up, straight and attentive, blue eyes sparkling at Phillip. One month out of school, and she was telling Sara how to do her job.

Something inside Sara's mind felt heavy. It was like a wad of gum that was stuck inside her brain, sticky and dirty, promising to stay there for a long time. She tried to dismiss the incident as a one off, but it wasn't.

The weeks passed, and Sara watched as Ashleigh piped up at every meeting, voicing her opinions loudly, eagerly. Phillip ate up every word with relish, and Sara wondered how he didn't realize her comments were simply out of a college PR textbook.

Ashleigh was careful to stay close by Anna's side. She supported every one of her mentor's ideas with fierce loyalty and adhered to every one of her directions.

The Monday meetings soon became a quiet battleground, with Sara at one end of table, listening while the others talked and joked and made fun of Maxine and more recently, MPP Raji Shivani, who had made a semi-inappropriate comment that was published in the local paper. Phillip had taken the opportunity to bring the paper into the meeting and read the comment aloud. It was the basis for the newest round of jokes, which lasted the next few weeks.

Sara thought about the comments made by other MPPs, ones that were even more inappropriate and, in some cases, quite stupid. But Phillip didn't appear to notice these ones. In fact, once, when MPP James McCrae was in the hot seat for speaking off the cuff—the comment resulting in a Twitter frenzy—Phillip defended him, saying that sometimes people were simply caught off guard and everyone needed to get a life.

The wad of gum that was stuck inside Sara's brain grew stickier. She found herself counting down the minutes during every Monday meeting until it was over and she could escape into her office, or sometimes, into the recreation centre foyer to watch the simple actions of the community members as they entered and exited.

When Ashleigh had been at Albatross for just over six weeks, Phillip made an announcement at one of the Monday meetings.

"One of our centres has developed a new green initiative," he said proudly. "Yes. They actually have a group of seniors and students in the community who have formed a green committee and are leading an environmental charge. They are doing a summer clean up in the neighbourhood and have started going door-to-door to talk to residents about recycling and using water more efficiently for gardening, et cetera. It's really very progressive."

Sara felt a little pang of excitement. This would be an interesting initiative that could get some great media attention.

"So Mara has asked us to assign a public relations professional to the project. We'll have to develop brochures and press releases and organize a launch event. There will be media interest for sure. And, of course, the local politicians will want to show up to support the green project."

He paused and looked around and then smiled.

"And I've decided that Ashleigh will be the lead person on this project."

The room was quiet as all eyes turned to the gleaming intern. Sara's mind went numb. She looked directly at Phillip, mouth slightly open, words on her tongue but not cooperating with her brain to develop sentences. She had sent him an email a few weeks ago, forwarding a message from Ruth, who told her about the initiative. He never responded and now she knew why.

"Oh, and, of course, she will report to Anna, who will be her mentor throughout the project." Phillip smiled his big, wide grin.

Sara sneaked a look at Venah, who looked just as miserable as she felt. Finally they had something in common.

"I'm so excited. I have so many ideas!" The chirping words pierced the air in the room, and Phillip beamed.

"Great! And of course, Sara and Venah will be there to help you at the event. You'll need people to do the running around." He looked directly at Sara and giggled, as if he'd made a little joke.

Sara said nothing and put on her best contrived smile and nodded. But her stomach was turning, and the gum lodged inside her brain raised a sticky hand.

When the meeting ended, she walked back down to her office, feeling the routine of the green mile walk. As she sat in her office, she felt the tears threatening to burst, and she got back up again, putting her head down as she headed back through the hall to the washroom. Anna was coming down the hall from the meeting room, but Sara was lucky enough to duck into the washroom before the two collided.

As she shut the door of the stall, Sara sat down on the toilet seat and buried her head in her hands. Why this feeling of defeat? Was she jealous of Ashleigh? The twenty-one-year-old intern who just came out of school?

Yes, she was jealous. Resentful, confused. Ashleigh, the pretty girl who had gone to community college for three years, was now, less than two months into her first internship, being handed a high-profile, ground-breaking project to manage, and Sara was being asked to assist her.

In Sara's experience, projects like this one were not usually given to interns. Her internship duties had consisted of filing, helping senior staff with their stories, covering lame evening events only to have the story ripped to pieces by a senior reporter, or worse, the editor. It was about paying your dues, she was told, because interns were supposed to learn from those who had experience.

Was she being ridiculously insecure or was something wrong with what Phillip was doing? The very question confused her, as if she didn't have the right to question his decisions.

Besides, what would she say? "Hey, Phillip, do you like Ashleigh more than me? Are you going to give her my job?" The very idea was ridiculous because she had six years of experience on the intern. It could not and would not happen. Besides, what about the diversity factor? Didn't they hire her because they needed someone brown in their department so the community would feel more comfortable at their events?

As the thoughts and fears came flooding out with the tears, Sara felt a little lighter. Crying was therapeutic, something she'd accepted over the past few years, partly because of Catherine, who never hesitated to let the tears flow when she was upset.

Maybe Catherine could provide some insight into what she was feeling at work. She was having dinner with her and Giselle this Friday. Perhaps two objective views, especially one from a lawyer like Giselle, would bring some stability to her work again.

The tears stopped, and Sara listened carefully to make sure that she was the only person in the washroom. Perhaps someone had come in while her mind was in flux. But the stalls were quiet, so she slowly opened the door and walked out.

Her eyes were a little red, but thankfully she wore no eye make-up, so the streaks down her face were clear. Splashing a little water on her face to wash away the emotions and a quick pat to absorb the evidence with a rough paper towel and the frustration was gone, hidden behind an accepting smile. Satisfied, Sara walked out of the washroom and back to her office.

"What do you mean he gave her the lead role?" Giselle's head snapped away from the menu and looked directly at Sara.

"He said she would be overseeing the project. What else is there to understand?" Sara found that the only way to be friends with Giselle was to mirror her manner—bold, direct, and holding nothing back. Some days it wasn't easy, but tonight, each forceful word relieved Sara of some frustration.

"Yeah, I heard that. But she is an intern. Interns don't manage projects—they assist."

"He's giving her an opportunity," Catherine's voice piped in.

"Yeah, the opportunity is the internship. Sara, seriously, did you talk to him about this?"

"I sent him an email from Ruth and expressed my interest in working on the project."

"But did you talk to him after he announced that an inexperienced intern would be running the show on a big initiative?"

Sara paused and sighed. "No."

"Well, that's it then. You need to speak up."

"I don't know if that's the best idea, Giselle," said Catherine.

"Why not?"

"Come on Giselle, you don't want her to lose her job."

Sara blinked hard and looked directly into Catherine's concerned eyes. Could she lose her job for speaking up?

The comment cooled Giselle's fire, and she paused, looking at her friends across the table. Her hazel eyes softened, "Okay, I see what you're saying."

She knew the realities of working environments, having been with a legal firm for some time. But her relationship with her friends sent her into protective mode, and she struggled between idealism and realism. Still, Catherine's words were clear.

"Sara, don't worry about it. Sometimes you just need to watch and be patient. She's only there for a short time." Catherine had been working as a political reporter since she graduated, and at first, the shock of seeing the corruption in politics up close was overwhelming to her positive disposition. But to do her job, she had to remain neutral and hide her disgust. There were times to stand up, but choosing those times wisely was important.

"Yeah, she's supposed to be leaving at the end of the summer. I guess he's just giving her a really good opportunity, so when she leaves, she has the experience to find a better job." As she said that, Sara wasn't convinced that her words held truth.

"Look, the guy sounds like he's being manipulated by that Anna person. She sounds like a bully, and maybe he just wants to keep the peace. I don't think it's about you as much as it is about her." Catherine sounded convincing.

"You know, I get what you're saying, Catherine. But Sara is the senior person in the department next to, what's his name, Phil?" Giselle looked over at Sara. who nodded. "And she should be the one who mentors the intern, not Anna."

"Anna's been there longer," Sara tested a defense.

"Yeah, so why didn't she get your job then?"

"I don't know. Maybe this place has a different way of working. It seems disjointed somehow. Titles don't reflect the actual responsibilities of the jobs." Sara was thinking out loud.

Giselle opened her menu and surveyed the contents. "Maybe. And maybe you should ask for an intern. Wait until after this little chick is gone. He can't say no."

"Yeah, that might be a good idea." Sara was tired of talking about work, and Catherine could tell, so she popped a new question: "Hey, so how is that cutie-pie Richard doing?"

Talking about Richard was an ideal distraction, hiding the sticky gum for the moment. Sara eagerly went into detail about her growing relationship.

Sara watched as Ashleigh flitted around for the next month, preparing for her big event. She was torn between jealous resentment and genuine affection for the young intern. Ashleigh was vibrant and outgoing, and there wasn't anything in her demeanour to suggest that she was gloating at her growing status.

But for the first week, she decided to stay away from Ashleigh's euphoria and watched helplessly as Phillip and Anna, and even Venah, coddled her and stroked her ego as she struggled to plan an event with little insight.

After the first week of observing from the safety of her office, she heard a soft knock on her door and saw blond stripes in her peripheral view. She stared at her screen for a moment and then turned to look into the eager blue eyes.

"Hi, Sara. Anna told me that you have a list of media contacts that I can use for my event that you can send to me." It wasn't a question. It was a command, and her voice was firm, expecting, but her eyes showed slight hesitation.

Sara saw Anna trying not to look at her through the glass of her office window. She paused for a moment, feeling suddenly protective over the list she'd worked so hard to create.

"Yes, I have a list. I can send it to you. Perhaps I can give you some insights into the different reporters and editors? Some are easier to deal with than others."

Ashleigh's answer burst from her pouty lips, "Oh yes, that would be great!"

"Great. When did you want to meet?"

"Um, I have some things to do right now, but how about this afternoon?"

"Okay, perfect. We can meet here after lunch, and I'll go over the list with you."

As Ashleigh bounced out of her office, Sara felt a twinge of empowerment. Perhaps this would be an opportunity to mentor someone and gain some experience of her own. Anna and Phillip probably didn't intend for this to happen, but that didn't matter. She was not simply going to hand over a list that she worked hard to develop through many years of building relationships with the media. Suddenly, Sara began to look forward to the rest of her day.

The hour of the meeting came, and there was no interference from Anna. In fact, she just sat in her office and didn't seem to be bothered about the two heads together in Sara's office.

Ashleigh asked a lot of questions and seemed very keen on learning. The talk moved from work to personal matters, and soon Ashleigh was telling Sara about the courses she was taking at school. It was interesting to hear how little the curriculum had changed from when Sara was in school just a few years ago. Although, at that time, social media was still very new, and the strategies they had learned were quite tame; people were still very afraid of having their information appear on sites like Twitter and Facebook.

Sara found herself fascinated by Ashleigh's take on social media because her generation grew up with the tools, which were as commonplace to them as television was to her.

As she got lost in the conversation, the sudden appearance of a figure standing in the doorway startled her, and she looked up to see Phillip frowning. Anxiety washed over her. He was upset for some reason.

"Hello." His voice was cheerful, but his face was tense. Sara desperately wanted to look over at Anna because her expression would confirm or deny if worry was warranted.

"Ashleigh, is Sara showing you the media list?"

"Oh yes, she showed it to me, and we were talking about some of the reporters and editors and also how to use social media."

"That's great. But Sara will be supporting you by dealing with the media, right?" His eyes were on Sara. "You can work with Ashleigh on the media advisory and the press release, and you'll be the contact for inquiries."

"Oh yes, sure, I can do that." She heard her own voice, as eager as Ashleigh's.

"Great. We need to make sure Ashleigh has all the support she needs so her event is successful." He shared a smile with the intern and walked out to visit Anna's office. He stood with his back to the doorway, his round frame blocking Anna from view as they spoke. Sara couldn't make out the words coming from their low voices, clearly intended not to be heard.

"Okay, well I guess you won't need the list then." Sara tried to make sure her voice was calm and easy going, fighting the emotions that were rising inside of her. Something was going on, and she wasn't sure what it was. "I'll just send the releases from my email."

"Okay, no worries." Ashleigh jumped up from the chair and picked up her notebook. "We can talk more about it when we need to do the release." Then her tone became more authoritative, despite the quick blinking of her eyes: "Why don't you work on the press release, then?"

Sara thought about that for a moment, unsure of what she was supposed to do. If she wrote it, then Ashleigh would edit it? That didn't make sense.

"Actually, it may be better if you drafted something, and then we can look at it together?"

"Okay." She backed away, accepting the decision. Phillip's back was still in view, blocking Anna's doorway and her face. Sara knew they were listening and wondered why she felt like she'd just done something wrong.

Sara woke up at 2:00 a.m. on the morning of Ashleigh's event. She changed positions for a few hours and fell into a light sleep until the alarm forced her to open her eyes. Tossing the covers aside, she jumped into the shower, soaking her hair with hot water and hoping the heat would soothe the tightness inside her head.

She was supporting Ashleigh today. It was a concept that she'd been wrestling with for a month. Sure, she'd been instrumental in helping with the media—crafting an advisory, a draft press release, reaching out to the reporters. But when materials went to Phillip for approval, his comments were always the same, "Has Ashleigh reviewed this?"

Somehow, Sara couldn't get past the irritating notion that she was the senior, full-time media person in the department. What exactly did an intern with three months of experience know about crafting a press release that would generate a good story?

It was a struggle, but true to her nature, Sara bit her tongue and smiled when Ashleigh tried to make changes. She would nod and diplomatically agree or disagree in an authoritative, adult tone, straddling the line between providing guidance and taking direction.

Sometimes there would be a "but, but ... in class, we were taught ..." When Ashleigh questioned Sara's approach to press releases, Sara responded calmly, "Yes, textbooks tell us that that is the ideal way to do it, but in reality, it doesn't always work that effectively. You should always know your audience, and in this case, the media is our audience, and we must first convince them why this is a story. Then they become the channel to the intended audience, which is the public."

Although her words came out smoothly, the anxiety she felt inside was overwhelming at times. She took breaks to sit in the foyer of the recreation centre and calm her senses. The tiny kids strolling from the day care to the courtyard, holding hands with friends, eyes shining and eager, were a welcome sight that shook away the silliness of her anxieties.

Richard had noticed that something was wrong and confronted her one evening.

"How's work? Everything going okay?" He had leaned over the table at the bar and taken her hand in his, his blue eyes shaded grey in concern.

"Work is good."

"Are you sure? You don't seem like yourself lately."

"What does that mean?"

"It means you're distracted, seem kind of worried about something. I'm guessing it's about work ... and not about us?"

"About us? No, Richard ... we're good, aren't we? Or are you trying to tell me something?"

"Nope, I'm good. Just making sure you're good." And with that, he leaned back and smiled. She knew how to change the subject.

The night before the event, she avoided him. She let his call slip into voicemail and then texted him before she went to bed to say that she was busy preparing for a work event the next day and would call him soon. A kiss emoji sealed the text, and his response was good: "k, talk to you soon, night."

As Sara approached the community centre that morning, her stomach twisted in knots. She returned to her car to sit and finish her coffee and calm down before heading inside. She watched Ashleigh bouncing in and out of the front doors, to and from her car with armfuls of boxes, Anna holding the door to the building, barking instructions.

Phillip's car wasn't in the parking lot, and Sara knew she had to be inside before he was. One last swig of lukewarm coffee, and she breathed deeply, ready for the day. Grabbing the media kits from her trunk, she walked to the building, casually and not quickly, smiling at Anna as she approached.

"Morning." Sara's tone was cheerful.

Anna returned the greeting with a forced smile and held the door while Sara stepped inside. Should she offer to hold the door, so Anna could get back inside? Sara decided against it. She suspected that no matter what she did, it would not be the right gesture and Phillip would hear about it.

So she walked inside and began to set up the media table.

Ashleigh leaped over immediately. "Hey, you got the media kits?" She grabbed one and opened it, leafing through the contents. "Great! Do you have the sign-in sheet?"

Sara smiled and pulled it out of another folder along with a pen.

"Good, good job." Ashleigh patted Sara on her shoulder.

"Thanks," Sara managed to say, feeling a little silly.

Phillip strolled in, followed by Venah, who regarded Sara through narrowed eyes, in her usual fashion. They both walked over to the media table.

Phillip picked up a media kit and opened it, looking at the Albatross backgrounder, the stats about green initiatives at Albatross, the stats about green initiatives in the city and surrounding areas, the contact information, the brochure about the partnering retirement home, and the press release.

"This looks great!" he said, walking over to Ashleigh. "Great job on this!"

Ashleigh beamed, and Sara stood behind the table, mouth open, slightly stunned. The media kit was hers. She put it together, wrote the press release and the backgrounder. Ashleigh merely looked it over and tried to add input.

Sara watched as Phillip and Ashleigh chatted and laughed. Finally, Phillip put the kit back down on the table and said, "I've got to pick up Adam. He's at home today, and Randi has to leave for a meeting, so I thought I would bring him here."

"Okay" was all that Sara could muster.

Phillip walked out the door, and Sara looked up to see Venah watching the entire scene, dark eyes amused. The feeling that washed over her was defeat. What could she do? Scream out to Phillip that she was the one who developed the media kit? Sara's eyes went to Ashleigh, who was standing proud in the middle of the room, streaked yellow hair sleek and contrasting her tight, black suit and red high heels. She looked like a star, an up-and-coming executive who climbed easily, without having to look down because she was certain the supports were there.

The foyer suddenly seemed huge. People were buzzing around, posing questions to Ashleigh, whose puzzled face turned to Sara each time, eyes big, imploring assistance. Sara stood behind the media table and watched, not moving, not attempting to help. She wanted to save the young woman, but her feet would not move.

Soon, Ashleigh began pointing towards the media table, and bearers of questions moved toward Sara . She had no choice but to respond. She knew most of the answers, and when she didn't, she simply found the person in the crowd who could respond accurately and walked the inquirer over to them.

A look in the intern's direction indicated some relief in the once panic stricken face. Sara felt a twinge of resentment. Here she was, helping someone who was junior, inexperienced, and taking credit for work that she was doing.

"Ashleigh, I need to go to the washroom. Can you cover?" Sara's tone indicated it was a direction, not a question. She didn't even wait for a response but casually made her way over to the washroom, stopping to chat with staff she recognized on the way. Suddenly, a figure appeared in front of her, a scarlet smile on a caramel background.

"Hello, how are you doing today?" It was Joan Rodriguez, the board chair. Sara had never been formally introduced to her; she extended her hand in a greeting.

"Hi there, Joan. I don't think we've formally met before. I'm Sara. How are you doing?" She managed a strong tone, despite the shivering of her spine. Was it the fact that she was the chair or something else that prompted that reaction? Sara couldn't decide at that moment but knew she had to continue the conversation.

"Yes, Sara, I'm great. Thanks so much for your work on this event and my speaking notes. I understand you wrote them?"

"Um, yes, you're welcome."

"They are very good. I like your writing style, Sara. They are just what I need to open up this event today."

"You're welcome. I'm happy to help. And don't hesitate to let me know if you need anything else. I'm here all morning."

"Of course I will. Thanks again."

Sara slipped into the washroom breathlessly. Closing the door on the stall, she then let her breath out, almost gasping. The board chair liked her notes! So then why did she hesitate to tell her that she was the writer?

Sara searched the back of her mind for something to explain the feeling of guilt that pressed onto her chest. It was Ashleigh's event, but that didn't mean she had to lie about her involvement.

She flushed the toilet and walked out to greet her face in the mirror. A dark-skinned immigrant looked back at her, gloomy complexion and dried lips, hair pulled back haphazardly and surrounded messily by escaped wisps. The circles under her eyes seemed prominent today, maybe from the lack of restful sleep. She released her hair from its clip and pulled it back again, tighter, hoping the contain the black wisps. The lip gloss that could provide some shine was in her purse, which was still at the media desk. But it didn't matter. No one was looking at her anyway.

A deep breath pushed her back into the main foyer, and she made her way to the media table where Phillip, Anna, and Ashleigh were talking to Joan and Mara. There was also little Adam, Phillip's son, sitting on a chair behind the table, reading what looked like a graphic novel. She approached him, smiling at his white blond hair.

"Hello," she said from the other side of the table. "Are you here to help?"

Light brown doe eyes surrounded by thick white lashes only natural in young children looked up at her. A blush told her he was shy, and then a soft voice, "I can help if you want."

"Ha ha ... no, it's okay. I was just kidding. What are you reading?"

Adam held up the book. A graphic novel it was. Sara had heard that these new types of comics were the key to getting boys to read. She smiled and asked if he liked it.

"Yep, I like this one. I have all three of them."

"Oh, you do? Is this the last one?"

"No, it's the second one. The first one was good, but this one is better. And my dad bought me the last one."

"Cool. So you like to read?"

"Yeah, but I like to play video games too."

"Ha ha, which ones do you like to play?"

Before he could answer, Phillip appeared.

"Adam, don't bother Sara; she has work to do."

"Oh, he wasn't bothering me, he was just telling me about his book and his video games ... " Her voice trailed off as she saw the stern look on Phillip's face as he grabbed his son by the shoulder and turned him around.

"Go over there and help Ashleigh," he said, nodding in the direction of the intern.

Turning back to Sara, he smiled, eyes stern, and said, "He really prefers blondes."

The words hung in the air, and Sara wasn't sure if she'd missed something. She watched Adam run off towards Ashleigh. Her eyes could not move from the figure of Ashleigh as she welcomed the small boy and took his little hand in hers. They matched. It seemed appropriate.

Sara stole a glance at Phillip, who was smiling adoringly at the vision of his son and the intern. She looked down at the sign-in sheet and noticed there was one reporter already there: Don. Looking around, she found the familiar face and walked over to greet him with a smile.

"I'm just going to say hello to Don," she said over her shoulder to Phillip.

"You didn't greet him when he came in?" The words followed her, but she didn't look back.

"Hey, Don! Great to see you! Thanks for coming."

"Hey, Sara. You know I'll always be here when there's a good story like this. Green community initiative run by a group of local seniors and youths—great local story. You're doing well here, eh? Everything that's come across the desk lately has been pretty good. Wasn't like this before."

"Yeah? Well, thanks ... I guess I've been helping somewhat. Is a photographer coming?"

"Yeah, he should be here soon. Looks like a lot of people here today. Should get some good pics. So can you hook me up with someone from Albatross? The ED, maybe?"

"Sure, you can talk to Mara, who is the executive director, and perhaps get a comment from the director of the centre, Maggie Carter. There she is over there. Come on, I'll introduce you."

Don followed Sara over to where Maggie was standing, her eyes watching over the scene of people filling the seats, staff helping seniors settle into seats.

Sara stayed within earshot of the interview. Reporters weren't keen on having the publicist hang around, but she wanted to hear Don's voice, taking her back to the days when she was the asker.

Besides, Phillip was watching and, most likely, Venah and Anna too. So she needed to look like she was paying attention to the questions and would be there to jump in if one was inappropriate or if Maggie needed help. Hands behind her back, she kept a half smile etched on her face and avoided the gaze of her colleagues. The centre was filling up quickly with seniors and youths in jade t-shirts, walking around chatting with other attendees, promoting the fact that they were part of the green committee.

Suddenly, she saw a man with a TV camera enter the foyer. Instinctively, she headed over to greet him. It was one of the Toronto television stations that rarely came out this far to cover a story. But it was a good story, and she reminded herself that the press release sold it well.

Sara searched the foyer to see Phillip's reaction. Surely, he would be pleased. But when her eyes found him, her smiled faded at the hard and almost annoyed look on his face as he stared at the camera crew and the South Asian reporter who was a familiar sight on the six o'clock news. As if he sensed her eyes, Phillip's gaze turned to Sara, and the moment their eyes locked, he forced a smile.

Sara smiled back, but the gum in her brain felt sticky again. A stale, gluey substance that would never melt. Whatever had annoyed him would have to be dealt with, but at that moment, she needed to do her job, so she created a smile and introduced herself to the reporter, ready to facilitate the interviews and the filming.

34

As soon as Phillip set his coffee cup down on his desk, Mara appeared.

"Good morning," she said with a smile.

He immediately felt annoyance rise inside his chest. He hadn't even sat down yet, and here she was, standing in his doorway, that smug look on her face. It was not yet nine o'clock, for goodness sake. While his mind was telling her where to go, his smile beckoned her in. She sat down in front of his desk.

At least she was smiling, he thought as he took the lid off his large double cream, double sugar Americano that cost him fifteen minutes of waiting in line at the Starbucks down the street. He took a large gulp of the sweet liquid, and it streamed through his body, relaxing his muscles as it made its way down to the pit of his empty stomach. He'd resisted the urge to purchase one of the breakfast sandwiches because Randi had made a comment about his bulging stomach last week.

Mara waited politely while he savoured the first mouthful and then slowly spoke.

"Well, how did you think the green event went?"

Phillip thought about the question for a few seconds, wondering where she would be going with this conversation. "I thought it went well. Maggie seemed quite happy, and we had some good media coverage. What did Joan think?"

"She was pleased. In fact, she wanted to know who on your staff took the lead."

The tone of Mara's voice made Phillip feel a little uncertain. He paused and took another sip from his paper cup before answering carefully. "Ashleigh took care of the details but was strongly supported by the entire public relations team."

"So Ashleigh was the lead?"

Another gulp added courage. "Well, technically she was the project lead, but

168

she's still new, so she was mentored by Anna. It was an opportunity for her to learn under the guidance of a skilled professional."

"Okay. I won't be telling this to Joan. If she knew that such an important event was left in the hands of an intern, she would not be comfortable with it. She thought Sara had the lead, since she saw her handling the media and she was very visible walking around and talking to the attendees and the staff ..." Mara looked Phillip directly in the eyes. She was looking for the truth.

"Sara handles the media relations. Her job is to make sure the media speak to the appropriate spokespeople. She wrote the speaking notes and the press release with Ashleigh. But the event was really managed by Anna, with Ashleigh executing."

"I didn't see Anna much."

"Well, that's the mark of a good leader. She stayed in the background to let her intern shine! But trust me, Anna oversaw the entire event."

"Joan was very impressed with Sara."

Phillip tried to keep his surprise hidden. Inside, he felt panic rise in his throat, but he fought to maintain his smile. His face, however, was a battle he would never win. The flush of red that he felt blossom on his cheeks was uncontrollable. He hoped his smile would outshine the heated look of fear that he was trying so desperately to cover.

"Really? I didn't realize she had talked to Joan. I noticed her with the media."

"I was watching her as well. She is quite social and can really work a room."

"Well, that's her job. She doesn't have Anna's years of experience at Albatross though. There are still some small details that she overlooks."

"I see. Anna was not visible. Joan only saw and spoke with Sara."

"What did they talk about?" Phillip couldn't help but blurt out the question.

"Something about the speech."

"Well, Ashleigh wrote the speech with Anna's help. Sara just helped."

"But you said earlier that Sara wrote it?"

"She helped. But Ashleigh is Anna's intern, and she supervised all of her activities and the logistics of the event. Sara was on support for media."

"Okay. We don't have to get into details of who did what. But I wanted you to know that Joan was pleased with Sara, and when she gets fond of someone new, she will try to work with her as much as she can. Joan can be very demanding, but she should not approach Sara directly. The protocol is that she comes to me, and I find the resources she needs. The board has only one employee, and that's me."

"Yes, that's clear to me. I will make sure Sara knows that she should not be approaching Joan, and that if the board chair approaches her, then she needs to tell me."

"Great. And good job on the event by the way." Mara's words filled the air as she turned and walked out of his office.

Once she was no longer visible, Phillip sat back in his chair and grabbed his coffee, chugging big gulps of what was lukewarm by now. Worry caused his forehead to crease, and then annoyance filled his mind. Anna should have been more visible at the event because now Sara was on Joan's radar.

Phillip was a skillfully strategic planner. He sat quietly, letting the thoughts mingle in his mind so he could determine the next course of action.

So Joan met Sara and believed she was the lead for the event. It was only one time and one event. He couldn't have pushed Ashleigh up front because Joan wouldn't have taken an intern seriously.

Although Joan had met Anna on numerous occasions, the plain, plumpish small-town girl didn't have an image that impressed or was even noticeable for that matter. She was hardworking, but not someone who walked into a room and captured the audience with their dynamism or engaging conversation. She was a background employee who did the grunt work, kept him informed about the other staff, and made him look good. Anna was valuable.

Sara was young and new to the organization, but she was, as much as he hated to admit it, a rising star. Phillip knew she had potential when he hired her, but he was certain he could keep her under his control.

The conflict with Anna could be easily managed, and so far he was doing fine. His conversations with Anna assured her that she was next in line for a promotion. He even made little jabs about Sara from time to time, when Anna seemed uncertain about his motives. They needed a diverse workplace, and Sara's presence helped improve their public image, he would say with a coy smile, silently confirming that a promotion for Sara would not happen at Albatross.

Despite the government's insistence on creating a diverse workforce, Phillip knew how the world operated. People hired people who resonated with themselves. It wasn't about being racist—it was about comfort level and, most of all, trust. Cultural backgrounds made for different values, morals, and ways of thinking. Sara was smart and capable, but he was not sure where she was coming from. Could he trust her to maintain his status? Or would she try and push him out someday?

And she just wasn't someone who Mara would put in a leadership role. There was no threat of Sara taking his job or even getting further than she was right now. So then why was he concerned?

The thought nagged at him, and as he drained his cup, he knew he had to take some action. He couldn't leave it the way it was because Joan could approach Sara at any time.

As he walked to the bakery around the corner, he strategized about approaching Sara to make sure she would not interact with Joan again. But then again, he wanted Anna to work directly with Joan. It was a tricky situation.

The waft of baked goods tantalized his nose as he opened the door, and he filed the dilemma away for a moment. The Danishes were freshly baked by the German couple who owned the place. They were filled with sweet apples and cinnamon and topped with brown sugar. Randi had suggested that he consider rethinking his diet, so he didn't tell her about the daily Danishes and didn't eat sweets around her. Their dinners out were rich and extravagant, but at home the meals were simple, mostly because he made them.

Armed with a warm paper bag, Phillip headed back to the office and resumed strategizing on the way. He would talk to Sara, and he'd get a little upset perhaps. Maybe he would bring Anna in for the conversation, and they would position it as a "team strategy." Yes, that would work. He would appoint Anna as the liaison between the board members and their department. The board could communicate through Mara, but if they wanted to speak with the public relations department directly, they would have to contact Anna or him, not Sara. Sara had little choice but to accept it.

By the time he reached the office, two minutes away, his stomach was grumbling. Rushing to his desk, he barely sat down before he tore open the bag and grabbed the Danish with his teeth, pulling a mouthful of sweetness. As the taste resonated with his senses, he sighed and sat back in his chair.

Sara stared at the meeting invitation. It requested that she and Anna meet with Phillip to discuss "board protocols." She sat in front of it for a few minutes, anxiously churning through her memories of the past event. Yes, she'd talked with Joan, but she hadn't said anything inappropriate as far as she could remember.

Joan asked about the speech she wrote, and it didn't seem necessary to tell her that Anna looked it over and made some changes. In fact, the changes were just for the sake of having some input—a different word here and there, a contrived key message that added little value to the speech, but Sara had complied. The initial themes and ideas that she developed were preserved. She'd worked closely with Ashleigh to show her how to weave ideas together, build energy with supportive quotes, and form a conclusion, all while keeping the audience engaged. But Anna did the final edit. Now she wondered if she should she have explained this to Joan.

Sara finally hit the accept button, and the meeting landed in her calendar. It was tomorrow at three o'clock. The end of the day on a Friday.

Richard was concerned. He tried not to show it on his face and carried on a normal conversation, slowly directing it towards the cause of his concern.

"So, did the media write any articles about the event?"

"Yep. They covered the event and wrote a couple of great stories." Sara heard her own reply and realized how flat it was.

"Were they good?" Hearing her tone, he persisted.

"What?"

"The stories … were they positive?" His hesitance made her look up, and when she gazed into his confused eyes, she realized she'd snapped at him.

Softer, she replied, "Yes, they were. Local media stories are mostly positive when it comes to events that will benefit the community."

"That's great, Sara. Did your boss say anything?"

She paused and realized that Phillip didn't say anything about the media coverage. And then, a small pang of hope rang in her mind—maybe that's what the meeting was all about? Maybe she was worried for nothing. Perhaps Phillip wanted to congratulate her on the success of the event.

She smiled and looked at Richard, seeing the relief wash over his face as her own lightened up.

"Not yet but we're meeting tomorrow to do a debrief."

"Good. I'm sure he was pretty happy about it. Media coverage is free publicity. We get lots of negative stories about the school board. Almost every day."

Sara knew how true this was. The media were always looking for dirt, and the schools were an easy target, accused of mismanaging taxpayer dollars and not allocating enough money for the kids, which was usually true but often exaggerated. A good news story was a boon.

Hope spread through her as she took a gulp of the almost warm, half-full glass of draft. She looked at Richard, her rising warmth spilling over into his blue eyes, causing them to crinkle with affection as he smiled.

It was just a month ago that she'd met his family after a casual invitation over text. His parents had an open house for the neighbourhood, an early spring tradition they held every year, and he asked her to stop by. Meeting his parents seemed like a big step, but then again, it was an open house, so maybe everyone was invited. She decided not to overthink it and showed up with an apple pie from the German bakery down the street, hoping it would be enough for all the neighbours.

She rang the doorbell and waited, but there were no sounds coming from the house. When a middle-aged woman with ash-blond hair opened the door, Sara wasn't sure that she had the right house.

"Hello! Sara? I'm Valerie, Richard's mother."

"Hi there. Um, I brought this for you." She held out the pie as she walked across the threshold. Richard appeared in the doorway of a nearby room, where she heard quiet talking, but not the boisterous noise of a neighbourhood group as she had imagined.

"Hey!" His blue eyes twinkled, and she immediately relaxed as he took the pie in one hand and put his other on the small of her back, ushering her into the room. His mother, still smiling, walked beside them. Sara wasn't sure what to say.

As she entered the immaculate living room, she saw a bigger group of people than the noise level indicated. She was relieved that the neighbourhood open house was not a mythical event.

She met his father and his sister and her family, as well as the neighbours, and each greeting was warm. Sara sat beside Richard for the afternoon, listening to the conversation as she sipped white wine and nibbled on double-cream brie, smoked gouda, and buttery crackers.

The crowd morphed a few times during the afternoon, and when Richard's mother switched on the lamps in the dimming room, Sara leaned toward Richard and said that she would be leaving. He picked up her hand and held it, right there in front of his parents. "Okay, I'll walk you out."

After goodbyes, Sara found herself beside her car with Richard, allowing herself to look directly into his sparkling ocean eyes as he leaned in and kissed her softly on the mouth. She knew that someone would be watching from the window, and she didn't care.

Now, looking across the table at this guy who'd taken her to meet his family and was obviously concerned about her mood, she allowed her fear of the work meeting to fade and changed the subject.

She was early. Anna had not yet arrived, so she sipped her coffee and tried to make small talk with Phillip. But he was uneasy, checking his emails and apologizing that he had to send one right away. This wasn't unusual when he was around her; Sara often envied his comfort around Anna and Ashleigh, sitting back and laughing for over an hour in Anna's office. When he had to approach her, he spoke quickly, balancing on the edge of his chair, getting the point across and then citing an urgent matter that needed his attention.

Now, he was staring at his computer screen, one hand on the mouse as he moved it around, clicking on emails and responding to them. Or pretending to.

Suddenly he turned his head, and she was certain she saw the relief transform his face as Anna walked in and sat down beside her. Phillip got up and closed the door.

Anna opened her notebook and looked at Phillip but didn't acknowledge

Sara. The office suddenly felt really small.

"So, here we are." Phillip placed both his hands on his desk and looked at the two women sitting across from him. "First, I want to thank the both of you for a great job at the event. Both Mara and Joan were very happy. Sara, thanks for the work with the media. The entire board will be happy to see the stories." Sara took a deep breath.

"In fact, Joan has already mentioned the stories to me. We'll be including the media clips in the next board meeting package ... " he hesitated, forcing the next sentence, "And she was thrilled with the speech. Thanks to both of you for working with Ashleigh on it."

He nodded and smiled directly at Anna, and Sara realized what was happening.

"It shows me how you both are honing and improving your leadership skills."

Sara saw Anna out of the corner of her eye. She was very aware of the wall that separated them.

"But I understand that Joan approached you, Sara?" Phillip's tone made Sara's stomach flip again. She looked directly at him, trying to hide the anger that was rising inside her.

Sara was ready. "Yes, she talked to me at the event."

"Well. Mara was a little upset about that. The board members are not supposed to talk to staff."

"She approached me." Sara tried to keep her voice steady.

"Yes, that may be the case, but did you tell her that you wrote the speech?" Phillip waited.

"I did write the speech." From somewhere inside her, the voice came out, and its strength surprised not only herself, but Phillip, whose eyes widened in astonishment.

"Well, it was a team effort, Sara. We don't take credit for work that is not solely ours. You may have written the first draft, but Ashleigh wrote parts of it and Anna finished it. She made significant edits."

Sara was shocked. Anna did no such thing. Her "edits" were small word changes. She had no writing talent.

"Joan said that she liked it, and I thanked her for her compliments."

"Perhaps that is the case, but Mara has made it clear that we do not talk to board members about work. They have only one employee, and that is Mara. Now obviously, we cannot walk away from board members if they approach us at an event. So there needs to be one point of contact for our department. It will be me, if I am around, but when I am not around, Anna will be the person to liaise with Joan and the other board members."

Sara knew what was happening, but was already deflated. To protest would be futile.

"We will start the process by having all materials go through Anna. So, if Joan needs a speech, Anna will send it to her. Once this pattern has been established, Joan will know who to speak with at events. Board members just need to be trained." He tried to get a laugh, but no one else caught the mood.

Sara said nothing. In her mind, she knew she had the senior role. But Anna had been at Albatross longer, and more importantly, she had Phillip's ear.

"This will set a process so the board understands that they shouldn't be speaking to the entire staff at events. It could get out of hand and soon they'll be sending emails directly to you. Sara, you don't want that. It's better to have one point of contact."

"Okay, that makes sense," Sara said in a voice she barely recognized as her own. The tone was strong, and even Phillip looked slightly puzzled. "Process is important. And of course, it's about the work that is delivered to them from our department; we are a team after all." She smiled at Anna, who blinked and stared straight ahead.

When the meeting ended, Sara headed to the recreation centre. The open foyer felt more welcoming than her own office. Something about the space, the staff, made her feel like the very reason for being at Albatross resided inside this space. There was such strong energy from people who walked through the foyer—the staff and the residents in the community—and it reminded her why she loved her job. As she sat on one of the benches, she allowed herself to think. What had just happened? She had written the speech! It was not a lie.

Instead of getting credit for a job well done, she was being forced to go through Anna. Punished.

Suddenly the door to the gym opened, and a flood of little kids ran out. The pre-school program. As she watched the tiny feet running across the floor, kids with eyes wide, mouths open, Sara couldn't help but smile. She got up and went back to her office.

35

She heard about the official promotion from Maxine. She didn't know if it was true, because the job had not been posted. Phillip said nothing about an official promotion and a manager title, only that Anna would be the board liaison, but when the email announcement corroborated Maxine's story, Sara felt her spirit fade.

She tried to work with the new process, hoping that it really was just a way to streamline the work to the board. But she found herself labouring over speeches, spending long hours researching and rewriting to accommodate Phillip's red-marked edits, only to hand them over to Anna to send to Joan. It was teamwork, she told herself. Until the day she was walking towards Phillip's office and heard Joan talking to Phillip and Mara.

"The speeches really are well written. You have quite a talent in Anna."

Sara waited for the correction, the teamwork message.

"Yes, she is very talented. She's quite a rising star." Phillip's voice.

"Well, I'm quite pleased. I got a standing ovation at the Rotary meeting the other night. They were quite impressed."

"Phillip has been working with her to hone her skills, but Anna has been with us for a long time, and her experience, not to mention her passion for Albatross, is reflected in the notes." Mara's voice.

Sara felt the tears flooding her eyes. She could not pass the open door. Turning around, she went the other way, keeping her head down, not conscious of anyone around her. The only place to go was the foyer of the recreation centre. When she reached the comfort of the foyer, it was filled with people. One of the classes was out. She walked out the door into the warm, late summer air.

Only when she looked up at the green foliage did she let the tears flow. Deep breaths put strength back into her body, and she quickly wiped away the tears that had spilled onto her cheeks. She didn't want to think about the words she'd heard. Why was she surprised? Did she really believe it was "teamwork?"

They were trying to make it seem like Anna did all the work, which she'd suspected for a while but refused to acknowledge. She'd filed it in the back of her mind and told herself she was being paranoid, but here it was, the truth. But why?

What was the benefit of pushing Anna into the star role? Sara was hired as the senior person. They could have given the job to Anna instead of hiring her, but they chose to hire someone from the outside. And now, she had been pushed up over Sara, bypassing protocol.

None of it made sense to Sara. Only in the weeks that followed did the story unravel. It happened fast, but time felt blurred to Sara, as if she were watching a clock melt, turning her head sideways to see if it was real or perhaps an illusion. Maybe she would move her head in the other direction, and something would snap, and she would no longer be at Albatross. It would all have been a piece of art.

Anna had been made board liaison manager, and Sara was supposed to write speeches and send them to her. Joan had decided she wanted to attend more events and promote the good work of Albatross. This kind of visibility would help them get more funding from private sector organizations through partnerships, she'd said. It was part of a new initiative that Phillip had worked on with Mara.

A new speech every couple of weeks was added to Sara's already full workload. She'd spend hours sitting at her computer, eating lunch while she worked, creating speeches that were welcoming and would draw in audiences. Occasionally, she'd put in a joke and hope Joan would use it. But she never saw the speech once she emailed it to Anna. She suspected that some editing was done before it was sent to the chair, but she didn't ask about it.

She kept writing and sending, and then other board members started going to more events, and Anna said they wanted speeches too. She started to fall behind in her own work. Maxine had a new project she was preparing to announce, and she'd asked Sara to create a press release and some background information for the website. When Maxine called her to ask how it was going, Sara realized she'd completely forgotten about it. Maxine was understanding, but Sara knew that she wasn't able to keep up and decided to talk to Phillip.

She knocked softly on his door, and he looked up, startled. Sara rarely approached him, and at first, he stared at her like a cornered animal, but then motioned for her to come in. She closed the door.

"Phillip, I see that there are a lot of speeches being requested by the board members."

"Yes, well, you know they are trying to go out and promote the organization.

The board members are our ambassadors, so they will need speeches."

"Yes, I understand. It's great that they are doing this. But I've received one speech a week over the past three weeks, and I'm having a hard time keeping up with my own work." She realized she'd blurted everything out too quickly. It sounded like she was whining.

"Okay." He looked at her seriously.

"Well, I am just finding that the speeches are taking a lot of my time, and I don't often have a chance to work on other projects. Like Maxine's new project that is coming up. We have to do an announcement, and she is thinking we need to invite the media for a press conference."

"Well, Maxine does not make those decisions," he snapped, leaning over the desk.

"Okay. So what should I tell her? Maybe you'd prefer to talk to her?"

"No, I don't need to talk to her. But she knows that press conferences are not usually held for small announcements like that one. Just let her know that you will do a press release."

"Okay, sure. So I was wondering if it's possible for Ashleigh to help with the speeches? She's a pretty good writer, and this could give her some experience in speech writing." Sara realized that she needed to make it sound like a benefit for Ashleigh and not relief for her. It worked. Phillip's eyes lit up as the words were delivered.

"Okay, that is a good point. Perhaps Ashleigh can take the smaller speeches for the board members. But not yet for Joan."

"Okay, that makes sense. Should I help her with them or is this something that Anna should supervise?"

Phillip's eyes widened. "Well, Ashleigh has written speeches before. She can do them, and you can have a quick look and send each one to Anna for a final look before she sends them to the board. But remember, Ashleigh will only work on the speeches for smaller events. I still expect you to handle the majority of them. If you have conflicts with other priorities, let me know, and I will help."

It didn't seem like much was being taken off her plate.

"Okay, so I will talk to Ashleigh then?" Sara watched him hesitate.

"Sure ..." And he got up and walked around his desk. The meeting was over.

But when she approached Ashleigh, the young intern was reluctant. "Well, I am pretty busy with my own stuff," she said, very defiantly.

"Phillip told me to talk to you about it." Sara tried to keep her voice calm.

"Well, I will have to talk with Anna about it," Ashleigh said, looking away. "I'll talk to her during lunch, maybe." The intern stood up, her crossbody Coach bag over her shoulder as she quickly made her way to Anna, who was waiting for their twice-a-week lunch date. When she came back to the office a couple of hours later, Ashleigh popped her head into Sara's office and confirmed that she would write a few of the smaller speeches under Anna's supervision.

A week later, Phillip showed up at her door. "Sara. How are things going?"

"I'm good. Trying to get this speech finished for this afternoon."

"Great. You're doing a great job with the speeches. Joan is pleased."

In the weeks that followed, she would vividly recall the comment and replay it as it came from Phillip's mouth.

"Okay, that's good to know," she said.

"Since the board members have been going out and speaking at other companies, we've been getting more recognition. And now we've been asked to participate in an event that the province is hosting. We're being asked to give a presentation on our diversity efforts. Venah has been working very hard with community centres across the city, and we have some good initiatives going on."

Sara still had no idea what Venah's role was. She knew that she was supposed to be helping community centres understand the needs of newcomers and their families, but she never saw anything come across Venah's desk.

Phillip continued, "So now Mara would like you and Venah to work on a speech for Joan for this event. The theme will be diversity, and we need to have some insight into the audiences that we serve. That's where you and Venah can put your heads together."

Anxiety filled her insides. Sara would remember sitting there staring at Phillip, uncertain how to respond.

"Well, what do you think?"

"Okay ..." She wanted to sound enthusiastic but wasn't sure if this was an opportunity or a trap. "Sure, when does it need to be ready?"

"The event is next Thursday, so you have a little over a week."

A fog took over Sara's mind, and her limbs started to feel heavy. A week to work with Venah on a speech. About diversity. To show how Albatross rolls out the red carpet for newcomers.

"Okay. I will talk to Venah."

"Wonderful!" And with that, Phillip got up and walked out of her office.

36

Venah welcomed Sara into her office, motioning for her to sit in the chair across from her. Sara kept her guard up, noticing the smile on Venah's face but also the way her eyes didn't meet her own. She felt the way a bird must when a cat is lurking nearby.

It was the first time that Sara had been alone with Venah.

"So, what is this speech going to be about?" Venah was always assertive in her tone.

"Oh, didn't Phillip talk to you?" Sara was a little flustered because she herself wasn't sure about the details of the event.

"No, he said you were writing a speech for Joan, and you needed my help."

"Oh, well, he told me that there is going to be an event with the province, and they wanted Joan to talk about the diversity initiatives that Albatross is undertaking."

"Ah, yes!" Venah pointed her finger in the air as if she'd had a revelation. "Okay, well are you taking notes?"

"Of course. I brought my notebook." A hint of annoyance slipped out.

"Well then, I have been doing some really great work with the recreation centres. Before I came to Albatross, they were not treating the seniors or the youths or any of the immigrant families with respect. They were not serving the right food, nor did they understand religious accommodation."

Sara jotted down the points.

"How did you find this out?"

"What do you mean? I just looked. I could see it! I talked to the families. People were going for recreational events and classes, and they could not eat because there were no vegetarian options, so they starved! Many could not communicate because the staff only spoke English, and there was no translation."

"Okay, I understand." Venah's aggression made Sara uncomfortable. "So you made them add vegetarian options and offer events and classes in different languages?"

"Well, I did more than that! I educated them on how to deal with different cultural ways!"

"Okay, so how did you do this? Did you conduct training on cultural sensitivity or put best practices into place?"

A slight pause and then, "I am working on the training and practices right now. It is not easy because we have many different cultures in the city. Everyone has their own preferences."

"Preferences? I'm not sure what you mean. Can you give me an example?"

"I've already given you examples. South Asians are mostly vegetarians. They need to eat food that they recognize from their homeland."

"Okay, and what about newcomers from Somalia or some of the other African countries where the families have escaped war?"

Venah looked startled. "They are Muslim. They do not eat pork, and many of the women wear hijabs."

"Yes, true, but they bring other customs with them, don't they? Maybe some cultural differences that we should be aware of? And also the trauma some have faced. You know, from the war-torn countries." Sara wasn't sure if Venah heard her the first time.

"Of course they bring different customs. But their religion is their strongest guide! This is what we need to be aware of!"

"So what other diversity programs do we have besides religious and dietary accommodations? Tell me about the cultural accommodation programs."

Venah said nothing for a moment. "I already told you, Saraswati. You are not listening. Religion is the strongest guide. We must support newcomers and allow them to practice their religion."

"Everyone is allowed to practice their religion. It's part of our constitution."

"Well, maybe it is, but it is not practised. People face discrimination every day."

Sara took a breath. Maybe she had been too forceful. "Yes, you're right. But maybe all we need is some cultural training so Canadians understand the differences that newcomers bring. Sometimes, many of the misunderstandings are the result of a lack of exposure. Maybe we could have cultural days where newcomers share their traditions?"

"You are not the expert here, Saraswati!"

The comment set a fire in Sara. "Maybe, but I do have some first-hand knowledge about being in a minority group!"

"Yes, but you are ashamed to even use your real name. What does this say to newcomer families when they see your name tag?"

"I already told you, my parents have always called me Sara. And my name is not the subject here." Her voice was low, calm but shaky.

"You do not understand diversity. Now, I must leave." And she got up, tossing her scarf around her neck.

Sara walked back down the hall to her own office and noticed Anna staring at her computer but not focussing. She had heard the conversation.

Once back in her office, Sara wondered what to do. She had little information for a speech and still couldn't package the diversity initiative in her mind. She opened one of the last speeches she'd written and started reading through it. Maybe she could simply modify this one and indicate that they were working on training programs.

An email came through from Maxine, and suddenly, she had a revelation. Of course. Maxine would know. She would have information for the speech since she'd watched Albatross evolve over the years along with the community. Sara picked up her phone and dialed Maxine's extension. A few minutes later, she was walking down the hall, notebook in hand, looking forward to a meeting that would give her information for a speech that would blow the board chair away.

Mara walked into Phillip's office and closed the door. He wasn't expecting her and was a little annoyed since his mouth was full and his Danish was only half eaten. Damn. Now it would get cold, and he'd walked to the bakery just to get one when it came out of the oven.

"Hi, Mara," he managed to say with a pleasant tone as he swallowed the sweet treat.

"Phillip," Mara said, eyes like stone. She was sitting back in her chair, but her hands were gripping the armrests. Phillip gulped.

"I just talked to Joan."

She spoke slowly, and Phillip knew that whatever was going to come out of her mouth was not good. He braced himself. "Okay. Is everything all right?"

"Well, I don't know if everything will be all right. All I know is that Joan complimented the speech that she delivered at the provincial event yesterday. She said it was one of the best speeches she'd ever read, and that she received a standing ovation for it, even from the premier."

"Well, that's great, isn't it?"

"Sure, unless you consider that she said Sara was one of the best speechwriters she's ever had."

Phillip felt the words hit him in the abdomen. For once, he had nothing to say.

"So, how did she come to this conclusion?" Mara's voice was controlled and calm, a capped volcano.

"I am not sure." Phillip's voice was almost a whisper.

"Find out." And she left his office.

Phillip waited for a minute to make sure she was gone and then hustled out of his office. He walked into Anna's office and shut the door behind him.

"Anna. How did Joan find out that Sara wrote the speech for the province's diversity event?"

"What do you mean?"

"I mean, Mara just came to my office and said that Joan said that Sara was one of the best speechwriters she had worked with." He watched the reaction spill across Anna's face.

"What?"

"Okay, so you didn't tell her?"

"Why would I do that? I thought we were trying to keep her from knowing?"

Phillip paused and chose his words carefully. "We are not deliberately trying to keep her from knowing. We want to make sure she follows the process."

"Okay, sure. But I didn't tell her anything. I just sent her the speech."

"Did Sara work with Venah on the speech?"

"As far as I know. They had a disagreement though. Sara challenged Venah on the diversity programs. Did Venah talk to you?"

Phillip thought for a minute. He remembered an email from Venah that said she wanted to meet, but he'd forgotten to respond—or maybe he did respond. His mind wasn't focussing.

"Well, I heard part of the conversation. Sara said something about the programs not being the right ones or something like that. And Venah got angry. So I'm not sure how much information she gave her."

"But you read the speech?"

"Yes, and I sent it to you."

Phillip tried to recall reading it. Yes, he did. He now remembered. "It sounded good. Accurate as far as I know. It talked a lot about the history of how the programs evolved."

"Yes, I noticed that. It all seemed factual. I checked it against the list of programs we offer."

"Well, then Sara probably told her. I asked her not to talk directly to Joan." Phillip got up from the chair.

"Okay, well she probably did because I didn't." Anna was satisfied. It must have been her because Venah would never give Sara credit for anything well done, especially to the board chair.

Phillip looked over at Sara in her office. She looked so innocent, and yet, what was she capable of? Did this little girl think she could push herself up the ladder by going behind his back? The board chair was also brown. Did she want Sara to move up into a position like his? Didn't they all look out for one another?

He was angry now. He realized he was staring when Anna said, "Phillip?"

"Yes. Okay. Just thinking about how to talk to her."

Anna couldn't stifle a smile. She wanted to see what would happen when Phillip confronted Sara. It would be about time. That girl felt she was better than everyone, and frankly, she was just a brown girl who was trying to force her way to the top. She had to be put in her place.

Sara could feel the tension as Phillip approached her doorway.

"Hi." Her voice sounded tiny.

Phillip closed her office door and sat down. He leaned over and closed the blinds in front of the big glass window so Anna or anyone else could not look in. Sara felt afraid. She was not sure what was about to happen.

"Sara, Mara came to my office today."

"Uh huh."

"And she said that Joan loved the speech you wrote. The one for the diversity event with the province."

"Okay." Sara was puzzled. So this was a good talk? She smiled, and then noticed that Phillip smiled back, in kind of a funny way.

"That's great. We are always happy when the chair is happy."

"Okay. That's good news."

"Yes. It is. Joan told her she was very pleased with your work. Did she tell you that herself as well?"

"No, I haven't talked to Joan."

"You haven't talked to her? You didn't ask how the speech went? I mean, we all want to know if the work we are doing is effective. Which makes sense."

"No, I saw her in the hallway, but I just smiled and said hello. You said it was better if we didn't approach the board members directly. I thought Mara didn't like it."

Phillip looked deeply into Sara's eyes. She was telling the truth.

"You are right. Mara prefers if we don't deal directly with the board members. That's why Anna is the liaison." He tried to sound professional, but inside he was yelling: *who the hell told Joan about the speech*?

"It was filled with great information about our diversity programs. Did Venah give you a lot of good information?"

"Um, well, I had a meeting with Venah, but she didn't have a lot of information. So I talked to Maxine."

There it was. Maxine. She told Joan. There was nothing he could do to stop her from talking to the board members. She'd been at Albatross longer than he had, and she did not report to him. But she did report to Mara.

"Maxine? She gave you the information?"

"Yes. I tried to get it from Venah, and she told me about the religious accommodations and said she was working on new programs that weren't finalised yet. So, I knew Maxine had been here for a long time and figured she could provide the history of how the programs evolved to meet the changing needs of the community."

It was a good strategy, and Phillip realized just how smart Sara really was. It worried him.

"Okay. Well that's good to know."

Sara didn't want to say anything else, but she knew that Maxine told Joan that she wrote the speech. So what? And she wasn't sorry that during her meeting with Maxine, she let a comment slip about the new process of sending everything through Anna. Maxine's eyes had narrowed at that revelation.

Phillip got up from the chair and opened the door.

"Phillip?" Sara's voice was soft and a little pleading.

"Yes?"

"Is everything okay?"

"Yes, of course." He closed the door again and said, "You know Mara; she gets paranoid when the board members talk to staff. She also likes processes to stay in place. Good job on the speech." He said the last words without looking at her and walked out of the office.

Phillip instantly began planning how he would tell Mara. He was a little giddy because this was finally the moment he'd been waiting for. Finally he would be able to put Maxine where she belonged, and that was out of Mara's favour.

Since she'd been promoted, the woman acted as if she was too important. There were many qualified candidates for that job, but Phillip suspected that there was some fear that hiring an external white person over Maxine would look racist, and they couldn't run that risk. He knew that the board had made the decision, which was usually not the procedure. Hiring staff was part of operations, and that normally fell under Mara.

He also knew that Sharon had talked to one of the board members about her replacement. He suspected she told them to hire Maxine, which secured the woman's position. Still, Maxine acted as if she had been the most qualified candidate for the job.

It irked him every time he attended a meeting with her. Her high and mighty comments, the way she challenged others annoyed him. But he was quick to nod his head and agree with her when she talked about newcomers and developing programs and changing policies to meet their needs.

At first, he was horrified. Why would they change long-standing traditions to cater to people who just came into the country? Stop reciting the Lord's Prayer at board meetings? Saying *happy holidays* instead of *merry Christmas*? What was that all about? He wasn't asking the Muslims to stop celebrating Eid.

But as the newcomer population grew, he realized he needed to show that he could adapt. He was progressive after all. He believed in equal rights. So while he didn't champion the initiatives, he let Maxine bring them forward and then he agreed.

It had worked in his favour: Mara asked him to hire the diversity expert. She didn't ask Maxine. And Venah was his choice, not Maxine's, even though she was part of the interview panel.

Phillip was a patient man, and he knew that in time, Maxine's belief in her own power would cause her to slip. And when she did, he would be there. That time had come.

Mara looked up from her computer screen to see Phillip's Cheshire cat smile. He had information. She immediately ushered him inside her office and gestured for him to shut the door.

"So, I talked to Sara." He leaned in and said the words almost in a whisper.

"And? What did she say?"

"She told me that she did not talk to Joan. She admitted that she went to Maxine for the information in the speech."

"Maxine? Why? I thought she was going to work with Venah?"

"Well, that's what I thought too. I will need to speak to Venah about it."

Mara leaned back in her chair, her brows furrowed. Phillip expected her to be pleased about the opportunity to reprimand Maxine. But she sat there and said nothing. She was thinking. Finally, she spoke, very matter-of-factly: "So Maxine told Joan. I have seen her talking to Joan in the hallway and in the lunchroom. I will talk to her about it. Thanks."

Was she dismissing him? Phillip was a little surprised. Usually Mara would engage in a bit of gossip, bordering on slander. But she turned back to her computer, indicating that he needed to get up and leave.

Mara was already deep in thought before Phillip left her office.

So it was Maxine. She was sure of it. And she could almost envision how it happened. Maxine often made a point to talk to Joan and drop hints about certain staff members.

Sara was young, and although she was smart, she needed to pay her dues. Promotion would not come without hard work and certainly not just because of her ethnicity.

Her own career path had been a steep slope, with few hands helping her climb and more feet kicking her down. But it made her try harder, work more, and push herself. It toughened her skin and taught her the game of politics. In the end, she came out wiser, more secure. She created a life for herself that no one could take away. She had a partner who adored her and a job that was stable. She was respected, and she'd done it on her own.

Sara and Maxine needed to realize that handouts did no favours. There were all types of people in the world who were capable of anything. If she simply smiled and let her staff get ahead with just average work, how would they manage when they left Albatross and encountered reality? No one else would give handouts. No. Sara needed to learn that the workplace was tough. She needed to experience unfairness and learn how to maneuver around the roadblocks. And she needed to respect those in authority.

She'd worked with Sara on one project, and while the work wasn't bad, her attitude irritated her. It is never about good work. No one will notice the work. They will notice the behaviour, the attitude. The willingness to please and the ability to let insults and unreasonable expectations slide without crying unfairness. Sara's attitude indicated that she truly believed that if she worked hard, she would get ahead. There was no self-awareness as to who she was and how others saw her. Not only that, she was not a pleaser. She dared speak back when Mara pointed out flaws. She had actually tried to say that Mara misunderstood. That type of defiance of one's superiors would not help Sara in the working world.

And now Maxine had given Sara an advantage. This was not good. So Mara had to find a way to reverse Maxine's mistake. It was for Sara's own good. She would be helping the young woman in the long run.

She picked up the phone and hit the speed dial to call Joan on her cellphone. She would schedule a lunch.

Sara had mixed feelings when Phillip told her that Joan liked the speech. There was something about his tone that contradicted the compliment. It was only later in the week, when he called her into his office, that she realized there was an issue.

She sat on the edge of her chair and looked at Phillip. His eyes were more grey today than blue. Sara forced a smile against her fighting nerves.

"So how are you doing, Sara?"

"I'm good, thanks." She felt impatient as she waited for him to get to the point.

"That's good to hear, Sara. How are you doing with the speechwriting? Are you enjoying it?"

"Yes, I am. It's a lot of work, but I'm learning a lot."

"Good. Now, I told you that Joan liked the speech."

"Yes, that's great that she was happy."

"And we talked about Anna being the liaison, right?"

"Yes."

"Well, the reason I brought Anna into that conversation was because she feels you are not working as a team member."

"What?" The word came out without permission.

"Anna has been here for a long time Sara—longer than you have been. Perhaps your role has a more senior title, but Anna knows the organization and how it works."

The comments slapped Sara in the face.

"Yes, Phillip, I realize that Anna has been here a long time, but I don't understand what you mean. How have I not been working with her?"

"I can't get into details about what she said, Sara. It would only be a 'she-said, she-said' situation. What I am trying to do is bring forward some constructive criticism from your colleague."

He made little sense. But Sara heard the sternness in his voice and realized that pushing for a concrete example would be futile.

"So. When you worked on the speech, did you include Venah?"

So here it was—Venah. She got to him first.

"I met with her, and we talked. But she ..." Sara stopped herself as she heard the defensiveness in her voice.

"Yes?" Phillip's tone told her that no matter her defense, he had already made up his mind.

"We couldn't seem to agree. She felt as if I didn't have her experience and knowledge."

"Sara, Venah is the diversity and community expert. The role of the speechwriter is to take the information from the subject matter expert and turn it into effective copy."

"Yes, that is true. And that's what I kept telling her, but I couldn't get detailed information."

"She says you were not respectful of her role and that you challenged her on her expertise."

"No ... I did not ..." Again, she had to stop herself from sounding defensive. "I was trying to understand what she was saying. I wanted more information about the diversity initiatives so I could include facts in the speech, but she didn't seem to have those details."

"Well, she wants an apology. She felt that you were disrespectful."

Sara's eyes widened. She opened her mouth and, despite her desire to retain her composure, she heard herself protest. "An apology? I didn't do anything wrong."

Phillip's expression turned from stern to sheepish. He knew. He'd pushed her too far, and she was pulling out the card she'd been holding onto. It was time.

"If I must apologize to her, then I want an apology from her. For challenging my name, for telling me that I am ashamed of my ethnicity, and for the comments about speaking Hindi and wearing a sari." The words came rushing out in anger and suddenly there was silence as she stared, confused, at Phillip's crimson face.

"Okay, I will talk to her," he mumbled after what seemed like minutes. "Thanks."

Sara got up and walked straight to the foyer of the recreation centre, out the front doors, and into the courtyard. Only when she found herself inside the gazebo did she give the tears permission to come out. But they didn't. Instead, her mind shifted to the notebook. The one with the comments about incidents with colleagues and beside each one, the date and time and witnesses. It was a good directive from Giselle. Evidence, she'd said. Just in case.

About a week after the meeting with Phillip, she got an email asking for another meeting—this time, a representative from human resources was on the invite list.

The meeting took place in a room at the other end of the building late in the afternoon. When Sara walked in, Cynthia from human resources, Venah, and Phillip were already there. The purpose of the meeting was to openly discuss Venah's issue.

Cynthia opened the meeting, saying that they were there so the two women could recount their stories, come to a conclusion and hopefully an agreement.

Venah started with hers. "I had opened my office to Sara with the hope that we could work on the speech together. I was trying to provide my expertise about cultural and religious accommodations, and then she started challenging me. I felt very disrespected, and so I believe I need an apology for her unprofessionalism."

Sara wasn't really shocked by Venah's haughty tone and waited until it was her turn to talk. Cynthia asked Venah to elaborate on what happened during the meeting.

"She came into my office and challenged me. She said I was not an expert, and she started challenging me on my knowledge. I do not need to explain my programs to her." Her voice was dramatic, close to hysterical, and Sara rolled her eyes. As if realizing that there would be few facts from Venah, Cynthia asked Sara to recount her side of the story.

"Phillip asked me to meet with Venah to get some information about Albatross's diversity programs for a speech Joan would be giving. I wanted details for the speech because we need to have facts to back up our statements. But

Venah told me that I was not the expert, and she challenged me over my name and the fact that it is a shorter version of my given name."

Phillip and Cynthia looked a bit confused. No one knew her name was shortened; it wasn't indicated on her resume since she had been called Sara at birth. What did it matter anyway?

"Well, I was going to give you details of the programs, but you were not listening. And you were the one who told me your full name." Venah did not look at Sara.

"Sara, is this true?" Cynthia asked.

"Is what true?"

"Did Venah try to give you the information?"

"No. I kept asking, and she didn't have any details."

"You were rude and disrespectful, and you owe me an apology," Venah said curtly.

"I didn't do anything wrong. Frankly, Venah, since you started here, you have disrespected me. You have challenged my cultural background by asking me to wear a sari and speak Hindi, and you keep calling me by a name that I do not use. I have told you that my name is Sara. If anyone deserves an apology, it's me.".

Venah's eyes were on the table, a strange half smile on her face. She said nothing.

Cynthia piped up quickly. "Venah, I don't think that an apology is necessary here. It sounds to me like a clear situation of misunderstanding, so I would like to ask that this situation be resolved and that we move on from here."

Phillip nodded. "Yes, I believe that is a good idea." His face was red and expression anxious, and Sara hoped he was afraid that she would accuse him of making sari comments as well. The thought danced in her mind, and although she didn't have the courage to put Phillip on the stand, she felt a little satisfaction at his fear. As she was relishing the moment, Cynthia suddenly adjourned the meeting, saying that she was open to talk again if the two women felt the need. But she concluded that the situation was resolved and they could move forward professionally.

Sara realized that both Cynthia and Phillip wanted to get everyone out of the room immediately before any more comments surfaced. Sara was certain that this would be the last of the issues at work—perhaps now she could just continue with her job without harassment. But she was wrong.

A few days later, Phillip called her into his office. Cynthia was also there. They explained that they had to provide her with a letter of all of the complaints against her from other employees as well as Phillip's observations of her

191

productivity. He handed her the letter, his eyes staring down at it as Sara took it from him, turned, and left the room.

At her desk, she put the envelope containing the letter inside her purse, packed up her few personal items, and left. She wouldn't read it until she was home, and when she did, it revealed that she was being put on notice for her lack of teamwork and mistakes she'd made, including asking about the anniversary date of Albatross. This was the first notice, she read. He was giving her time to change her behaviour and work on improvements. Then her performance would be reviewed.

Sara folded the letter and put it back into the envelope and into the bottom drawer of her desk, under a pile of papers. She didn't want it in front of her. Logging onto her computer, she immediately went to her Facebook page and checked the updates. Some days, getting lost in other people's life stories could make her own more bearable.

Giselle posted a picture of her new shoes, which she recently purchased from DSW. Sara laughed. Giselle could afford Jimmy Choos, but always said that her Italian grandmother would come back to haunt her if she knew that her granddaughter spent five hundred dollars on a pair of frivolous gold sandals that would hurt her feet.

Photos of their last dinner drew her to Catherine's page, and the wide grins of her friends during happy times eased Sara's anxiety. Dogs, cats, Catherine was always posting cute photos of animals. And then there was a baby elephant with a caption that read "Crush." Sara clicked on the picture, and it took her to a website with photos of baby elephants, ropes tied tightly around their feet and secured to posts so that they could barely move. Their tiny heads leaning back, trunks flailing, ears flapping, eyes in shock and pain as they absorbed the sting of a whip. She couldn't look away. Photo after photo of baby elephants enduring beatings; Sara needed an explanation, so she scrolled down to the article.

Baby elephants are taken from their mothers when they are born and deprived of sleep, food, and water in a tortuous ritual called "the crush," which is meant to break their spirits so they can be controlled by their owners, who use them to provide rides for the tourists.

Shock hit her senses, and Sara closed the page, ran into the bathroom, stood over the toilet, and threw up. The taste of vomit and bile in her mouth forced her to gargle with water and wash the pain from her face. Exhausted and defeated, Sara lay down on the cold tile floor. What seemed like hours later, she got up and went into the bedroom, noting the darkness of the room. It was late, and she fell asleep.

The crying of a baby elephant as a whip lashed across its delicate face jolted her out of sleep. Sara sat up in bed, breathing heavily. She couldn't go back. She would call in sick tomorrow and maybe the rest of the week. Something inside her brain said that she should not go back to Albatross.

38

It took a week of hiding inside her apartment with sleepless nights and several bottles of wine before she decided to pick up the phone and call Giselle. She needed a straight shooter who could give her the best advice. Catherine would just console her, and pity would not help.

"Hey, babe, what's up? Haven't heard from you in a while. Been busy with that cute boyfriend of yours, huh?"

"Yeah, sort of."

"What's wrong, Sara? I can hear something in your voice."

"Giselle, I've taken sick leave from work. I couldn't handle it anymore … I need your advice."

"Hey, sure, no problem. What are you doing tonight? I can leave at six and meet you at your place. Actually, let's meet for dinner. That pub around the corner from your place with the great poutine? I'll pick you up."

Giselle was a litigator who handled divorce cases, and she knew the law. Since the day that Sara vented about Ashleigh's lead role on the environmental project, Giselle had replaced her tough, sarcastic comments with ones that were quieter, practical. Their dinners together became a source of comfort. Sara found herself talking more about her job, as her two friends listened quietly, injecting comments that gave Sara the external views she needed.

Poutine ordered, Giselle leaned back and sipped a glass of red and listened to Sara's account of the meeting with HR.

"If you made mistakes, the employer has a right to reprimand you. The letter is just their way of providing you with that notice."

"Sure, but what about the mistakes that Venah or Anna make? And Ashleigh, she makes lots of small errors. But they have never been reprimanded."

"Not that you know of. Perhaps behind closed doors. But even still, this is about you, not them."

"I know. But what about the sari comments and chastising me for not speaking Hindi?"

"Yes, that's a human rights violation, and you could have a case there."

"But it's my word against theirs, right?"

"Yes, unless you have witnesses. Maxine maybe?"

"I am not sure. She didn't hear the comments."

"But you've kept the journal that I suggested, right?"

"Yeah, I have it. Still, I don't understand how my notes would be evidence. I mean, anyone can write notes at any time."

"Yes, that's true. But you have times, dates, and quotations, which may be more than they have. A journal holds more credibility than you might think, as long as you kept it up with details."

"Yeah, I've been keeping it up to date."

"I think you need to consult a lawyer, Sara. A good employment lawyer can handle this case and get you a proper settlement. Unless of course you want to go back to Albatross? A lawyer can negotiate a deal where you return under different circumstances."

"No, I can't go back. I can't work there anymore."

"Okay. Perhaps you need to take some time and get your head together. In the meantime, I know someone who can help. We went to law school together, and he's smart and tough. He's cute too." She added the last part with a wink and reached over and squeezed Sara's arm.

"Well, that's just what I need, a cute lawyer. You know I already have Richard!"

"Yes, Mr. Wonderful. But a cute lawyer is better than a not-so-cute lawyer. But listen to me, now I'm violating the human rights code. A person should not be judged by their race, religion, sexual orientation, or gender."

"Ha ha, I won't report you. Hey listen, thanks for this, Giselle. I feel like I'm being such a whiner though. Going to a lawyer for this kind of nonsense; it makes no sense."

"I know. But these things happen when you're interacting with humans in a competitive work environment. An objective solicitor is there to help."

"I didn't think it was competitive. I thought I was just doing my job."

"I know, babe. We are all just trying to get through our days by doing the best we can. Sometimes, that's not enough, and I'm sorry you went through that. You seemed so happy there."

"I'm not sure," Sara sighed. "I really loved working with Maxine and Ruth, but the constant struggle and the feeling of being on the outside all the time— sometimes as if I wasn't even there."

A waft of melted cheese cracked the mood as the waitress put down two steaming bowls of poutine in front of them. Giselle took a sip of wine and smiled at her friend. "Bon appétit!"

As Sara picked up her fork, the thought settled in her mind. She would hire a lawyer and ask Albatross to pay her a severance so she could leave quietly. True to her word, Giselle passed along the number for Aaron Finlay, and Sara made the appointment for the following week.

Sara avoided Richard for a little while. She needed some time to adjust after leaving Albatross, so she told him that she had the flu and was at home recovering. It wasn't really a lie. She was not well. But she continued to answer his texts and even talked to him on the phone a couple of times, keeping the conversation brief. Her voice was soft and dull and according to Richard, she sounded sick.

For Sara, there was an illness inside her body—a dull ache that rendered her physically weak and emotionally drained. She was useless.

She ate very little, but when she did, it was grilled cheese, chased down by mouthfuls of cheap, red wine, which numbed her brain and forced her to sleep for a few hours before she woke in the middle of the night. Then she would roll over on her back as her mind raced in circles around questions and confusion. When the sun rose and threw shards of light through her blinds, she felt sleep pushing her eyelids closed, and she would rest, getting up finally at ten to sit numbly in her apartment until it was time to do it all over again.

The lawyer's office had leather couches in the waiting area, and an older lady with coiffed blond hair sat behind a dark mahogany desk. As Sara sat nervously on the edge of one of the couches, she wondered if she would be able to afford the fees.

She was nervous. Was this the right thing to do? She hadn't told Richard because she was uncertain about what his reaction would be. Would he be disappointed in her? Or, worse, embarrassed for her?

The memories started to flow into her mind, triggering the anxiety inside her body, her stomach, her heart. It had been a month since she filed for sick leave. She remembered speaking with her doctor, who didn't even try to talk her out of it. The physician's eyes had been filled with concern as she sat silently and listened. Then she took out her notepad and wrote a letter stating that Sara needed some time off.

She couldn't even take the letter to the office. Instead, she asked them to email her the necessary documents, and she would mail them back with the letter. Human resources at Albatross didn't argue, and the email came just an hour later.

"Sara?" A male voice shook her back to the present, and she looked up into the hazel eyes of a handsome face. His curly red hair was short and his features bold, framed by a light spattering of freckles. He looked mixed. She smiled and stood up.

"Hi." She reached out and shook his extended hand.

"I understand that you're a close friend of Giselle's." Aaron chatted as he escorted her into a meeting room with a round wooden table and soft, green chairs. Pale yellow walls created a background for a vibrant watercolour of flowers, and bright sunlight streamed through the room. Sara imagined the scent of spring in the air and felt her body relax into her chair as she placed the thick folder onto the table.

Aaron's eyes flickered to the folder as he leaned in slightly and started the conversation.

"So, thanks for coming in, Sara. As you know, this consultation is to get more details about your case, and then we can determine the next steps, whether you want to negotiate a settlement or move forward to litigation."

He was very formal but seemed slightly nervous. It made Sara a little uncertain. Was he the right lawyer to handle her case?

"Okay, I understand," she said.

"Great," he said, leaning back in his chair. "Now, I've reviewed the information you sent me, but I just need to hear the story again from your perspective, which will help me fill in some gaps about the situation, so I can advise you better."

Sara suddenly felt overwhelmed. She wanted to tell her story but her emotions felt like a cap blocking the words in her throat; she had to take a deep breath before she could begin. But where to begin? Before her mind could form a strategy, her voice pushed forward.

"Okay. I left my job. My boss gave me a letter putting me on notice ... he said the staff had complained, but they were making me work long hours; they promoted my colleague over me and kept saying I was making mistakes, but they weren't my mistakes ... they asked if I would wear a sari, speak Hindi ..." Her voice trailed off as she saw the confusion in Aaron's eyes.

When she stopped talking, he smiled and leaned in a little. "Okay, so you quit?"

"No, I went on sick leave. I couldn't stay there. I talked to my doctor, and she said I needed to take some stress leave for a while."

"Okay, so what led you to make an appointment with your doctor?"

His tone was calm, and Sara realized she'd been talking very fast, gasping for air in between words. She took another breath and looked into his kind eyes, and she recounted the meeting and the letter in detail.

"Okay, so let's backtrack a bit. Tell me about what led to the meeting with HR."

As Sara regurgitated the story, she felt emotions rising in her throat. She swallowed several times and heard her voice cracking. But she managed to keep her composure, partly because Aaron was writing as she spoke, his eyes firmly planted on the paper. And, when he did look at her, his face was void of emotion.

"You gave me notes on those details?"

"Yes, I included all of the notes that I took while at Albatross."

"Do you have anything in writing about the sari comments, or was anyone else privy to these comments?"

"I have my own notes, but that's all."

Aaron wrote something down, but Sara knew that it would be her word against everyone at Albatross's. Maybe it was futile.

How she would tell Richard was another issue that she wasn't ready to face. Would he see her differently and possibly even leave her? Sara wondered if she had the strength to handle losing him as well as her job.

Finally Aaron began to speak again. Yes, she had a case. He needed to further review all of the information she gave him, but by the sounds of it, a severance was possible. He had previously negotiated settlements and this case, while troubling, was not uncommon. The amount that she could get, however, was still up in the air. She'd only been with Albatross for two years, and according to employment standards, companies were required to provide one week per year of employment. However, given the sari comments and the fact that Anna was promoted over her, a senior employee, the company could be forced to give more. A few months perhaps, Aaron suggested.

That didn't seem like enough to Sara. She had rent to pay and groceries to buy, and she had to live. She shook his hand, and as she walked out of the office, she started to wonder if she had made a big deal out of nothing. People got notices from work all the time, and they just dealt with it. Maybe she needed to go back and work on her performance. Maybe Phillip was right—she wasn't working well with either Anna or Venah, and so what did she expect? She had to improve her teamwork skills.

But by the time she reached her driveway, the thoughts that had been rolling around in her head formed a perfect sphere, and the truth was clear. She had done nothing wrong. Her mind was set on the decision—she would fight.

39

Phillip stared at the email, his eyes fixed on the law firm's logo in the signature at the bottom. Then he stared at the sentences indicating there was an attached letter. Slowly, he got up from his chair and closed his office door. Sitting back down, he stared at the attachment without opening it.

He decided to google the name of the law firm, and he found that it was a small firm, in a sketchy part of the city. Boutique wasn't a word he would use, but more like independent. Interesting. It peaked his confidence, and he directed the cursor over the attachment.

But he froze and quickly closed the email. Time for a coffee.

As he exited the office in search of a hot caffeine jolt, he ran right into Mara. Her eyes were wild, and she held a piece of paper in her hand. Instinctively, he backed into his office and shut the door.

He sat down on one of the armchairs and faced Mara. She was grasping the letter tightly, and she was visibly shaken. He had never seen her this ruffled before, and he found himself quiet.

"I got this today. It was in my mail. Sara has hired a lawyer and is accusing us of human rights violations and is asking for a settlement so she can leave Albatross. Did you know about this?"

"I haven't opened any emails yet, but I remember seeing something with a lawyer's address." His voice was calm despite the anxiety that was rising inside him.

"What happened?"

"I talked to Sara about Anna's title change and also the fact that she needs to be more of a team player." He paused. "I also gave her a written warning."

"Warning? In writing? I didn't see a letter of warning."

"I don't know that we talked about it. I didn't think you wanted to be bothered with trivial staff issues. She *does* report to me," he said cautiously.

"Yes, she does. But in a case like this, I need to be aware. What is this accusation about the sari? Did someone tell her that she needed to wear a sari for an event? The letter states that both you and Venah asked her to wear one."

Phillip hesitated.

"Phillip?"

"Venah talked about the two of them dressing traditionally for events so they could represent the diversity of Albatross. I may have agreed with that suggestion."

"Did you tell her that she needed to wear a sari?" Mara repeated the question.

"I don't remember saying it in those words. I agreed with Venah's suggestion, as I would with any suggestion that could be beneficial to promoting diversity in our organization."

Mara looked directly at him. Even though his answer made sense, he knew she saw through him. He also knew that the comment could be considered a human rights violation. By the look on Mara's face, Phillip understood that Albatross could be at risk, and that he, the head of public relations, was facing serious accusations.

The director rose to her feet and put her hand on the doorknob. "I'll need to contact our legal advisor. I will set up a meeting." And she walked out of the office, morphing back into her usual stoic demeanour.

Anna felt trouble in the air when Phillip came into her office and closed the door. Sara would be off on leave for a little while, he explained in a very professional tone, and he wanted Anna to take over her projects and assign some work to Ashleigh, whose contract had recently been extended.

He didn't elaborate on the purpose behind the leave, and Anna knew better than to probe. Her instincts told her why Sara was away, and secretly she felt relieved. When Phillip gave her the promotion, she suspected that it would cause some upset in the department.

Anna knew that her promotion would affect Sara the most. After all, now she was in a management role, and although she earned it, it appeared as if Sara was passed over. Perhaps she would quit. Sara made her nervous, but even more so, her attitude was off-putting. Her mouth smiled, but she always seemed to be judging everyone with her patronizing nods of agreement in meetings and her arrogant comments about her own work.

If Sara was upset about Anna's promotion, then she could take it up with Phillip. But he wouldn't change his mind about it, nor would he promote Sara.

They couldn't have two managers—it would look foolish, like they were creating jobs and sticking manager titles on them so they could look important.

The leave wasn't for personal reasons. It had to do with work. Anna was sure of this much. But surely, the young woman could not have taken leave just because she was upset about the promotion? That would be ridiculous and yet so thrilling. Imagine, Sara jealous of her.

Richard rolled over and stroked his girlfriend's dark, silky hair. Her body rose slightly with every soft breath. He was glad that she'd finally fallen into a deep sleep, but as he looked at her face, he saw the wrinkled forehead of someone who was in distress.

She rarely talked to him about her issues. The only time he ever saw her vocalize her emotions was that night at the bar, when Maeve brought the redhead over to meet him. He knew that Maeve was trying to set him up because, for some reason, she didn't understand why he would be interested in Sara.

He realized how it must have looked when he was sitting at the table with the two women. Sara had every right to be jealous, but he couldn't have admitted Maeve's intentions at the time. It would only have made the situation worse, and Sara even more insecure. So he had downplayed it.

The comment about preferring redheads had been a stupid one, and he was waiting for the right moment to rectify that notion in Sara's mind. He didn't like redheads and wasn't sure why he would even say something like that.

Sara had not brought up the incident again, but he couldn't help but wonder if her change in mood had something to do with him. She wouldn't say.

All he knew was that she was taking some time off work to sort out some things and decide what she wanted to do in her career. He'd asked about her reasons, but she wouldn't provide any details.

He remembered the first time they met. It was at the local coffee shop around the corner from his place. They had been chatting on a dating site for about a week—it was time to either move on to someone else or agree to a face-to-face. He'd been chatting online with several women at the time, but he knew that meeting Sara was a given. She looked pretty and laid back in her pictures, and he loved the way she wrote.

But the most alluring part of her was her dark skin. Flawless in the pictures and even more so when he met her. Like a sheath of silky liquid, milk chocolate that glistened in the light.

Growing up, he always found himself attracted to the girls in his classes who looked the least like the women in his family. His sister and mother were both blondes with pale, pink skin. So when he first kissed a girl in grade five, he opened his eyes, and when he saw the faded freckles against the white skin, he pulled back, envisioning his cousin Emily. He turned around and left her standing alone in the park where they had met an hour earlier.

After this happened, Richard started to wonder if he was gay. He didn't think he was attracted to boys, but the girls with the pale skin and freckles didn't appeal to him either. Perhaps that was why he shied away from kissing that girl.

And then, a month later, he saw her. Her family had just moved from Kenya, and the teacher introduced her as Niara. Her skin was dark, and her eyes were large and round. Richard was entranced. She was beautiful, delicate, and he wanted to kiss her. He welcomed the desire that she stirred inside him, and even though he never dated or kissed her, he always considered her his first.

Sara moved in her sleep, and the memory of Niara faded as Richard jumped back to the present. He moved closer to her warm body and circled her with his arm. Whatever she was going through would come out when she was ready. For now, he would protect her. He loved her.

40

Anxiety became a constant. Sara spent much of her time in front of her laptop, staring at the screen. When late afternoon came, she would venture into the kitchen to pull something together only in an effort to stop the stomach rumbles.

She didn't tell her parents that she was on stress leave. They wouldn't understand the kind of stress she was encountering. Everyone had to work, pleasant or not, and unless there was a physical illness, no one in her family ever took sick leave.

She could hear her father's voice: "So they promoted someone over you. It happens all the time, Sara. Do you know how many guys have been promoted to manager, and I have been there longer than them? Be thankful that you have a good job."

True statements and yet she couldn't accept it. Anna's promotion was disappointing, but the comments about the sari, the way Phillip ushered Adam away from her, the long hours that were just not acknowledged or appreciated. Only Maxine valued her. Or did she?

Just after she officially signed up for sick leave, Sara decided to talk with a counsellor who was part of the employee assistance program offered by Albatross. Perhaps she was missing something; perhaps she was just being paranoid, and maybe the counsellor could provide an objective point of view.

The woman in her fifties with dyed red hair was based out of an Albatross recreation centre and counselled staff as well as community members. She was well qualified, and she also knew the players, which Sara suspected was the reason she was nodding in agreement during her explanation.

"So you have taken some time off to get your thoughts together?" The counsellor's name was Rose, and her voice was calm, without judgement.

"Yes, I took sick leave. It seemed the most appropriate thing to do since I just couldn't ... "

"I know; it's okay. This is what short-term benefits are for. It's good to get your mental health back to a place where you can function in a good state."

"But I can't go back ... I mean, I'm not sure if I will be able to go back."

"Well, that is your choice. But don't make that decision right now. Take some time and think about it."

"I don't know what I did wrong ... I don't think they want me back." Sara sounded shaken.

"Perhaps you didn't do anything wrong. I can understand why you would be upset if someone asked you to wear traditional clothing. And having someone promoted over you can be unsettling. It's natural to feel slighted."

"Maybe I wasn't doing a great job after all. Otherwise, he wouldn't have promoted Anna."

"Don't go there. This is not about that; this is about how you feel right now. They've been there a long time and have been doing whatever they wanted." The last statement stopped as quickly as it was blurted out. Sara looked at Rose's face, shocked at the judgement. Rose changed the subject. "When we are emotionally wounded, we tend to be hard on ourselves. Blaming yourself will not help."

"I'm just trying to be realistic. Maybe I could have done something better."

"Maybe. And yes, it's good to reflect. But you need to be positive and look after yourself, so you can get better."

As Sara drove home after the hour long session, she could not help but wonder about the comment that Rose blurted out. Was it on purpose? What history did she know about Phillip and Anna? Had this happened before?

She mentioned the conversation to Aaron, but he didn't say much. It was speculation.

It was only a week after meeting with Aaron that he sent her a first draft of the letter. As she opened it and looked at the harsh words, she felt anxiety. He was accusing Phillip of asking her to wear a sari and supporting Venah in her chastisement of Sara for not speaking Hindi, which was a human rights violation. In addition, he had passed Sara over for promotion and did not provide a fair recruitment process. Despite all of this treatment, Sara had been asked to apologize to her colleagues for what they deemed was unfair treatment of them.

"It sounds so harsh," she said to Aaron over the phone.

"Well, it is supposed to generate a reaction. This is your recollection of what occurred, is it not?"

"Yes, but what if they say it's not true..." In Sara's mind, this was a given.

"Well then, I would like to leave it as is." Aaron was firm, but gentle.

"Okay, sure. I trust you."

"Great, who should I send it to?"

Sara gave Mara's name along with Phillip's. Aaron said he would email them the letter, copying their assistants in the process.

When she hung up the phone, Sara sat on the couch for a while. What would happen when they got the letter? What would Natasha and Irene think when they read it? Although she knew this was what she wanted, Sara could not help the sick feeling inside her stomach. It was really going to happen. She could not look at the letter again and decided not to check her email for the rest of the day. Instead, she got into bed and curled up in the fetal position under the covers.

Waiting. She knew that the email would have been received by now. Aaron had indicated that they could go to litigation, but the idea of confronting Phillip and Anna in a room, face to face, was too much to bear. They could lie, Aaron said. It happens all the time. Or they could say that they didn't remember. That happened as well.

So then, why go to litigation? It wasn't like in the movies. There was no background music for motivation, nor was there a bold witness to come forward and corroborate her story. Maxine, maybe … although, would she stick her neck out and put her job on the line? Call her, Aaron suggested. Maybe she would.

What would she say to Maxine? That she was the victim of discrimination? Sara couldn't get the idea cemented in her mind. All she knew was that she was tired and she was discouraged, and she was not even sure that she was cut out for another job—any job.

She agreed to see Richard on the weekend, realizing that she could only put him off for so long. Besides, she needed the comfort and missed the way his blue eyes softened her. He showed up at her place with a bag of groceries in one hand and a bouquet of flowers in the other. She couldn't help but smile when she opened the door to her apartment. In usual Richard fashion, he leaned in and kissed her as he handed her the bouquet.

She had never talked to him about the real reason she was on leave, so she didn't tell him about the legal case. It would ruin their evening, and all she wanted was to curl up in his arms. Dinner would be okay as well, since she hadn't eaten all day.

"I thought I would make dinner tonight," he said, walking into her tiny kitchen and unpacking the bag. Sara saw crusty bread, chicken breasts, mushrooms, onions, and peppers. Her stomach instinctively grumbled. She hadn't eaten a full meal in a few days and the thought of chicken cooked with a mix of savoury veggies with bread and butter sparked her appetite.

"I brought some red wine." Richard held out a bottle of Henry of Pelham baco noir, and Sara smiled as she took the bottle and opened the drawer for the corkscrew. "I know red doesn't really go with chicken, but I am not a fan of white. And you aren't either, right?" He knew her well.

Her eyes didn't leave him as he took over her tiny kitchen. She didn't want to talk. It was far more peaceful to watch Richard as he rolled up his sleeves, washed his hands, and started preparing the meal.

Sara sipped wine and watched as he pounded the chicken breasts, seasoned them with salt, pepper, and garlic, and set them aside to marinate for a few minutes. Rummaging in the top drawer, Richard pulled out a knife and started chopping the vegetables. He julienned the peppers and then sliced the mushrooms and onions. She swallowed the wine and thought for a moment. Mushrooms. The gum in her brain felt sticky, and she stared as the blade slipped through each one. Swigging back a gulp of wine, Sara shook her head, dislodging the gum. Soon, it would be gone.

"What are you making?" She managed a question as the wine seeped into her senses.

"My version of chicken piccata." He smiled at her, eyes twinkling.

"Mmmm … sounds great!" She meant it and felt the wine hit her empty stomach, sending a wave of relaxation through her body.

She watched as he pan-fried the chicken and set it aside. Then he sautéed the onions, peppers, and mushrooms, and put that aside. He put some butter in the pan, added some white wine vinegar, capers, and then some lemon juice to make a sauce. He put the veggie mixture into the sauce and then poured the whole thing over top of the chicken breasts that lay in the dish.

It was a delicious meal. Every bite of the succulent chicken soaked in the buttery lemon sauce filled her taste buds. She pulled apart the bread, buttered each piece and balanced sautéed, savory vegetables on top, and popped them into her mouth, embracing the full, rich taste.

Richard watched her and smiled, and then she realized she was eating as if she were at home with her parents. It was as if her mom had just made baigan choka, and she was scooping up mashed, garlicky eggplant with warm pieces of handmade roti. She paused for a minute, wondering if she came across unsophisticated, but his eyes were filled with affection. "It's so good," she said. "Thanks."

"Sure. I'm glad you are enjoying it."

"I didn't know that you were such a great cook. Did your mom teach you?"

"Yes, a little. But I worked in a kitchen in university. It helped pay the bills for a couple of years. Plus, I was fed really well. Good gig."

"That is a great gig. I wish I had done something like that. I can cook a bit, but I've never made anything like this."

"That's okay ... I don't mind being the cook."

As Sara ate, she looked down at two slices of red pepper on her plate, both curled side by side in a pool of butter; off to the side lay a lone mushroom slice, shades of brown and black separated from the twin red curls.

"Something wrong?" Richard's voice jolted her. "Is there something wrong with the veggies?"

The words stuck in her throat. The sight of the vegetables on the plate was familiar, and yet she wasn't sure how. It seemed like minutes before she choked out the answer, "No, they're delicious."

"You've eaten all of them, except for those few."

"Richard, what do you prefer? Peppers or mushrooms?"

"I like them both. Why?"

Sara looked down at her plate again. Maybe he did like them both. Maybe he, like most men, liked all vegetables; he didn't have to choose one over the other.

"But if you could choose one, which one would it be?"

"Mmmm ... I really like mushrooms," he said. "There are all kinds of exotic mushrooms. These ones aren't just regular mushrooms—they're porcini mushrooms that I got from the health food grocery on College. So they're special."

Sara looked up into his eyes and smiled. He'd put a lot of effort into the meal because he knew she was going through a difficult time. He'd stopped probing after a while, and she realized that she'd been unfair in withholding the information and not opening up to him.

She'd been uncertain about his feelings for her. At first, she couldn't dismiss the notion that she was just a passing fancy, a brown girl to have a fling with until he was ready for a real commitment with someone of his own race, perhaps someone with alabaster skin and light brown freckles on her shoulders. But now, it seemed ridiculously insecure.

Suddenly, she realized that there was nothing to fear. Her comfort level with Richard had evolved naturally, seamlessly, and she hadn't been fully aware of it until just now, as she speared both peppers and popped them into her mouth, saving the last mushroom to end the lovingly prepared meal. For the first time in a long time, Sara allowed herself to relax.

"Richard, I want to tell you why I am really off from work."

He looked into her eyes and smiled, and she started to talk.

41

The picture that accompanied the article was a good one. Mayree usually felt uncomfortable posing, but the newspaper had a professional photographer who seemed to find the exact second that she wasn't aware, capturing a natural moment. They were, after all, telling her story, and she couldn't hide behind words and be anonymous anymore.

Filing the human rights claim had been a hard decision. She would still be at work while the tribunal investigated the claim, which meant seeing Tina every day. But she reassured herself that the claim wasn't against Tina, and that she had no real connection to the board members. When they attended meetings or events, Mayree knew she could easily hold her head up and do her job without acknowledging the tension.

But then there was Mara.

The idea of facing the stone-eyed executive director was frightening. She knew that Mara would resist the claim and drag it out and, furthermore, she would be very offended. Mara was powerful and would use her position to fight the claim, destroying any credibility that Mayree had. Winning seemed almost impossible. But when she met with the lawyer and presented all of the facts that she'd collected over the years, he urged her to file. It would be a matter of public record, and perhaps it would force Albatross's hand into a settlement.

The outcome was uncertain. Mayree could state that she wanted a facility director role as a remedy, if the claim went through. But the organization could draw things out, and there were so many loopholes. Albatross could say that there was nothing available, or they could put her in a place that was very far away from where she lived or very difficult to manage. Perhaps the best outcome would be a settlement and some satisfaction in the process, knowing that her claim would build awareness among the board of directors and prompt some change in the hiring practices. Deep down, Mayree knew that her hopes of being promoted after being with Albatross for fifteen years would not materialize.

It was a fact that all of the facility directors were Caucasian, and yet she had still tried to break into that circle. Mayree worked her way up to assistant faculty director after working in three different community centres as a youth program manager. She also spoke Punjabi, Hindi, and French, and she founded a drop-in program for South Asian seniors. It was a service for seniors who so often spent their days at home alone, watching the slow hands of the clock. Some would be waiting for their grandchildren to arrive on a school bus, so they could begin their work as caretakers until parents returned home from work.

Mayree knew many seniors in her community lived this lonely existence. So she initiated the program, which provided seniors with fitness classes, social events, and community lunches to enjoy together. It was a ground-breaking program for Albatross, and although she was recognized for her contribution, it did little to help her secure a leadership role.

It wouldn't have been as upsetting if it weren't for the fact that promotions always went to those who were junior in experience, fair haired, and privileged.

The rejection always came in the form of a formal, templated letter with Mara's signature. There was never a telephone call and no acknowledgement about the decision from Mara when they crossed paths at Albatross events.

When Phillip's friend got the last FD role, Mayree decided it was time to take action. Janine, the woman who beat her, had been a youth program manager and had only been with Albatross for five years. Prior to that, she had worked as a supply teacher and had been unsuccessful at getting a full-time teaching role.

But her experience in teaching helped push her to the top of the list—that was the explanation that Cynthia, the human resources manager, had given Mayree when she challenged the decision.

"What about my experience with Albatross? I have been here for fifteen years, and six of them in an assistant FD position. Doesn't that count for anything?" Mayree had tried not to sound hysterical, but she had gotten frustrated at Cynthia's stoic expression and disinterested responses.

"Yes, they do. You were a very strong candidate. But the other candidate was the more suitable fit."

"Suitable fit? I'm not sure I understand the term. Can you elaborate on the requirements for 'fit'?

Cynthia refused the bait. "Mayree, you are a good assistant FD, and there will be many more opportunities. I encourage you to apply again."

Cynthia's canned message indicated that it was time to end the meeting. So Mayree put on her professional face, smiled, and thanked the manager for her time. She left work, resisting the urge to confront Mara in her office. But when she got home and talked to her husband, he was outraged.

"It's time to call Rohan," Arjun said quietly.

Rohan was a family friend who was an employment lawyer. Over the course of his career, he had outed many employers for discriminatory practices.

"Okay, let's invite him for dinner." Mayree was determined, especially with the encouragement of her husband.

And that's how it began a year ago. And now, she was no longer at Albatross, having taken sick leave. It had been more difficult than she imagined.

She had talked to Tina and mentioned that she was going to file a claim, fully anticipating that Tina would understand. Sure, given her position, Mayree did not expect her to actively support the claim or get involved. But she believed that Tina would accept the decision and just continue on with her job as if nothing was going on. After all, the claim did not mention or affect Tina in any way.

At first, Tina seemed unruffled. Her eyes had widened a bit when Mayree spilled the news over frothy cappuccinos in a café far from Albatross. But she nodded and then leaned in, and, as predicted, inquired about her name in the claim. Mayree smiled, put her hand gently on her superior's, and said, "Absolutely not. You have been wonderful to work with. You were the one who gave me the support I needed to launch the seniors' drop-in program. This is just a formal claim to prompt an investigation into my failed attempts at moving into a leadership role. I am convinced that the process was flawed somehow. And sadly, it feels like discrimination."

Tina's pale eyes darkened a little as she sat back in her chair.

"Okay, then. You know that I cannot get involved, but you still have a job at Albatross, and as long as the claim does not hinder your work in any way, I am sure it will be fine. I would ask that you not share this news with the staff, since this kind of action can make some people nervous."

Mayree wanted the staff to know, but decided it was best that it did not come from her. She'd gotten along well with most of the staff, and there had been a few offline discussions about how it was not easy for visible minorities to move into leadership positions. A few had commented that Mayree had done well to make it as an assistant FD—she was the only person of colour who had managed to break into such a role.

But, for Mayree, it wasn't enough.

After filing the human rights claim, she and Rohan were enjoying a cup of tea and reviewing their strategy, and he suggested that she may want to call up a reporter from one of the city's dailies. Rohan knew a particular whistleblower who would use the freedom of information process to get a copy of the claim and perhaps write a story that could ignite a fire under Albatross's leadership.

Leaking the story to the media was not something Mayree had considered. Tina had asked her to keep it quiet so as not to create negativity or fear among the staff, but if someone happened to read it in the paper as they sipped their morning coffee, it wouldn't be her fault.

She thought about the idea for a few weeks. It would take weeks for the claim to be reviewed by the Human Rights Tribunal, and even then, it could be rejected. But the fact was the claim would be accessible in the meantime. She decided to contact the reporter.

Now, as she skimmed the article without actually comprehending the words, Mayree realized how long the past year and a half had seemed, and how much had changed.

Soon after the claim was filed, there was little change in Tina or the staff. If they knew about the claim, no one asked, and Mayree didn't share, as was her promise to Tina. But, along the way, something changed. Tina started declining lunch invitations and began saying that she was too busy for coffee. When Mayree met with Tina in her office, they went through work items and then Tina would get up and walk around her desk, saying that she had work to do or another meeting to attend. It was obvious—Tina wanted to distance herself.

Mayree was certain that when the claim was submitted to Mara, there had been a discussion. Of course, Tina feared for her own job, and it was just natural survival tactics. But it was hurtful.

So she decided it was best not to keep in touch with Tina when she took short-term leave. If there were work-related questions, Mayree insisted that Tina could reach out, but she knew that there would be no questions.

That was almost a year ago. She had managed to survive at work for just over five months, and now she was staring at her story in the newspaper—her picture on the front page. Albatross was being accused of systemic discrimination. The Human Rights Tribunal had reviewed the claim with all of the evidence, including her notes, and decided to move forward and conduct an investigation into Albatross. And now, the entire company, as well as the entire city, would know.

42

She could go back to being a reporter. The thought rolled around in Sara's mind as she perused articles online. Headlines were different these days, she noted. Racier, more sensationalistic. She moved the cursor to her favourites bar and clicked on the tab for the *Community Reporter*. That was when she saw the headline:

Human Rights Tribunal to investigate Albatross Community Services for discriminatory hiring practices

It took a minute before the words sunk in. The woman in the picture, standing in front of the community centre, looked familiar. Sara clicked on the link and began to read the story. The woman, Mayree Grewal, was quoted. Her allegations were troubling—she had applied for the position of facility director twice and had not been successful; she had many years of experience, and yet the promotions were given to those with less experience but lighter skin and Anglo names. There had been obstacle after obstacle, the article read.

Sara read the entire story and then just sat in front of her computer. There it was. The brown elephant in the room had stood up and announced its presence.

The response came quicker than Sara had anticipated. When she looked up the name of the assistant facility director on Albatross's website, there was no email address listed. But Sara knew how the addresses were formed, so she typed out mgrewal@albatross.ca, wrote a short email, and hit send. She simply introduced herself, mentioned the media story, and indicated that she too had some work-related problems at Albatross. It didn't feel right to include details.

There was no telling how the woman would respond—if she would respond. Sara was a stranger, and perhaps there had been many emails from people who read the story. After all, it was on the front page of the local paper.

It was a few hours later that Sara received the response, which included a telephone number and a request to speak in person. As she stared at the screen, Sara felt frozen for a moment. She could call Mayree, but what would she say?

Albatross had not yet responded to Aaron's letter, so there was no reason she couldn't talk about it. He advised her to use good judgement about what she said, but until there was a signed contract with a clause forbidding her to speak, she was free to tell her side of the story.

Now that an opportunity presented itself, Sara wasn't sure what to do. Was her story the same as Mayree's? Sara closed her computer and slipped into a pair of flats. She was feeling restless, and she was out of wine. It was a good time to take a walk over to the liquor store on Bloor Street.

There was a slight breeze flowing through the late summer air, signalling the transition to fall. The street was strangely quiet, the way it was during the day when people were locked away in office buildings. She looked at the time and thought about her old office at Albatross. She would be sitting at her computer, perhaps working on a press release or a project with Maxine.

When she made the decision to go on sick leave, she had called Maxine and told her. Maxine listened quietly and then spoke after a short pause. "Sara, I'm sorry this has happened. But I have to admit, my dear, that I am not surprised. You and I both know how this organization works. Phillip would never have allowed you to get close to the board chair. Putting Anna in the middle stops you from climbing over him."

"What do you mean? I don't want Phillip's job ..."

"Well, maybe not now. But you would have grown into a professional who could have replaced him. And with the need for diversity, you would be a good candidate."

"But Mara would never consider that option."

"Maybe not Mara but perhaps Joan and the rest of the board. Look, Sara, I'm not saying that would have happened, but ever since the whole diversity initiative came about, much of the leadership at Albatross has been feeling protective of their jobs and their normal routines. No one likes change—you know that."

"Yeah, I suppose. But look at you. You're one of the few managers here, and you seem so unruffled, untouchable really."

Maxine laughed. "It wasn't always like this, Sara. I had to fight every step of the way. And don't think that the struggle has stopped. Just because I changed my hair, doesn't mean they have accepted me fully."

"Your hair?"

"Yeah, I used to straighten it."

"Oh right, I've seen pictures of you and Sharon. But I'm not sure I know what you mean. What does your hair have to do with anything?"

"I worked in the field, at a rec centre, for a few years before I decided that I wanted something more. When I was looking to transition to an office role, I had braids down to my shoulders. Long braids of my real hair that I loved."

Sara tried to picture Maxine with long braids as she listened to her story.

"And I got lots of interviews, but I wasn't getting offers, even for entry-level roles. I complained to my mother, worried that I'd spent years in school, getting a master's degree, and now I couldn't even get a job as an administrative assistant. And you know what she said to me?"

"What did she say?"

"She told me to take out my braids and straighten my hair. And when I asked why, she said, 'Maxine, your braids make you look too ethnic, too black. Straighten your hair, girl, stop wearing big earrings, and start dressing conservatively. White people don't want a black girl in the office who looks too ethnic.'"

Maxine's candor pushed Sara into silence. She opened her mouth, but no words were brave enough to surface.

"I started straightening my hair from that day on. And it helped me land the job here at Albatross. So when I started the job, I kept straightening my hair, damaging it, really, until just after I got the manager's job."

"And that's when you grew the afro?" Sara's voice was timid.

"Yes. After I landed a management position, I waited four months, just a bit longer than the probation, and I stopped processing my hair. The growing out period was not easy, so I braided it at first." She laughed at the memory. "You should have seen Mara's face! And Phillip's!"

"I can't believe that. Why would they care about your hair? It's beautiful the way it is now, so elegant. I told you that when we first met."

"Yes, you did. And maybe it's nothing more than a nice hairstyle to you, but to some people, it's a look that they are not ready for. And you, my dear, are someone they want in the room, but they don't want you to make too much noise or be too visible."

"Decoration," Sara said. "A dancing Shiva on the mantelpiece."

"Yes."

As she neared Bloor Street, Sara filed the conversation back into a neat folder in her mind. Suddenly, she didn't miss her office at all. She realized that she would never again sit in the grey swivel chair, in front of the second-hand laptop, with a view of Anna on one side and a broken-spirited tree in the parking lot on the other.

Sometimes, when she was stuck on formulating a thought into words, she would turn and look at the tree, analyzing the lines that made up each green leaf and the contrasting sharpness of the grey bark in the winter. How it adjusted to its environment so easily, roots firmly planted as it grew a little each year, quiet and unassuming and protected on the Albatross property. If one of the branches grew too close to the building or dared hinder the path of oncoming pedestrians, there would be action taken and the rogue branch would be cut, its tender bark sawed away from the living host. But in the year and a half that Sara worked at Albatross, the tree stayed the same and remained untouched and, except for her occasional stares, unnoticed.

The honk of a car startled Sara and alerted her to the busy street, the smell of exhaust around her. She crossed at the lights and headed up to the liquor store on the corner.

Two bottles of wine that she favoured were on sale, so Sara quickly made her purchase and walked back to her tiny apartment. A woman pushing a stroller walked past, cellphone to her ear, and a man walking a dog on the other side of the street pitched his cigarette on the ground. A few kids on their bikes suddenly came around the corner and whizzed past her, and Sara instinctively turned to watch as they swerved around the woman with the stroller, who didn't flinch.

Once back in her apartment, Sara could not stop herself from opening her email. Emails usually appeared on her phone at least ten minutes after they hit her computer, but once she checked, there was nothing new. She read Mayree's email again. It was three o'clock and the email had been sent at quarter to two. Still too soon. Perhaps she would call after dinner.

The thought of food made Sara's stomach grumble, and she opened the fridge. Somehow, she thought to buy wine but forgot to stop at the grocery store. There was cheese and a few slices of bread, but grilled cheese had lost its appeal due to overindulgence. Perhaps she could go out for dinner. She hadn't seen Richard since earlier in the week, and after telling him about her situation at Albatross, their relationship had eased into a comfortable pattern once again. She sent him a quick text, knowing that he would be on his way home from work soon.

He responded within a few minutes, agreeing to meet at the pub for dinner at six. He needed to finish a few things at work and stop at home first.

Sara looked at the clock. She had three hours to wait, so she picked up her phone and opened Mayree's email. The phone number was highlighted, indicating a link, so she tapped it and waited while it rang.

"Hello?" The woman's voice had a slight accent—English.

"Hello, um ... Ms. Grewal? My name is Sara ... I sent you an email?"

"Oh, yes. Hello, Sara. Thanks for calling. How are you doing?"

"I'm good. Thanks for responding to my email. I, um, I read the story in the paper, so I thought I would reach out."

"Yes. Well, thank you for reading and for reaching out. The reporter did a good job of telling the story. I am sorry to hear that you also had some work issues with Albatross. Are you still working there?"

"No, I am taking a leave of absence. Sick leave, or short-term leave, I guess ..."

"I think I remember seeing you Sara. I was there visiting the lady in public relations ... "

"Anna?"

"Yes, that's right, Anna."

"Yes, I used to work with her."

"Well, I am sorry that you are on leave as well. Just like me. It has been hard, as you read in the paper. But Sara, this isn't the best way to have this conversation. I wonder if you would like to meet for a coffee and have a talk? I would like to hear about your situation if you are comfortable talking about it."

"Yes, I would like to talk about it. When do you want to meet?" Sara heard the eagerness in her voice and made a mental note to be less anxious.

"How about tomorrow? I live close to Albatross on the northwest side of the city."

"I'm in the south part of the city, but I am happy to meet you. Where can we meet?"

"There's a Starbucks at Finch and Highway 27. How about one o'clock?"

"Okay, that works for me. I will see you then. Thanks very much."

"Sure. I'm looking forward to it, Sara."

The conversation was over, and Sara sat down on her couch. How was this possible? A coincidence ... or could there really be an issue at Albatross? How could two brown-skinned employees be off on sick leave, both with human rights issues? Sara stared out of the window at the brick wall and wondered. It seemed unreal.

Sara sat nervously, sipping green tea and looking at the door. The Starbucks was located in the neighbourhood Sara had grown up in, and it hadn't changed much except for the influx of newcomers. It was an interesting area with blocks of middle-class bungalows inhabited by long-time residents who dared remain in their homes despite the growing population of low-income families, mostly newcomers who resided in lofty, aging apartment buildings.

The clientele of the coffee shop was a tidy microcosm of the area. A group of Somali men sat together at a table, drinking hot beverages and engaging in a lively discussion, while lone patrons in power suits and funky shoes sat engrossed in their laptops. A scattering of students from the nearby college, earbuds replacing the café noises with downloaded top 40 hits, typed furiously as deadlines loomed. An older Caucasian man sat at a table near the window, peering at a newspaper through bifocals.

"Sara?"

Sara looked up to see the woman she'd seen in Anna's office that day so long ago. The woman who had glanced in her direction and smiled as she walked away.

"Yes, Mayree?"

"Yes, hello. Nice to meet you." Mayree held out her hand, extending long, elegant fingers crowned with clear polish.

"Thanks for meeting me." Sara didn't know what else to say but managed, "Are you getting a drink?"

"Yes, perhaps I will. I'll just leave my bag here." The woman was tall, with shiny black hair cut into a neat bob that showed the back of her neck. Her complexion was light brown, and her features bold, and if Sara didn't know better, she would have mistaken her for someone with a Mediterranean background.

As Mayree went to the counter, Sara's eyes followed the elegant woman, puzzled that she was the person who was accusing Albatross of racial discrimination.

"So Sara, I was very pleasantly surprised to get your email. But, of course, I am disappointed and sorry that you are going through this." She put her hand softly on Sara's as she finished.

There was something about her tone and smile that threw Sara a little. Mayree seemed very controlled, as if she knew the exact right words to say. Polished, confident—she could have been a politician, or even the board chair of Albatross.

"Thanks," Sara managed to say, a little intimidated.

"So, how are you feeling?"

"I'm doing okay. I was surprised to read your story, though. I had no idea that something like this was happening at Albatross."

"Well, it is unfortunate. I didn't think it would come to this. But as you can see, it is happening."

"The story says that you applied for a facility director role a couple of times? But it was given to a junior person both times?"

"Yes, twice beaten out by younger women with less experience. And yes, both were Caucasian but don't get me wrong, I have no issue with the race of the women. I don't want to come across racist by any means—if they'd had more experience, then I would not have had an issue. But neither had even half of my

217

experience. So naturally, it made me wonder what the issue was."

"That doesn't make much sense."

"No, it doesn't. But one was friends with Phillip Williams, and the other was a friend of Mara's wife or her former colleague or something like that. Also, there are no visible minority FDs at Albatross, and with the community changing, you would think that it would be a consideration when hiring."

Mayree's voice started to get a bit emotional, and she took a breath. Sara could tell that she was not only frustrated, but hurt. It was the same feeling that was sitting inside her, close to her heart, that feeling of complete sadness that weakens the spirit, the mind, and the body.

She lifted her cup to her mouth and sipped the lukewarm tea. "I thought they were supposed to be hiring employees who reflected the community? I think, actually, that was why I was hired ..."

"They are. And they will say that they have employees who reflect the communities. But they don't have to promote these employees to leaders. In fact, there are no visible minority leaders at Albatross."

"Maxine?"

"Yes, but she is a manager. Look at the directors, even at the administrative level, HR for example."

Sara knew this was true. Cynthia was Caucasian. Many of the frontline staffers at the centres were of African descent, some of Asian and South Asian descent. But Mayree was correct, none of the leaders were ethnic. And at the head office, she and Venah were among a handful of visible minorities.

"So did they explain why you didn't get either job? Did you ask why the other candidates were picked?"

"Yes, I did. But the answer was always the same—their experience and skills made them stronger candidates. I have nothing against Cynthia because I know she just does as she is told. But I cannot elaborate anymore. It is frustrating. Or was, anyway."

"So you filed a complaint with the Human Rights Tribunal?"

"Yes. My lawyer felt that it would, at the very least, push Albatross to look at their hiring practices and implement some kind of change. There are recommendations that can be implemented based on the information in the claim."

"But will it help you get an FD job?"

"No, I am not sure that will happen. At this point, I am not looking to continue working with Albatross. I just want the organization to take some responsibility and to create some change so that this does not continue to happen. For people like yourself, so you can one day become a leader at Albatross."

"I don't know that I will go back."

Mayree's passion cooled a bit, and she leaned in. "Yes, tell me what happened."

Sara recounted her story as Mayree nodded in sympathy. The words tumbled out of her quickly, more smoothly than in the past. She finished suddenly, and as her mind caught up to her words, she felt a little embarrassed and bent her head to sip her now cold tea.

"You did the right thing by contacting a lawyer," Mayree reassured her.

"Well, I think you were brave to file the claim. I can't imagine doing that. We haven't even received a response from Albatross yet."

"When did your lawyer send the letter?"

"Last week."

"It takes time. They usually stall to buy themselves a bit more time and, frankly, to wear you down. I filed over two years ago, and we are still negotiating. It has been difficult though, which is why I chose to leave." Mayree's tone changed, and Sara looked into her dark eyes to see sadness, vulnerability for the first time.

"I can imagine."

"I worked at Albatross for fifteen years, and I worked evenings and weekends to make sure the programs were running effectively and the community's needs were met. I implemented the seniors' drop-in program—so many South Asian seniors are now spending their days with their friends instead of at home. Do you know how many people sponsor their parents and then leave them at home alone all day? Some of them get sick just from loneliness and isolation. My own mother lived in my brother's home for years, and when she had a stroke, there was no one around. She just lay there for hours until my sister-in-law came home and found her." Mayree's eyes were filling with emotion. "I wanted to make sure that seniors had a place to go, within walking distance of their homes or at least within walking distance of the bus."

"I heard about that program," Sara said and smiled, hoping she could reassure Mayree somehow. "It's a great program. But I thought that Tina had implemented it?"

"Ha! Of course. That's what everyone thinks. Tina supported me, but I worked on the funding proposal with the facility staff, and I presented it to the board along with Tina."

Sara didn't know what to say. It all seemed unbelievable and silly. Surely people were not that petty. This was a professional work environment at a non-profit organization that provided services to communities. They were all working for the greater good.

"Sara, I have another appointment in half an hour; sorry, I didn't realize the time. But I would like you to come to a meeting next week at my house. It's just a gathering of Albatross employees who are going through the same issues."

"There are more people?"

Mayree laughed. "Yes, there are four others. Three have settled their claims with Albatross, and one is still negotiating. No one else has gone to the Human Rights Tribunal, but they can tell you a bit more next week."

"Okay, sure. Can you send me the details?"

"Yes, I'll email them to you. Sorry, I must run. But thanks for taking the time to meet with me. I hope to see you next week!" Mayree extended her hand again and then walked away.

Sara sat at the table and didn't move for a few minutes. There were others.

43

Aaron's message was brief. Give him a call. Instinctively, Sara knew there was a response from Albatross. A jolt went through her body, and she had to sit down. So Phillip and Mara were now aware of the situation. It was too late to turn back now.

It took her twenty minutes to dial Aaron's number.

"Hi, Aaron. It's Sara."

"Sara, hi. How are you?"

"I'm good. What's up?"

"Albatross sent back a response. I wanted to touch base before I sent it to you." His voice was void of all emotion. He was all business.

"Yes, sure. I'm at home. Go ahead and send it."

Why didn't he just tell her what the letter said? Sara didn't want to read it; she felt anxiety rising in her chest and was afraid. Surely Mara and Phillip would be angry.

Suddenly, the email was there, in her inbox; she stared at it for a minute. Her shaky hand cupped the mouse, and she managed to click on the email and open the attachment.

Her eyes focused on every word, each one evoking a pang of emotion when it hit her senses. It was a strong, direct response, saying that her claims were false, but that they were open to resolving the situation. That was it?

She picked up the phone and called Aaron.

"I just read it. It seems okay ... but they denied making the sari comments, and they said that they followed process with Anna's promotion."

"They always deny the claims. Admitting to them on paper means they are admitting fault. Overall, it is a very positive response. They want to resolve this as quickly as possible. They don't want us to proceed to litigation."

Sara didn't want to go to litigation either. The thought of facing Phillip, Mara, Anna or Venah in a court was too much for her to bear. She just wanted to let it all go and try to get another job.

"What do you think we should do?"

"I'm going to give their legal counsel a call and get a sense of their position. I'll get back to you. Don't worry, Sara; it sounds to me like they don't want to drag this out."

"Okay." Sara hung up the phone and sat back down on the couch. The television was on, but she couldn't see or hear the program. This could not be happening to her. She did nothing wrong.

Richard was at work, and if she sent him a text, he would respond, but then it could throw off his day. So she decided against it.

When she'd told him about her case, he had listened intently, his eyes shadowed in grey.

"I'm sorry, Sara. I had no idea that this was what was going on at your workplace." His voice was quiet.

"I am not sure how it got to this point." Sara was hoping he could tell her.

"Promoting a junior person to a role above you is kind of breaking process, isn't it? Is there a union?"

Sara thought for a minute. No, there wasn't a union for the administrative employees. She wasn't sure if there was one for the staff at the centres, but that didn't include her anyway.

"No, I don't belong to a union. And I don't know the process for hiring either. Perhaps Anna really was the most suitable candidate for a manager's role."

"Why do you say that? She was junior to you, right?"

"Yes, but the board forced them to hire me. They can't go around hiring people simply based on skin colour. They need to hire based on skills!" Sara heard herself and saw Richard's eyes soften at her emotion.

"But is it about merit? Look at the workforce and the leadership. How do you think it got that way in the first place?" Richard stroked her hair as he spoke, strength in his words.

As much as he made sense, inside her mind there was doubt. Maybe she could have done something differently—acted differently towards Anna. She could have reached out and been the bigger person. But then again, Anna went behind her back and complained to Phillip, as did Venah.

Richard didn't say too much more. He seemed distracted somehow, as if something was annoying him. Sara kept waiting for him to say something that would bring more clarity to the situation, but that didn't happen. So she changed the subject and asked about his work instead. He smiled and started to talk, but she noticed his eyes were not agreeing with his smile. Instead of the shimmering blue, she was certain that she saw a storm brewing. But she sipped her wine and lost herself in a teacher's story and didn't ask if something was bothering him.

Richard loved Sara's body. She was slim but rounded in places his hands could find and caress easily. After they left the pub and went back to her apartment, he found himself making love to her more assertively than usual, and he noticed her pulling back slightly a few times, seemingly surprised.

He wanted to protect her, but his mind was filled with rage and embarrassment. When she had told him the reason she was at home, he sat very still, eyes not moving from hers. Richard had had no idea that his beautiful, intelligent girlfriend was facing discrimination at work. He knew it happened, because he saw it at the school, but not to Sara.

He'd been a teacher for five years and had watched the hiring process many times. The union had a process based on seniority, but promotions always seemed to go to those closest to the principal or vice principal.

Over the years, he noticed the pattern—the successful candidates were almost always Caucasian.

When he started at the school, straight out of teacher's college, he didn't see it. There were only six department heads, and he didn't pay much attention to their race. It just seemed normal. But as some of them moved on or retired and were replaced with other Caucasians, the pattern became undeniable. None of the talented teachers who were non-Caucasian got to become department heads. But it was never spoken about. Just a quiet discomfort in the air when he saw who hadn't been promoted. He was certain that others saw it, and he wanted to bring it up, but didn't. It was the elephant in the room that was waiting for a brave soul to point it out.

Dave, his running buddy who met him for drinks on weekends and lived just down the street, had been a science teacher for seven years. Despite his intellect, Dave had an ability to reach students by relating to them easily. Students excelled in his class, and in Richard's opinion, Dave was university professor material. Dave was also black.

When he applied for the role of head of the science department, Richard was certain that it was just a formality. Dave would get it. He was always the go-to guy when the other science teachers had questions. He even looked the part— tall, thin, round glasses. The typical science geek, he joked to Dave one morning at breakfast after a run.

But the job was given to Larry, who had also been at the school for seven years. So it wasn't based on seniority. Larry was smart, but he was uptight, tense,

223

and a bit paranoid. He wasn't well liked by his colleagues or the students, but he was close to the principal, and he was Caucasian.

Dave never wanted to talk about it, dismissing the topic if Richard asked. It was fine. He was happy to have had the opportunity. There would be another position at some point.

So when Sara poured out her own story to him, Richard felt the sting of injustice as he had when Dave was passed over.

But he didn't say anything about it to Sara. How could he admit that his own race was responsible for oppression despite the fact it was the new millennium. The world preached that racism was in the past. It wasn't cool. The posters with images of cultural mosaics, the messages of diversity, inclusiveness—was it all just spin?

Now tonight, after dinner at the pub, she told him about her conversation with Mayree. He made a mental note to read the article and do a little Google search about the case. But it made him angry, and after listening to her for a bit, he let her change the subject and leave the topic sitting in the corner. He couldn't offer much advice anyway, and she had a lawyer who would handle it.

Mayree's house was on a corner lot on a quiet street, not too far from the Albatross building. Sara was cautious as she drove to the location, since it was just before the end of the work day.

She parked her car on the street. She saw a few other cars close to the house and realized the gathering had begun.

The living room was cozy and dimly lit. There were trays of appetizers sitting on the coffee table, and Mayree offered Sara a glass of wine, which she gratefully accepted.

There were five other people in the room, drinks in hand, munching on the crispy, spicy snacks and making small talk. Sara was quiet as she observed the guests and nibbled on a small potato cake topped with a savory tamarind chutney that made her taste buds tingle.

A middle-aged black woman sat beside a black man in his thirties. He was cute, fit, and she liked the way he smiled at her. Blushing, she turned her eyes to see three brown-skinned people: a man and a woman about her age, and an older woman who was watching her curiously. The woman was plump with red hair, perhaps in her early forties, and was dressed in business attire.

"Why don't we get started?" Mayree's voice was strong as she entered the room. The buzz of conversation stopped, and she had everyone's full attention. "I'd like to thank you all for coming today. I know it's a weeknight, and you have to be up early tomorrow. So thank you for taking this time. Tonight, we have a new member joining us. While I welcome Sara to our group, growing membership is a bit bittersweet since we are here to support others who have faced discrimination, and new members indicate that the issues are increasing. But, we are here to build a network of strength in an attempt to promote change and break the glass ceiling. So Sara, welcome and thanks for joining us."

Sara smiled and said hello as she looked around the room at the smiling faces.

"Why don't we all go around the room and introduce ourselves so Sara can put names to the faces?"

The middle-aged black woman was Christine, and the cute guy beside her was Mark. Donald was the only brown-skinned man and beside him were Shivani and Natasha, the red-haired woman in the business attire.

"So today, we are going to talk about the upcoming annual general meeting of the Albatross board and our plans to attend. But before we do, let's have some updates from the group. Who wants to start?"

Natasha put up her hand.

"Natasha, go ahead."

"Today, I had a meeting with Eva and Cynthia from HR to review why I didn't get the promotion. The reasons given were the same excuses that we have all heard before. It was based on the qualifications of the candidates and the specific skill set they required. Amanda, apparently, has managed to acquire management skills in the two years she has been with Riverpark." Natasha's voice had a slight South Asian accent laced with English undertones.

"Amanda van Horten?" Mark asked.

"Yes," Natasha nodded.

"I thought she was only hired last year?"

"Two years ago. She's young, yes, and she's smart. But I've been at Riverpark for ten years. I cannot keep doing the job of a youth counsellor forever." Natasha sounded a little whiny to Sara.

"She's only been a youth liaison for two years, and now she is your manager?"

"Yes, but she was previously at another centre and has about seven years of experience in total. But the role of liaison is junior to the role of counsellor, so I asked why she was promoted ahead of me, and they said that I was doing such a good job in my current role that it would be a shame to have to replace me."

Mayree sighed. "Of course. They always make it sound as if they are doing us a favour. We are valued."

Nods around the room indicated that this was a common theme.

'Will you seek legal counsel?" Christine asked.

"I am not sure yet. Perhaps. But then I will have to leave my job."

"Not really. You can still work. Check with the union rep." Mark suggested.

"Sara, are you comfortable telling your story?" Mayree asked. The group of supportive faces gave her the courage to nod and begin.

She spoke slowly, trying to convey each detail objectively, without emotion. Her eyes focussed mainly on Mayree but looked around the room a few times. She heard gasps when she delivered the sari story and the one about Phillip pulling Adam away from her because he preferred blondes.

When she came to the part about the letter putting her on notice, Sara felt the emotion rising in her throat. Pausing for a deep breath, she looked down and blinked several times to make sure the tears stayed inside her eyes and did not shame her. When she looked up, she caught the eye of Mark, whose own eyes emanated confusion, concern. Sara looked away and continued, keeping the story about the letter as brief as possible. It wasn't such a big deal—it was just a letter.

When she finished, the room was quiet. Then Mark spoke. "Oh man, Sara. That's crazy."

"I am utterly stunned." Shivani's voice.

"Real sorry, Sara." Donald's accent was thickly Caribbean, and it reminded her of one of her uncles. "But you know, you can't stand up."

"Stand up?" Sara's eyes matched her confused tone.

"Yeah, you push dem back. A double whammy. One, you are brown. Second, you stand up. They don't like that."

The words hung firmly in the air, hard and cold and real. She didn't know how to answer. But the words came slowly: "Maybe ... but my story is probably not much different than everyone else's here?" Sara heard herself sounding a little defensive. "Aren't we all standing up now?" She looked to Mayree for help.

"Yes. We are. " Mayree's voice was clear.

Sara lowered her eyes. She didn't want to be a victim. She didn't know where she stood.

"I didn't get a promotion either. And I asked about it, so now I know I won't be considered because I spoke up." Mark added.

"Me either. I was passed up like Mark, and I talk to dem. So I going to retire now. But let me tell you, no one ask me to wear anyting because of my colour or racial background. And if dey did, well I would tell dem about it." Sara couldn't help but smile as Donald's voice brought her memories of family gatherings. She found out later that Donald was a custodian who had been repeatedly denied a supervisor position. He had been with Albatross for eighteen years.

Sara looked at Mayree and saw a slight frown on her face. As if on cue, Mayree spoke up, shifting the angle of the conversation. "Sara, we are all truly offended that you were treated in such a disrespectful manner at Albatross. All of us have been prevented from moving up into senior positions. These are clearly

226

cases of discrimination. Now, let's move on to our strategy for the board AGM at the end of the year."

The conversation shifted, and Sara listened. The group was planning to attend Albatross's AGM in December. Mayree was hoping the board of directors would respond to her claim by then. If not, she was going to talk to the reporter from the *Community Reporter* and let him know that he should attend the AGM and ask a few questions.

The entire group was encouraged to sit in the audience in the hope that their very presence would put pressure on the board; in Mayree's case, she hoped it would push Albatross to settle her claim quickly.

Sara realized that it meant facing Mara and Phillip. Would she have to acknowledge them or would they all pretend they were strangers, ignoring the past two years of interacting so closely with one another? Her stomach flipped, and she remained quiet while the rest of the group discussed their plans. Mayree would get there first and hold a section right up front for the rest of the group. Then they would walk in one by one and sit together along one row.

Looking at the group, Sara felt as if she were far on the other side of the room, watching the tight knit group as they strategized.

Suddenly, she wondered if she'd made a mistake reaching out to Mayree and attending the meeting. She was not an activist, and she didn't want revenge. All she wanted was a settlement so she could pay her bills until she could find another job. This group wanted to make a statement.

Yes, they all seemed to have reasons for their anger. Being passed up for promotions time and time again is frustrating. But she didn't really get passed up for a promotion. She didn't even apply for a manger's role. Hers was a simple case of not fitting into the department anymore. They had Anna and Ashleigh, who would, no doubt, be promoted very soon.

She stood up, and Mayree looked at her, concern on her face. "Are you leaving, Sara?"

"Um, yes, I should be getting home. Thanks for inviting me."

"Of course. I'm pleased that you were able to join us this evening. And thank you for sharing your story. Do you think you will be able to make it to the AGM in December?"

"Sure, I will do my best to attend."

Mayree put her hand on Sara's back and walked her to the hallway. Once they were away from the group, she said in a low voice, "Sara, I know this is a difficult time. This meeting must have been a bit overwhelming for you. But everyone here has faced the same issues and is very supportive."

"Thanks, Mayree. I'm glad I was able to meet with the group. I didn't realize that there were so many people in the same situation."

"There may be more, but some employees are afraid to come out and talk about it. They have families to feed, and they need their jobs."

"I know." Sara felt silly. She had no family that relied on her. "Um, can you let the group know that I am leaving? I didn't want to interrupt the conversation."

"Sure, will do." Mayree's words were barely out when Mark appeared.

"Leaving so soon?"

She couldn't help but blush. He was taller than she realized. "Yes, I should get home. Nice to meet you."

"Yeah, hey, good to meet you, Sara. And sorry again that you went through that experience. It's that kind of thing that needs to stop. Are you coming to the next meeting?"

Mark wanted to keep the conversation going. But she felt tired, weak, and wanted her bed. And Richard. She wanted Richard's arms around her.

"Sure. Mayree will let me know?"

"Yes, I will send an email." Mayree's voice was warm.

"Okay. Thanks. Have a good night." And with that, Sara bolted out the door and down the street to her car. She drove until the house was no longer visible in the darkness, and then she burst. The cry from her mouth released tears, and she sobbed as she drove home. But the reason for her distress wasn't clear. The group was supportive, and Mayree was welcoming. So why was she upset?

44

It was snowing a little. Flurries. Winter was coming early perhaps. Phillip didn't realize he was staring out the window until he heard the whistle of his cellphone. It was a text from Randi. He read it and smiled. Usually he would text her back right away, but he didn't have the energy and put his phone down on the desk.

The events of the past month had been trying. He was weary of discussions with Albatross's lawyer while Mara's sharp eyes peered closely at every word that formed on his lips. Putting on a smiling face at staff meetings and lying about Sara's leave was becoming more and more difficult. Anna knew that there was an issue, but he never explained the details.

He hadn't expected so much drama from one issue. Albatross had dealt with many employee issues in the past. Some cases had even gone to litigation. So why was this one so tense?

Sara's accusations made him angry. She twisted the facts to make them look nasty. He was not a racist, nor did he discriminate against her. He was being a manager and making decisions based on his knowledge and expertise. Anna deserved the promotion, and she was doing a good job.

So the sari comment backfired. He meant well, but Mara was outraged, as was the lawyer. It violated the Human Rights Code, apparently.

And what about asking Sara to work for Ashleigh? Why would a senior employee need to report to an intern? Phillip didn't back down on this one. He was hoping that the entire team would be supportive in mentoring the young intern. It appeared discriminatory, the lawyer argued. It could be construed as putting Sara in a subordinate role to an intern, despite her senior status, and in conjunction with the other allegations, it could support the discrimination accusation.

"Did you tell Sara that Adam preferred blondes and discourage him from interacting with her?" At this question, Phillip felt outraged. It was his son, and

229

as a parent, he had the right to determine who his son interacted with. Besides, it was meant in a joking way.

Although Randi would have some insight, he didn't share the issue with her. He told her that Sara took some time off for personal reasons, and they were taking the opportunity to restructure the department to better meet the needs of the organization. Perhaps Ashleigh could move into a permanent role, and Anna would be his second in command. Ashleigh fit in so well at Albatross. Cute, perky, smart, and full of energy, she would do well in a higher position.

He knew that Sara would not come back. He didn't want her back. Having her in the department had been challenging. Her very presence created drama. Drama from Anna, complaints from Venah, and Sara was unhappy.

The more she was ostracized, the harder she worked, and the more she excelled in her role, the angrier the other women got. It had been painful to watch as Sara tried hard to prove herself, not realising that she was giving the other women more cause to dislike her.

It reminded him of high school. Girls always hated the pretty overachiever with the good grades—especially if the overachiever happened to be brown.

Taking a deep breath, Phillip pulled himself back out of Sara's corner and reminded himself that the issue would be resolved in time. Albatross would pay her a settlement, and she would go away, and he would go back to his department with a staff that worked together to get the job done without drama. He just needed to wait for this storm to pass.

That little bitch. That was all Mara could think. What kind of young woman runs to a lawyer and whines about work? Files a claim just to get money. So that was what Sara was all about. Money.

Her accusations were ridiculous. So Anna was promoted. So she had to help Ashleigh with her project. Okay, perhaps Phillip should not have asked her to wear a sari, but he explained his reasons.

It wasn't the first time that Albatross had to deal with such a situation. That other woman, Mayree, was following through with a human rights claim.

News of Sara's case had been leaked to Joan. Probably through Maxine—another whiner who pulled the race card at every turn. Joan had quietly questioned her about the situation, and asked if there would be any public issues. Sara was the media contact after all, and they had to keep this out of the media. Mayree had already gone to the paper, and two cases of discrimination was too much for Albatross right now. They could be at risk of losing credibility with their partners.

It would be resolved, Mara assured her. It was a simple, disgruntled employee claim, and perhaps they would have to pay a little settlement, but it would be worth it to be rid of her. Employees who were unhappy were not productive, and while Sara did some good work, it was time for her to go.

Joan seemed fine with the answer, but the next issue was troubling. Apparently, the last speech she'd received was not well written. It wasn't nearly as engaging or effective as the previous ones, and there were several grammatical mistakes that Joan had to change herself.

Mara said she would look into it. Perhaps the department was overloaded now that they were down one person. Joan accepted the response and reminded Mara about the upcoming AGM. She would need a really strong speech, and, of course, they needed to invite all of their community partners, as well as Minister Boland. She wanted media coverage as well.

"Yes, I did not forget. Phillip and his team are working on it, and from what I have heard, the planning is well underway. It's going to be a great event!"

As Joan left her office, Mara felt a heaviness inside her chest. Phillip had not discussed the AGM with her. In fact, with Sara's claim and Mayree's story in the paper, Mara had forgotten to ask him about it.

She sighed and sat down in her chair. She would discuss it with him ... she just needed a few minutes to get her head together.

Anna looked at Phillip and just blinked. The last two speeches had grammatical mistakes—did she not proofread them? Yes, Anna insisted.

"Who wrote the speeches?" Phillip asked quietly.

"Ashleigh wrote the first drafts, and then I edited them."

Phillip said nothing for a minute. He knew it was his responsibility to look over all content before it went to the board chair. He thought back, wondering how it had been done in the past. Right. Sara would write the speech, and he and Anna would review it before Anna sent it to Joan. But lately, he'd been skimming the content, relying on Anna to do the final edit.

"Okay. Well, moving forward, it makes sense for me to review the speech before it goes to Joan."

"You always review them." Anna's face was serious, and her tone accusing. She thought Phillip was reviewing them in detail. She admitted that writing wasn't her strongest skill.

When Anna asked where Sara was, Phillip explained that she was on leave for personal reasons. But Anna knew. She knew he'd been having meetings with the legal counsel and Mara, and she put the pieces together. Sara had gone to a lawyer.

Phillip had told Anna about the letter he was sending to Sara about her performance. But Anna never saw the letter. She didn't really have serious complaints about Sara and didn't really intend for it to go that far. Sure, there had been a couple of mistakes, but maybe she had blown them out of proportion. But Phillip wrote the letter and never showed it to her. She'd never gotten a chance to say if the complaints were inaccurate or unjustified.

She decided not to bring it up with Phillip and hoped that it would be the end of Sara. She didn't like her all that much. Everyone talked about what a skilled writer she was and how she was so admired by the staff at the community centres, but Anna didn't think she was all that great. She was hired because of the colour of her skin. If she wasn't brown, she would never have received the job.

Sara didn't want to open the attachment. She could always ask Aaron to read it to her, but a lawyer's time is money. She knew that it contained all the final details of the settlement from Albatross.

She took a deep breath and opened it. Surprisingly, Albatross was being very accommodating. They came up with a settlement figure that was higher than Sara had expected. They had only been negotiating the settlement for a few weeks.

"They wanted to resolve this quickly," Aaron explained.

"Do you think that Mayree's claim and the story in the paper has something to do with why this is happening so easily?"

"Perhaps. It's likely that the organization doesn't want to face any more bad publicity. It's likely that they want to keep this claim from going to litigation."

"But we talked about that. I am not going to litigation." Sara was afraid that he wanted to steer her in a direction she didn't want to go. Her parents were still not aware of the situation, but if she went to court, they would need to be told.

"Yes, but they don't know that." Aaron's twinkly smile and calm voice always reassured her. He was a good lawyer.

Sara reviewed the details of the settlement. She had to read the email a few times before she realized that it was over. This was what she wanted. Albatross agreed that Sara could use up all of her sick leave with pay, and she had one month remaining. Then, she would receive a settlement that would last her for four more months—more if she lived frugally for a while—and a reference letter that outlined her accomplishments. She would also qualify for employment insurance. She would be fine.

As she read the details, Sara didn't consciously make her mouth open to allow the gasp to escape, nor did she realize there were tears rolling down her face. She felt the relief in her body as it rid itself of the toxins. It was over.

45

Sara wasn't sure how to tell Mayree about her settlement. The former Albatross colleague was still struggling with her own human rights claim, and it sounded like the organization was dragging it out.

She had agreed to attend the board AGM in December, and Mayree was hosting three planning meetings to prepare. But after signing her name on the settlement contract, three times, and receiving the funds in her bank account, Sara found herself backing away a bit.

Should she attend the AGM with the disgruntled group? Mayree was still angry—to the point where she seemed to be on a path of revenge more than one of justice. She had worked at Albatross for years, and her work-related stories sounded so unfair that sometimes Sara found them difficult to believe.

Was Albatross so blatant in their favouritism? Did they really hold Mayree back because of her race? Is that why Phillip promoted Anna? Was the organization really fostering a culture of discrimination?

The week after settling, Sara didn't contact Mayree or anyone else from the group. She received emails about the upcoming meetings but didn't respond. Her mind was racing. There were too many thoughts and anxieties that she couldn't control.

So she focussed her mind and body on Richard. He was thrilled when she told him about the settlement, and they celebrated with a nice dinner at a quaint restaurant in her neighbourhood and a romantic evening back at her place.

Richard had been supportive throughout the entire ordeal. But Sara hadn't told him all the details of the case, nor did she tell him about Albatross's AGM. She wasn't sure how he would react if she told him that she was going to face her former colleagues at Albatross along with Mayree and a bitter group of employees.

The fear that the media would attend was high in her mind, and Sara made up her mind that she would not speak to them if she went to the meeting. She couldn't anyway. Part of her settlement included a confidentiality agreement that forbade her from discussing the settlement or the details of the case.

Perhaps Mayree would forget about her. Perhaps the group would go to the AGM without her support. As the weeks rolled on, Sara read countless emails from the group, but didn't respond.

When Mayree called, Sara looked at the number and watched the phone ring. If she didn't answer, there would be a message, and if she chose to ignore it, there would be another phone call. So she picked up.

"Sara, hello. How are you?"

"Hi, Mayree. I'm good. How about you?"

"I'm fine, thanks. A bit frustrated lately. Albatross has not yet responded to our last letter, which was sent over a month ago. My lawyer is not sure what they are doing. But anyway, the group is still moving ahead with our attendance at the AGM. Did you get my emails?"

"Um, yes, I did. Sorry I have not responded ... " Sara had no excuse.

"How is your settlement coming along?"

"Well, actually, Albatross settled with me last week."

A pause and then, "Sara, I am so happy for you." Another pause. "Are you happy with the outcome?"

"Yes, I am. I'm just glad that it is finally over."

"Good, I am really happy for you. I know that the other members of the group were quite concerned about you after hearing your story. They have asked about you."

"Have they? That's really sweet."

"Yes. Many of them are still waiting for a resolution or are very discouraged at the way Albatross has disregarded their claims. They really need some hope, and I think you will be able to give it to them by sharing your results."

Sara thought for a moment. Yes, Mayree would not let her walk away.

"Okay, well, I can do what I can."

"Great. So you will be at the meeting on Wednesday evening?"

"Yes, I'll do my best."

"The group would love to hear your story."

"I am not able to say too much because I signed a confidentiality agreement."

"Yes, of course. But it is reassurance enough to know that you were able to finalize something. It gives the group some hope."

"Okay. So I will see you on Wednesday."

"Thank you, Sara."

As she hung up the phone, Sara still felt hesitant. But she gave her word, and she would go to the meeting. As far as attending the AGM, she was still undecided.

Christmas was looming. Advertising kicked off the premature start of the season as soon as Thanksgiving ended, and suddenly people were scrambling to get their lists together. Christmas carols dominated the radio stations and played in all the stores to cajole shoppers into the giving spirit.

Christmas with Sara's family was a lively two-week event. Lots of relatives gathering at various homes to stuff their faces with traditional Caribbean fare fused with Canadian modifications. Usually, Sara loved this time of year, and the thought of bringing Richard home for Christmas was still floating in her mind. He had already asked, but she had not yet committed.

"So, we're still seeing each other's families for Christmas? My mom asked if you were coming for dinner." They were at her place, eating take-out shawarmas and watching the news.

Sara waited until she swallowed the garlicky mouthful and said, "I usually have Christmas dinner with my family. Not sure I can miss it. But maybe Christmas Eve? Or lunch? Um ... and you can come when you like as well."

His face brightened as if he were waiting for her to say it out loud again. "Okay, when do you want me to come? What day?"

His eagerness made her nervous. Her parents knew that she was dating someone, and they were open to having him over for Christmas. In fact, her mother was pushing for it. Sara was getting close to thirty, the age where singlehood started to become worrisome.

"Okay, maybe I could go to your parents' place for Christmas Eve?" she suggested.

"We don't usually do much on Christmas Eve."

"Hmm ... I can visit your parents early Christmas Day, but I have to be at my parents' dinner. I am not sure how we can do this."

"What time is your dinner?"

"Oh, we eat pretty early because it's more like a late lunch/early dinner. All of the relatives start arriving by one. We may eat at around five-ish."

"We can do both, then? I can stop in at your parents' place early, have a small bite, and then you can come to ours for dessert? We eat at seven. But we have dessert in the family room with our coffees."

"Okay, that works." She couldn't help but smile at his eagerness. He really wanted her there. She envisioned sitting at his parents' dinner table with the linen napkins and crystal stemware. Fancy. It would be nothing like hers. Although her mother had nice glasses and cloth napkins, they didn't eat around the table because there were too many people. The food was laid out on a long table, and everyone ate buffet style, but on her good china plates that were reserved for special occasions. He would enjoy it, she thought, and suddenly, her mood lifted.

"Sara, what do you think about setting a limit on Christmas presents?" Richard turned to look at her.

"A limit?" Oh, he was concerned because she was not working right now. Something warm stirred inside her.

"Okay, sure. What were you thinking?"

"Twenty-five dollars?"

"Really? Okay, if that works for you." Sara knew she could find kindness dancing in his blue eyes.

She attended two more meetings at Mayree's home. The group was getting excited and quite organized with their strategy. The local reporter had been contacted and was planning to attend the AGM, along with a few other reporters from ethnic papers.

She was amazed to learn more about the stories of her colleagues. Mark, the cute guy who smiled at her during the first meeting, was an assistant recreation manager who planned sports programs for youths. He had a master's degree in physical education and had been with Albatross for nine years. He had applied for the role of manager when it became available, but it was given to a younger, less experienced man who happened to be from a prestigious wasp family in the city.

Christine had been a program manager and had been with Albatross for almost fifteen years. She applied for the program director's position twice, only to be told that she came in "second place"—both times. It was not an easy role to fill, and the Caucasian candidates picked by Albatross had struggled to relate to the newcomer youths and had both quit after just a couple years in the job. The role was now open again, and Christine was hesitant to apply, but Mayree and the group were urging her not to give up. Christine, however, wasn't sure she could go through it all over again.

Shivani had a master's degree in health administration and was facing an uphill battle in her attempt to obtain a management position. And Natasha was an administrative assistant struggling to become an executive assistant, even though she had a bachelor's degree in business administration. At this point, Donald was simply trying to convince himself that retiring early would be better than becoming a supervisor.

It was overwhelming for Sara. How could this be possible? Were these colleagues simply just not good at their jobs? Maybe it was a really big coincidence. As the stories unfolded during the meetings, Sara felt fear rising inside her. She had settled her claim and was no longer an employee of Albatross, but these people were still there, except for Mayree.

Yet, despite the stories of injustice, the group seemed somewhat accepting of their situations. It was surreal to Sara. There was some natural bitterness, but they all appeared to accept that this was how it was and their goal was to get around it. They weren't asking for acceptance into the elite classes. They just wanted a chance at a better job so they could support their families and make a difference in their communities.

Sara began to wonder if she actually fit into the group. Was her desire to fit in with the city's elite or did she really want to contribute to the community? After the second meeting, she left quickly because the air grew thick and her head began to ache.

She didn't fit at Albatross because they did not want her. But she wasn't sure that she was part of this group either—the underdogs, the ones who might very well get promoted after a long fight, but never accepted. Tokens.

When she was with Richard and his family, was she accepted or was she still a token?

She skipped the last meeting of the group. It was held two weeks before the Albatross AGM, which seemed less appealing as it drew nearer.

"You have to go," Richard's voice was stern. Sara wondered why she told him in the first place. They'd had a few glasses of wine over dinner, and she was feeling warm and cozy beside him on the couch when the talk came up.

"How can I face Phillip and Mara?" she said quietly.

Richard stroked her hair. "Yeah, it won't be easy. But you settled your claim. You won."

"I didn't win. I lost my job. I was weak ... I ran away."

There was a pause. She knew that Richard didn't know what to say.

"I did, didn't I?" She pushed. She sat up and looked into his eyes.

"No. You fought. You got out of a situation that was not working for you. You were unhappy over there."

She sighed. Maybe she did, but she felt weak.

"If you don't support the group at the AGM, then you will be weak."

It was true. She was running away and hiding. She was ashamed of being associated with the group—the elephants in the room who decided to stomp and rage so they would be noticed.

"Okay." And she leaned in and kissed him, and the conversation ended.

The clock said 6:12 p.m. The AGM would start in forty-eight minutes. She had enough time to get there and slip into a seat quietly. No one would notice. When it was over, she could melt into the crowd and disappear.

6:16 p.m. She sat on her bed and looked out the window. She had showered, but was still in her robe. She got up and walked into the living room and checked her email. She had not responded to Mayree's last two emails with updates for the group. Mayree had not called her recently or asked if she was going to the AGM. So maybe she didn't need her to be there.

6:21 p.m. Sara pulled on black tights, a skirt, boots, and a blazer. Business casual. The white button-up shirt made sure of that.

Maybe a glass of wine. She poured a quarter of a glass and took a sip. It tasted like metal. Maybe it was just the taste in her mouth. She went into the bathroom and looked at herself in the mirror. Lip gloss applied, she smoothed her hair.

6:34 p.m. Oh no. She would be late. She couldn't let anyone see her walk in. Sara pulled on her red coat and ran out the door and into her car. Adrenaline, deep breaths, anxiety rolling in her stomach, snow falling on her windshield.

The parking lot looked the same. She looked over at the tree, the one that lived outside her old office. It was bare, quiet, and unassuming. It was a stranger to her now.

She opened the familiar doors and walked down the hall to the boardroom. The doors were wide open. A few people stood outside including the reporter, who glanced curiously at her as she approached.

Sara paused and breathed, walked in and paused. As if drawn by a magnet, her head turned to meet Maxine's eyes. She had not spoken to Maxine since she had left Albatross. The large brown eyes crinkled, and there was the bright smile. She nodded and her expression said she was still there. Sara dropped her keys, and all eyes looked up. She made her way to Mayree and the group, and suddenly, her eyes found Phillip, Anna, and Venah in their seats. Anna's and Venah's eyes were wide. Phillip was staring at the ground, his face red.

Sara took a seat and looked ahead at the board, sitting at the front of the room, Mara at the same head table. The director looked directly at her, and Sara didn't avert her eyes. Mara looked away.

She looked at the other members of the group and smiled. Mark nodded at her, and Natasha reached over and squeezed her hand. Mayree gave her a regal smile and patted her arm. It didn't matter where she fit. She was visible.

Acknowledgements

Thanks to Jim Nason and everyone at
Tightrope Books for believing in the story.
Much gratitude to the readers of this book.

About the Author

Since she was acclaimed by her Grade Five teacher for story writing skills, Priya Ramsingh has recognized her calling as a writer. An English graduate from Carleton University, Priya spent twenty-two years in communications, with nine as a freelance writer. *Brown Girl in the Room* is her first novel.